STRING OF PEARLS

Book One of "A Cord of Three Strands" Series

Lydia Moen

Elk Lake
PUBLISHING

Elk Lake Publishing

String of Pearls, Book 1 in "A Cord of Three Strands" Series
Copyright © 2015 by Peggy Byers, Ann Guyer, Nancy Willich
Requests for information should be addressed to:
Elk Lake Publishing,
PO Box 4043
Atlanta, GA 30024
Create Space ISBN-13 NUMBER: 978-1-942513-42-1

All rights reserved. No part of this publication, either text or image may be used for any purpose other than personal use. Therefore, reproduction, modification, storage in a retrieval system or retransmission, in any form or by any means, electronic, mechanical or otherwise, for reasons other than personal use, except for brief quotations for reviews or articles and promotions, is strictly prohibited without prior written permission by the publisher.
Published in association with Joyce Hart, agent, Hartline Literary Agency

Cover and graphics design: Anna O'Brien
Editing: Deb Haggerty and Kathi Macias

All Scripture taken from THE HOLY BIBLE, NEW INTERNATIONAL VERSION®, NIV® Copyright © 1973, 1978, 1984, 2011 by Biblica, Inc.® Used by permission. All rights reserved worldwide.

Dedication

To Lydia Genrich, Ada and Ellida Moen, three loving women of faith, who believed in and lived God's Word to Joel (1:3). *Tell it to your children, and let your children tell it to their children, and their children to the next generation.*

Acknowledgments

We are grateful to the following who offered assistance and encouragement: Debby Nolan, our first editor; Joyce Hart at Hartline Literary Agency; Kathi Macias, Deb Haggerty, Fred St. Laurent at Elk Lake Publishing; Beth Adams, Jon Woodhams, John Blase, Susan Meissner, James Scott Bell, and all our ACFW friends and advisers.

Chapter 1

Ellen Bailey turned her back on the oppressive grayness outside the large windows overlooking Pearl Lake. *Why did I agree to this? There's nothing here for me.* She reached above the stone fireplace and nudged the right side of the gold-framed painting just a touch higher, then stepped back. Her eyes lingered on the artist's image of the ruby red stream of brake lights and warm haze of street lights along Washington, D.C.'s Potomac River at dusk. She felt a familiar dampness tracing down her cheek. Home was just outside the nation's capital—not in the middle of nowhere—Water's Edge, Wisconsin.

Ellen and Bob had moved into one of the three homes on Lakeshore Lane when he was forced out of his job and into early retirement. She hardly knew her neighbors. Her only friends lived half a continent away.

Before her husband came downstairs and caught her crying again, Ellen grabbed her gray L.L. Bean slicker and headed out the door. The late-afternoon mist enveloped her as she made her escape. Ellen trudged up the driveway and turned onto Lakeshore Lane. She reached the stop sign at the end of the worn gravel road just as a jagged streak of lightning ripped across the sky.

Lydia Moen

"Are you kidding me? I hate this place! I can't even go for a walk."

As the drizzle intensified to a steady rain, she pulled the hood over her head and hunched her shoulders, retreating turtle-like into the protection of her slicker.

Ellen barely heard the car skidding toward her. The horror of recognition hit just as the car struck. A terrified scream pulled the air from her lungs. Ellen Bailey lost consciousness as the impact thrust her against the base of a pine tree.

Maggie MacDonald's golden retriever whined and jostled the novel out of her hands. "Are you suggesting we go outside, Sammy? Great idea. Let's do it."

The retired teacher, who had lost her husband the previous year, stretched and smiled at the scene outside. *I can't imagine living anywhere else. I'm so blessed to have a home on Pearl Lake.* Maggie reached down, snapped on Sammy's leash, and ruffled his ears.

"Okay, Sammy. I'll just grab my raincoat." Maggie retrieved her cell phone from the shelf under which her keys hung. As she stood on the porch, protected from the rain, a dark sedan raced down Lakeshore Lane. "Turn your lights on!" she yelled.

"Evidently, Sammy, Mr. Bailey hasn't acquainted himself with Wisconsin laws yet."

She'd scarcely spoken the last word when a chilling scream pierced the air.

Wanda Santiago put down her paintbrush and switched on her studio lights. Her gray tabby stretched, yawned, and squinted at her owner from her window-seat perch. "Did you hear the thunder, too, Purrdita? I bet I forgot to close the car windows."

Wanda hustled out the door. As she reached her aging station wagon, the clouds opened up. She jumped into the front seat and cranked the handle of the passenger-side window. "Next car…automatic windows…a must!" Wanda knelt on the front seat and stretched for the handles in the back. She jumped and looked around in horror when her posterior hit the horn. As she dashed back toward the house, a high-pitched shriek brought her to a standstill. She whirled around and scurried up the lane.

"Bob, what happened?" Maggie bent down and observed the rhythmic rise and fall of Ellen's slicker. She looked up at her neighbor's husband. "Thank God she's still breathing. Have you called 911?"

When he didn't answer, Maggie stood up. "Are you okay, Mr. Bailey?" She grabbed his arm, and he turned to her. She stared at his expressionless face then pulled out her cell phone.

"Hello. We need an ambulance at 121 Lakeshore Lane." Maggie put her index finger to her lips when Wanda arrived, quieting the questions that were about to tumble out of her friend's mouth. Then she continued with the 911 operator. "Yes, the victim's name is Ellen Bailey. She was hit by a car." There was a pause, and then Maggie said, "No, she's unconscious but breathing. She has a few scratches on her face, but there's no other obvious bleeding. Yes, of course, we'll do that immediately."

Maggie put her hand over the phone and turned to Wanda: "Go into my house and get that throw from the back of the rocker. We need to keep Ellen as warm and dry as we can until the ambulance gets here. And for heaven's sake, Wanda, grab one of my coats for yourself."

"I'm not going anywhere until someone tells me what's going on here. Bob, what happened?"

Maggie squeezed her friend's hand. "Wanda, this is an emergency. We can talk later."

Maggie watched Wanda hurry into the house, and then she resumed her conversation. After assuring the operator she would stay on the line and learning that help was on the way, Maggie turned to Ellen's husband. "Bob…Mr. Bailey, do you have any umbrellas in the car? We need to shelter your wife from the rain."

When there was no response, Maggie raised her voice. "Did you hear me, Bob? Are you all right? Your wife needs your help."

"I'm sorry. It was an accident. I didn't mean to hit her." He stood motionless, staring at his wife's twisted body.

Maggie ran over to the car, opened the back door, and found two umbrellas wedged in the pockets behind the front seats. She forced one of them into his hand, "Here, Bob. Hold this over your wife's face until the ambulance arrives. I'll open this other one so we can give her a little more protection from the rain."

Maggie raised her eyebrows, scrutinizing her new neighbor as he stared down at his wife. They stood in silence until Wanda returned with the blanket and gently laid it over Ellen. "I let Sammy in. He was sitting right by the door. Such a sweetie!"

The sound of approaching sirens broke the stillness, and Maggie spoke into her phone. "I can hear the emergency vehicles now. Thank you for sending help."

Bob Bailey shivered as he sat on the vinyl chair in the air-conditioned waiting room, his wet clothes clinging to his body. A fishing hat shielded his eyes from the bright lights, but he kept his gaze directed at the floor. He clenched his jaw as the policeman fired another question at him.

"Let's try it again. Can you tell me exactly what happened, sir?"

"I already told you. It all happened so fast. One minute I was in the car, and the next minute an ambulance was pulling up in front of me."

"Where were you going, sir?"

Bob crossed his arms. "I don't remember."

"So you don't know where you were headed?"

"How many times do I have to tell you? No, I don't." Bob shook his head and drew in a long breath.

"Was it raining when you left your home?"

"What am I supposed to be, buddy, the weatherman?"

"Do you have any idea how fast you were going at the time of the accident?"

"No!" Bob's voice echoed off the cement walls.

"Have you been drinking?"

"No, I haven't, and I don't appreciate all these questions."

Bob glanced over at his two neighbors sitting across the room and lowered his voice. "This is humiliating. I'm an attorney. I know my rights, and I know all the right people in all the right places in Washington, D.C."

Bob stood and turned his back on the interrogator as the emergency room nurse approached him.

"Mrs. Bailey has returned from the MRI; you can see her now."

Bob glared at the young deputy, who fell in step behind him.

Wanda and Maggie picked up their purses and headed for the parking lot. As they approached Maggie's car, Wanda heard men's voices behind them. She poked Maggie, and they turned in time to see Bob Bailey walking between the officers toward a police vehicle.

The two women slipped quickly into Maggie's car and stared.

Lydia Moen

Wanda saw the color drain from her friend's face as they watched their new neighbor secured into the rear of the cruiser. She noticed Bob's head was hanging down when the car pulled out of the parking lot.

Wanda slumped back in her seat. "Oh, Maggie, do you think Bob tried to kill Ellen?"

Chapter 2

Ellen sensed the presence of people in her room before she heard their whispers. She opened her eyes slowly, wincing at the brightness that surrounded her.

"Oh, Ellen, we didn't mean to wake you."

Ellen turned to face the voice and saw two women, one wearing soft blue and the other in vivid pink and green. "I know we've met, but I don't recall who you are, and I don't know where I am."

Ellen tried to remember who was whom when the visitors reintroduced themselves as her neighbors. *Maggie MacDonald: short silver hair, my height, average weight, and pastels. Wanda Santiago: black ponytail, short, plump, and neon.* When they told her she was in the hospital in Water's Edge, Wisconsin, Ellen's eyes widened. "What did you say? Why am I in the hospital? What happened to me?"

The woman who had introduced herself as Wanda placed a vase of flowers on the bed stand. "Not to worry, sweetie. You were in a little accident. You'll be back next door to me before the paint dries on my latest landscape."

The other visitor, Maggie, walked over to the side of Ellen's bed. "I'm sure the doctor will explain everything later, dear. Your job now is

Lydia Moen

to rest and recover. This is an excellent hospital with wonderful medical personnel. We're helping with your recovery the best way we can. We're praying for you. Would you mind if we said a short prayer while we're with you?"

"Whatever. I'm not sure it will do any good, but if you want to, go ahead."

Ellen crossed her arms and watched them bow their heads. She gazed out the window until she heard "Amen."

"That's very sweet. Thank you, ladies. It was nice of you to visit." Ellen rubbed her forehead, and her eyelids drooped. When she opened them again, the two women were gone.

Maggie pulled up to the stop sign and looked over at Wanda. "Poor Ellen. Her face!"

"I hope they don't let her have a mirror." Wanda pulled down the visor and looked at her own reflection. She turned her head from side to side and removed the purple scrunchy from her ponytail. Then she combed her hair with her fingers, replaced the band, and raised the visor.

"I guess we shouldn't be surprised by the bruises on her face," Maggie said. "After all, she was hit by a car. But I am surprised that Bob Bailey isn't there with his wife. Aren't you?"

"I bet they locked him up."

"Oh, for heaven's sake, Wanda."

"No, I'm serious. I think we should check out their house on the way home." Wanda rubbed her hands together.

"I don't know what to think. Bob certainly was evasive yesterday. Something didn't seem right. I would have expected a high-powered attorney to react better in an emergency." Maggie raised her eyebrows. "Do you think his being so indecisive is an act?"

"I've seen it happen in my crime shows."

Maggie wasn't surprised that Wanda's sources of information were TV police dramas. She knew her friend was addicted to them, even though Wanda frequently vowed she wasn't going to watch them anymore.

"I suppose we could go over to their house and make sure he's okay." Maggie turned onto Lakeshore Lane.

"I think you should park your car on the road, and we'll sneak up on him."

Maggie shook her head. "Wanda, that's ridiculous. I'm not going to sneak around our neighbor's house like a peeping Tom."

When Maggie pulled into the Bailey's driveway, she spotted Ellen's van parked in the garage and pointed it out to Wanda. "He must be here. There's her van, and we saw the police take his car."

Maggie headed for the Bailey's porch. "Well, let's go to the door and see if he's all right." When doorbell ringing, knocking, and yoo-hooing didn't work, Wanda walked over to the shed, peeked in the window, and shook her head. Then the two of them continued around the house, finally spotting Bob down by the lake.

Wanda marched onto the dock, her enormous pink and purple tote bumping off her hip as she approached their neighbor. "Bob, we've been looking all over for you. We couldn't imagine why we didn't see you at the hospital. We had a lovely talk with your sweet wife. Poor thing hadn't had a single visitor all morning."

Bob crossed his arms and scowled. "What did she tell you?"

Maggie joined them at the end of the dock. "Ellen seemed pretty confused. You'll probably want to get over there in time to talk to the doctor. I believe they may keep her for a day or two."

"Oh, really?"

Maggie raised an eyebrow and peered at him over her glasses. "She asked about you."

Ellen's husband stood up. He put his hands in his pockets and kicked a pebble into the water. "What did she want to know?"

Before she could answer, the conversation was interrupted by the sound of Maggie's phone ringing. She pulled it out of her small white clutch purse and glanced at the screen. Excusing herself, she walked away before speaking.

When she finished the call, Maggie stepped back on the dock. "I'm sorry, Bob, but that call was important. I'm afraid we're going to have to leave." She tugged on Wanda's sleeve and tilted her head toward the shore.

Wanda continued to talk with Bob as Maggie pulled her away. "When you visit your wife today, tell her we'll stop by to see her again tomorrow."

Wanda fanned herself as Maggie drove the two of them to the police station. "Maggie, why do you think Carlos wants to talk to us? We told him yesterday that we didn't see the accident. Do you think he's questioning everyone who's had contact with the Baileys? Of course, we'd be at the top of the list, being neighbors and all."

Wanda's eyes flashed as she grabbed Maggie's arm. "We better get our stories straight before we get there."

Maggie shook Wanda's hand off. "Mercy. You could have caused an accident. And I thought you were going to stop watching so many police dramas."

"They're not dramas. They're educational documentaries. You could learn something by tuning in once in a while, Mrs. MacDonald."

Maggie grinned. "I guess I'll just have to rely on your expertise, Mrs. Santiago."

Wanda waltzed into the Water's Edge police station and extended her hand to the desk sergeant. "Good morning, Mary Jo. Carlos is waiting for us. We'll just go right in."

Before the officer could answer, Wanda tapped on the chief's door and peeked inside. "Yoo-hoo! It's your cousin's wife and her neighbor reporting as requested."

Chief Gallego waved Wanda and Maggie into his office and hung up the phone. "Have a seat, ladies. I'm surprised you got here so quickly."

Maggie peered over her glasses at Carlos. "I hope we're not interrupting anything."

"I can get back to him later, and I appreciate your coming in."

Chief Gallego addressed his first question to Maggie, while Wanda surveyed the collection of wanted posters, police alerts, and evidentiary photos lining the office walls. "Excuse me, Carlos. Maggie, can I pour you a cup of coffee?"

Maggie gulped. "For heaven's sake, Wanda. Carlos is a busy man. We can have coffee later."

Carlos looked down at his notepad. "I'd like to ask you a few questions, too, Wanda. Mr. Bailey seems quite confused. I wonder if there's a member of the Bailey family we could contact to clarify the situation."

"The Baileys just moved in. Of course, I took them peanut-butter treats as a welcoming gift, but I haven't found out much about them yet. If it would help your investigation, I could do a little digging."

"Thanks, Wanda. I'll let you know if we need your assistance."

Maggie took a deep breath and tapped her foot. "I think they have a daughter in the area, and that's one of the reasons they moved to Water's Edge."

Carlos looked at Maggie. "Just a couple more questions. Is either of you aware of any problems in their home? Have you overheard any arguments or seen any bruises on the wife?"

Wanda leaned her arm on his desk. "Carlos, do you think he's abusing her?"

"I certainly hope not. But we have to ask these questions, or we wouldn't be doing our job."

"Of course. Go on." Wanda sat back.

"Any bruises?"

The two women looked at each other and shook their heads.

"So, that's a no. Now to continue, have you had an opportunity to observe Mr. Bailey's driving habits? Did you ever see him speeding or driving erratically?"

Maggie nodded. "He drove by just prior to the accident. He was driving too fast, and he didn't have his lights on."

Carlos jotted a note on his yellow tablet. "Perhaps you've noticed behavior that might be brought on by drugs or alcohol?"

Wanda gasped, stood up, and put her hands on the chief's desk. "I should have thought of that. Crimes are like puzzles. Now it all fits. We were at the Bailey's when you called. Bob was just sitting on the dock, staring at the water. He hadn't even been to the hospital. He had no idea how Ellen was doing or when she'd be coming home. I bet he's on drugs."

Carlos frowned. "Maybe he isn't very eager for her to return."

Ellen winced at the sudden glare from the long bulb directly over her bed. "Turn that off!"

Bob apologized and hit the switch again.

Ellen rubbed her eyes. "That's better. Thanks. Have you been here long?"

"I just got here. I thought you were coming home."

"Seriously? Coming home! What are you thinking?"

Bob slumped into the only chair in the room. They sat silently in the dark for a long time.

"Who brought the flowers?" he finally asked. "They look pretty, as much as I can tell in the dark."

"I don't remember who brought them. I thought maybe you did."

"I don't think so, but I would have if I'd thought of it."

"Bob, tell me what happened. How did I end up here?" Ellen twisted her wedding ring.

Her husband didn't answer.

The darkness in the room gave way to soft ambient light as a nurse opened the door.

"Hi, Mrs. Bailey. We're changing shifts now. My name is Sharon. I'll be with you for the next twelve hours. How are you feeling?"

"My head still hurts, and everything's a little jumbled in my mind."

The nurse moved quietly around the room, checking Ellen's vital signs, IV, and monitors.

"Are you Mr. Bailey?"

Ellen answered for her husband. "Yes, this is Bob." She cringed when she looked more closely and realized he was wearing the same gray sweatshirt and jeans that seemed to have become his uniform lately. She nearly groaned when she noticed his dirty fishing hat as he nodded at the nurse before crossing his arms and closing his eyes.

Ellen turned her face to the wall. The only sounds she heard after that were the quiet shuffling of the nurse's feet and the door closing. Moments later the door closed once more, and she knew Bob was gone.

Ellen shoved the breakfast plate with its half-eaten helping of runny oatmeal, cold toast, and pre-packaged jelly to the side of her tray table.

She flopped her hand down on the complimentary copy of what she assumed was the local paper. She didn't have any enthusiasm for reading it, but she was bored.

LOCAL MAN HITS WIFE WITH CAR

"Hah! That's the lead story in this backwoods town?" Ellen slowly shook her head, fell back against her pillows, and closed her eyes.

Thirty seconds later, her eyes popped open, she sat up straight, put on her glasses, and grabbed the *Lake Breezes*.

"Oh, no!"

Robert Bailey…wife, Ellen…Lakeshore Lane…new residents… husband, no comment…wife, unavailable…Water's Edge Hospital… under investigation.

Ellen threw the paper on the floor and collapsed into her pillow, covering her face with her hands.

Chapter 3

"It's time, Sammy! He'll be here any minute." Maggie's companion wagged his tail, as she paused to look in the mirror, put on a touch of lipstick, and fluff her hair. The two hurried down the brick path and were waiting for him at the dock's end when he pulled up.

Charlie Bingham delivered mail by boat from Memorial Day to Labor Day throughout the community of lakes in central Wisconsin. He shared the neighborhood news as he motored from dock to dock. He wasn't a gossip, more like a slice-of-life journalist.

Maggie couldn't contain her grin as she greeted the lean man whose skin bore the signs of his many hours in the sun. "Good morning, Charlie. I've been watching for you. Do you have anything of interest for me today?"

"Today's *Lake Breezes*, and you'll want to read the front page."

Charlie laughed when Sammy nudged his hand. "Not today, my friend. I'm sure Maggie wants to see the paper right away. How about if you carry the rest of the mail back to the house?"

Maggie felt a slight flutter in her stomach when Charlie's hand brushed hers as she reached for the paper. After the postman placed the remaining envelopes in her dog's open mouth, Maggie chuckled.

"Thanks, Charlie. I don't know which one of us is more eager to see you each morning, Sammy or me."

"I hope it's you, Maggie. I suspect Golden Boy is happy to see me because he knows he'll get a treat for retrieving your mail."

"Seeing you is enough of a treat for me." Maggie felt her face flush as soon as the words escaped her mouth. She kept her eyes on the newspaper but felt Charlie's attention fixating on her, as she fumbled to unfold the publication and look at the front page.

Maggie rubbed her forehead as she read the headline. "I can't believe this is the lead story."

"I'm afraid when a husband runs into his wife with his car, it's big news anywhere. Do you know how Ellen's doing?"

"I don't think she broke anything. By the looks of her face, her head got the worst of it."

"What a shock. I can't imagine how her husband must be feeling. I've talked with him a couple times, and he seems like a nice guy. Very smart."

Maggie frowned. "That's the odd thing. Wanda and I had the same impression. He's a smart man, but he says he can't remember anything about the accident."

"I'll stop in and see him after I finish my route. Maybe I can get a better handle on it. He could probably use a friend right now."

"You're so thoughtful, Charlie. It's one of the things I admire about you." They both blushed at Maggie's compliment.

Then Charlie's voice softened. "How are *you* doing?"

Maggie understood what Charlie was asking. Mac, her beloved husband—and Charlie's close friend—had died a year earlier. "I'm doing okay, Charlie." Maggie smiled. "I don't get hit with waves of grief quite so often these days."

"Losing a spouse is tough. It took me a while to figure out who I was without Fae. I imagine it's the same for you."

"That's exactly what it's like. It's good to have a friend who understands." Maggie and Mac had helped Charlie and his wife through the final five years of her life and his recovery after her death.

Charlie gave Maggie one of the crooked smiles she found so endearing, tugged on his Florida Gators cap, and then slowly steered his boat away from the shore.

She beamed when Charlie turned and gave her a salute from Wanda's dock next door. Then she opened the newspaper again and started reading it as she walked up to the house.

Maggie peered over her glasses at Sammy as she set down the newspaper. "I finished today's crossword in less than fifteen minutes. That's my second-best time. Now I need to call Wanda."

Maggie picked up the phone and dialed her friend's number.

"Maggie, have you seen the paper? I can't believe they used our names without even checking with us. I'm surprised they didn't plaster our pictures next to the headline."

"I'm just glad they didn't publish our ages." Maggie chuckled and then furrowed her brow. "I hope Ellen hasn't seen it. What a way for the Baileys to be introduced to their new hometown!"

Before Wanda could respond, Maggie continued. "I'm really calling to see whether you're all booked up for the day. If not, could you squeeze in lunch with me? I'd like to see your designs for the community center walls."

"Lunch sounds great, but my plans for the murals are still a little sketchy."

Maggie tapped her foot and nodded. "I thought that might be the case. Maybe we can do a little brainstorming. I'll pick you up at—"

Lydia Moen

Wanda interrupted. "Just a minute. It sounds like there's an emergency next door. Hang on."

Maggie pressed her ear against the phone and heard Wanda's footsteps, the squeak of a window being shoved up, and muffled angry voices. The minute Maggie heard her friend retrieve the phone, she demanded, "Wanda, what's going on?"

"We need to get over to the Baileys' on the double. The police are there, and some woman is attacking Carlos. Call 911 and tell them an officer needs assistance."

"Let's not be too hasty, Wanda. I don't think we should run over there without more information. Is Carlos alone?"

When she received no answer, she said, "Wanda, are you there? Wanda?" When Wanda still didn't respond, Maggie ran out the door.

She arrived at the Baileys' driveway in time to see the chief holding a red-faced, thirty-something female at bay while keeping a firm grip on Bob Bailey's shoulder. She spied Wanda peeking out from behind a large pine tree, tiptoed over, and tapped her on the shoulder.

Wanda whirled around, threw her hand over her mouth, and whispered, "Are you trying to give me a heart attack? Anyway, I'm glad you're finally here. Did you call for reinforcements?"

As Maggie started to answer, Wanda pulled her further behind the tree and put her finger to her lips. "Keep your voice down!"

Maggie nodded. "I haven't called yet, but I have my cellphone. Let's stay back for a few minutes. Carlos seems to have this under control."

Maggie and Wanda turned their attention to the female's continuing rant. "This is outrageous. What kind of rinky-dink police department are you running here? Do you have any idea who my father is? This man has devoted his entire life to the law. To think he would intentionally break it is ridiculous. I demand an explanation."

"Deputy Berger, would you assist Mr. Bailey, please? Let's step over here, Ms. Bailey."

"My name is no longer Bailey. I'm Elizabeth Rosen. You may have heard of my husband, David Rosen. He's a defense attorney and quite well known in legal circles."

When Wanda rolled her eyes at her friend, Maggie raised her eyebrows and shook her head.

"I apologize, Mrs. Rosen. I'm not familiar with your husband's work, but I am familiar with my job, which is to follow the orders of the district attorney. Now, if you'll step over here with me, Deputy Berger will help your father into the squad car."

Maggie wasn't quick enough to keep Wanda muzzled. "Carlos, is this absolutely necessary?" Chief Gallego spun around like a giant top, his cheeks flashing crimson. Maggie thought the color was not unlike that given off by the flashing light on the top of his patrol car and was quite relieved that he kept his pistol holstered.

Always the gentleman, Carlos recovered in time to suggest that, after he had a moment alone with Mrs. Rosen, it would be helpful if the ladies would assist her in any way they could. "I'll speak with you later, Mrs. Santiago." He turned his back on them and ushered the Baileys' daughter to the other side of the police car.

Maggie couldn't help overhearing the chief's explanation.

"Your father and mother were involved in an incident two days ago that left your mother in the hospital and your father with some legal problems. Your mother's injuries are not life-threatening, and as I understand it, she will, in all likelihood, be released from the hospital soon. The district attorney ordered us to arrest your father for inattentive driving and reckless endangerment. We have no choice.

"I'm confident that with both your husband's and your father's experience in legal matters, you're familiar with the process involved. Let me assure you that we'll treat your father with the utmost courtesy in this difficult situation. However, we *are* going to take him down to the station. You may feel free to call me at any time and see your father during our visiting hours. Here's my card. The hours are on the back. Good morning."

With that, Chief Gallego put his hand on Mrs. Rosen's elbow and guided her back to the waiting women. Maggie's heart warmed as she watched her friend open her arms and gather in the young lady. She knew Wanda was doing for the Baileys' daughter what generations of caring women have done for those who have less experience dealing with life's trials.

"It's going to be okay, sweetie. You'll see. We'll get this mess all straightened out, and before long, it will be nothing but a nasty memory. For the time being, you can lean on us."

The young woman sobbed openly, but it was apparent to Maggie that Wanda's soft shoulder and comforting words worked on her as well as they might on a toddler who was scooped up by his mother after taking a tumble. Her breathless sobs gave way to fast-flowing tears before the inevitable staccato sniffles and, finally, the stillness of exhaustion.

"I guess it's time we introduced ourselves to you. The woman who's hugging you is your parents' next-door neighbor, Wanda Santiago. I'm Maggie MacDonald, and I live in the first and only other house on the lane. We've barely gotten to know your parents, but we're concerned about your father and praying for your mother's speedy recovery."

"I'm Lizzy Rosen. Do you know how my mother's doing?"

"We visited her yesterday. She's going to be fine, dear. I'm sure you'll both feel better when you see each other." Maggie nodded toward the door. "Let's go inside and discuss how we can best help you."

Wanda and Lizzy settled onto the couch. Maggie pulled her chair closer to them and began. "Apparently what caused the police to be concerned was your father's unwillingness to share any details of what happened. He seemed very reluctant to answer their questions."

Lizzy's hand shook as she gripped the arm of the couch. She leaned forward to brace herself on the coffee table as she rose.

Maggie and Wanda watched in silence as Lizzy crossed to the window in slow motion and stared out at the lake. After several minutes, she turned to face the two women. "As shocking as this is, I'm not surprised."

Chapter 4

Bob muttered to himself as he paced back and forth in the eight-by-ten room like a dog in a kennel. "This is ridiculous. I have no idea why I'm here. They obviously don't know who I am."

He pushed up the sleeves of his gray sweatshirt and turned to face the officer who entered the room.

"Please have a seat, Mr. Bailey. As I told you earlier, I'm Chief Gallego, and I have the reports from the accident in which you were involved."

Bob jammed his hands in his jeans pockets. "I have no intention of sitting down, and I am not interested in your reports. I want to know why I'm here."

The chief placed a number of papers face up on the table.

"Mr. Bailey—"

"I'm waiting for your explanation," Bob interrupted.

"As I was saying, this report contains the findings on your car's mechanical condition. Our investigators found no evidence of problems with the car's brakes, steering, or fuel system."

"Of course, they didn't. I keep our cars well maintained." Bob picked up the report and started to fold it.

"We're going to have to keep that document, Mr. Bailey."

Bob threw the papers across the table. "Fine! But I'd like a copy for my files."

"No problem. I'll have one made for you. Now this is the actual report from the scene. I've put a check mark next to the pertinent information."

"Just give me a copy of that too."

"Mr. Bailey, you were involved in an incident that sent your wife to the hospital. We're conducting an official investigation here, and we'll do whatever's necessary to get the information we need to conclude that investigation."

Bob shook his finger at Chief Gallego. "Now hold on a minute. I demand—"

"Mr. Bailey, sit down."

Bob jerked out the chair, sat down, and crossed his arms.

"Thank you. What we're looking at here is the evidence we've collected from the scene. It indicates that you never applied your brakes."

"Evidence? I don't know who collected your so-called evidence. Would it be the Water's Edge Police Department, or are you the entire investigative team?" Bob stood up and shoved his chair back, grabbing the papers as he rose. "And for that matter, why are you wasting your time questioning me? Things a little slow around the lakes, buddy?"

The chief grabbed the edge of the table with both hands and leaned toward Bob. "Mr. Bailey, would you kindly put the reports back and sit down? Being uncooperative isn't helping either of us. If you could please just fill in some details."

Bob slammed his chair down and hit the table with his fist.

Chief Gallego grabbed the papers on his way to the door. "Sergeant, we're finished here. Please escort Mr. Bailey to a cell."

Ellen's cheek chafed against the pillow's dampness. She turned it over to find a drier spot to burrow into, but her movement pulled the IV that pierced the back of her hand. It was no use. She was awake. But she had no idea what had happened to her life. When had things gotten so out of control? She knew only that she felt cold and alone.

Ellen kept her eyes closed, searching for the sleep that eluded her. But a familiar scent pulled her further into consciousness. Not antiseptic. Sweet. Not sugary. Floral. Not overwhelming. Subtle. "Lizzy?"

"Mom, yes, it's me. I've been waiting for you to wake up."

Ellen winced as she rolled over a few degrees at a time. "I'm not really awake now, and I'm not sure I want to be."

"We're so worried about you."

Ellen looked up at the ceiling. "I don't think your father's very worried about me. He hasn't even been here to see me today."

"Mom, please don't say that. You know we love you. I was so concerned when I couldn't reach you that I took the day off from work and drove over this morning." Lizzy reached for her mother's hand, but Ellen pulled it back.

"Whatever. You've fulfilled your obligation; now you can leave."

"Mom, I don't understand how you can say that. Why are you so mad at me?"

"I'm not mad at you, Lizzy. My head aches. My whole body aches. I'm in the hospital in some small town in Wisconsin where I don't have any friends. I miss my home, my life."

Ellen pulled a tissue from the box at her side and winced as she dabbed the tears running down her cheek. She drank a couple long sips of water, leaned her head back on the pillows, and closed her eyes.

Lizzy picked up the newspaper and put it on the tray table. "Do you

Lydia Moen

want me to turn on a light so you can look at this?"

"No, I don't want a light on, and I certainly don't want to look at that paper."

"How about if I read it to you?"

Ellen grabbed the paper and tossed it at Lizzy. "Read it to yourself. Everybody else in town is going to…if they haven't already."

Maggie sat in her car outside Wanda's house, fiddling with the buttons on her lilac blouse. After five minutes, she quit tapping her foot, put the crossword puzzle from the newspaper back in her small clutch purse, and headed for the door.

"Come on in. I'll be right there."

Maggie raised her eyebrows and looked at her watch. "Do you need help?"

"Just give me a second. I don't want you to see this mess."

"I've seen it before," Maggie said under her breath as a smile stole across her face.

Twenty minutes later, after locating Wanda's gold sandals, keys, and lime green tote bag, they found a quiet table at the Water's Edge Inn. "Can you believe we have a felon in our neighborhood?" Wanda asked.

"For heaven's sake, I think he was just taken in for questioning."

"Well, I know, but the circumstances don't lie. I can't count the number of police shows I've seen where a woman is killed, and it's almost always the husband."

Maggie looked around the room. "Wanda, here comes the waitress. Please keep your voice down."

After they ordered their meals, Maggie got down to business. "I can't wait to see what you're planning for the community center murals. Your artwork will sure brighten up the place."

Wanda gulped. "I haven't gotten much done yet, but I did take pictures of every room in the center." She dumped the contents of her large tote bag onto the table and pawed through the pile. Maggie pulled out a half-dozen photographs.

"Oh. I thought you were going to do some scenic photos around the lakes." Maggie started tapping her foot.

"I thought you wanted me to take pictures of the rooms."

"Wanda, we need measurements of the walls, not pictures of the rooms." Tap-tap-tap.

Wanda grabbed the photos out of Maggie's hand and threw them back in her bag. "Well, I'm sorry, Mrs. MacDonald, but you didn't make your requirements clear. Furthermore, this is my project. I'm the artist, and I know what I'm doing. If you want to be in charge of a project, why don't you get one of your own?"

Maggie had to do most of the talking over lunch, and Wanda maintained her unusual silence on the ride home. As soon as Maggie pulled into the Santiagos' driveway, Wanda bolted from the car. A horn blared behind them, and both women froze.

Maggie almost fell out of the car. "Thank heaven you honked, Lizzy. I could have backed right into you."

"Oh, Lizzy! I almost had a heart attack," Wanda blurted as her hand flew to her chest.

Lizzy slammed her car door. "I just left the hospital, and I'm on my way to the jail. Please tell me this is all a bad dream."

"It is like a bad dream, dear. How can we help?" Maggie walked over to the Baileys' daughter.

Wanda joined the others. "Yes, sweetie. 'Though one may be overpowered, two can defend themselves. A cord of three strands is not quickly broken.' Ecclesiastes 4:12, one of my favorite Bible verses."

"Mine, too." Maggie nodded and embraced both women.

Lydia Moen

"I could sure use your help." Lizzy shook her head. "Can you go to the jail with me?"

Maggie approached the front desk. "Hello again, Mary Jo. Lizzy Rosen is here to see her father, Robert Bailey."

"One moment, ma'am." The desk sergeant hit the intercom button on her phone. "Chief, there are three women here to see the suspect you brought in this morning."

Maggie cringed when she saw Lizzy's head drop into her hands at the reference to her dad as a suspect. She was relieved when Carlos came right out and led them to his office.

Lizzy hesitated in the hallway. "I'd like to see my father right away."

"Your father is safe and comfortable, Mrs. Rosen. I'm sure he'll welcome a visit from you. However, first I have a few questions."

"Wanda and I will just wait in the lobby so you can have some privacy, Lizzy. We'll be right here if you need us."

"I'm so grateful you came with me. Would you mind staying with me?"

The two women looked at Carlos. When he nodded his head, all three followed him into his office and sat down. "This is not an interrogation. You weren't even at the scene, Mrs. Rosen. But perhaps you can provide some background information that'll be helpful."

"I'll do anything I can to help resolve this ridiculous situation and get my father—the suspect, as you like to call him—out of here and back home, where he belongs." The words tumbled out of her mouth, and Maggie put a comforting hand on Lizzy's arm.

"Your father isn't cooperating with our investigation and will be held here until we can clear this up. He claims to have no recall of the accident, and he can't, or won't, tell us where he was going. He

34

was examined at the hospital and apparently suffered no injuries that would cause this kind of confusion or amnesia. Do you know of any circumstances that would support his apparent loss of memory?"

Lizzy's voice trembled. "Yes, I do. Although a definitive test isn't possible while he's still living, last year doctors diagnosed that he was in the early stages of Alzheimer's disease."

Maggie glanced at Wanda and saw tears well up in her eyes. She clasped Lizzy's hand in both of hers. "I'm so sorry, dear."

Carlos leaned forward, his brow furrowed. "That explains much of what we've witnessed," he said, more to himself than to Lizzy.

The two women stayed behind when Carlos escorted Lizzy to her father's cell. Upon returning to his office, he asked Maggie and Wanda to wait for him by the front desk while he made a phone call. Maggie watched him place the call through the glass wall that stood between the chief and the lobby. He was on the phone for a long time, and from what she observed, he did more listening than talking.

When he came out of his office, Wanda stood up. "Thanks for taking care of everything, Carlos. Maggie, you pull the car around. I'll wait here for Lizzy, and we'll bring Bob out as soon as they spring him."

"Not so fast, Wanda. The legal process works at its own pace. What seems obvious to you may be more complicated than you think."

Maggie jumped in. "But he's innocent. Surely you can't keep him in jail now that you know about his condition."

Carlos sighed and shook his head. "It's not my decision, Maggie."

Chapter 5

Ellen Bailey, Wanda Santiago, and Maggie MacDonald lived on Pearl Lake, one of the nineteen connected bodies of water known as the *String of Pearls*. The lakes were central to the daily lives of those who resided on their shores and regarded them as extensions of their homes.

As usual, Maggie and Sammy were on her dock when Charlie pulled up. "Good morning. I'm glad you got here early. I imagine you're wondering about my neighbor."

Charlie turned off the motor and held onto the dock. "Yeah, I sure am. There was no sign of him when I stopped by yesterday afternoon, and your car was gone too."

"We were both at the police station."

"The police station?" Charlie's mouth fell open.

Maggie cringed. "I guess I should have called you."

She gave Charlie a quick summary of Bob's incarceration and Lizzy's revelation that her father had Alzheimer's. "I hope Carlos will be able to release him today."

Charlie nodded. "That poor guy. No wonder he couldn't remember what happened."

Lydia Moen

"From what I know about Alzheimer's, they're going to need a lot of help." Maggie felt Sammy's paw on her pant leg and bent over to ruffle his ears. "I believe my friend's reminding me to get the mail."

"I've got it right here, Sammy." Charlie reached into the bag behind him, then turned and handed several envelopes and flyers to Maggie.

She released a sigh as she quickly shuffled through them. "Nothing from overseas. I haven't heard from Josh in over a week. I'll be so relieved when my grandson's tour of duty is over and he's back home. I can't imagine how hard it must be for young service families."

Charlie raised an eyebrow and leaned toward Maggie. "Maybe you'd be interested in that new church project to help families of military members stationed overseas."

"Charlie, that's the answer! You asked me how I'm adjusting to life without Mac yesterday, and Wanda told me I need to stay out of her project and get one of my own. Now you tell me about this opportunity to serve military families. It's perfect!"

Maggie grinned and nodded her head at Charlie's response. "We could do it together, Maggie," he said, his eyes shining. "We can help another serviceman's family, since we can't really do much for Josh. I miss having him around too, you know. Fishing's a lot more fun when you're with a buddy, and I bet he's a mighty good fisherman."

Sammy whined and peered down into the water. Maggie spotted a good-sized bluegill swimming past. "Oh, oh. I think Sammy heard you say 'fish.'"

In the process of lunging at the bluegill, Sammy's shoulder knocked Maggie in the knees and she tumbled toward Charlie and his boat. A former shortstop with the Water's Edge Walleyes, the postman knew how to play his position. Maggie landed safely in his outstretched arms.

The fishing expedition was much more successful for Charlie than for Sammy. Foiled in his attempt to snag his trophy, the wet dog jumped back up on the dock. He marched up to his people and shook. Maggie disentangled herself from Charlie's arms while he tried to protect his mail bag.

"Mercy, Charlie, are we breaking any laws by my being in your mail boat?"

"Not yet," he replied with a wink.

After Maggie finished toweling off her soggy doggy on the porch, she decided to take him for a walk. "Sammy, I need to stop by and apologize to Wanda first. Would you like to have a play-date with Purrdita?" The golden retriever wagged his tail and nuzzled Maggie's arm. "I thought so." She fastened his leash, and they were out the door.

When they reached Wanda's place, Maggie rang the bell and called out a yoo-hoo.

"Come on in and have a seat."

Maggie grabbed a pile of papers off the living room couch, not yet sure if she should try to sit down before they talked.

Wanda re-scrunchied her ponytail as she entered the room. "Oh, I was thinking about sorting through those today. Just throw them under the coffee table, will you?"

After straightening the papers, Maggie bent down and placed them on top of an existing mound. She walked toward her friend, extending her arms. "I'm sorry about yesterday. I've been thinking about what you said, and—"

Wanda met her halfway. "Maggie, you know me. It's always a drama, and I have to be the star."

"I love you just the way you are, dear. And what you said about getting my own project made a lot of sense. Interestingly you aren't the only one who has me thinking about that. Charlie helped me see that I need to redefine my life without Mac." She shrugged. "I'm no longer a teacher. I'm no longer a wife. I have to figure out who I am."

Wanda gave Maggie an extra squeeze. "Well, sweetie, you may no longer be those things, but you'll always be my *amiga querida*, my dear friend."

"And you, mine."

Maggie glanced across the room as she and Wanda sat down on the couch. "Just look at those two," she said, pointing to Sammy and Purrdita lying side by side on the Persian rug. They were exchanging friendly licks and nudging each other with their paws. The noises they made seemed almost like conversation.

She patted Wanda's hand. "They're just like we are—great friends who love to chat and are there to put an arm around the other one whenever it's needed."

Wanda rolled her eyes and grinned. "At least we don't have to lick ourselves off after we're together."

Maggie laughed, and both sets of friends continued to converse in their respective languages.

Maggie beamed at Wanda's reaction to her description of the ministry to help military families. "That's perfect for you," Wanda exclaimed, her face lighting up. "Josh and his parents will really like that. So you and Charlie will be doing that together? How convenient."

Maggie could feel the heat rising in her cheeks and decided to change the subject. "Have you heard from Lizzy this morning?"

"No. I was hoping she'd called you. She said she'd let us know as soon as her dad was freed. You know, I never really thought that sweet man could have been trying to kill his wife."

Maggie raised her eyebrows. "I'm ashamed of what I thought. He needed our sympathy, not our suspicion.

"Alzheimer's," Maggie said, shaking her head. "Bob wasn't trying to be evasive. He really couldn't remember what happened."

Wanda jumped up when the phone rang. "Good morning. This is Wanda."

She covered the receiver with her hand and whispered, "It's Lizzy."

She redirected her attention to the phone. "I'm so glad to hear your voice. How soon will your dad be able to come home?"

Maggie snapped her fingers at Wanda and pointed to the phone.

"Just a minute, Lizzy. Let me put you on speaker. Maggie and I have been waiting for your call." Wanda pressed the speaker button.

"Hi, Maggie. I'm glad you're both there. I just got off the phone with Chief Gallego. They're processing the paperwork right now. My dad should be released within the hour."

"Praise the Lord!" Maggie's response was immediate.

"The D.A. has agreed to close the investigation into the accident. But Dad's driver's license will be revoked until he passes both Wisconsin's written and behind-the-wheel tests. I'm afraid this may be the end of his driving, and that'll be hard for him."

Maggie looked over at Wanda when she heard Lizzy sigh. "Yes, it will, dear. But it might have been much worse. Your mother could have been hurt more seriously or even killed."

"You're right. We were really lucky. In fact, we just found out Mom's about to be released too. I'm at the hospital now, so I can take her home with me. Could you pick up my dad? Mom doesn't even know he's been sitting in a jail cell all this time."

Maggie stood up and signaled Sammy to come. "We'll be there in ten or fifteen minutes."

That afternoon, after delivering Bob safely home from the police station, Wanda plowed through two boxes and several paper bags full of recipe cards, magazine articles, and photos. She dumped the containers onto her living room floor and pulled out a dozen pictures from the piles. With the photos spread out around her, she closed her eyes and picked up the first picture she touched. "Ooh, I love this one! Kids swimming. What could be better?" She slid it under the coffee table.

"Now I need one for the senior daycare center." It took two blind tries to touch the right one this time. The winning photo captured an elderly gentleman in a red driving cap sitting on a park bench. "Perfect. I wonder if that squirrel joins him every day for popcorn."

Before Wanda could select a third picture, the phone rang.

"Good afternoon. This is Wanda."

"Are you okay, querida? I can barely hear you."

Wanda squealed. "Alberto, it's you!" She raised her voice a couple of notches and hollered into the phone. "Maybe it's a bad connection. Can you hear me now?"

"Loud and clear."

She started pacing back and forth. "I miss you so much. When can you come home?"

"Is everything okay?"

"I'm just lonesome for you. I'm always a little disorganized when you're on one of your mission trips." Wanda slid the photos into an existing pile under the coffee table. "The house is a mess, and Maggie's anxious to get the murals for the community center started...and finished. I'm feeling very stressed."

"I'm a little stressed too. How about if we take a walk down to the lake together?"

Wanda raced to the kitchen. "Great idea. I'll bring the peanut-butter treats and iced tea."

"Oh, I can smell them—almost taste them."

"I'll have a couple for you, querido." The sound of her hubby's infectious laugh warmed her heart. After pouring a glass of iced tea and filling a small plate of treats, Wanda slipped on her gold sandals and strolled down to the gazebo.

"Okay, Alberto. You close your eyes, and I'll tell you what we're seeing. First of all, the pines across the lake are standing on their heads."

"Standing on their heads? What happened?"

Wanda laughed at the concern she heard in Alberto's voice. "The trees are fine. It's their reflections in the water that are upside down. I think God is so happy with them He wants us to see them twice."

"You are indeed an artist, querida. You're painting a beautiful picture for me. I can see it all the way from Mexico."

Wanda beamed at Alberto's compliment and took him on a visual tour of Pearl Lake. Having added the last detail to her masterpiece, she tried to swallow the lump that grew in her throat. "You know, it's much better in real life. And it's much better if I can hold your hand while we walk. I need you, Alberto. When can you come home?" Wanda wiped her tears with her sleeve.

"I don't know how soon that will be, but as much as we miss each other, we know we're never alone. Let's pray together."

When her husband finished his prayer, Wanda added, "And, heavenly Father, please send my Alberto home quickly."

Chapter 6

Ellen's headaches persisted after she came home, and her face looked like she'd been the loser in a boxing match. Neither she nor Bob were sleeping soundly in their new house yet. As a result, Ellen wasn't getting up as early as she usually did. When the phone rang at eight in the morning, she answered in a hoarse, sleepy voice.

"Hello."

"Hello, Bob. This is Tracy Evans."

Ellen hit the speaker button and cleared her throat. "Tracy, it's me."

"You're there! I didn't expect to reach you."

"Then why did you call?" Ellen rubbed her hand over her forehead.

"Because I wanted to find out what's going on out there. You sound terrible. Is it true you were run over and Bob has been arrested for trying to kill you?"

Ellen sat up and flung her legs over the side of the bed. "Seriously? Where did you hear that? I can't believe that ridiculous story has reached D.C."

"Then it's not true? Oh, thank God! Lizzy called a friend of hers, and that friend's mom knows a member of my golf foursome, and she called me. What's the real story, and how are you?"

"I'm feeling just fine. You know, it's an hour earlier out here. I was just sleeping a little later this morning."

"Ellen, half the morning's gone. I've already done my three-mile run and met Cynthia for coffee. I promised I'd call her as soon as I spoke with you."

Ellen cringed at the thought of the story streaming through the capital's legal community and started to counteract it with a slightly under-blown version of events.

Tracy interrupted. "You need to get back to civilization, Ellen. I was never in favor of your moving way out to the north woods of Minnesota."

"It's Wisconsin, Tracy."

"Whatever. You need your friends at a time like this. A few mornings of shopping and afternoons of bridge by the pool at the country club, and you'll be back to normal. The fall lines are in at Nordstrom's and Lord and Taylor."

"Don't even get me started, Tracy. You have no idea how much I miss D.C. I don't fit in here. Seriously, I feel like I'm in a foreign country." Ellen stood up and sauntered to the window. Then she turned her back on the scene outside and plodded back to bed. "I never wanted to move, and it's even worse than I expected. All my friends are back there. Everything I liked to do is back there. And I'm stuck here."

"You know I'd love to have you visit whenever you can, Ellen. Oops, I just realized we'll have to cut this short. I have my weekly appointment with Maurice in an hour. Let's talk again soon."

As Ellen put down the receiver, the image of Tracy getting pampered at the spa slithered unwelcome into her brain. She rubbed her forehead and winced with pain. Squeezing her eyes closed only brought up the next slide in the show: Tracy on the phone with Cynthia, gazing across the river from her Watergate apartment balcony, while she spread the news about the Baileys.

Memories of luncheons in Tracy's elegant dining room and cocktail parties on Cynthia's terrace flooded her mind. *How I loved going out for lattes and shopping at the Georgetown mall. Now I'm reduced to grabbing a coffee at the grocery store.*

Ellen dragged herself out of bed and walked stiffly down the stairs. As soon as she focused on the painting of D.C. hanging above the living-room fireplace, her eyes filled with tears. Head pounding and hands trembling, she staggered into the kitchen and opened the bottle of pills her doctor had prescribed for pain.

Maggie's hand groped awkwardly as she tried to find the phone on her bedside table. Who could be calling so early?

"Hello, MacDonald residence."

"*Hola*, Maggie."

Maggie sat up, fluffed her hair, and straightened her flowered nightie. "Alberto, what a wonderful surprise. I hope everything's all right." Maggie waited for his response, reminding herself that he couldn't see her and she probably didn't need to shout just because he was in Mexico.

"Thanks for asking, Maggie. Everything's fine. I'm calling to see if you might be able to pick me up at Central Wisconsin Airport around six-thirty tomorrow evening. I've made plans to fly home and surprise Wanda, but I could use a ride to Lakeshore Lane if I'm going to pull it off."

Maggie sat up straighter. "I'll be happy to pick you up, Alberto. Wanda will be ecstatic. She's been very lonesome for you. And so have I, my friend. Just email me your flight information."

"I'll send it right away. Thank you, Maggie."

Ellen sat down on the loveseat in front of the painting of her beloved Washington, D.C., placing her vial of pain killers on the coffee table.

She closed her eyes, breathing in again the smell of the Potomac River and the cherry blossoms, hearing the buses rumbling as they fought their way through the early morning traffic, feeling the jostles of morning commuters streaming up marble steps into the office buildings where the nation's business was conducted. Vibrant, exciting, alive.

She opened her eyes and looked again at the pills, picked them up and counted them.

She leaned into the overstuffed back of the loveseat and closed her eyes again.

Ellen remained still for several minutes, listening to the steady rhythm of her own breathing. Then she reached for a tissue.

"Hi, Charlie. I've got some news for you today, but you can't tell anyone else."

"I love a good secret, and I know how to keep them."

Maggie crouched down, put her face next to his ear, and whispered, "Alberto's coming home."

His surprise came out in a near-shout. "Alberto's coming home?"

"Shush. I thought you said you could keep a secret. It's a surprise."

"I'm sorry." After a quick glance at the Santiago's empty dock, Charlie turned his face back to Maggie. "When's he coming?"

Maggie stood up and stepped back. "Alberto called this morning, and he wants me to pick him up at the airport tomorrow evening."

"That's great. We could have dinner on the way. I've wanted to check out the new—"

Maggie tapped her foot. "Charlie, Alberto asked *me* to pick him up."

"I just wanted to help."

She put her hands on her hips. "I'm quite capable of driving myself, thank you very much."

"Alrighty then." Charlie pulled away from the dock.

Maggie waited for his farewell salute, but it never came.

Ellen stared at the picture of D.C. She straightened her back, wiped the tears from her cheeks, and clutched the bottle of pills. As she stood up and crossed the living room, she spied Bob sitting on the dock.

Running up the stairs, Ellen marched into the bathroom and deposited the pill bottle in the medicine cabinet. She jerked the closet door open and snatched the largest suitcase from the shelf. After she stuffed it full, she hauled it downstairs and out the door. She slung it in the back of her van and jumped in the front seat. Gravel shot out from under her tires as she escaped down Lakeshore Lane.

Ellen arrived at the airport entrance in less than an hour. She pulled into the long-term parking area and yanked out her cellphone. Lizzy answered on the first ring, but Ellen did all the talking.

Maggie set down her novel when she heard the phone. "Hello, MacDonald residence."

"Hi, it's Lizzy. I just got off the phone with my mom. She's going back to Washington!"

Maggie nearly fell into a chair. "Is there an emergency, or has she been planning this trip?"

Lydia Moen

"I think she's running away. I'm worried about both of them. She's in no shape to be traveling, and I'm not sure my dad can take care of himself."

"Of course you're concerned. I'll talk with Wanda. We can keep an eye on your dad and take care of his meals." Maggie picked up her clipboard and started a to-do list.

When Lizzy offered an apology, Maggie said, "Don't be silly. I'm grateful you called. Jesus told us to 'love thy neighbor,' and it's easy to love your folks."

Maggie winced when she heard Lizzy's sharp retort. "Jesus? I haven't seen any evidence that He even knows my parents."

"Yoo-hoo. It's Maggie."

"Come on in to the kitchen, sweetie. Let me get some of this stuff out of your way." Wanda slid several piles of mail and newspapers to the end of the kitchen table.

Maggie slumped into a chair, tossed her clipboard on the table, and ran her hands through her hair.

"What's wrong, querida?"

As Maggie explained the situation, Wanda sat open-mouthed across from her. "I can't believe Ellen would just take off like that. How's Bob handling it?"

Maggie peered over her glasses. "He doesn't even know she's gone."

"Well, someone has to let him know."

"Yes, and assure him that we'll fix his meals until she gets back."

Wanda raised an eyebrow. "Is she coming back?"

"Let's just pray she will." Maggie tapped her pencil on the clipboard. "Now, I'd like to make a schedule for meals and checking in on him. He'll need transportation too, since he doesn't have his license."

"I'm tied up tomorrow, but I'm free the next day, and I can help with meals anytime."

"That works for me. I have some errands to run tomorrow afternoon, and I can take Bob with me. He might enjoy riding along." Maggie added that to her list.

"Why don't you call Charlie and see if he can handle a couple of evening shifts?"

Maggie gulped. "Will you call him?"

"No. You call him." Wanda tilted her head and smirked. "What's the matter? Trouble in paradise?"

Maggie kept her eyes glued to her clipboard. "I'd just rather not speak with him right now, and I think he feels the same way about me."

Wanda stood up. "I'm not going to get in the middle of your little spat. You're a big girl. Call him yourself." She handed Maggie the phone.

"Tracy, it's so good to see you. Thanks for letting me visit on such short notice." Ellen stood at her friend's front door and traded air kisses.

"Ellen, you look even worse than I imagined. You're black and blue all over. We'll have to get you in to see Maurice."

"May I come in?"

Tracy opened the door wider and stepped back as Ellen struggled with her bag.

Ten minutes later, the two women were sipping wine and chatting as they looked out at the twinkling lights along the Potomac. "I have the painting you and Cynthia gave me hanging over our fireplace in Wisconsin."

"You should have a D.C. picture in every room. Let's go to one of the galleries while you're here."

"Fabulous!" Ellen pushed her glasses on top of her head and took another sip of wine.

Tracy stretched her arms out, encompassing the view. "I doubt if you have anything out there that compares with this."

"Well, the lake is—"

"Yeah, full of water," Tracy scoffed.

Ellen summoned up a quiet chuckle and took a long sip of wine.

"I've already talked to Cynthia. The two of us have a date for lunch tomorrow with Laura. I'm sure you'd be welcome to join us."

"Who's Laura?"

"She's the new you. Her husband replaced Bob at the firm. Laura's a doll. She's jumped right in—Christmas ball, hospital charity, Smithsonian auction…."

Ellen struggled to keep her eyes open. Sometime later, she heard glass clinking. She sat up and saw Tracy gathering up the remnants of their wine and cheese.

Ellen cleared her throat. "I must have dozed off."

"No problem. It's good to see you. I'm glad you're here. Now make yourself at home. I have an early day tomorrow, so I'm going to bed."

Ellen watched as Tracy turned off most of the lamps in the room, leaving her guest sitting in near darkness. The lights across the Potomac blurred, and Ellen lowered her head onto the arm of the couch.

I'm home. So why doesn't it feel like it?

Chapter 7

After an early morning kayak ride, Maggie stood across the living room from the window she gazed through. She hadn't moved in five minutes. The same wasn't true for Sammy, who paced back and forth at the door.

"Lie down, Sammy. We're not going anywhere near that dock this morning."

Her eyes darted to the television screen, where a morning news show was broadcasting live from the war zone.

Maggie grabbed the remote, turned up the volume, and sat on the edge of the ottoman. She leaned forward, wringing her hands as the helmeted, flack-jacketed newsman reported on a battle involving Americans. *Oh, no! I wonder if that's where Josh is. Lord, please keep my grandson safe.*

Maggie peered intently as the cameraman panned a group of soldiers hunkered down in a bunker. She flinched and covered her ears when she heard a shell explode near the scene. *Those poor boys. Heavenly Father, please protect them.*

The newscast ended, and Maggie hurried to the window. Her mailbox

Lydia Moen

flag was down. "Okay, Sammy. We can go now."

Maggie's shoulders slumped when she rifled through the usual flyers and letters to "Occupant." She walked her dog slowly back to the house and closed the door behind them. Her phone was ringing as she came in with the mail.

"Maggie, is that you?" the voice on the other end of the line had a frantic and hushed quality to it.

"Wanda, what's wrong? Are you all right?" Her near-whispered response echoed her neighbor's breathlessness.

"No, I'm not all right. Come right away. I need your help now."

"I'll be right over."

Maggie ran along the well-worn path that cut between two of the cedars in the hedge separating the Santiago yard from her own. She knocked on the door and opened it at the same time. Heavy drapes darkened the living room, but a sliver of light escaped from beneath the studio door. As Maggie reached out to grab the knob, the opening door smashed into her hand.

Ellen turned over to put her arm around her husband. "Bob?"

She kept her eyes clamped shut against the pain that gripped her whole body. "Bob? Where are you? I need my pain pills."

Ellen groaned as she pushed herself up then opened her eyes. The view in front of her was not just a painting of the Potomac; it was real. She gasped, got up from the couch, and straightened her wrinkled clothes. "Tracy?"

She found a note on the kitchen counter. "Gone to the club then lunch with Laura. Back by 3:00."

Ellen crumpled up the note and threw it in the wastebasket on her way out of the room.

Maggie and Wanda stood staring at each other, the *a cappella* aria of screams rising from their throats like the high notes reached by two tomcats fighting over a back fence. The studio lights fell on a torrent of papers of all colors, sizes, and sorts as they floated down from Wanda's raised arms.

"God help us!" Wanda's face turned as white as her capris were fuchsia.

"What? What?" Maggie's hands flew to her chest.

"Oh my heavens, Maggie! Are you trying to give me a heart attack?"

"I could ask you the same thing."

Wanda bent over, put her hands on her knees, and took a couple deep breaths. "I was just going to open the door for you. Come and sit down at my desk."

Maggie scanned the room. "Don't you have another chair? Mercy, how do you ever find anything in this mess? You sounded panicky when you called. What happened?"

"I've lost them." Wanda jerked her large turquoise pendant back and forth on its chain.

"You've lost what?"

"The photos for the murals."

Maggie's mouth dropped open. "You're kidding."

"No, I'm not kidding. I can't find them anywhere." Wanda pulled her ponytail out of the fuchsia scrunchy and attacked her hair like Purrdita after a ball of yarn.

"Do you have any idea where you left them? The kitchen, the living room, upstairs?"

Lydia Moen

"If I knew that, they wouldn't be lost, would they?"

Maggie peered at her over her glasses. "I'm just trying to help."

Wanda rolled her eyes. "Well, you're not."

"What would you like me to do?"

"I don't know. I thought you'd tell me. You're the only person I've ever known who actually keeps her pictures in albums."

"Where do you keep yours?"

Wanda clenched her teeth, turned, and stabbed a finger at the pile of boxes and bags in the corner. She kept her back to Maggie.

Maggie's eyes widened as realization hit her. "You're right. I'm not helping. Perhaps I'm the wrong person for this." She closed the studio door behind her on her way out.

Ellen rummaged through her carry-on and finally dumped the contents onto the couch. She grabbed her cellphone, and ten minutes later, she was booked on a flight.

She walked slowly over to the window and gazed down at the foggy scene below her. She closed her eyes and drew in a deep breath. Then she grabbed her suitcase and turned her back on Washington, D.C.

Not long after she'd left Wanda's, Maggie headed over to the Baileys' place. When there was no answer at the door, she walked around the house and spotted Bob on the dock.

Maggie sat down on the bench next to her neighbor. "Catching anything?"

"No, and I'm beginning to wonder if there are any fish in this lake." Bob reeled in his line. "What are you up to?"

"We have a date to pick up Wanda's husband at the airport."

"That sounds good. I'd forgotten. I seem to be doing a lot of that lately. Is it time to go?"

Maggie stood up. "If we leave now, we can grab an early supper on the way."

"Sounds good. Let me check with Ellen. Would it be okay if she went along?"

Maggie didn't answer for a few seconds. "Of course, she's welcome, but I don't think she's home now."

"Let's check up at the house." Bob put down his pole.

When they climbed the porch steps, Bob held the door for Maggie. Her eyes opened wide as she scanned the kitchen—drawers half open, dirty dishes piled precariously on the table, and an open jar of mayonnaise on the counter.

"Maybe Ellen's upstairs. I'll be right back."

Maggie got busy as soon as he left the room. She loaded the dishwasher, tidied up the kitchen, and had plenty of time to straighten the living room before Bob returned.

"I'm sorry, Maggie. I can't find my keys anywhere."

Maggie bit her lower lip. "Bob, your license was… You don't have to drive. I've got my car right outside."

Maggie glanced at the clock on the dashboard: 6:25. They were just going to make it. The quick supper had taken much longer than she anticipated. Bob had difficulty figuring out the menu, and he took so long in the restroom that she almost asked the waiter to check on him. Maggie raised her eyebrows when her companion, sporting his customary gray sweatshirt, jeans, and fishing hat, stopped at a table to introduce himself. The second time it happened, Maggie walked over, smiled, and took Bob's arm. "We'd better be on our way so we aren't late."

After parking the car, Maggie led Bob into the airport. She had a gift for caregiving honed over years of teaching and then during her late husband's battle with cancer. "I'm so grateful you could come with me, Bob. I'm enjoying your company."

Bob beamed. "Me, too."

"*Hola*, Maggie."

A striking figure with short black hair sprinkled with gray walked up to Maggie, picked her up, and twirled her around before gently setting her down and bowing to her companion. Maggie giggled and blushed. "Bob, this is Alberto."

They chatted for a few minutes until Maggie said, "If you don't need help with your luggage, Bob and I will get the car and bring it around to the front of the building."

Alberto winked and nodded. "I've learned to travel light. I'll watch for the car." He headed off to baggage claim.

Ellen was awakened by the pilot's announcement. "We'll be arriving at Central Wisconsin Airport right on schedule. It's currently 6:15 local time. Flight attendants, please prepare for landing."

As soon as the seatbelt sign went off, Ellen stood up. She exited the plane and made a quick stop at the first restroom she passed then headed to baggage claim. She stood back as travelers from a previous flight collected their bags. A handsome gentleman with salt and pepper hair smiled and nodded as he moved around her and headed to the exit.

Chapter 8

As he walked along the shore from Maggie's house, Alberto could see light from his home flickering through the trees. He breathed in the clean smell of pines and the freshwater lake. When he heard a loon, he returned its call as if to say, "I'm home."

He stepped onto the large lawn leading to their house. Light shone from several rooms, but the tiny sparkles he'd seen flickering through the trees came from Wanda's studio.

The sight brought an involuntary grin to Alberto's face. "She's home." Wanda was the first and only woman he'd fallen in love with, and he couldn't wait to see her face and hold her tight.

Alberto walked up the path leading to the door. He could see Wanda's shadow on the studio wall. He opened the door slowly and crept into the foyer. He set down his duffle bag, slipped off his shoes, and tiptoed toward the open studio door.

Alberto stood in the doorway and breathed in the scene. Purrdita was asleep on the window seat, and his beautiful wife was at her easel with her back to him. As she did so often when she painted, she was singing. He raised his eyebrows at the sight of a painting of himself in a Milwaukee Brewers cap on her easel.

Lydia Moen

His entrance had gone unnoticed. Purrdita was lost in sleep, and Wanda was lost in her painting. Alberto didn't want to startle his wife, but he couldn't resist the urge to creep over to her easel and put his arms around her.

The minute Alberto's hands touched Wanda's waist, she let out a scream remarkably akin to that of a screech owl, and whacked him on the head with her palette. In his fumbling attempts to protect himself, he knocked the palette into the air and across the room.

Paint splashed everywhere—on Wanda, on Alberto, and even on Purrdita, who let out a shriek not unlike Wanda's, and headed for the door. Every bit of fur on the cat's body stood on end. Her eyes, which were usually closed or exposed only as tiny slits, were the size of billiard balls. And although her claws were fully extended, she was unable to get any traction. She exerted an enormous amount of energy, her four legs spinning like the wheels of a fast-moving train, but Purrdita was finding it impossible to get out of the station.

Maggie dropped her clutch purse in a chair and picked up the phone. "Hello, MacDonald residence."

"Hi, Maggie. This is Charlie."

"Yes, Charlie." She frowned as she paced back and forth in the darkened room.

"Am I interrupting? Is this a bad time?"

"No, not at all. What is it?" Maggie sat down and tapped her foot.

"Uh, I missed you at the dock this morning. Did Alberto get in on time?"

"He did."

"Wish I could have seen Wanda's face. He's been gone so long."

Charlie paused. "Uh, the reason I called...we've been assigned a military family."

"Really? Do we know them?" Maggie stood up and switched on the kitchen light.

"It's the Jeffersons. They have two youngsters and one on the way. They live over on Seventh Street."

"I don't think I've met them. Do they go to our church?" Maggie strolled into the living room and turned on the end table lamps.

"I'm not sure, but church membership isn't a requirement. In fact, one of the goals of the ministry is to reach out to the community. The church is sponsoring a get-acquainted ice cream social at seven tomorrow evening. If that works for you, I can pick you up about ten minutes before."

Maggie flicked on the porch lights. "I'd like that. Thanks for getting us signed up. I'm looking forward to meeting our family. You're really good for me, Charlie."

Ellen kept her hand on the door and eased it closed. *He must have every light in the house on.* After putting her suitcase down, she paused, took a deep breath, and entered the living room. Her husband stood in front of the television, fumbling with the remote.

Bob looked up as she came in the room. "Ellen, I can't get this to work. Can you help me?"

"Seriously? Bob, I just walked in the door." Ellen crossed her arms and stared at him.

"Perfect timing. I just got home too."

She looked down and twisted her wedding ring. "Where were you?"

"Maggie and I picked up a friend of hers at the airport."

Lydia Moen

Her eyes widened, and her mouth dropped open. "You were at the airport?"

"We wanted you to come with us, but I couldn't find you. I can't get the news on. Can you fix this thing?" Bob handed her the remote.

Ellen turned on the news while Bob settled into his recliner. She walked back into the kitchen, grabbed her suitcase, turned off the overhead light, and slipped up to their bedroom. After unpacking her bag, she threw the navy blue blazer, khaki slacks, and the rest of her travel clothes into the hamper. Then she treated herself to a long, steamy shower.

Bob entered the room and turned the light back on just as Ellen was settling into bed. Hearing the noise from the television Bob had left on, she got up and dragged herself downstairs. She turned off the television and the table lamp next to Bob's chair. As she reached for the light that illuminated the painting of Washington, D.C., over the mantel, she paused and shook her head. She yanked the tiny cord and walked away from the darkened picture.

The next morning, the Santiagos sat at the breakfast table. When Alberto reached for Wanda's hand, she almost purred. "I've dreamed about this day. I've prayed about this day. And here you are—the man of my dreams, the answer to my prayers."

Alberto chuckled. "Well, you can get used to it. I plan on having breakfast with you every morning for a long time."

Wanda's eyes followed her husband as he crossed the room to refill his coffee cup. She felt the familiar lump rising in her throat. "Is that a promise, querido?"

"I think so. The church has asked me to serve as chaplain for The Harbor at Water's Edge. I'd also like to get involved in the adult daycare program at the community center."

Wanda jumped up and hugged him. "Praise the Lord! We can even carpool to the center."

"That would make driving to work a lot more pleasant for me. By the way, how are the murals coming along?"

They sat back down. Wanda winced and stared at her coffee cup. "Not that well."

"Let's talk about that. What's the problem?" Alberto reached over and put his hand on hers.

Wanda's eyes filled with tears. "My photos for the murals are lost."

Alberto paused and ran his hands through his hair. "Wanda, we need to get you organized. I have a couple days before I go back to work. I'll call Maggie and ask her to help."

Wanda held up a warning hand. "Stop right there! I don't need or want Maggie's help." She threw her damp tissue on the table, shoved her chair back, and flounced out of the room.

Next door, Maggie and Sammy strode across the lawn. "Come on, Sammy, we're going to clean out the shed today." They went in together—she to clean, he to sniff.

First Maggie moved Mac's fishing gear onto the lawn. "I'll save this for Josh." She looked over at Sammy. "Maybe you and I can even do a little fishing before he comes home."

Josh was their oldest grandson. He and his grandfather had fished for hours together. Maggie was eager for the opportunity to continue growing the relationship where Mac and Josh had left off—sitting on the bench at the end of dock, fishing poles in hand.

Dear Lord, please protect him and bring him home soon. She repeated the silent prayer that came to mind a dozen times a day.

As she moved in an orderly manner through the items in the shed, Maggie spotted a small wooden box on an upper shelf. *I wonder what this is.*

The walnut box with Maggie's initials inlaid in oak was a work in progress, something Mac must have started. *I bet this was a surprise for the wedding anniversary we never got to celebrate.* She collapsed onto a stack of boxes and let herself cry—soft drops that felt like sad little kisses on her cheeks.

For the first few months after Mac died, Maggie had tried to suppress her tears. She didn't want her children and grandchildren to worry about her during their own time of grief. And she didn't want others to see her sorrow as a lack of faith.

Then one day, as she and Wanda sat chatting in the Santiagos' gazebo, a sudden and unexpected wave of grief washed over her. She couldn't hold back the tears.

Wanda, who loved God above all others, had spoken from His Word. "'Jesus wept.' That passage gives us permission to grieve. So weep, Maggie. The tears are from God. Let them heal you."

After a few minutes, Maggie pulled her elbows off her knees, dug a tissue out of her pocket, wiped her eyes and nose, and got back to work. Within seconds, her companion let out a series of loud barks. She looked over at him just in time to see an animal scurry out from under the tarp Sammy had been scratching. Maggie ran from the shed with her arms flapping in the air. "Help me!" she shrieked. "Somebody, help me!"

Wanda slammed the door and marched down to the lakeshore. She stomped to the end of the dock. Then she noticed Ellen Bailey coming toward her in a kayak.

Taking a deep breath, Wanda waved at her neighbor. "Yoo-hoo, Ellen. You're back! We missed you."

She steered the kayak toward Wanda. "Thanks for noticing. Bob didn't even realize I was gone."

"Men." Wanda looked back at her home and rolled her eyes. "How I envy your being out on the water. I'd like to escape for a while myself. I've always wanted to kayak, but I'm sure it's much too hard for me."

Ellen pulled up in front of the Santiagos' dock. "Would you like to try it?"

Wanda took a step back. "Oh, dear. I don't think there's room for both of us in your little boat."

"That's probably true." Ellen put a hand over her mouth and cleared her throat. "We have two kayaks. Just walk over to our dock, and I'll help you get started."

Wanda felt trapped as she hustled along the shore toward her neighbor's dock. *How did I get myself into this? And how in the world can I get out of it?*

By the time Ellen had docked her kayak, Wanda had arrived at her friend's dock. The next words popped out of Wanda's mouth before Ellen even climbed out of her kayak. "Ellen, you're a sweetie for inviting me, but I'm just not dressed for this. I've got these capris on and this big old T-shirt. I can see from your darling outfit that I should be in a swimming suit or shorts. Maybe another day."

Ellen smiled. "Your clothes are fine. I only have time for a short ride anyway."

"Well...okay. I'm game—I guess. But remember, I'm a novice."

"Here, let me help you," Ellen offered. She held the small boat steady against the dock and guided Wanda as she placed one gold-sandaled foot and then the other into the cockpit.

Lydia Moen

Once seated, Wanda raised her paddle over her head. "I passed the entrance exam!"

The two women paddled to the other side of the lake. Wanda, determined to show Ellen she was a natural athlete, surged ahead. Her kayak tipped precariously as she peered over the side. "Oh, Ellen, look at all those plants down there. I may just shift my specialty from *land*scapes to *lake*scapes. God's been nudging me to get out here. I never would have seen them if you hadn't invited me along today. We'll have to do this more often."

"Yes, perhaps we can. I'm glad you're enjoying it."

Wanda looked over her shoulder at Ellen. "Sweetie, do you mind if I ask how you keep so trim?"

"I was born with a high metabolism."

"What a blessing. I was born with a big appetite." Wanda shook her head. She quit paddling and let Ellen catch up with her.

As they glided along, Wanda noticed her partner seemed more relaxed. Ellen laid her paddle across the kayak, leaned back, closed her eyes, and lifted her face toward the sun. Observing the golden highlights in Ellen's shiny, brown hair, Wanda reached up to her own black ponytail. She removed and replaced the scrunchy, then grabbed her paddle before it slipped into the water.

Ellen took a deep breath. "Hmmm, this air is so fresh. In D.C., we'd be more apt to smell bus exhaust."

"We do have clean air here, but I bet you miss Washington."

Ellen didn't respond. She stared silently at the far shore. After a moment, she looked at her watch and frowned. "I really should get back to Bob."

Wanda hesitated and then answered in a hushed voice. "Yes, I should probably get back to Alberto too."

As soon as they reached the dock, Wanda stood up in the kayak, raised the paddle high above her head, and shouted, "I did it!"

No sooner was Wanda's proclamation of victory out of her mouth than her kayak tipped over and she tumbled into the water, arms flailing madly and legs thrashing like a school of fish in a feeding frenzy. She ended up submerged in the shallow water.

After one still moment, in which all of the lake seemed to hold its breath, Wanda's long, black, curly ponytail emerged amidst much sputtering and gasping.

Ellen extended a hand to her new kayaking partner. "Oh, Wanda, I'm so sorry. I should have warned you about not making sudden moves. Are you all right? What can I do to help?"

"How about grabbing that gold sandal before it floats away?"

"Wanda Dobinski Santiago, what in the name of heaven are you doing down there?"

Wanda recognized the controlled and authoritative voice. She looked up from the water and sputtered at her husband, "I'm kayaking. What does it look like I'm doing?"

Surprisingly Maggie's nearly hysterical pleas for help were answered.

"Maggie, what's the matter?" Charlie shouted. "What can I do?"

"Oh, Charlie, I'm being chased by a huge rodent! He's in the shed. Help me, please!"

Charlie sprinted toward the shed and stepped inside, while Maggie watched from a distance, clasping her hands in front of her face. She heard thrashing about and saw Sammy run out the door. There was more thrashing, followed by a long period of quiet, then Charlie came walking out the door with a butterfly net extended in front of him. Maggie could see the apparently lifeless form of a tiny mouse at the bottom of the net.

She peered over her glasses. "Mercy, Charlie, you didn't kill him, did you?"

"Oh, no. I knew you wouldn't approve of that. He may have passed out from fear, but he'll be fine. I checked all around the shed, and he was the only critter in there. I'll just take him with me across the lake to the big field and let him go." Charlie was a catch-and-release kind of guy.

"Thank you. I appreciate your assistance, but I don't want to hold you up any longer."

"I'm glad I was here to help. I was just putting your mail in the box when I heard your screams." Charlie winked and gave her a salute. "Don't forget to pick it up."

Maggie blushed. "I won't forget." Then she winked back and returned the salute.

After Charlie left, Maggie decided to call it a day on cleaning the shed. As she switched off the light, she spied the box that Mac had been making for her. She stared at it for a moment, then picked it up with both hands and held it close as she ambled back to the house.

The handsome gentleman offered a hand to Ellen. "Let me help you up on the dock."

As she reached out to him, her eyes narrowed and she tilted her head. "Do I know you?"

With Ellen on the dock, Alberto turned and pulled Wanda onto the dock as well, while Wanda introduced her new friend to her husband.

Alberto shook Ellen's hand. "I'm glad to meet you. No, I don't think we've met before. I've only been two places since I returned last night—the airport and home."

Ellen snapped her fingers. "That's where it was. I saw you in baggage claim."

Wanda moved closer to them and shivered. "I hate to interrupt, but I have to run home and change into something dry. Before I get all prettied up, I need a picture with my kayaking instructor. Alberto, do you have your cellphone with you?"

When Alberto pulled out his phone, Ellen moved off to the side. "That's not necessary. Just get a picture of your wife."

Wanda drew Ellen into a drippy hug. "Get back here! I would never have dared to get into that tiny boat if it weren't for you."

Alberto focused the cellphone on the two women. "Say cheese!"

Ellen had to laugh. "What else would we say? We're in Wisconsin!"

"Nice job, ladies. I got two good shots, and you can see the kayaks in both of them."

"Thanks for the ride, Ellen. It was a splash!" Wanda chuckled as she headed back home. "Now you two get acquainted. I'll be back in a flash."

Ellen grabbed a towel and dried herself off as she and Alberto moved to the bench. "So where were you flying in from?"

"Mexico. I was returning from a two-month mission assignment. What about you?"

Ellen shifted and looked down. "I just took a quick trip to D.C."

"It's helpful to be able to stay close to friends after you move away."

Ellen held back tears for the umpteenth time that day. "Yes, that would have been nice."

Alberto reached into his pocket and handed her a card. "I can't take the place of your friends, Ellen, but if you ever want to talk, I'm a pretty good listener."

She looked at his card. "Oh, that's right. Wanda told me you're a pastor. But we aren't members of your church."

Lydia Moen

"You don't have to belong to our church. Keep the card. You may not need it now, but I'll be available if you do. Frankly, since I just got back home, I'm looking for customers." He winked and added, "Of course, there's no charge."

Ellen flicked the corner of the card with her thumb. She looked out at the lake for a moment and then back at Alberto. "Thanks for the offer, but I'm really fine."

Chapter 9

Maggie's smile broadened as Charlie pulled his boat up to her dock. He tugged on his UCLA cap before reaching into his bag and handing most of her mail to Sammy.

"And this one's for you!"

Maggie grasped the letter and clasped it to her chest. "It's from Josh!"

She twisted the hem of her pink cotton sweater as if she were a young girl talking to her boyfriend. "Charlie, I notice you're ahead of schedule today. Would you have time for a glass of iced tea and a muffin?"

Charlie turned off his engine and tied up his boat. He hopped up on the dock and followed Maggie to the house. She walked slowly and felt his hand in the small of her back as they approached the porch.

When Maggie came back with the drinks and muffins, Charlie stood up and waited for her to sit before slipping back into the chair next to hers. "You'll probably want to get right to Josh's letter, so I'll just sit here and enjoy the day and the refreshments while you read."

"That's so like you, Charlie. But the letter can wait." Maggie thought about saying more but held back. Her heart was racing, and she could feel the flush rising in her face.

Charlie took a big gulp of his iced tea and picked up a cranberry muffin. "These look terrific, Maggie. Did you bake them?"

"I did." She paused for a minute and then, looking down at her plate, added, "I was hoping I'd have someone to share them with."

"I'm glad I'm able to accommodate you, ma'am." Charlie's grin was contagious.

"Before I forget, I want to thank you for your chivalry during the rodent attack the other day. I found the butterfly net beside the mailbox. Thanks for returning it."

"Happy to be of help. I let the little guy out in the field as promised. He laid there on the ground for a second—I think he was playing dead—then ran into the brush."

"I appreciate everything you do for me, Charlie, including the detailed report."

Sammy put his nose under Charlie's arm and gave it a not-too-gentle shove, almost spilling the iced tea.

"Sammy. What are you doing?" Maggie's question sent the golden slinking a few feet away, where he plopped down with a heavy sigh. "I'm sorry, Charlie. I think he's a little jealous."

"Well, maybe he should be."

"I wonder what Ellen is doing." Bob set his fishing pole down on the dock and sauntered up to the house.

"Is lunch ready yet?"

He found Ellen's note on the counter telling him about the fruit plate and croissant she'd left in the refrigerator.

"I think I'd rather heat up this leftover pea soup."

Bob grabbed the plastic container, set it on the stove, and turned on the burner. Then he headed out the door, hopped in his car, and backed out of the garage.

A familiar woman with a long black ponytail waved him to a stop. "Hi, neighbor! I've brought you some sweet corn from the vegetable stand. It was picked this morning."

"That looks great, but I have to get going."

"Okay. Is Ellen home?"

Bob scratched his head and scowled. "I don't think so."

"I'll just leave it on your kitchen counter."

"Thanks. It sure is a beautiful day." Bob gave her a thumbs-up as he pulled out of the driveway.

Ellen leaned back into the soft vinyl chair, her feet resting on the matching foot stool. She closed her eyes and relished the gentle massage of the stylist's fingers. She breathed in the conditioner's lavender mint fragrance. The steady pulse of the warm water carried her to the brink of sleep.

Two hours later, Ellen emerged from the New You salon feeling exactly like its name. She found an easy listening station on the car radio and rolled her window down. By the time she reached the four-way stop, she was singing along with Celine Dionne.

She looked in the visor mirror and smiled as she fluffed her shiny brown and golden hair. Ellen did a double take when she pushed the visor back up and caught sight of a large sedan going past in the opposite direction. *Hmm. A navy blue Cadillac. I thought Bob had the only one in town.* Ellen bit the inside of her lip and shook her head. *It couldn't be.*

Lydia Moen

Wanda twisted her multi-colored ceramic necklace and frowned. *That's strange. Bob's driving again. I'm kinda surprised he got his license back so soon.*

She smelled the smoke as soon as she entered the house and dashed into the kitchen. "Ellen, are you in here?"

When she saw the flames, she dropped the bag of corn and ran to the stove. The black, acrid air stung her eyes and burned her throat. She lurched back, assaulted by the heat.

"Lord, help me!" she gasped. "What should I do?" Wanda's eyes darted around the kitchen. She snatched a placemat from the table, wrapped it around her hand, and turned off the burner. Choking and gulping for air, she stumbled to the phone and dialed 911 on her way out the door.

The aroma of coffee wafted in Bob's window, and he followed it. Pulling sharply into a space in front of the Java Joint, he cut off another car. When the driver beeped his horn, Bob smiled and waved. He hopped out and took a seat at one of the outdoor tables.

He ordered a large coffee and a caramel roll, closed his eyes, and tipped his head up to catch the full warmth of the noonday sun. A copy of the *Lake Breezes* left on the table held no interest for him, so he gave it to a couple of teenagers sitting nearby.

The waitress returned with his order, and Bob reached for his wallet. "Do I pay...?" He scratched his head and looked under the table.

"Is something wrong, sir?"

Bob checked his pockets again. "My wallet's missing."

"I'll look around inside and see if anyone's turned one in."

She returned a moment later and shook her head. "No luck. Do you live in town?"

"Yes. We just moved here."

"Welcome to Water's Edge. This is my mom's shop. We'll make this one on us."

Warmed by the coffee, the sun, and the friendly waitress, Bob headed down the road a half-hour later. He sang along with the radio, making up his own words to the familiar tune. His eyes scanned the stores on either side of the street as he passed by. He never looked in his rearview mirror until he heard the siren.

The officer approached Bob's open window.

"Did I do something wrong?"

"Mr. Bailey, I'm sure your driver's license hasn't been reinstated. You can't be driving without a valid license."

Bob slumped in his seat.

"I'll give you a ride home, and we'll have a deputy bring your car over later today. Make sure this never happens again, and I'll let you go with a warning."

Ellen and Bob ate at the Water's Edge Inn that evening. When they returned home, Bob headed down to the lake, and Ellen hustled over to the ringing phone and put it on speaker. "Hello."

"Hi, this is Smokey the Bear," Wanda chuckled. "How are you and Bob and the house doing?"

Ellen flipped her glasses on top of her head. "Things are pretty much back to normal, whatever the new normal is. We're lucky there was a nice breeze, so the smoke cleared out quickly. Thanks to you there was no significant damage. I don't know how we'll ever repay you."

Lydia Moen

"No repayment required. But if you insist, how about another kayaking lesson? I'm dying to check out those lakescapes again. That little dip I took didn't dampen my enthusiasm a bit." Wanda laughed at her own joke.

"Fabulous. We just got back from dinner." Ellen glanced at the lake. "And Bob is on the dock fishing."

"I'll be right over."

"I'll get the paddles and lifejackets. And, Wanda, thanks for calling."

Ellen walked out the door and saw Maggie sitting on the dock next to Bob. Both of them had fishing poles, but they appeared to be doing more talking than fishing.

She could hear Wanda singing before her kayaking partner popped into view. She was a vision in pink, from the straw hat with a ribbon tied under her chin to the flowered T-shirt and matching capris. Ellen looked down at her tan polo shirt and navy shorts with matching tennis shoes and sighed. *Maybe a little more color isn't a bad idea.*

"I'm prepared this time." Wanda held up a foot. "I'm wearing my floatable flip-flops."

Ellen laughed. "Excellent! And they match your capris and pedicure perfectly."

"Well, I am an artist; I should know how to coordinate colors."

Once the two women were in their kayaks, they paddled out onto the lake, waving at Bob and Maggie as they passed the end of the dock. Wanda called to Maggie, "Popcorn and lemonade in the gazebo after kayaking. Just the women, Bobby. You'll have to entertain yourself."

"Aw, shucks!" he hollered back.

They paddled for about fifteen minutes across two lakes before Ellen led them down a channel and into a small cove in the woods. "Bob and I found this spot the other day."

"I love watching the two of you kayak together," Wanda said. "It reminds me of Maggie and Mac."

Ellen stopped paddling and looked at Wanda. "I know she misses her husband, but she seems to be doing pretty well."

"Maggie has the assurance that she'll see him again in heaven, and she knows he'd want her to make the most of her time here. She trusts God's timing and plan for her life."

Ellen shook her head. "It must be nice to be so certain."

"It's wonderful—blessed assurance, as the hymn says." Wanda burst into song.

Blessed assurance, Jesus is mine.
Oh, what a foretaste of glory divine.

When Wanda started singing, Ellen pressed her lips together and raised her eyebrows. But the setting was serenely beautiful, with water so clear they could see rocks, small shells, and an occasional fish. Magnificent birches hung over both banks, and water lilies marked their liquid road. A blue heron surprised them when it flew out of the cattails along the shore and landed at the top of a tree just to their right. Ellen kept her paddle out of the water and leaned back against the cushion. She closed her eyes and listened to the words of Wanda's song.

...watching and waiting, looking above,
filled with His goodness, lost in His love.

Half an hour later, the kayakers joined Maggie in the gazebo. Wanda grabbed a handful of popcorn. "Mmm, mmm. Thanks, Maggie. I'm starving from all the exercise. I'll get the lemonade."

Ellen cleared her throat as she looked out at the lake. Then she turned to Maggie. "Thank you for spending time with Bob. It was such a relief to get out and not have to worry about him. I assume you heard the fire trucks this afternoon."

"Actually I was gone at the time, but Wanda called to let me know you were both okay."

Lydia Moen

Wanda bumped the door open with her hip and placed a tray of lemonade on the table. "Since it's girls' night at the gazebo, Alberto went over to your house, Ellen. He's going to talk Bob into watching a Brewers' game."

"Oh, Bob'll be thrilled." Ellen flopped back in her chair and let out a big sigh.

"It's been quite a day, hasn't it?" When Maggie leaned forward and looked up, Ellen met her gaze, nodded her head, and closed her eyes.

The three women sat without speaking for several minutes before Ellen broke the silence. "I realize we haven't known each other very long, and I'm normally a private person, but I need to talk with someone about Bob."

Her gaze took in both of her new friends. "His Alzheimer's is really becoming a problem. This afternoon's fire is the latest and scariest example. Did you know Chief Gallego caught him driving today and brought him home in his police cruiser?"

Maggie gasped. "Thank the Lord it was Carlos that intercepted him!"

"Seriously. In D.C., we'd be sitting in night court right now."

Wanda shook her head. "Oh, Ellen, I could have stopped him. I talked to Bob just as he was leaving. I assumed he'd gotten his license back." She reached over and put her hand on Ellen's. "Alzheimer's is such a difficult disease."

"It's affecting everything in our lives. He forgets to do things all the time. I keep finding piles of fishing tackle on the kitchen table. We're constantly looking for things he's lost and eventually finding them in bizarre places, if we find them at all. It never ends."

Ellen leaned forward and folded her arms on the table. "I'm getting completely frustrated. I've even started losing my temper with him. Then I feel guilty for being impatient."

She shook her head. "I can't lean on my daughter. She's too busy. I can't count on my D.C. friends. They've gone on without me. I feel so alone. I know I should be strong enough to handle this, but…"

Ellen's face crumpled and she dropped her head onto her arms and wept. Wanda stroked her back as Maggie moved her chair next to their distraught friend's. When Ellen's body stopped shaking and her sobs subsided, she heard Maggie's whispered prayer.

"Heavenly Father, comfort Your child, Ellen. Help her know she's not alone. Show us how to love our neighbor as You love us, Lord. Thank you for bringing Ellen and Bob to our shoreline, and bless them with Your love and peace."

Chapter 10

Wanda tiptoed out of the bedroom and down the stairs. Purrdita made even less noise than Wanda until her mistress started fixing the morning's kibbles. "*Meeoooww! Meeoooww! Meeoooww!*"

"Shhhhh! We don't want to wake Alberto. I'm hurrying, Purrdita. I want you nice and full, so you'll be sleepy when I start your portrait. Let's put your bowl here in the studio window seat to make sure you're in this breathtaking sunlight."

Wanda went back to the kitchen, grabbed a breakfast bar and a diet root beer, and returned to her studio. By the time she'd set up her easel and gathered her paints and brushes, her subject was snoring softly.

She sketched.

She sang.

She squinted.

She sighed.

And then...Alberto entered the studio.

"I thought I heard someone down here. I bet I know what you're doing."

Wanda stepped out from behind the easel, batted her eyelashes at her husband, and pulled him by the hand. "Well, come on around here and take a look, Pastor Santiago."

"Mrs. Santiago, are you inviting me into your studio to see your sketches?"

"Why, Pastor Santiago, I think you've found me out."

Alberto lifted her off her feet and swung her around before depositing her gently next to himself. She tilted her head back to accept his kiss. When she opened her eyes, she saw that he was squinting at the portrait of Purrdita. She pulled away. "What are you frowning about?"

"Why are you painting a picture of Purrdita when all you can talk about is getting the murals done?"

"How can I work on the murals if I don't have the pictures?"

"When are you planning to look for them?"

"I don't know. Maybe when I find someone who's willing to help me."

Wanda turned her back to her husband and stared out the window. After a moment, she bit down on her bottom lip and faced Alberto. With reddened eyes and quivering jaw she stuttered, "Nothing I do pleases you. I don't keep house. I don't know where I put the pictures. I don't even paint what you want me to paint. Alberto, I don't tell you what to say in your sermons, so please don't tell me how to run my studio."

Ellen felt refreshed after her morning jog and shower. She fixed breakfast for Bob and herself and then headed out. She met Alberto at the door to the church offices. "Thanks for making time for me."

"It's good to see you, Ellen. I'm glad you called."

Ellen sensed that Alberto was trying to put her at ease by recounting the events of his surprise homecoming. As he finished telling the story, they reached his office. She was laughing almost uncontrollably, breathing in gulps, eyes overflowing.

The tears triggered by Ellen's laughter soon turned to sobs. Offering her one of the two easy chairs in front of his office fireplace, he took the other for himself, handed her a box of tissues, and sat back.

Ellen wiped her eyes and looked down at the tiny shoulder bag in her lap. She fiddled with its strap. "I'm sorry. It's been a rough couple of days."

"Give yourself a break, Ellen. You've been through a lot, not only in the last few days but in the last few months. How's your home? Did you have any serious damage from the fire?"

Ellen felt her face flush. She cleared her throat. "No. It was really lucky that Wanda showed up when she did, or we might have."

A single tear trickled down her cheek before a flood of thoughts tumbled out of her mouth. "...the accident...the fire...the driving..." She took a deep breath and hesitated. "I'm embarrassed about my escape to D.C. You must think I'm a horrible person. I can't believe I just took off like that. If something had happened to Bob, I would never have forgiven myself."

"I understand." The pastor's gentle smile felt like a warm hug to Ellen. "Caregiving for a loved one is a demanding job that nobody applies for. One of the biggest mistakes caregivers make is assuming full responsibility for the person they're caring for. You can't do it alone. And you've already made a good decision by moving closer to family."

Ellen sat up a little straighter. Her tears were softer now, no longer an uncontrollable torrent. Alberto leaned forward in his chair. "Perhaps it would help if you could get some consistent relief from the never-ending burden. Are you aware of the community center's adult daycare program?"

Ellen stood up and glared at the pastor. "Seriously? Daycare? Alberto, my husband doesn't need a babysitter!"

Maggie walked up to the bait shop. A sign on the door read, "Back in 30 Minutes."

She folded her arms and tapped her foot. Then she walked around to the side of the shop.

"Neil, I've been looking for you." Maggie shouted across the alley.

Neil Olsen had just secured a padlock on the wide overhead door of a small unmarked building. He gave Maggie a quick tip of his fishing hat and hurried across the alley to meet her.

"Hi, Maggie."

"Hello, Neil." She peered over her glasses and pointed to his sling. "What happened to your arm?"

"Oh, it's just a little bursitis. Sorry if I kept you waiting."

"No apology necessary." Maggie raised an eyebrow. "I've never understood these signs. How do your customers know when thirty minutes started? It could have been one minute ago or twenty-nine minutes. Perhaps a clock face showing the time you'll be back would be more helpful."

"I'll take that under advisement."

The bell on Olsen's bait shop door jingled as the two entered. "I haven't seen you in here for a while. How's everything going?" Neil checked his watch.

"You're right. It's been a while. I haven't done much fishing since Mac died. But I have new neighbors, and he's an avid angler. I thought I'd treat us to some fresh bait. What are they biting on?"

"These grubs are selling well." Neil looked up as the bell over the shop's door jingled.

Maggie turned around. "Hello, Joe. How are things at the Treasure

Chest?"

Joe shrugged. "Same as usual."

"I didn't know you were a fisherman. Mr. Olsen highly recommends these grubs."

"Oh, he's not here for bait. Joe and I have some business to discuss." Neil hustled around the counter, put the grub container in a bag, and handed it to Maggie. "Is there anything else I can get for you?"

"No, thank you. I'll pay for these and be out of your way." Maggie opened her purse.

"I'll just start a tab for you. Good to see you again."

Maggie frowned and hurried outside. She paused at the curb. When she looked back, the door was closed, and Joe's hand was turning the *Open* sign around.

Maggie had just gotten in her car when her cellphone rang. "Hello?"

"Oh, hi, Alberto. What's up?"

After a pause, she said, "Sure. That's a great idea. I'll pick up something for lunch and be there in twenty minutes."

It hadn't taken Wanda long to escape the problems at home and find a little comfort. "I'll take one of the chocolate frosted with sprinkles. And a large chocolate mocha with extra whipped cream." Wanda tucked into one of the booths near the back of the Java Joint with her cupcake, waiting for the mocha to be delivered.

Her eyes devoured the cupcake. She drummed her fingers on the Formica. Then she picked up a copy of *Lake Breezes* and slid the cupcake behind it. She peeked over the top of the newspaper, retrieved the cupcake, and slowly submerged her finger into the rich, dark frosting.

She closed her eyes and plunged the decadent delicacy deep into her mouth.

"Excuse me, Mrs. Santiago. Here's your mocha."

Wanda started choking and covered her mouth with a napkin.

"I didn't mean to scare you. Are you all right?"

Wanda nodded her head.

On her way out of the coffee shop a little later, she stopped to dig in her polka dot tote for her keys. It took a while, but she found them. She looked up and spied a notice for a nearby craft show benefitting wounded veterans. "That might be just the inspiration I need."

After two hours of strolling up and down the aisles at the VFW hall, Wanda drove back to Lakeshore Lane. She waltzed in the door. "Alberto, you're home."

The pastor greeted his wife with a peck on the cheek. "I was starting to wonder where you went. I've got a surprise for you."

Wanda caught a glimpse of a pastel blue sleeve behind Alberto's back. "Oh, Maggie. This is a surprise! What's gone on here while I've been out?"

Alberto grinned and shook his finger at her. "We'll show you, but first you have to close your eyes."

She obeyed and immediately felt Alberto's and Maggie's hands in hers. A tingle ran up and down Wanda's back as she allowed her companions to lead her from the room.

"Tah dah!" the conspirators chimed in unison.

Wanda's mouth dropped open as soon as she opened her eyes. "What have you done?"

"Do you like it?"

Wanda spun around, eyes glaring, and poked Alberto in the chest. "If you didn't want me to paint, why didn't you just tell me?"

"What do you mean? Don't you like it? Now you can find everything."

"I won't be able to find anything." She paced around the room, her arms sweeping over the uncompromising, un-artsy, un-Wanda order of her once free-spirited studio. "My paints are all mixed up. Where are my sketches? And you moved my easels!"

Alberto reached for her hand. "But, Wanda—"

She swatted him away. "I'm going to my room. Call me when I have my studio back." She whirled around and stomped out the door and up the stairs, then hollered down to Alberto, "My ancestors built and enjoyed this home for its surroundings and peacefulness, not for extreme, stifling organization." Her ancestral home shook as she slammed the bedroom door behind her.

Shortly before dinner, Ellen went out to check on Bob. She stepped over the boxes that covered much of the floor and watched as her husband moved tools from one box to another. "How are the plans coming for turning this into your workshop, honey?"

Bob's face lit up like a lighthouse beacon. He wiped his hands on his gray sweatshirt and dusted off his jeans. "I've already hired a handyman. We're going to put shelves over here and pegboard up over there for saws and hammers."

Ellen watched quietly, encouraging Bob from time to time by asking a question. He spent the next ten minutes describing in detail exactly what he wanted where and why.

She couldn't decide whether the tears burning the back of her eyelids were tears of joy or sorrow. Her husband was back! She knew it wouldn't last long; he'd slip away again. She didn't know where he went, and if or when, he'd come back. But at this moment, Bob was here...with her.

"It sounds like a great plan, Bob. I can't wait to see what you do.

Lydia Moen

I'm going inside to check on dinner. By the way, what's the handyman's name?"

Bob handed her a dirty business card. "He stopped over this morning."

Ellen frowned. "Hmm. Ray Hoffman. Did you get any references on him?"

Wanda left the bedroom and headed downstairs as soon as she heard the outside door close. Alberto met her on the seventh step.

"I'm sorry," they both said at the same time.

They grinned at each other, and Alberto led Wanda toward the kitchen. "Before Maggie went home, she and I planned another surprise for you. We're pretty sure you'll like this one."

Her two best friends had made dinner, set the table—complete with lighted candles—and selected soft music for the CD player.

"Now this is the kind of surprise I like," Wanda cooed.

Alberto pulled out a chair for his bride. When she was seated, he got down on one knee. "Querida, forgive me. You're right. That's *your* studio. You're the boss in there. I know I bungled it today, but I'd like another chance to help."

Wanda put her hand on his cheek. "You and Maggie had good intentions, but ever since you got back from Mexico, I've felt like you've been trying to change me. Alberto, are you unhappy with me?"

He sat down across from her. "I love you, Wanda, just the way you are."

Tears tumbled down Wanda's cheeks. "I know I need to be better organized. But that's not who I am. I'm not a librarian who shelves every book according to the Dewey Decimal System. I don't want to

88

spend my life filing papers, organizing art materials, and cleaning house. I want to paint, and sing, and love God."

Alberto reached across the dinner table and took her hand. "And that's what you should do. But what would you think about getting some cleaning help?"

Wanda wiped away her tears. "Oh, Alberto! Can we afford it?"

He looked into her eyes and squeezed her hand. "Can we afford not to?"

Maggie was waiting in the driveway when the car pulled up. "Charlie, you're right on time."

"I wouldn't want to get in trouble with the teacher for being tardy." Charlie winked.

Her eyes widened as they pulled into the church parking lot. "Good heavens, I had no idea there were so many military families in Water's Edge."

As soon as the two pinned on their nametags, a small boy ran up to greet them. "Hi. I'm James, but everyone calls me Junior."

"I bet you're Mrs. MacDonald and you're Mr. Bingham." A tall, pregnant woman extended her hand. "We're the Jefferson family. I'm Tamara, and this is my daughter, Jessica."

"How did you know who we are?" Maggie asked, stooping down to shake Junior's hand.

"Look at our nametags. They match. We all have golden retriever stickers."

Charlie held out his hand to the young boy. "You're right."

Junior looked up at his mother. "Can we get in line for ice cream now?"

As soon as they were seated at a table, Maggie asked Tamara when she had last spoken with her husband.

"We saw him tonight!" Junior shouted between spoonsful of ice cream sundae.

Charlie's spoon stopped halfway to his mouth. "You saw him tonight?"

Tamara answered for her son as he hopped off his chair and joined a group of children at the other end of the room. "We video-chat with my husband whenever he has access to a computer. It's great. We get to see that Daddy's okay, and Daddy gets to watch his kids growing—including the one that's yet to be born."

Maggie leaned forward and whispered. "When's the baby due?"

"I'm hoping both Daddy and baby will be here before the leaves fall."

Maggie turned to the little girl beside her. "Your daddy and a new sister or brother. Wouldn't those be the best presents ever?"

Jessica's black curls bounced as she nodded her head. Then she held up her doll to Maggie. "I want a baby sister just like this."

Maggie touched the hem of the doll's dress. "She's beautiful. Does she have a name?"

"Jenny."

Maggie winked at Tamara. "That makes sense. Do you know what you're going to have—a Jack or a Jill?"

Tamara laughed. "We don't know yet, but we do know its name will start with a J."

Charlie grinned as he joined the conversation. "I found picking a name was one of the hardest parts of having a baby."

"You wouldn't think that if you were a woman." Tamara and Maggie exchanged a chuckle and a knowing glance.

"You're absolutely right. I don't know how you gals do it." Charlie pushed his chair back. "Now I'm going to see if I can get in on the fun at the other end of the room. I think I can still color inside the lines."

Maggie's heart warmed as she watched Charlie squat onto a tiny chair next to Junior's and put his arm around his new five-year-old pal.

Later that evening, Maggie sat at the kitchen table, Mac's handmade gift in her hands. She opened the lid, rested her chin on her clasped hands, and stared into the empty box. After several minutes, she nodded her head and smiled. She carried the keepsake upstairs and set it on the bed before placing her large jewelry box beside it. Then she sat down and pulled out the top drawer of the bigger case.

Her hand trembled as she picked out the delicate gold cross Mac had given her on their first anniversary. She could almost feel his hands fastening the clasp at the back of her neck as she positioned it in the new box. Each piece she touched brought back memories of Mac—anniversaries, birthdays, vacations.

The ringing of the phone shattered Maggie's mental mosaic of their times together.

She glared at the intruder before picking it up. "Hello, MacDonald residence."

"Is that you, Maggie?"

"You know it is, Charlie." She jiggled her foot and waited for him to speak.

"I really enjoyed this evening. Tamara and her kids are great."

"Yes, I could tell you and Junior bonded quickly. Jessica's a little shy but very sweet. Their mother's doing a nice job of raising them."

"I'm sure it's not easy. I think we can be a big help to her."

"Is there something in particular you wanted, Charlie?"

"Er, well, yes. I wondered if you would like to go to the band concert with me tomorrow night."

Maggie's gaze settled on Mac's walnut box.

"Maggie? Maggie, are you still there?"

"I'm sorry, Charlie. I'm still here, but I don't think I can make it tomorrow."

"Have I done something to upset you?"

Maggie could hear the concern in Charlie's voice. "No, you haven't done anything wrong. I'm just a little tired."

"I'm sorry I bothered you. Get a good night's sleep."

"I'll do that. Thank you for understanding." Maggie stared at the phone in her hand for a moment before she set it back down. Then she put both boxes on her dresser and got ready for bed.

Chapter 11

Sammy's barking woke Maggie with a start.

"What? What's wrong?" A loud pop made her jump. "Sammy, did you hear that? I think it was a gunshot."

Sammy paced and growled and barked again.

"Hush, Sammy. I need to hear." She stopped talking and forced herself to breathe.

Flowered nightie askew, Maggie reached for the flashlight on her nightstand. She didn't turn it on but instead tiptoed across her bedroom, raising the flashlight above her head. If she hadn't been so frightened, she might have laughed at the picture she made—a five-foot, five-inch grandmother, creeping toward the hallway, armed with nothing but a flashlight.

Sammy gave a long, deep-throated growl then panted like a chain smoker climbing a long flight of stairs. He finally sat with his ears raised and head cocked.

"Good boy," she whispered. "You're a good watch dog. You probably woke the whole lake with your barking."

Maggie crept down the stairs, her flashlight still unlit and held overhead. "Sammy, come. Stay right next to me." He leaned against her leg and inched along beside her.

Maggie pressed her back against the door jamb leading to the dining room, crouched down a bit, then turned and slithered into the room. Keeping her back against the wall, Maggie sidestepped to the kitchen doorway.

Then she heard it.

Click.

She felt lightheaded. She shivered. She tried to hold her breath but needed more air. She gave in, exhaled, then drew in another breath.

And then, just as she was about to enter the kitchen—

Click.

Maggie was right in thinking she wasn't the only one on the lake to be awakened that night.

Wanda's head jerked up. "Who's there? Don't try anything! I've got my pepper spray aimed at the door."

"Dios mío. ¿Qual es el problema?"

She grasped the dislodged purple curler that hung in front of her nose and rewound the lock of black hair. "Alberto, keep your voice down." Then she shouted, "And my husband's here too. You better get out while you can."

Alberto sat up and rubbed his eyes. "Who are you yelling at?"

"Whoever just broke into our house."

Alberto froze then tilted his head toward the door. "I don't hear a thing, Wanda. Pleasant dreams." He plunked back down, turned on his side, and pulled the pillow over his head.

Wanda pushed up the sleeve of her NYPD pajamas and shook her fist in the air. "My husband's cousin is the chief of police. He'll be here any second. This is your last warning."

Ellen, too, stirred in her sleep. *Was that gunfire?* A dog barked. She reached her hand out to touch her husband's shoulder. "Bob, Bob, did you hear...? Bob?"

The other side of the bed was empty. Ellen glanced at the clock—just past midnight. Bob had been snoring when she came to bed at ten.

She raced downstairs. "Bob, where are you?" She checked the kitchen, the entire first floor.

The sudden clanking of metal drew Ellen to the garage door. She froze. *Is Bob in the garage at midnight, or is it someone else? What if it is Bob and that noise I heard was him being shot?* She held her breath and nudged the door open.

Maggie didn't make a sound. She didn't even blink. She scanned the room, her eyes resting on the glow over the kitchen window. She watched the illuminated second hand move rhythmically around the clock face. *Click. Click. Click.*

She cleared her throat and patted her partner. "Oh, for heaven's sake, Sammy, it's just the clock."

She inspected each room on the first floor, examining every space large enough to be used as a hiding place. All clear.

She was about to go back upstairs when Sammy started growling again. He led her into the living room and straight to the large picture window overlooking the lake.

Through the fog, Maggie could see a figure on a boat or raft that appeared to be just leaving her dock. She backed away from the window and watched as the silent, low-lying craft slowly disappeared into the mist.

"Is that what you heard, Sammy? I don't like the idea of someone hanging around our dock in the middle of the night. But I shouldn't worry. Mac always said you were the best security system we could have."

Sammy cocked his head at the mention of Mac. Maggie reached down and ruffled his ears. "You miss him, don't you, boy? I do too. If he were here, he'd tell us to go back to bed. Sammy, come. Let's try to get some sleep." Although Sammy had his own bed, on this night the two remaining members of the MacDonald family would sleep in Maggie's.

"Dear Lord, protect us," she prayed as she pulled the covers up under her chin.

Just as she was drifting off to sleep, she heard a vehicle go by. *That sounded like a pickup. Who would be driving down our lane at this time of night?*

Wanda was almost certain she heard a truck on the road behind her house. She glanced at the bedside clock and then at the window. She frowned and shook her head.

She had no idea what had disturbed her sleep, it was obvious Alberto wasn't concerned. She shrugged. Maybe she'd just had a nightmare. Whatever it was, Wanda decided God would protect her and her husband.

She reached for the remote and put on her headphones. As soon as her head hit the pillow, Wanda flicked through the channels until she heard wailing police sirens and squealing tires from a favorite crime show. The familiar sounds comforted her, and ten minutes later they were accompanied by the rhythmic crescendos of her snores.

As Ellen opened the door to the garage, her husband turned and stared at her.

"Bob, you scared me. It's the middle of the night."

He crossed his arms and glared at her. "I'm trying to get organized."

Ellen shivered. "Didn't you hear those gunshots?"

"What gunshots? I heard some noise, but I thought it was just some kids with fire crackers."

"Seriously? I could swear I heard gunshots. Then, when I couldn't find you, I was frantic."

Bob walked over, placed his hands on his wife's arms, and looked into her eyes. "Ellen, calm down. Everything's all right."

She pulled away and walked toward the door. "No, it's not all right. It's not all right at all. Bob, it's the middle of the night. You need to get some sleep."

"I guess I am kind of tired."

"Let's go back in the house." Ellen flipped off the garage light and locked the door behind her.

Once inside, she said, "You go on ahead. I'm not ready to go up yet." She watched Bob climb the stairs and heard his footsteps in their bedroom.

Ellen's shoulders slumped as she shuffled over to the fireplace. She folded her arms and rested them on the mantel. Her head resisted but then submitted to the pull of the painting—the city she'd left behind. A tear trickled down her cheek as she turned on the TV and sank into Bob's recliner. Ellen put her head back and closed her eyes. She listened to the sound of her own breathing. She allowed her shoulders to sink into the chair, then her arms, her neck, her head....

Lydia Moen

The grating voice of the gadget salesman startled Ellen awake. She shivered and massaged the back of her neck. She stood up, walked over to the set, turned it off, and paused for a moment to look at the lake. She squinted and leaned closer to the glass. *What's out there?*

She shook her head. Probably just her imagination. She rubbed her eyes and dragged herself to the stairs, then grasped the mahogany railing and pulled herself onto the first step. She paused and then pulled herself onto the next.

As she entered the bedroom, she saw Bob, already asleep on his side of the bed, his face turned away from her. She crawled in and put her arm around his shoulder.

Chapter 12

The second cup of coffee hadn't worked. Maggie tore the messy attempt off her clipboard, crumpled it, and threw it at the wastebasket. After several moments of tapping her pencil on the table and staring at the blank paper in front of her, she drew a line down the middle of the page. She wrote Mac on one side and Charlie on the other.

A few minutes later she sat back and studied the four items in each column. She shook her head, let out a deep sigh, and tossed her pencil on the table.

As she headed outside, she mentally added a couple points to Mac's side. When Sammy nudged her, she brushed him aside and continued on to the dock.

"Good morning, Maggie."

"Mercy, you startled me, Charlie." Maggie felt her face flush. "Your motor's so quiet you can really sneak up on a person. Perhaps it'd be wise to give people a little warning when you're approaching their docks."

"Would you like me to use my air horn?"

Maggie peered over her glasses, grinned, and shook her head. "That won't be necessary."

Charlie put the mail in Sammy's mouth. "Hey, Maggie, what did you do with that bench from the end of the dock?"

Maggie's eyes darted to the now-empty space the rickety wooden seat had occupied for years. "Oh, no! I didn't even notice it was missing. Mac made that bench." She wrinkled her brow as she focused on the lake. "You know, I did see someone prowling around here last night."

Charlie scowled. "What do you mean, 'prowling around'?"

"Sammy and I heard gunshots around midnight. When I got up to investigate, I saw an unlit boat near the end of our dock."

"You got up to investigate? Why didn't you call me?" He shook his head. "Well, I'm here now, and the mail can wait." He turned off the motor, tied up, and hopped out.

"Now as you can see, we're both just fine." She patted Sammy's head.

The postman grabbed Maggie's elbow and steered her toward the house. "I want you to tell me everything that happened. I'll need paper and a pencil so I can write it all down while it's fresh in your mind."

Maggie stopped. "This is entirely unnecessary."

Charlie turned her so she faced him. "I promised Mac I'd look out for you, and I intend to keep that promise."

When they reached the porch, Maggie took the mail from Sammy and put it on the table. "Let's sit out here, Charlie. I'll try to make this fast, especially because you're already running late. I'll be right back with a clipboard."

As soon as she reached the kitchen, she tore off the top sheet, glanced over her shoulder, and stuffed it in a drawer. She took time to pour them each a cup of coffee and added a plate of blueberry muffins to the tray.

Charlie was pacing on the porch when she returned.

"Thank you, Maggie. I didn't expect a coffee break today. Now you talk, and I'll write."

"Good morning, Wanda. Sorry I'm late." The postman pulled up to the dock, slipped his engine into neutral, and handed her a small bundle of mail.

"Isn't it a glorious day?" Wanda spread her arms out. "God's palette is truly amazing. Everything I paint is just imitation."

She smiled. "I remember one time when Maggie and I were walking in Crystal Lake Park. We came upon a small family of deer. Was it six or seven?"

Charlie cleared his throat. "I wouldn't know. I—"

"I whispered to Maggie that I wished I had brought my camera...."

Charlie grabbed his clipboard. "Yes, well, I—"

"And I can still see the mamas looking over their spotted babies as they—"

Charlie tapped a pencil on the clipboard. "Wanda, Wanda..."

The artist blinked her eyes, shook her head, and looked down at the postman. "I'm sorry. Did you want to say something?"

"Actually, yes. I wanted to ask if you heard any strange noises in the night. Maggie and Sammy had quite a scare. She woke up to what she thought were gunshots."

Wanda's hands flew to her heart. "Oh, no! Not Maggie! Was she hurt?"

"She's fine, and so is Sammy. But the bench is missing from the end of her dock. Did you see or hear anything unusual?"

"Here I am prattling on about deer. Are you positive Maggie's all right?"

"Absolutely. We just shared coffee and muffins. She's fine." Charlie positioned the pencil over the clipboard. "Now about last night—"

"She invited you in for coffee and muffins?" Wanda raised her eyebrows. "Hmm. Does she do that often? This is very exciting."

"Wanda, I'm running a little bit late. About last night—"

"Of course, Charlie." Wanda added as much as she could to the information he had already gathered.

Satisfied he'd finally gotten all the information he could from her, he said, "If you remember anything else, please call me. I'm going to take my notes to the police station after work. Now I should be on my way." Charlie put his motor in reverse and touched the brim of his Notre Dame cap.

Wanda headed up the well-worn stone steps toward the house. Although no one would accuse her lawn of being manicured, she thought it acceptable—if she thought about it at all.

She delighted in the Black-Eyed-Susans that spread willingly and willfully along the foundation of the old, older, and oldest parts of the big home. Constructed initially as a two-room log cabin, the home had been subject to rambling yet charming additions by succeeding generations of Wanda's family. As the house expanded outward and upward to accommodate more children and activities, the log exterior had been maintained.

As the sound of the mail boat motor faded into the late-morning stillness of the lake, Wanda's soft singing replaced it.

When morning gilds the skies, my heart awakening cries:
May Jesus Christ be praised!

Refreshed from her jog and shower, Ellen handed a cup of hazelnut coffee to her husband and sat down beside him. She pushed her sunglasses up on top of her head. "Here comes the mailman."

Bob furrowed his brow. "Who's coming?"

"*Shhh*. It's the postman." Ellen scowled. She stood up and walked to the end of the dock.

"Hello. How are the Baileys this morning? What flavor is the coffee today?"

"We're fine, and it's hazelnut." Ellen crossed her arms. "Do you have a package for me? I'm waiting for fabric I ordered from a store in D.C."

Charlie turned around in his seat and handed her a large box from the back of the boat. "This may be it. My wife liked to sew, but she bought her material from the store on Main Street. Have you been in there yet?"

"Seriously? I doubt they have the selection I'm used to." Ellen took the package from Charlie and turned her back on him.

"That's probably true, but the owner's really nice, and I'm sure she'd be happy to order anything you want."

She looked over her shoulder. "Thank you. I'll keep that in mind."

"You're welcome. I apologize for being late this morning. I've been doing more talking than delivering today."

Ellen handed the package to Bob and turned around. "Is there something going on that we should know about?"

"I'm afraid there is." Charlie reached for his clipboard. "Did either of you see or hear anything suspicious last night, maybe around midnight?"

"We did. Bob thinks it was kids shooting off fireworks, but I think it might have been gunshots. Why?"

"The one thing I know for sure is that someone took the bench from Maggie's dock." Charlie told them what he had learned so far and added Ellen's comments to his notes.

Ellen twisted her wedding ring. "I can't believe this. I thought we were moving to small-town USA—smog-free, worry-free, and crime-

Lydia Moen

free. Whatever."

"Water's Edge *is* small-town USA. It's always been the kind of place where people don't have to lock their doors. But you're right; this is unsettling. I'd appreciate your keeping an eye out for Maggie's bench. Her late husband made it years ago. It was old, but it meant a lot to her."

"We will." Ellen pulled her sunglasses back down over her eyes.

Bob gave Charlie a thumbs-up. "It's a beautiful time of year."

Charlie returned the gesture as he prepared to leave. "That it is, especially here on the lakes. We're glad you're here, and I hope you'll come to feel the same way."

Ellen's thoughts flashed through her mind like an annoying TV commercial—the fire, Bob getting picked up by the police, her finding him in the garage in the middle of the night. She headed for the shore, grabbed the broom, and started sweeping. The rhythm of her strokes, almost frantic at first, gradually became more measured. The knots that had gripped her neck and shoulders loosened as she reached the dock's end and sat down again.

As she turned to Bob and put her hand in his, Ellen's face softened. "I've got some errands to run later today. Would you like to go with me?"

Ellen closed the bedroom door and spoke quietly into the phone. "I'd like to speak with Pastor Santiago, please." She sat on the edge of the bed and cupped her hand around the mouthpiece. At last his voice came on the line.

"Hello, Alberto," she answered, keeping her voice at just above a whisper. "This is Ellen Bailey. I called because I've been thinking about your suggestion regarding adult daycare."

Ellen glanced at the closed door. "Bob and I are going over to check out the community center this afternoon. I wondered if you might meet us there 'by accident.'"

She listened for a minute then said, "Thank you. We'll plan to get there a little after one." Ellen heard footsteps and glanced at the door again. She dropped her voice even lower. "I really appreciate this. We'll see you over there. Goodbye."

As soon as Maggie and Sammy got back from the dog park, her phone rang. "Hello, MacDonald residence."

Her neighbor's words shot out like pellets from a BB gun.

As soon as she was able to get a word in, she said, "Wanda, slow down! What's wrong?"

"I've been robbed. That band of vandals that's been terrorizing our little community has struck and wounded me personally."

Maggie stood up, grabbed her cellphone, and headed toward the door. "Wanda, hang up *now*. I'll call 911 immediately. Do you know how to apply a tourniquet?"

"Maggie, for heaven's sake, I wasn't speaking literally. I'm not bleeding. I didn't even see the thieves."

"Then how do you know they were there? Was your home ransacked?" Maggie sat back down, wondering how Wanda would know if her home had been ransacked. In fact, it might actually be more organized after a good ransacking.

"Maggie, please get hold of yourself. You're so dramatic."

Maggie bit her tongue, but she couldn't help rolling her eyes.

"No one actually came in the house," Wanda explained, "but someone must have sneaked into our yard and stolen our shore light."

"What light, Wanda? I don't even remember you having one."

Lydia Moen

Maggie thought back to the other night when she had returned late from Wanda's. She was grateful Wanda had lent her a flashlight because the path was so dark.

"We have a light on the post down by the dock. The fact that it hasn't been working for a few weeks—or maybe it's been a little longer—doesn't really matter. Our security light is gone. I'll be honest, Maggie. Right now, I'm not feeling very secure."

Maggie decided not to mention that if the light had been working, it might not have been stolen. Instead she replied, "Do you think we're being targeted? It's clear to me that these things aren't just lost. They've been stolen."

Maggie made a note on her to-do list. "We have to be more vigilant. We had that excellent talk on Neighborhood Watch. Remember that nice young officer who came over and described the program to us?"

"Good thinking! I'll call the police right now."

Maggie raised her eyebrows. "You're going to bother the police about the grand theft of a broken light?"

"I certainly am, and I'll tell them about your missing bench too."

"I guess that's probably a good idea. Maybe they'll have the patrol car come down our lane more often." Maggie shivered as she turned from the phone.

Ellen slipped on her silver and black designer sandals and looked in the mirror. The silver bling on her black scoop-necked blouse worked well with the black capris she'd found in a local boutique. "At least there's one decent store in this town."

"Did you call me?"

Ellen looked up as Bob entered the room in his now familiar "uniform"—gray sweatshirt, blue jeans, and fishing hat.

She crossed her arms. "I called you five minutes ago. And you can't wear that." She snapped her fingers toward the bed. "I set out a polo shirt and slacks. And put on some decent shoes."

Bob crossed his arms. "I don't need you to tell me what to wear."

"Well, obviously you do. You've worn that same outfit every day this week."

Ellen cringed as the red crept up Bob's neck and past his clenched jaw. She took a step back. "You win. But at least take off that dirty fishing hat."

"No way!" Bob pulled the hat further down on his head and glared at Ellen. "I'm ready. Are you?"

"Whatever. Let's get going."

Ten minutes later, the Baileys walked up to the Santiagos at the front desk of the community center.

"Look who's here!" Wanda gave Ellen a quick hug and then put her arm through Bob's.

"Bobby, I'm so glad we ran into you. I want to show you my plans to beautify this place. I'm quite an artist, you know."

Bob fell right in step, and the two headed off together. Ellen smiled and shook her head as she watched Wanda, dressed in a lime green and purple outfit, arm-in-arm with Bob in his gray sweatshirt and fishing hat.

Alberto chuckled and winked at his neighbor. "She's good."

"You planned that, didn't you?" Ellen shook a finger at him.

"I thought we might need a few minutes to talk, just the two of us. Let's go check out the adult daycare center."

Ellen didn't respond. She rubbed the back of her neck and looked at the floor.

She felt Alberto's light touch on her shoulder and gave him a tentative smile when he said, "I'll stay right with you. It's this way." And he guided her to a door simply marked "WELCOME."

Lydia Moen

As they entered, Ellen drew in a deep breath and then exhaled. Her eyes scanned the room: two men huddled over a cribbage board, a small group gathered around a table making sundaes, and a teenager played a Bing Crosby tune on the piano while several seniors sang along. "Where are the people in wheelchairs, nodding off in front of the TV?" she whispered to Alberto.

"Ellen, that's not what this place is about."

Ellen turned around when the door opened behind them.

"What are you two doing here?" Bob's eyes sparkled.

Wanda rubbed her hands together and glanced over at the ice cream table. "I bet they're here for the sundaes—just like we are."

A woman came up to them. "Hi, Wanda. Alberto, I heard you were back in town. It's good to see you again." She held out her hand to Ellen. "I'm Ruth Butler, the community center director."

Ellen shook her hand. "I'm Ellen Bailey, and this is my husband, Bob."

Wanda put her hand on Bob's shoulder. "They live next door to us. By the way, did I hear the word 'sundaes'?"

"You're just in time." Ruth chuckled. "Help yourselves. There's plenty for everyone."

Wanda pulled on Bob's hand. "I think I see hot fudge. Let's go."

As soon as the sundae scoopers left, Alberto and Ellen followed Ruth into the daycare office. Ellen watched Bob through the glass wall. Her eyes filled with tears as she absorbed the picture of Bob digging into the ice cream while his new friends took turns trying on his fishing hat.

She turned to the director. "I'd like an application for my husband, please."

Maggie took a second look at the ten-year-old red station wagon and turned into the next available parking spot. She nodded her head as she checked out the license plate: LAKEMAIL. She stopped to look at her reflection in the window of the pharmacy, fluffed her hair, and pinched her cheeks. With a winning smile on her face, she opened the door of the Java Joint.

The waitress behind the counter looked up at the tinkling of the bell. "Hi, Mrs. MacDonald. I bet our coffee's better than you ever had in the teachers' lounge."

"I'm sure of that," Maggie said. She looked around for Charlie.

"Are you meeting someone?"

Maggie's face turned a deep crimson as she looked into the corner booth.

"On second thought, I don't have time for coffee today. I'll stop in another time."

Maggie spun around and headed out the door. The welcoming bell clanged a little louder on her way out.

Chapter 13

Wanda carried a small plate of peanut-butter treats and a pitcher of iced tea down to the gazebo. "Can you believe how well the visit to the community center went?"

Alberto pushed the Brewers cap back on his head and nodded. "It did, thanks to you. If you hadn't gone with me, things might have turned out differently. You have such a wonderful way with people."

Wanda batted her eyes at her husband. "Oh, do you think so, Alberto?"

"You know it's true, querida. It's one of the things that makes you such a good pastor's wife. Adult daycare will be a tremendous help to Ellen, and Bob seemed to fit right in."

"He sure did. Those people are really fun. I had such a good time that I volunteered to help with the adult daycare activities. I think my first project will be finger-painting with chocolate pudding. Bob obviously has a sweet tooth."

Alberto frowned. "Are you sure you'll have time for that?"

Wanda pulled the scrunchy from her ponytail, ran her fingers through her hair, and replaced the scrunchy. "I thought we were getting a cleaning lady."

"I haven't found anyone yet, but I'll keep working on it."

Wanda jumped up and threw her arms around her husband's neck. "Wonderful. It's so good to have you home, Alberto. Remember when you were in Mexico and I had to give you a visual tour of Pearl Lake?"

"Your tour was amazing, but it's much better in real life." He picked up her hand and kissed it. "I couldn't do that from Mexico. It's good to be home."

As Maggie pulled into her driveway, she spotted Wanda and Alberto in their gazebo. She threaded her way through the gap in the cedar hedge.

"Hi, sweetie. Come on in." Wanda's hands flew to her heart. "Maggie, your face is so flushed. Are you okay?"

Alberto stood up. "Have a seat, Maggie. I'll pour you a glass of iced tea."

Maggie sank down into a chair. "Thank you. I'm really fine."

Alberto handed her the tea and put his hand on her shoulder. "Are you sure you're all right?"

Maggie nodded her head and smiled at her neighbor.

"In that case, I don't mean to be rude, but I promised Bob I'd stop by to see how his workshop is coming along."

As soon as Alberto left, Maggie put her elbows on the table and her head in her hands. "I just completely embarrassed myself in front of Charlie and everyone else in the Java Joint."

"Oh, you're always exaggerating, Maggie. Tell me what happened."

Maggie drew in a deep breath and looked up at her friend. "I saw Charlie's station wagon in front of the coffee shop. I parked my car and practically ran inside looking for him. I behaved like one of my love-starved students."

"Was he there?"

"Oh, he was there all right. But he wasn't alone."

Wanda gasped. "Who was he with?"

"I didn't stay long enough to find out. But it was a woman, and I've never seen her before." Maggie picked up a napkin from the table and dabbed her eyes.

"Wanda, it's all my fault. He called me yesterday and asked me to go to the band concert tonight. I turned him down and told him I was too tired to talk. I've been thinking a lot about Mac lately, and I feel guilty about enjoying Charlie's company. He probably thinks I'm brushing him off. Maybe he's decided to pursue other options."

"Don't go anywhere, Maggie. I'll be right back."

When Wanda left, Maggie stood up and walked out to the end of the dock. *Heavenly Father, please show me what to do. I'm not doing well on my own. Am I being unfaithful to Mac by enjoying time with Charlie, or have you put this dear man in my life for a reason?*

She heard the porch door close and hurried back to the gazebo. She was seated in her chair like an obedient student when Wanda returned.

Maggie recognized the handwriting on the sealed envelope as soon as Wanda passed it to her. "Maggie, your sweet husband gave this letter to Alberto and me shortly before his glorious entrance into heaven. He asked us to give it to you when the time was right. Something tells me this is that time. Take it home and read it when you're alone."

Alberto picked up the shiny power drill from Bob's workbench. "You have every tool I can imagine here, Bob."

"Yeah, buddy, but I can never find the right one when I'm looking for it. I'm so disorganized."

Alberto put his hand on Bob's shoulder. "We have the same problem at our house. Wanda and I have been talking about hiring a cleaning lady to help bring some order to our chaos. If you hear of one, let me know."

"Lookin' for a cleaning lady?"

Alberto turned toward the gruff voice and extended his hand. "Hello. I'm Alberto Santiago."

"Alberto, this is…" Bob scratched his head.

"Ray Hoffman." The unkempt man shoved his hands in his pockets.

Alberto put the drill back on the workbench. "So do you know someone who cleans houses? My wife and I are in the market."

Ray stared at the floor and scuffed it with his dirty boot. "The missus is looking for work. She can clean, and we could sure use the money." He lifted his head and glanced at Alberto.

The pastor smiled and nodded. "God works in mysterious ways. I thought I was just coming over here to look at Bob's shed, but I was also sent here to meet you. If you give me your number, I'll have Wanda give your wife a call. What's her name?"

"Rita. Give me your number, and she'll call your wife."

Alberto wrote the number on the back of one of his business cards, handed it to Ray, and turned to his neighbor. "So how did you two get to know each other?"

Bob frowned and rubbed his chin. "He drove by one day and asked if I needed any work done. Isn't that right, buddy?"

Ray nodded and shrugged his shoulders.

Bob slapped him on the back and beamed. "He's going to help me turn this shed into a workshop."

Alberto raised his eyebrows. "Ray, are you a carpenter or an electrician, or do you do it all?"

"Any work I can get."

"Well, it looks like you can find plenty of work around here for you and your wife."

"Yeah. Maybe our luck's finally going to change."

Maggie opened her Bible to 1 Corinthians 13 and tucked Mac's letter inside. She closed her eyes and bowed her head. After several minutes, she straightened up and headed into the kitchen.

She fed and walked Sammy.

Made herself a salad.

Cleaned up the kitchen.

Then she picked up her Bible, walked out to the porch, and sat in Mac's chair.

Maggie kept the envelope in her Bible as she murmured the familiar words. "*...if I have a faith that can move mountains, but have not love, I am nothing.... Love is patient, love is kind...It always protects, always trusts, always hopes, always perseveres. Love never fails. ...And now these three remain: faith, hope and love. But the greatest of these is love.*"

Maggie closed her eyes and leaned her head back. She listened to the waves lapping against the shoreline and heard the chimes from the Chapel on the Lakes.

Maggie couldn't remember the first time she'd seen Mac, but she could still see the half-smile he wore like a watch. He almost always had it on, and when he didn't, Maggie could tell he wasn't totally comfortable.

Mac was great-looking, the kind of guy whose life is a little easier because he's handsome. But the substance of him was even more attractive. He was a strong Christian, always thinking of others first, treating everyone with respect, and living with style—Golden-Rule style.

Maggie's canine companion leaned against her leg and put his head on her lap. "How do you know just when to do that, Sammy?" She stroked his silky ears. He raised his eyes at her touch and gave her hand a gentle lick. She gave his big head a generous hug.

She looked down at the envelope: *Mags*. She smiled and rubbed her thumb over his pet name for her. Her finger shook a bit as she slid it under the flap and gently broke the seal. She pulled out the single sheet, smoothed the creases, and placed it on her open Bible.

There is a time for everything...
a time to weep and a time to laugh,
a time to mourn and a time to dance

Maggie,

I've asked Alberto and Wanda to give this to you when the time is right. As you read these words, I trust that time has come.

God, through the author of Ecclesiastes, teaches us that life is divided into seasons. Your season of mourning is over. It's time for you to dance, Mags. Don't hesitate out of a misplaced sense of loyalty to me.

We promised to be true to each other "'til death do us part." And we both kept that vow willingly and faithfully. But death has parted us for now.

Are you feeling God nudging you to move on? I suspect you are. God's timing is perfect. Embrace this season of your life with love, joy, and peace.

I love you,
Mac

As she slid the letter back into the envelope, she heard the unanswered call of a loon across the water.

Sunday mornings were a time of reunion, reflection, and rejoicing for the parishioners at Water's Edge Bible Church. Maggie's family had always sat in the fourth row on the right side. Wanda's had preferred the left side about midway from the altar. Charlie was more comfortable in the rear.

Now that Alberto was part of the ministerial team, Wanda sat in the second row next to the center aisle. After Mac's death, Maggie had moved up to sit with Wanda. And today, Charlie strode up to the front and sat next to Maggie, who immediately dropped her hymnal and bulletin while fluffing her hair. Wanda retrieved the fallen items for her flustered friend and greeted Charlie with a broad smile and a wink.

Maggie joined in the warm, welcome-home applause Alberto received from his congregation as he stepped up to the pulpit. She closed her eyes and whispered the words of the 23rd Psalm along with her fellow parishioners. The video of Mexican children performing the same verses in Spanish brought Alberto's recent mission to life for Maggie.

Charlie stood up immediately after the sermon. Maggie's first thought was that he had been so carried away by Alberto's message that he was going to give him a standing ovation. Thankfully, he just quietly exited the pew. Then, fearing that he might be ill, Maggie leaned over to Wanda. "Do you think one of us should go with him?"

Wanda smiled and nodded her head toward the front of the sanctuary. There stood Charlie with a microphone in his hand. Maggie sat transfixed, her eyes never wavering, her hands clasped as she listened to Charlie sing:

I am weak, but Thou art strong;
Jesus, keep me from all wrong;
I'll be satisfied as long
As I walk, let me walk close to Thee.

Her vision blurred as the river of words flowed from Charlie's lips into her heart.

As soon as the service ended, Maggie reached for Charlie's hand and enclosed it in both of hers. "What a blessing. I had no idea you could sing so beautifully, and I needed to hear that message today." She squeezed his hand, and he returned the gesture.

Wanda popped her head around Maggie's shoulder. "Great job, Charlie. How about if the three of us corral Alberto and go to the marina for Sunday brunch?"

Maggie looked up at Charlie and shrugged.

"That works for me. Maggie?"

"Let's do it."

"Alberto, look. The Baileys are here." Wanda detoured past the buffet on her way to Bob and Ellen's table. She closed her eyes and breathed in the blended aromas of the bacon and sausage before her nose pulled her to the chocolate croissants and Belgian waffles swimming in maple syrup.

"Excuse me. Are you in line, ma'am?" If the question hadn't awakened Wanda from her caloric reverie, the woman's powerful perfume would have.

Wanda sneezed and took a step back. "I'm sorry. I didn't mean to sneak in line, sweetie. I'm just window-shopping now, but I'll be back to try a little of everything. Let me know which are the must-haves." Wanda pointed to the table where Alberto and the Baileys were sitting. "I'll be right over there with that handsome gentleman and the adorable couple."

Bob stood up as Wanda approached, and Wanda gave him a hug.

"Oh, Bobby, this is a special day. We get to have brunch with you and your lovely wife."

"It sure is a beautiful day. I've been saving this for you." Bob pulled out the chair next to him.

"I'm glad you two got the big table. Maggie and Charlie are right behind us."

"Charlie?" Ellen tilted her head to the side and pursed her lips.

Alberto put his hand on Ellen's shoulder. "Charlie Bingham, the guy in the university cap who pulls up to your dock every day in his red, white, and blue boat."

"Oh, that Charlie. I didn't realize you were friends."

Before Alberto could respond, Wanda jumped up and waved her hands, "Maggie, Charlie, over here."

Maggie walked straight over to Ellen and hugged her. "It's so good to see you. You look wonderful. How are you feeling?"

"Much better, thanks. It's good to see you too, Maggie. Hello, Charlie." She turned to her husband. "Bob, let's go over to the buffet. It looks like the line has thinned out."

Once everyone had a full plate and had returned to the table, Maggie asked Alberto to say a blessing. Wanda peeked up before Alberto finished and noticed Ellen was fidgeting with her silverware and Bob had started eating.

Wanda attacked her carb-rich selections as soon as she heard the "amen." As she worked her way around her plate, she observed her tablemates. Charlie and Maggie didn't seem to be very hungry. They mainly talked to each other. Alberto, Bob, and Ellen discussed Bob's plans for his workshop. When they mentioned Ray Hoffman, Wanda broke in, a huge smile on her face. "Don't forget about Rita. Ellen, did Bob tell you Alberto's going to treat me to a cleaning lady?"

"No, he didn't. You'll have to let me know if she's any good."

Lydia Moen

"Speaking of cleaning, I'm going to spend tomorrow morning finishing up my shed," Maggie chimed in.

"Finally. What's with the mess in your yard?" Wanda rolled her eyes.

Wanda poked Alberto when she saw Charlie put his hand on Maggie's arm and heard him volunteer, "I can explain that."

Maggie swatted Charlie's hand with her napkin. "Oh, no you won't. That story stays between the two of us."

Wanda leaned forward and took a deep breath but closed her mouth when Alberto squeezed her hand. She made a mental note to worm the details out of Maggie later. "Anyway, what are you going to do with all that stuff, Maggie?"

"I thought I'd drop it off at Carnegie's Treasure Chest, but it's going to take me a lot of trips in my little car."

When Wanda offered to drive her, Alberto chuckled. "Have you looked at the back of your station wagon lately?"

"You have a point." Wanda shrugged and picked up her croissant.

Ellen set her napkin on the table. "What's Carnegie's Treasure Chest?"

Wanda wiped most of the chocolate off her mouth. "Nobody but Maggie calls it that. It's really Joe's Junkyard. Go a mile past the ice cream store on the edge of town, and you'll see it on the left."

Maggie peered over her glasses. "It *is* a treasure chest. I've acquired a number of gems from Joe over the years."

"Seriously?" Ellen picked up her tiny shoulder bag and began fiddling with the strap. "I have to admit, I've never been to a junkyard before. Why not? We can take my van."

"It'll be an experience." Maggie smiled at Ellen. "Thanks for offering to drive. We can probably do it in one trip."

Wanda looked up. "Can I tag along?"

Ellen's face brightened. "Absolutely."

"Just give me a call when you're ready." Wanda grinned at her two friends. "We'll be a cord of three strands."

Maggie tilted her head and looked over her shoulder. "Charlie, did you mean to turn this way? Lakeshore Lane's back there."

Charlie looked over at her and chuckled. "You caught me, Maggie. Let's take a little drive. I think I have some explaining to do."

"You don't have to explain anything to me." Maggie tapped her fingers on the armrest.

"I think maybe I do. I saw you come into the Java Joint yesterday. And I'm pretty sure you saw me."

Maggie felt her face flush. "I did, and I know I acted like a fool."

"I was beginning to wonder if our friendship mattered to you. I have to admit it made me feel better to see you glare over at me and storm out of there." Charlie winked at Maggie while they waited for the light to change.

"Maggie, the woman I was with—"

"Charlie, I—"

"The woman I was with is an old friend of Fae's. When I found out she was coming through town, I wanted her to meet you. But I felt you needed some space, and I understand that."

"And I did need space. It's only been a year since Mac died. But I enjoy being with you, Charlie, and I was feeling guilty about that." Maggie turned her head and looked out the window.

Charlie put his hand over hers. "We both were blessed with wonderful marriages, and the four of us had great times together."

"That's true." Maggie squeezed Charlie's hand. "But Fae and Mac are both in heaven now, and we're still here."

Lydia Moen

Chapter 14

"A five-letter word for animal restraint." Maggie tapped her pencil on the newspaper. "Second letter's E."

She felt the nudge but couldn't keep her pencil from swiping across the puzzle. "What is it, Sammy?" Maggie looked down and started laughing when she saw what was dangling from his mouth. "You are so smart. L-E-A-S-H. I can't believe you brought it to me just so I could finish the crossword. I bet you had an ulterior motive. Want to go for a walk?"

Sammy wagged his tail and turned several circles.

Maggie picked up the phone and hit her neighbor's speed-dial number.

"Hello."

"Hi, Ellen, this is Maggie. How are you today?" Maggie snapped Sammy's leash onto his collar.

"I'm fine, thanks. Is it time to go to the Treasure Chest already?"

"No, not for a couple hours. Right now I'm going for a walk and wondered if you'd like to join me."

"Fabulous. I cut my run short this morning, and I need to keep my endorphins going."

Maggie grabbed two water bottles. "Good. I'll meet you on the lane."

She watched Ellen swing her arms and bounce along as she approached, calling, "Hi, neighbor." Ellen picked up the pace and jogged the rest of the way. She came to a sudden stop.

"Sammy, sit. Shake hands with Ellen." Sammy sat, put his right paw up, and wagged his tail.

Ellen stepped back and put her hands in her pockets. "My goodness, he's big. What kind is he?"

"He's a golden retriever." Maggie lowered her voice. "But he thinks he's a human."

Sammy wagged his tail as if indicating his owner was correct.

"Well, I've never had a dog, or any pets, but he seems like he's very well-behaved."

"He loves going on walks." As the three started off, Maggie handed Ellen a water bottle and made sure she stayed between her two companions. "I'm sure you'll become great friends."

Ellen didn't respond.

"It's a nice walk to the dog park, and Sammy can run and play with his canine friends in the large fenced-in area while I introduce you to the other dog owners."

Ellen continued to remain silent.

"I love watching the dogs play endless games of you-chase-me-then-I'll-chase-you and I-can-open-my-mouth-wider-than-yours. And, oh, I almost forgot Sammy's favorite: mark-your-attendance-with-a-pee-mail-note-on-the-tree."

Ellen smiled and chuckled. Her pace slowed as the trio reached the dog park. "I'll just wait outside the fence."

Maggie stopped and put a hand on Ellen's arm. "You don't have to be a pet owner to come in. And I'm sure you'll enjoy meeting these folks."

"Well, maybe for a few minutes. I really should be getting home. I've got some things to take care of before we go to the Treasure Chest."

"We won't stay long." Maggie looked down and said, "Sammy, sit." He obeyed immediately, so she reached down and removed his leash. "You've been looking forward to this, haven't you, boy?"

Ellen hung back and watched Maggie open the inner gate. Sammy scampered into the park and was met by a number of his friends. They got reacquainted while Maggie addressed some of them by name. "Hi, Luna. Trover, how are you doing? Hello, Reggie. Where's Dixie?"

After the formalities, Sammy led the dogs off to enjoy the freedom of the park, and Maggie introduced Ellen to the "parents" of Luna and Dixie. "Who's the new dog?" Maggie pointed to a brown mixed-breed. "I don't think I've seen him before."

"I'm not sure." Dixie's master scowled. "In fact, I haven't even figured out who brought him in."

Maggie peered over her sunglasses, keeping an eye on the stranger. "That's unusual. Didn't the owner read the sign on the gate? It clearly states that dogs must be supervised by a responsible adult."

Maggie noticed Ellen begin to twist her wedding ring as soon as the subject of the errant dog came up. Ellen grabbed Maggie's arm. "Which one is it? Is it the one with Sammy? That big spotted one?"

Maggie patted Ellen's hand but focused her attention on the energetic group of dogs Sammy was leading. "I don't see him right now. Should we get out of the sun? There's a pretty path through the woods."

"You go ahead, Maggie. I'm enjoying the warmth, and there's a nice place to sit right over here by the gate."

At that moment, one of the humans threw a tennis ball across the park, and the canines responded with a cacophonous chorus and a thunderous stampede.

Lydia Moen

Dixie was mostly Labrador but must have had some greyhound in her because she tore across the grass well ahead of the pack. She scooped up the ball and pranced toward her master.

As Dixie moved in the onlookers' direction, the unsupervised dog caught up with her, snarled, and knocked her to the ground. The other dogs raced to the aid of their friend, and a full-fledged fight ensued.

Ellen ran through the gate, slammed it behind her, and screamed, "Maggie, get out of there. Hurry!"

Bob jammed button after button on the TV remote, turning the volume up and down while trying to change the channel. He hurled the offending device across the room and stormed outside.

"What's wrong with me? I can't do anything anymore." He spied a stone on the driveway and launched it into the air with his foot.

"Hey, Bailey. What do you think you're doing?"

Bob looked up and saw the handyman rubbing his leg. "Sorry, buddy. I didn't see you."

"Have you got a minute? You still haven't told me where I'm supposed to put the shelves."

"I'm on my way to the shed now. Can't wait to try out my new power drill."

"Er... I don't want any help. Just tell me where you want the shelves, and I'll put 'em up myself."

Bob rummaged through boxes, piling tools and hardware on the workbench. "I know it's here somewhere. Have you seen my drill?"

Beads of sweat rolled down the handyman's forehead, his gaze frozen to the floor. "I have to run." Ray Hoffman bolted out the door.

"Okay, buddy, I'll see you later." Bob went back to his search. He looked up when the pickup rumbled to life and then ducked behind the boxes at the sound of three short bangs.

Ellen's jaw dropped when Maggie put two fingers to her mouth and let loose a piercing whistle. Sammy raced up to his owner and sat obediently at her feet.

Dixie's master ran at top speed into the midst of the fray, as did the other owners. Almost as quickly as the fight began, the dogs were pulled apart and under the control of the humans. That is, with the exception of the lone dog who started the melee. He was lying on the ground, his chest heaving with each breath, his frightened eyes wide open and watery, and several obvious wounds turning parts of his brown coat red.

Ellen's legs felt like Jell-O as the trio walked down the hill toward Lakeshore Lane. "That was frightening. I'm glad to be out of there. How did you get Sammy to mind so well?"

"Mac taught me how to whistle when we went to football games in college. Once we got married, we always had dogs, and that's the signal we give them to come immediately."

Ellen drew in a deep breath, sighed, and looked at Maggie. "What do you think will happen to that other dog? Is he going to die?"

"I don't think his wounds are serious. He'll be taken to the animal shelter and receive medical attention there. Hopefully his owners will claim him, and he can go home. If he's not picked up within a certain number of days, he'll be made available for adoption. Perhaps his next owners will be more responsible."

Ellen shook her head. "His owners shouldn't be allowed to have pets if they aren't going to keep them under control."

"I found it!" Ellen had grown accustomed to looking for Bob's misplaced items. But finding the remote underneath the TV stand, its back off and battery hanging out, shocked her. "Here it is, honey. What happened to it?"

Her husband wandered into the living room and took the remote from Ellen. "You broke it. Now what are we going to do? I was going to watch the evening news."

"Bob, we just had lunch." She snapped her fingers. "Give it to me."

A few minutes later, with the Nationals hosting the Brewers on the large screen and Bob settled into his recliner, Ellen sneaked out the door.

She backed her van up to Maggie's shed and hopped out. "Looks like you're ready to load."

"Not quite yet, sweetie." Wanda emerged from under a huge pink and orange hat. "She's giving away some scrumptious stuff. Look at this gorgeous flower pot. I can't believe she's taking this to the junkyard."

"Treasure Chest, Wanda." Maggie walked up to Ellen and gave her a hug. "It looks like you've recovered from our morning at the dog fight."

Wanda's hands flew to her heart. "Dog fight? Is Sammy okay?"

Ellen pushed her sunglasses on top of her head. "Sammy was awesome, and he's fine. We'll tell you all about it on the way. Maggie, what can I do?"

Ellen and Maggie loaded the van, while their friend continued inspecting the merchandise.

Wanda held up a pottery lamp. "How much do you want for this, Maggie?"

Maggie peered over her glasses. "For heaven's sake, Wanda, it doesn't even work."

"It's beautiful. I bet Alberto could fix it. I can put it on the dining room buffet. If I turn the chip toward the back, no one will even see it."

"It's yours, as long as you don't tell Alberto that I'm contributing to your conglomeration of collectibles."

Ellen looked at Maggie. "Are we ready?"

Maggie winked at Ellen. "We are. How about you, Madame Treasure Hunter?"

Wanda put the lamp back in the shed, picked up her tote, and climbed into the car.

As they drove to the junkyard, Maggie thanked her friends. "I don't think I could have finished the job without your help, ladies."

"Happy to be of service." When they answered in unison, Ellen smiled and nodded at Wanda in the rearview mirror.

She glanced at Maggie. "It must feel good to get this done. I still have boxes to unpack from the move."

"Me too," Wanda piped up from the back seat.

Ellen peeked back at Wanda. "I thought you'd lived here for over twenty years."

"We have, sweetie, but I like to take my time."

The three women chatted as they drove, and it wasn't long before Maggie told Ellen to turn into a gravel driveway. She pulled the van up to an eight-foot-high rusty gate. "Carnegie's Treasure Chest, Established 1948."

Maggie reached over and tooted the horn. While they waited to get inside, Ellen scanned the amazing collection beyond the gate—appliances under a corrugated metal roof, tires in a heap near dilapidated vehicles, rusty lawn mowers and gardening tools next to the woods at the back of the property.

She gulped down a swallow as a man with brown, stringy, longer-than-average hair and a scraggly beard approached. The man's baseball cap hid the upper half of his face. She shuddered. "You two go ahead. I'll just wait in the van."

Ellen felt Wanda's gentle poke on her shoulder. "Oh, come on. You'll love it."

Maggie waved at the man and then turned to Ellen. "Just pull the van inside far enough for the gate to close. Joe likes to keep the yard secured at all times."

Once inside the gate, Wanda opened Ellen's door. "Don't worry, sweetie. It'll be fun."

Ellen didn't hesitate when Maggie insisted she and Joe would do the unloading. She followed Wanda to a pile of picture frames. While her neighbor searched through them, Ellen wandered over to a large white-washed barn near the woods. The doors were ajar, and she stepped inside. The building was piled high with furniture—desks with broken legs, armchairs with only one arm, tables and chests in desperate need of refinishing.

"Can I help you with something, ma'am?" Ellen swung around. Joe Carnegie was just a step away.

She backed up but looked directly at him. "I hope I haven't intruded. My husband and I moved here recently, and I just wanted to see what you have to offer."

Joe's smile was frozen on his face. "Why don't you call before you and your husband come over, and I'll make sure I'm available to show you around?"

As she strode back to the van, the image of an old bench flashed into Ellen's mind. She had glimpsed it in a darkened corner seconds before the proprietor startled her. A shiver ran down her spine.

Maggie met her at the van. "We thought we'd lost you. Are you ready to go?"

"I sure am." Ellen jumped into the driver's seat and turned on the engine.

So this guy was a big-shot Washington lawyer? He can't even remember where his hammer is. This is gonna be easy. Ray Hoffman pulled the hammer from its place on the wall in front of Bob and handed it to him. "Is this what you've been looking all over for?"

Bob took the hammer and set it down on the workbench. "Thanks. Where should I put these power tools?"

Ray groaned and shook his head. "Wherever you want. You're the boss."

"Now, what's your name again?"

"Same as it was the last time you asked—Ray."

"Right. I'm Bob."

The handyman laughed out loud. "Yeah, I know."

"It's kind of dark in here. When are you going to put up some lights?"

Ray crossed his arms and glared at Bob. "Like I already told you, an electrician has to do that."

"Oh, right. I forgot."

Ray picked up the electric screwdriver and turned it on and off. "By the way, if you want me to pick up that shelving, I'll need some money."

Bob pulled out his wallet. "How much do you need?"

"I have no idea. I think it might be easier if you just give me your credit card."

"That sounds good." Bob handed his gold card to the handyman.

"See ya later." Ray's usual scowl morphed into a nasty smirk as he hopped into his truck and pulled the glove box open. He tossed Bob's card inside and slammed the compartment closed. The handyman whistled as he started the truck engine and sped away.

Lydia Moen

Ellen was still a little shaken when she got home from the encounter at the junkyard, but she had to get right back in the van. "Bob, it's time to leave."

"Where are we going?"

"Seriously?" She took a deep breath. "Today's the day we take our driver's tests. I hope you've been studying."

"I guess I know how to drive a car, whether it's in Washington, D.C., or here. It's about time I got my license back."

Soon Bob was installed in a booth and focused on the computer screen. Ellen shook her head as she watched him skim the questions, quickly click on an answer, and move on.

"Next." Ellen went up to the counter for her eye exam and photo. As she was writing her check, she heard Bob paged and saw the back of her husband's gray sweatshirt, blue jeans, and fishing hat approach another DMV employee.

"Here's your temporary license, Mrs. Bailey."

Ellen turned back to the clerk. "I'm sorry. Can you repeat that?"

"This is your temporary license. Carry it whenever you drive until your permanent one comes in the mail. It should arrive within three weeks."

As Ellen tucked her license into her purse, she heard her husband shout: "What do you mean I didn't pass the test? I've been driving cars since before you were born. I don't need a computer to tell me how to drive. I want my license. Now!"

Ellen could hear the frustration in the clerk's voice. "I'm sorry, sir, but you didn't pass the test, and you can't get your license until you do."

"I demand to see your supervisor!"

Ellen pushed her way to the front of Bob's line, ignoring the protests directed at her.

"Hey, lady, what do you think you're doing?"

"Wait your turn like the rest of us."

Grabbing her husband by the arm, Ellen tried to pull him away from the counter. "Please, Bob, don't make a scene. Let's just get out of here."

"Let go of me, Ellen. I'm not leaving here until they give me my license." Bob scowled at his wife from behind a face red with anger.

"C'mon buddy. You flunked your test. Move aside."

"Yeah, man, who do you think you are? You're holding up the whole line."

Ellen pulled on his arm. "Bob, come on. Let's go."

His shove sent her reeling into the young man behind her.

"Watch out, lady."

"I'm sorry." Ellen struggled to regain her balance and keep her tears in check.

Bob elbowed past Ellen and grabbed the teenager by the collar. "Don't you talk to my wife like that!"

"Hey, Grandpa, she started it. Get your hands off me." The teen pushed Bob. He bumped into Ellen, and she ended up sprawled on the floor, looking up into the stern face of the DMV security guard as he spoke into his radio.

Wanda picked up the phone. "Hello."

"Is this Mrs. Santiago?"

"Yes, this is Wanda."

"This is Rita Hoffman. My husband said you're looking for cleaning help."

Lydia Moen

Wanda thrust her hands heavenward. "Praise the Lord! I'm so glad you called, Rita. How soon can you start?"

"When do you want me?"

Wanda pulled a stack of papers off the table and shoved them in a drawer, bumping it shut with her hip. "Tomorrow morning would be great. We live right next door to the Baileys, so you can ride over with your husband. I'll be ready for you at nine."

Before the phone was back in its stand, Wanda shrieked, "Alberto! Come quick. It's an emergency."

She heard her husband's heavy footsteps as he hustled down the stairs and into the kitchen.

"What's wrong? What's the emergency?"

Wanda shook her head and flapped her hand at her husband. "Oh, Alberto, you're so dramatic."

Alberto ran his hands through his hair.

"Rita called. That's the emergency. She's coming tomorrow. We have to clean this place up before she gets here."

"But I thought we were hiring her to clean."

"We can't let her see our house like this. She'll quit before she starts. You begin in the living room, and I'll work on my studio."

Wanda worked tirelessly. First she moved a pile of papers from the desk next to the bookshelves. Then she moved a box of papers from the bookshelves to the table. Next she picked up some catalogs, looked around for an empty spot, and placed them on the desk. Twenty minutes later, she heard a cry from the living room.

"Wanda, I found them!" Alberto came running into the studio waving a folder and a bunch of photographs over his head.

Before she could reply, the phone rang. Wanda hugged her husband while she answered it.

"Uh-huh...uh-huh...uh-huh. We'll be right there." Wanda set

down the phone and turned to Alberto. "Hurry! This time it's a *real* emergency."

Wanda tapped her husband's shoulder. "What's happening? I can't see." Then she peeked under Alberto's outstretched arm, and finally faked a move to the right but passed him on the left.

"Wanda, get back here," he shouted over the din of agitated voices in the police station.

Wanda nudged the uniformed woman beside her. "What's going on?"

"Those three," she answered, stabbing her finger toward Bob, Ellen, and a teenage boy, "started a brawl at the DMV. We called the police, and they hauled them down here and made us come too."

Wanda screamed when the teenager shoved Bob. Then Ellen pushed the boy, and he yelled, "Look, Grandma, I already warned you and your husband to keep your hands off me."

Bob stepped in then and shook the teen's shoulders. The two faced off, and Bob raised his fists. Wanda clapped her hands and yelled, "You go, Bobby!"

The next thing Wanda knew, a scuffle broke out, with her husband somehow in the middle of it.

The crowd froze at the screech of a whistle. "Now everyone just settle down, or I'm going to arrest all of you for breach of peace, disorderly conduct, public endangerment, and anything else I can come up with."

The officer pointed at Wanda and said, "Pastor and Mrs. Santiago, sit down over there. Mr. and Mrs. Bailey, on the bench. Young man, I'll start with you. Follow me."

Wanda watched as Carlos led the boy through a door marked

Lydia Moen

Interview Room. She looked around the lobby and raised her chin, as well as her voice. "Your cousin sure knows how to take charge, Alberto. He undoubtedly prevented a serious injury. I can picture him on a police reality show—such a handsome man." Wanda closed her eyes, allowed a slight smile to slip across her face, and sighed.

Chapter 15

A knock on the shed window brought an ear-piercing scream from Maggie's throat. A familiar face peered through the dusty glass, and Maggie brought her hand to her chest. "Mercy. You scared me to death, Charlie."

"I'm sorry. I'm just dropping something off."

"Can you give me a few minutes?"

"Sure, I'll wait on the porch."

Maggie paused a moment, peeked out the window, and scooted to the kitchen door. Once inside, she washed her hands, whipped off her scarf, and fluffed her hair on the way outside.

She sat down next to Charlie. "I didn't expect a visit from you this afternoon. This is a nice surprise."

"I have another surprise for you." The postman handed her a letter from Josh.

"Oh, Charlie, another letter from Josh! Thanks for bringing it over. This is truly a special delivery."

Maggie opened the letter and read out loud:

Lydia Moen

Hi Grandma,

Wow! The care packages you sent were awesome. Please thank your church group for putting them together. How did you know just what to send? The beef jerky, chewing gum, and hard candy were all big winners. Don't tell the guys in my unit, but I kept all of Mrs. Santiago's peanut-butter treats for myself.

It was nice of you to send the Bible. I plan to get into it when we have some free time.

Remember how when I was little Grandpa and I would spend hours sitting on his bench, taking turns tossing pebbles into the water? We'd try to count the ripples as they spread out in larger and larger circles, but we never could. Grandpa always said the ripples seemed endless—you could never tell how far they would go. He had a wonderful way of teaching me about life through simple, everyday examples. I think about those ripples now when I give a piece of candy to a child. Hopefully I'm touching some lives over here, and the ripple effect will be positive.

I've been picturing you and me sitting on that bench, talking and fishing. I'm hoping to fix it up for you when I come home. I know Grandpa would mostly "catch and release," but if we catch a big one, I'll clean it if you'll cook it.

I love you, Grandma,
Josh

Maggie took off her glasses and wiped her eyes.

Charlie reached for her hand. "He's a great kid."

"I just wish he could tell me where he is. I know that's not allowed, but I'd love to know that he's not on the front line." She shook her head. "I hate watching the news, but I can't help myself. I keep hoping to catch a glimpse of him, and yet..."

"I'm sorry, Maggie." Charlie put his arm around her, and she rested her head on his shoulder.

After a few minutes, he patted her knee. "An early supper might be a good distraction. My treat."

Maggie leaned forward and drummed her fingers on the arm of the loveseat. "I'd like that, but I'm such a mess."

"You look fine to me." Charlie winked. "But let's do something casual. How about the root beer stand on Emerald Lake?"

"That'd be great. I haven't been there in ages. And how about a twilight kayak cruise when we get back?"

"You betcha." Charlie gave her hand a squeeze as they walked across the lawn to his car. Maggie smiled up at him and squeezed back.

Ellen barely recognized the face that stared back at her from the ladies' room mirror. She winced as she pulled the comb through her snarled hair. After splashing cold water on her face, she scrubbed the mascara smudges under her eyes and succeeded only in replacing some of the black with red. *This would have made a stunning driver's license photo!* She tossed her cosmetics in her tiny shoulder bag and pushed through the door.

Wanda met her on the other side. "I don't know how you do it. You've gotten yourself all fixed up." She grabbed the scrunchy from her ponytail, did a quick finger comb, and replaced the band.

"Thanks for having Carlos take care of getting our car home, Wanda. I don't think I could drive now."

Alberto and Bob were waiting for them in the car. The pastor pulled out of the police station parking lot. "I called the pizza place, and we can pick up our order on the way home."

"I'll throw a salad together." Ellen leaned her head against the window and fiddled with her purse straps.

Lydia Moen

"No, you won't." Wanda put her hand on the back of Ellen's seat. "Bob and I can do that. You just put your feet up and relax, sweetie."

"What's the matter, Ellen?" Bob asked. "Are you sick?"

Alberto looked in his rearview mirror. "It's been a long day, Bob. We'll all feel better when we get something to eat."

A short time later, the group walked into the Baileys' home, pizza in hand. Wanda busied Bob in the kitchen while Ellen and Alberto went into the living room.

Ellen collapsed on the love seat. "Thanks for coming to our rescue. I don't know how things got so crazy." She looked at her hands and twisted her wedding ring. "One minute I was picking up my driver's license, and the next we were at the police station. Bob flunked his driver's test and was completely out of control."

Alberto paused before responding. "How about if I pick up Bob tomorrow morning and get him started in the adult daycare program? He seemed to like it there, and if I were you, I'd need a break about now."

Ellen shook her head. "We've already imposed on you and Wanda enough. I can't ask you to do that."

"You're not asking. You know, Ellen, God's Word says, "Two are better than one, because they have a good return for their work: If one falls down, his friend can help him up." This is an opportunity for me to help you. Next time, I may be the one needing help."

"Thank you. I'll make sure Bob's ready on time."

Wanda heard the doorbell ring promptly at nine the next morning. "Alberto, can you get that? It must be Rita. I'll be right down." Wanda shoved her NYPD pajamas under her pillow before throwing the spread on top. She kicked several pairs of shoes under one of the two easy chairs and swept everything on her dresser into the top drawer.

When she reached the top of the steps, Wanda paused. Alberto and a petite twenty-something girl stood just inside the door. She noticed the girl's eyes and smile just barely fit into her face.

"Rita!" Wanda floated down the stairs with her arms stretched out to embrace her new cleaning lady.

Rita took a tiny step backwards but smiled and accepted Wanda's hug. "It's nice to meet you, Mrs. Santiago."

"Oh, sweetie, call me Wanda."

"Okay, Wanda, where do you want me to start?"

"Anywhere you think is best except my studio," Wanda said, pointing to the closed door off the living room. "I'm working on some murals for the community center—adult daycare, childcare, lunchroom, and library so far."

"Oh, they have childcare there?"

"Yes, they do." She smiled. "I haven't even asked you if you have children."

Rita's eyes danced. "Not yet, and Ray doesn't want me to tell anyone, but I'm expecting."

"Praise the Lord! You must be so excited. I promise I won't say a word to anyone." Wanda put her arm around Rita's waist and led her to the kitchen. "Now we must be very careful. No heavy lifting. Take frequent breaks. In fact, let's take one now."

An image of Lizzy getting on the bus for her first day of school flashed through Ellen's mind as she watched Bob and Alberto drive off to daycare. The sound of water running in the kitchen sink drew her eyes away for a moment. She turned off the faucet, and when she looked up, the car was out of sight.

As Ellen slowly scraped, then rinsed, then loaded the breakfast dishes into the dishwasher, she cringed at the memory of their argument over what he should wear that morning. He'd wanted to wear his gray sweatshirt and jeans, but Ellen had insisted on a nice pair of casual slacks and navy blue sport shirt. Dropping a plate that crashed to the floor brought on a torrent of tears. She raced upstairs and threw herself on their bed.

In time the tears dried up, and Ellen dragged herself off the bed and into the bathroom. She opened the medicine cabinet and reached for her pain pills, but drew her hand back. She grabbed the countertop and clenched her jaw. Her hand shot back to the pill bottle and knocked several other bottles off the shelf. She ignored the mess and struggled with the cap. It wouldn't come off. She read the directions on the lid, lined up the arrows, and tried again.

The ringing phone interrupted her, and she dropped the bottle in the sink and ran to answer it.

Maggie hadn't entertained very much since Mac died. Now she whistled as she set the table for lunch. Then she stood back. A frown creased her face. She stood with her arms crossed, then nodded her head, grabbed her garden shears, and went outside. By the time she returned with a small bouquet of zinnias and Queen Anne's lace, the phone was ringing.

"Hello, MacDonald residence."

"Hi, sweetie." Wanda's voice always made Maggie smile. "It's all set. Ellen and I will be there at eleven-thirty."

"Wonderful. I just picked flowers for the table, and lunch is ready." Maggie reached for a vase and filled it with water.

"Your timing is *perfecto*. Poor thing. She sounded pretty weak on the phone."

Maggie shook her head. "I can't imagine having to send your husband off to daycare. She really is going through a dark valley. And she's trying to do it all on her own."

"God didn't place them here by accident, Maggie. He wants us to reach out to her, and He'll let us know what we need to do and when to do it."

Ellen rang the bell, and the door opened immediately.

"Hello, Ellen. Come right in." Maggie gave her a warm hug. "I'm glad you could squeeze Wanda and me into your schedule again today. It's so hard when you're settling into a new home."

Ellen nodded and looked around. "Where's Sammy?"

"He's at the groomers. He'll look ten pounds lighter the next time you see him. And before I forget, thanks so much for your help yesterday. Joe Carnegie might be a little brusque, but he comes from a wonderful family. I don't know him very well, but what I know, I like."

"Yoo-hoo." The kitchen door flew open, and Wanda blew in. "Am I late?"

Maggie glanced down at her wristwatch as she hugged her friend. "Perfect timing."

Wanda passed the hug on to Ellen. "I assume Bob and Alberto got off alright. How did the rest of your morning go?"

Ellen grabbed a tissue from the box on the counter. She dabbed her eyes and blew her nose. "I'm so sorry. I don't know what's wrong with me."

Lydia Moen

"Give yourself a break, sweetie."

"I agree," Maggie said. "Let's just relax in the living room for a few minutes."

Ellen sat on the edge of the couch cushion twisting her wedding ring. She looked up at the two women. "Thank you for including me today. You must be wondering who you let into your neighborhood."

"We didn't just include you, Ellen. You're the reason for the lunch."

"I don't understand why, Maggie. We've been nothing but a nuisance since we moved in."

Wanda got up and plopped down next to Ellen. "Nuisance? You two are the classiest people we've got on this block—next to Maggie, of course."

She smiled. "When Alberto went into the seminary, the kids and I moved in with my folks. I fought it because I thought we'd drive them crazy. But God insisted, and He knows what He's doing. Turns out my parents needed us as much as we needed them."

Ellen narrowed her eyes and looked at Wanda. "But you were family."

"And so are you, sweetie."

Maggie stood up. "We live within fifty feet of each other. We're the closest thing to relatives we all have." She gestured toward the kitchen. "Let's finish this discussion over lunch."

Ellen set her cellphone next to her plate. "I just want to make sure the daycare center can reach me if they need to."

"As long as they offer ice cream, Bob'll be fine." Wanda licked her lips. "He really enjoyed himself the other day."

Maggie peered at Ellen over her glasses. "I've heard wonderful things about that program. I was talking with Joyce King the other day. Her husband's been participating for several months, and she said it's made a huge difference in both their lives. It's a blessing Bob was able to get involved so quickly."

"After yesterday, I'm surprised they even took him." Ellen cringed and glanced at Wanda.

Maggie raised her eyebrows. "What happened yesterday?"

"Wanda didn't tell you? When we had the accident with the car, my friends in Washington couldn't wait to spread an exaggerated account to each other."

"Well, Wanda hasn't told me anything, and you don't have to either."

Ellen put her elbow on the table and rested her forehead in her hand. "Do you have a copy of the paper? It's probably on the front page."

"That little incident won't be in the paper." Wanda gave a sketchy account of yesterday's events.

Maggie shrugged her shoulders. "That doesn't sound like such a big deal."

"Well, Wanda has been kind enough to leave out the embarrassing details."

"I would *never* want to be accused of embellishing." Wanda smacked her hands down on the table. "Besides, I'd rather talk about me. Did I tell you I have a new cleaning lady?"

Ellen sat back in her seat and smiled. She listened. She talked. She laughed. And she didn't think about Bob for the next hour.

Maggie served dessert—root beer floats in chilled soda fountain glasses with straws and long-handled spoons.

Ellen swished her straw around the edge of the glass. "What a fabulous idea, Maggie. What made you think of this?"

Maggie blushed. "To tell you the truth, I had a spontaneous date last night."

"How exciting!" Ellen giggled. "Do I know the lucky man?"

Wanda clapped her hands. "Of course you do. It's got to be Charlie."

"The mailman?" Ellen lifted an eyebrow and stared at her hostess.

Maggie returned Ellen's gaze. "Charlie Bingham is one of the finest men I've ever known."

Chapter 16

Ellen was at her desk before the sun rose. She opened her stationery drawer and pulled out a stack of three boxes. As she placed the winter scene cards off to the side, her eyes rested on the monogram below. She opened the box and rubbed her hand over the engraved Alexandria address. Then she closed the lid, shrugged her shoulders, and tossed the box in the wastebasket.

She gazed at the wildflower bouquet on the third choice. *Perfect.* She picked up her pen and began writing. When she was finished, Ellen addressed, sealed, and stamped the envelope and took it down to the dock. A narrow pink glow peeked above the eastern shore. She checked her watch and pulled the tape measure out of her pocket.

Ellen's plan was perfect, except for one rather large detail. The second she stepped onto Maggie's driveway, she heard a low bark. Hoping the dog's mistress was still asleep, Ellen hurried to the shed Maggie had just cleaned out.

Maggie woke with a start. "What is it, Sammy? Are you hearing noises again? It's probably a deer on an early morning walk, but I'll check it out."

Maggie scanned the yard from her bedroom window but couldn't see anything that would cause Sammy to go on alert. The bathroom window, however, looked out toward the road. From that vantage point, Maggie saw her new neighbor standing next to the shed door. She was just about to open the window and call to her when Ellen reached for the latch. *What's she doing out there?*

Maggie yanked her hand back and stepped away from the window. She watched as Ellen glanced around then scurried to the far side of the shed. Moments later, she sneaked out of the yard and down the lane.

Maggie frowned. *Does she have something in her hand?*

Maggie scowled. *When did things start disappearing?*

Maggie grimaced. *Wasn't it right after the Baileys moved in?*

"Hi, Charlie. I have a little treat for us this morning." Maggie winked. "And I also have a proposition."

"This has been one of my favorite stops for quite a while, but it's recently grabbed hold of first place all by itself." Charlie hopped out of the boat and sat in one of the chairs Maggie had brought down to replace the missing bench. She held out a tray with two iced coffees and two cranberry-walnut muffins and waved it under his nose. Charlie raised his eyebrows as he helped himself to one of each.

Maggie sat down in the other chair, placed the tray on the dock, and picked up the remaining coffee and muffin.

"Alrighty then, now that you've bribed me, what's the proposition?"

Maggie took a bite out of her muffin, had a sip of her coffee, and looked out at the lake. "I had lunch with Wanda and Ellen the other day. We're getting to be quite a threesome, and I'd like to host an informal dinner for them and their husbands. I was wondering if you'd be willing to co-host it with me."

Charlie set down his coffee and muffin. He leaned forward, closed his eyes, and folded his hands.

As Charlie paused, Maggie said hurriedly, "That's okay, Charlie. I can do it on my own. But I would like you to come."

"I'd love to entertain with you, Maggie. I'm thrilled that you asked me, and I accept your proposition."

Maggie reached over and took Charlie's hand. She looked into his eyes. "Thank you. This is a big step forward for me."

Wanda held the gazebo door open. "Come on in, sweetie. The coffee's hot."

"A small thanks for your help." Ellen handed her a fruit plate. "You and Alberto are awesome."

Wanda plucked a strawberry from the plate and took a bite. "Mmm, yummy. You're going to get me eating healthy if I don't watch out. I'll bring donuts tomorrow, and you can do the coffee."

Ellen shook her finger at Wanda. "Then it's kayaking in the afternoon to burn off the carbs."

Wanda rolled her eyes and laughed. "Alberto loves having Bob's company on the way to work in the morning. How does your hubby like adult daycare?"

"We call it the *office*." Ellen giggled.

"Oh, that's so cute! He goes off to work every day."

"Exactly. Just the way he's done for his entire career."

"So your schedule's pretty much the same as it was in D.C." Wanda popped a grape into her mouth.

Lydia Moen

"His might be, but not mine. I used to leave the house when he did. I ran from volunteering at an art gallery to chairing a fundraising meeting and then raced home to get ready for an evening gala."

"Sweetie, you must have been exhausted." Wanda fanned herself with a paper plate. "Alberto doesn't think I can handle a little volunteering at the community center."

"What are you doing over there, Wanda?"

"My first event is tomorrow. I'm taking everyone from the office on an outing."

Ellen grinned. "I'd love to be a fly on the wall."

Wanda brushed a fly off the fruit plate and nodded at Ellen. "We'll probably have plenty of flies, but I'd love to have you join us. I could use the help."

Ellen rubbed her hands together. "Where do I sign up?"

"You just did." Wanda raised her coffee, and the two volunteers clinked cups.

Ellen hummed as she took the steps up to her house two at a time. A splash of pink in the side yard caught her eye, "Aah, peonies." She detoured to the shed for a pair of garden shears.

Ellen froze when she saw the rusty blue pickup in the driveway. Then she circled the vehicle, looking in all directions as she went. She tiptoed over to the door of the shed. It was slightly ajar. She nudged the door open just far enough to peek inside.

"Mr. Hoffman?"

Ellen sucked in her breath at the sudden crash inside the shed. Ray Hoffman's head snapped around, eyes enormous in his scruffy face. At the same time, his callused hands slammed the lid on the cardboard box at his feet. "Mrs. Bailey?"

"Yes."

"What do you want?"

"I wanted to meet you. How is the work coming along? Will you be finished soon?"

"I don't know. Your husband isn't real sure about what he wants."

"I trust you have experience with this type of renovation, Mr. Hoffman. I haven't seen any plans, but I assume you prepared a drawing for my husband to approve. Did you get a permit?"

As the color drained from Ray Hoffman's face, Ellen knew her suspicions were correct. There were no plans. There was no permit.

Wanda spent much of the next morning gathering food and drinks for the adult daycare outing. When the doorbell rang, she ran down the stairs. "I'll be right there." She pulled the door open and huffed, "I'm running a little late. Thanks for walking over. Can you carry this?" She thrust a cooler into Ellen's hands.

On the drive over, Wanda filled Ellen in on the plans for the afternoon. "Neil Olsen, the founder of Olsen's Marina, is bringing a pontoon boat over to the community center pier to take the office staff out for a tour of the lakes. Neil provides the boat, the fuel, the music, and the clever dialogue. Our jobs are to make sure everyone wears a life jacket and to provide the refreshments."

At the community center, Ellen gave Bob a quick hug while completing the nautical outfit she'd convinced him to wear with the fishing hat he'd left on their dock.

He scratched his head. "What are you doing here?"

"Wanda and I are the refreshment ladies today."

Lydia Moen

Wanda peeked out from behind Ellen. "Hi, Bobby. Are you ready to go cruising?"

"It sure is a beautiful day."

Wanda marched onto the boat and waved a small American flag. "Ahoy, mateys. We'd like to welcome you aboard the USS Happy Mariner. Your captain today is Neil Olsen. Ellen Bailey is the deck hand, and I'm Wanda Santiago, your first mate."

It seemed she had undivided attention, so she continued. "As you come aboard, the deck hand will give each of you a Coast Guard-approved lifejacket. We ask that you abide by the regulations and wear them at all times while aboard the ship. Refreshments will be available throughout the voyage. And finally, we want you to relax and enjoy yourselves as you cruise through our very own liquid gems—the String of Pearls."

With that the captain blew his horn and broadcast Glenn Miller's *String of Pearls* over the PA system. The attendees threaded their way onboard, donning their identical bulky white lifejackets. They sat close together on the benches encircling the deck. Wanda stifled a laugh. *They look like a human string of pearls.*

"The galley is open." Wanda threw open the lid of the cooler. Half a dozen "pearls" bounced off each other as they rushed to the refreshments. *Oops, the string just broke.*

A few minutes later, Wanda noticed Ellen loading the cooler lid with soft drinks, cheese curds, and apple slices. Ellen circled the deck, offering them to the cruisers who chose to stay seated. After everyone had snacks, she visited with people who were by themselves.

Wanda, the unofficial cruise photographer, pulled out her camera.

"Bob, stand next to Neil. Put the captain's hat on." Click. "Great!"

"Elsie, move closer to your handsome husband." Click. "Bingo!"

A few photos later, Ellen snatched the camera out of Wanda's hand.

She directed her to sit in the captain's seat and wave her little American flag. When Wanda resisted, all the other cruisers insisted, clapping their hands and shouting, *"Wanda, Wanda, Wanda!"*

Before they left the boat, Wanda arranged for one of the community center employees to take a picture of the whole group, including Captain Olsen. "Crowd together so they can see us all. Ellen, put your arm around Mr. King. Check the office bulletin board next week to see your shining faces."

Everyone said it was the best office party they'd ever attended.

Ellen slipped into the back seat of Wanda's station wagon. "Bob, you sit in front. I'll be fine in the back."

"I'm sure you'd prefer not to sit next to me." Bob jerked open the car door.

Ellen whipped around. "What did you say?"

"I said you'd rather be sitting next to Mr. King."

Ellen tilted her head and frowned. "Mr. King? Who's that?"

"Don't try to play dumb. I saw you hugging him when we had our picture taken."

"Seriously?"

Wanda glanced at Bob. "I asked Ellen to put her arm around Mr. King. He's very unstable on his feet."

"Don't stick up for her, Wanda. I know what I saw."

Ellen put her head in her hands. "Bob, please, this is embarrassing."

"You should be embarrassed. You were hanging around him all afternoon."

Ellen crossed her arms, turned her head, and stared out the window. Wanda got out of the car as soon as she pulled into the Baileys' driveway. She opened the back door for Ellen. "Sweetie, do you want me to come in for a little while?"

Ellen put her hand on Wanda's arm and spoke in a hushed voice. "Thanks for asking, but that's not necessary. Wanda, I'm so sorry. It's the disease. He'll probably forget all about it."

While Wanda gave her a quick hug, she whispered in Ellen's ear, "Call us if you need us. Anytime, day or night."

Chapter 17

Ellen looked in the bathroom mirror, put on lipstick, and frowned at the dark circles under her eyes. After she smoothed the bedspread for the third time and reorganized the four books on her bedside stand twice, she turned and gazed at the bedroom door. Reluctantly she reached for the knob and drew in a deep breath.

She stopped in the living room and stared at the painting of D.C. that hung over the mantel. She shook her head and closed her eyes.

A few minutes later, she entered the kitchen, walked to the refrigerator, opened the door, and studied the contents before closing the door again. She placed the coffee server under the faucet and stared out the window as the water ran in the pot and overflowed.

"Good morning, sleepy head." Ellen flinched at the touch of Bob's hands on her shoulders. She glanced down at the sink and turned off the tap. Then she slowly turned around and faced her husband.

Bob pulled her rigid body into his arms. "How's the love of my life doing this morning?"

Ellen leaned back and cleared her throat. "I'm okay. How are you feeling?"

"Never better. What should we do today?"

Lydia Moen

Ellen laid her hand on the gray sweatshirt that covered her husband's chest. She stepped back and squinted up at him. "I don't know." She snapped her fingers. "How would you feel about a visit to Carnegie's Treasure Chest? We could even do brunch at the marina."

"That sounds good."

"I'll call Joe Carnegie. You wait for me in the van."

Ellen got hold of the junkyard owner, ran a comb through her hair, and freshened her lipstick. She grabbed her purse and hurried down the steps. When she opened the garage door, Bob was nowhere in sight. She looked across the yard and saw him standing on the dock, rod and reel in hand, and fishing hat on his head.

"Bob, what are you doing? Mr. Carnegie's at the junkyard now, but he's leaving in half an hour."

"I thought I'd do a little fishing."

Ellen clenched her teeth and spun around, hollering over her shoulder, "Bob, we're going to the junkyard. We're supposed to be there in ten minutes. Come on, let's go."

"Why didn't you tell me you wanted me to go somewhere?" Bob stomped up the dock. "Let me put my stuff away."

"*No!* Just leave it there."

During the drive to the junkyard, Ellen told Bob that she wanted to check out the barn for Maggie's bench and Wanda's security light. "He might even have some secondhand tools you'd like for your workshop."

Ellen turned onto the gravel road just as Joe Carnegie's pickup exited the junkyard and came toward them. Ellen waved at him to stop, and he slid to a halt next to them.

"Sorry, you'll have to come back another day." He tipped his dirty ball cap and skidded off, kicking up a trail of stones and dust behind him.

Ellen slammed both her fists against the steering wheel. "Seriously?" She shook her head. "He could have waited for us. And he was so rude. There's something about him...."

Bob leaned over and squeezed Ellen's hand. She looked into his eyes and took a deep breath. "I love you, Robert Bailey. We can still have brunch at the marina."

"That sounds good." Bob nodded his head and stared out the window.

When they got to Olsen's Marina & Grill, Lynn Olsen showed them to a sunny table with a large green umbrella that provided shade over two of the four wicker chairs. They chose seats on the sunny side so they could absorb both the warmth and the view of the lake.

The couple shared a light lunch and discussed their new life in Water's Edge. Ellen was beginning to appreciate the slower pace and the lack of traffic, such a relief after driving in Washington, D.C. She spoke of their new neighbors and how much she enjoyed kayaking on the crystal-clear lakes. Her new relationships with Wanda and Maggie had begun to lessen the sadness she felt about leaving her long-time home.

Ellen stopped her chatter. Her narrowed eyes scanned the lake. "What are you staring at, Bob?"

"I'm watching that gorilla. I think he's about to jump in the lake."

"Gorilla? What are you talking about? Where?"

Bob's voice echoed across the water as he shoved his chair back, almost tipping it over. "Can't you see it, Ellen? It's standing on that green dock!"

Ellen glanced around the restaurant. It was filled to capacity, but the other diners were fully engaged in their own conversations. She lowered her voice: "Are you kidding? That's a poodle."

"You better get your eyes checked. I know a gorilla when I see one."

Ellen gazed at the man she thought she knew so well. *Is he hallucinating?*

The waitress approached them. "Is there anything else I can get for you, Mrs. Bailey?"

Ellen looked down at the napkin she was twisting in her fingers. "Please just bring me our bill."

"I have it right here. Thanks for coming in. It was nice to see you again, Mr. and Mrs. Bailey. I hope you'll be regulars at the marina."

Ellen looked into the waitress's eyes and smiled. "Thank you. We really appreciate the nice service." Then, taking her husband by the hand, she pulled him out of his trance.

As they left the restaurant, Ellen stopped and stared at Joe Carnegie's truck shooting out of the alley next to the bait shop. *So this is where he was going in such a hurry.*

"Okay, Sammy. It's time." Maggie opened the pontoon gate.
Nothing.
"Okay, Sammy. Jump on."
More nothing.
"Sammy, let's go for our ride."
Sammy lay down on the dock, his head between his paws.

"Mac's not coming. You can do it, and so can I." Maggie grabbed Sammy by his lifejacket and backed herself onto the boat, pulling Sammy's front half on with her. Then she got behind him and pushed until, at last, more of the dog was on the boat than off.

At that point, the golden jumped up and ran to his accustomed spot, exactly front and center. He turned slowly and looked at Maggie as if to say, "Come on, let's get going."

As the boat headed into the open water, Maggie took a deep breath, then another. She pushed the throttle forward to increase the speed and shouted, "Yeehaw!"

Mercy, did I just say that? I've turned into a boating cowgirl. She looked around to see if anyone had heard her, but the only witness had four legs.

Although Mac had been the captain and she the first mate, Maggie knew the route as well as he. She had denied herself the pleasure of the lakes for too long. On one of their last boat rides, Mac had said, "Some of our happiest times have been on these lakes together. Do me a favor, Mags, and have some fun out here for me."

Maggie screened the passing shoreline watching for friends. She waved to anyone she saw on land or lake, not wanting to offend someone she knew.

Suddenly the engine began to sputter, and a puff of smoke rose from the back of the boat.

Wanda stood in the center of her studio, arms folded, head tilted, and eyes narrowed. Five easels fanned out in front of her. Four of the boards were empty. Every square inch of the middle one was covered with postcards featuring scenes from the String of Pearls or pictures from her files.

Wanda grabbed the paint brush out of her ponytail and tapped it against her palm. Then she turned on her heel and flew up the stairs. When she returned several minutes later, she walked up to the center easel. She carefully draped the object in her hands on push pins holding several of the pictures.

Lydia Moen

She backed away, paintbrush secured between her teeth, and squinted. "Yes!"

"Yes, what?" Alberto strolled into the room.

Wanda almost swallowed her paintbrush. "Alberto, I'm going to have to get you a bell like Purrdita's if you keep sneaking up on me."

Her husband chuckled "What are you doing with Grandma's pearls?"

"Oh, Alberto, they're the heartbeat of my murals. Grandma would love it. And I've finally figured out exactly what I'm going to do for the first one." Wanda pointed to the middle easel. "Can you picture it?"

Alberto put his hands on his hips and tilted his head from side to side. "Well, not fully. Why don't you tell me about it?"

Wanda grabbed a wooden folding chair and placed it in front of the easel. When Alberto sat down, she leaned over and gave him a kiss on the cheek. Then she stepped up and, using her brush as a pointer, gave a short discourse on every item displayed—not in order, but randomly, as she did all things.

"I envision a medley of scenes…pines on the big island…boats crowding the marina…an eagle against a blue sky…kayaks stacked against a stone wall…. No people. Just scenes around the lakes. And then, weaving through all this natural beauty will be a stunning string of pearls, a smiling face shining out from each precious gem."

Wanda beamed when Alberto stood up and came toward her with arms spread wide. She leaned into him, returning his warm embrace. He brushed a lock of hair from her face as she looked up at him. "Mi querida, you amaze me. I love the excitement in your voice and the sparkle in your eyes when you're in the midst of creating. This plan you have for beautifying the community center is worth waiting for. It will broadcast the message that the real pearls in our lives are not from an oyster's belly but are all around us—our families and our neighbors, the old and the young, the weak and the strong."

The motor died. Maggie sat in the captain's chair, head bowed and hands clasped.

The response to her prayer was all that she could have asked for and more than she expected. She spied Charlie's dark green fishing boat, fluffed her hair, and waved her arms to attract his attention.

When he pulled alongside, Maggie tossed him a line. "Charlie, you are a real Godsend. One minute Sammy and I were skimming across the water. The next minute the motor conked out. Now we're stranded."

"I'll tie up my boat to yours and see what I can do." He sat down in the captain's chair and pushed the button to raise the motor. Then he walked to the back of the boat and inspected it.

While Charlie checked the motor, Maggie chattered. "This is the first time I've taken the boat out by myself. I don't know what I would have done if you hadn't come by. I'm sorry to cut into your fishing time, but I'm grateful to see you. I just hope there isn't anything seriously wrong with the boat."

"The fish can wait. I doubt it's anything serious, Maggie, but you'll need a mechanic to look at it. For now I'll just tow you home. Or if you'd like, I can tow you to the marina and then drop you off at your dock."

"Are you sure your little boat can pull mine?"

Charlie nodded and put his hand on her shoulder. Maggie leaned into him, her head fitting into the crook of his arm. The resulting hug was both natural and comfortable and might have lasted longer if a slow-moving Chris-Craft hadn't passed by.

Neil Olsen called out, "Maggie, Charlie, do you need any help?"

Lydia Moen

Ellen pulled into Wanda's driveway when she spotted her neighbor out watering her garden. She waited for Wanda to turn around and greet her.

After a minute, she called out the window, "Hi, neighbor." She waited some more.

Ellen opened the door and stepped out of the van. "Hi, Wanda."

Still no response.

Ellen hesitated and started to turn back to the van. *Oh, she's probably just thinking about something,* she told herself and then walked up behind the pre-occupied gardener and tapped her on the shoulder.

Wanda screamed, spun around, and blasted Ellen full in the face with the spray from her hose.

Ellen shrieked and dodged to escape the water, but there was no escape. Wanda, working feverishly on the nozzle, continued to douse Ellen wherever she darted.

"I can't turn it off. I can't turn it off!" Wanda's voice was an octave higher than Ellen remembered.

"Seriously. Just drop the fool thing!"

Unfortunately, Wanda obeyed instantly.

"Run for your life," Wanda shouted as the hose whipped around.

Ellen pulled up the neck of her Lands End shirt to cover her head. "This is insane. Where's the faucet?"

"It's right next to…"

Ellen was unable to decipher the next words out of Wanda's mouth but was able to determine the direction of the faucet by Wanda's skid marks through the well-watered garden. She had lost her footing and slid to a stop right under a tomato plant, having taken out several feet of topsoil on her way.

"I've got it!" Ellen yelled as she reached the faucet.

Wanda pulled a carrot top out of her mouth. "*Ay, caramba.*"

Her husband came charging out the door and into the yard. "Is everyone all right?" He saw his wife on her back in the garden. "Wanda, what are you doing?"

"Alberto, what does it look like I'm doing? I'm transplanting the carrots."

"You'd better sit down, Maggie. After I start my engine, I'll have to go full-speed ahead to pull your pontoon boat. That tow rope will—"

Maggie interrupted him as she peered over her sunglasses. "Don't worry about me, Charlie. I've been around boats all my life."

"Just the same, I'd feel better if you—"

"Charlie, I appreciate your rescuing me, but I don't need advice about how to take care of myself on my own boat."

Maggie planted her feet sailor-style and held onto the railing at the bow, midway between the two ropes attached to either side of both vessels. She nodded to Charlie and gave him a thumbs-up.

Charlie grimaced and shook his head, started the engine, looked back over his shoulder, and rammed it into gear.

Maggie's head lurched back and forth like a schoolyard tetherball during recess. But her hands gripped the rail, and her skid-resistant shoes prevented a humiliating hurdle into the lake. When Charlie killed the motor, Maggie bent over laughing. She gave Charlie a sheepish grin and headed for the captain's chair. She paused, rendered a snappy salute to Charlie, walked over to the side bench, and collapsed onto it.

Lydia Moen

Ellen tried to pry her hand out of Wanda's muddy grip, but her friend held on tight. "Wanda, what are you doing?"

"We're going for a swim. Last one in is a chipmunk's granny!" Wanda pulled her toward the lake.

"Are you kidding? You might be going for a swim, but I'm not." Ellen dug her heels into the soggy soil.

"Oh, yes you are, Ellen Bailey." Before Ellen could react, Wanda wiped mud off her arms and smeared it onto her friend's.

Ellen's jaw dropped, and her eyes widened.

The two women stood stone-still, staring at one another.

"That does it!" Ellen pushed her way around Wanda, and the race was on.

Ellen surfaced just in time to shout, "Wanda's a chipmunk's granny! Wanda's a chipmunk's granny!" before the loser cannonballed in.

"Bailey wins by a splash." Alberto arrived at the dock, towels in hand. He helped each of the contestants up the ladder.

Ellen immediately dried off, spread her towel on the dock, and sat down. She closed her eyes and lifted her face to the sun for a moment. When the dock started shaking, Ellen jumped back up just in time to see a dripping Wanda chasing her husband toward the shore. "Come on, Alberto. Give the chipmunk's granny a little sugar."

"Oh, so it's sugar you want." Alberto turned abruptly, and Wanda crashed right into him. Her husband picked her up and heaved her over his shoulder.

Ellen's mouth dropped open as she watched Alberto thunder down the dock and into the water, his wife pounding on his back and hollering, "Put me down!"

The pastor and his wife emerged coughing and sputtering. Ellen laughed until her sides hurt. "You two have completely destroyed my image of church people."

Chapter 18

Maggie looked at Charlie when Lynn Olsen asked where they would like to sit. "We'll take that spot in the shade." He put his hand in the small of Maggie's back and steered her to a table. As he pulled out her chair, Maggie noticed their hostess was barely stifling her giggles. She assumed Lynn was amused at the sight of her former teacher on a date with the postman. Maggie caught Charlie's eye, tilted her head toward the hostess, and he winked.

When they were both seated, Maggie reached for his hand. "If it weren't for you, Sammy and I would still be sitting in the middle of Jade Lake."

He rubbed his thumb across the top of her hand. "If it weren't for you, I'd still be sitting in the middle of Ruby Lake, fishing all by myself. I've done a lot of that the past five years. This is much better."

They both drew their hands back as the waitress approached. "Are you ready to order?"

Maggie winced at the unopened menu in front of her. Charlie smiled at the waitress. "What's the special today?"

"Fresh walleye. It's really tasty. And you get to choose two sides."

Maggie nodded when Charlie looked over to her and raised his eyebrow. "We'll take two of those." They finished ordering and handed their menus to the waitress.

Maggie cleared her throat. "You taught me a good lesson today. I should have followed your advice from the start. You'll have to be patient with me, Charlie. I've become used to making my own decisions, and they're not always good."

"I'm a very patient man, Maggie. And you'll need patience with me too. I have to admit I started the boat a little more forcefully than I had to."

"I was pretty sure about that." Maggie laughed. "And I deserved it. Now we really need to talk about tomorrow night."

"I'm looking forward to it. Do you have a to-do list for me?"

Maggie peered over her glasses at him, and he winked back.

"I'm not much of a cook, but I'm a mean grill man. How about if we introduce Bob and Ellen to Wisconsin bratwurst?"

"Well, I was planning on serving…" Maggie's eyes widened as she brought her hands to her mouth. "Bratwurst will be perfect."

"Are you sure?"

"Absolutely. I'll whip up some potato salad and fix a bowl of fresh fruit. What do you think of brownies with vanilla ice cream and hot fudge sauce for dessert?"

Charlie whistled and rubbed his hands together. "Alrighty then. I'll stop and get the ice cream on my way over."

"That would be a big help. The other thing we need to talk about is getting together with our military family. I can ask Tamara if she and the kids would enjoy coming over and spending time at the lake. We could have a picnic."

Charlie rubbed a hand on his forehead. "Would it be easier for you if we had them over with the Santiagos and Baileys?"

"It might be easier, but we should probably get to know the family better ourselves first. And I'm hoping you and Ellen will get better acquainted. She's becoming a good friend, and she doesn't really know you very well. It's important to me that you know my friends and they know you."

"Then it's important to me, too."

Ellen sighed when she saw Bob walk out onto the dock with his fishing gear. Alberto stood up and reached for the gazebo door. "I'll go see if we can pull that angler away from his favorite pastime and get him to spend a little time with us."

Ellen tilted her head and looked up at the pastor. "Could you wait just a bit?"

Alberto sat down, and Wanda moved over to sit next to her friend. "What's the matter, sweetie?"

"It's Bob. I was so embarrassed when he accused me of flirting with Mr. King. That's actually why I stopped over this afternoon. I wanted to apologize." Ellen kept her gaze on her wedding ring and twisted it back and forth.

"He did seem really upset. How did it go after I dropped you off?" Ellen could hear the concern in Wanda's voice.

"I set some food out for him and spent the rest of the evening working on a project in my sewing room. We hardly talked to each other until this morning. Then he acted like nothing had happened."

Alberto sipped his iced tea and then looked at Ellen. "Someone once told me that the only good thing about having Alzheimer's is that you have only happy memories. I can't prove that, but the dementia patients I minister to at the Harbor recall lives of accomplishment, laughter, and vitality. God's great mercy at work." Alberto smiled and shook his head.

"That's encouraging, but we're not at that point yet." Ellen turned her attention to her husband, sitting on the dock and staring at the water, fishing pole in hand.

She broke the silence that followed. "I also need to tell you about something that happened at the marina this morning." She paused, massaging her brow with her hand as she moved her head from side to side.

"Ellen, take your time. We know this is difficult." Wanda sat back.

"I...I...I'm afraid Bob might be having hallucinations." Ellen shivered and dropped her head into her hands.

Maggie hustled home after the early service to get ready for the evening's cookout. She had just put the potatoes on the burner to boil when the phone rang.

Before she could speak, Maggie heard a familiar voice. "Hi, Grandma. This is Josh."

His voice startled her, as it always did. It sounded so much like Mac's...not deep, but masculine...not loud, but husky.

"I can't believe you're calling." Maggie dropped onto the closest chair.

"Everyone in our unit got phone cards in a care package sent to one of my buddies. I decided that card was meant for you. How are you doing?"

"I'm fine, dear. What about you? Are you staying safe?"

"Yeah, Grandma, I am. But you know I can't say much about what's going on here. Tell me what's happening there."

"Well, let me think." Maggie tapped her fingers on the table. "I've been spending a lot of time with Wanda. And Alberto's home."

"Mrs. Santiago must be happy. Say hi to them for me."

"I've also gotten to know the couple that moved in next to them. Ellen Bailey, Wanda, and I have become quite a threesome. We go kayaking, take walks, and have lunch— you know, retired lady things."

"It sounds like heaven to me. Have you done any fishing?"

"A little over at the Baileys' with Ellen's husband, Bob. But I can't wait until you get home and we can fish together." Maggie cringed when she thought about Mac's missing bench.

"Have you caught that big bass that's been toying with us forever?"

"Bob's not the fisherman that you are. We mainly put our lines in the water and talk."

"That works. What else have you been up to?"

Maggie put her finger to her lips. "Josh, don't tell your parents, but I've been dating a little."

"Way to go, Grandma! Who's the lucky guy?"

"Do you remember Mr. Bingham?"

"You mean the guy who brings the mail by boat?"

"That's the one." She felt her face redden.

"I remember him. He seemed nice. Weren't you and Grandpa friends with him and his wife? She died a long time ago, didn't she?"

She nodded, though she knew he couldn't see her. "Yes, we were all good friends. She passed away five years ago, and now Charlie and I enjoy spending time together."

"I'm really happy for you, and I promise to keep your secret."

He hesitated before continuing. "Grandma, I want you to know I've started reading that Bible you sent. Chris, the buddy of mine who gave me the phone card, has one too. The two of us started reading together, and a bunch of other guys have joined us. I just thought you'd want to know."

Maggie raised her head heavenward and closed her eyes. When she opened them, she felt a tear trickle down her cheek.

Before they hung up, Josh said, "You may not hear from me for a while. We won't have access to phones or mail, but don't worry."

"I'll try not to worry, and I will be praying. Charlie's praying for you too."

"I love you, Grandma."

"I love you too, Josh. Thanks so much for calling. Be careful. And Josh, thank Chris for me."

Maggie fluffed her hair before greeting Charlie at the door. He handed her a bouquet of red roses and stargazer lilies. "I'll be right back with the ice cream and bratwurst." Maggie stifled a squeal while savoring the sweet scents of the flowers. Her pulse quickened as she watched Charlie hop down the steps and sprint to his car.

She looked at her watch and hurried back to the kitchen to select a vase. As she swapped Charlie's flowers for the casual daisies and Black-Eyed Susans she'd picked earlier, she heard him come in the door. Her eyes glistened as she faced him. "Charlie, it's been a long time since anyone's brought me flowers. I'm glad they're from you."

"So am I."

The two stood side by side at the counter. Charlie sliced the melons. Maggie washed and removed the stems from the berries. A slow smile emerged on her lips when she peeked at the neat slices of watermelon, cantaloupe, and honeydew piling up on the cutting board next to hers.

"Maggie, do you have something in the oven?"

Realization hit her, and she felt her eyes go wide. "The brownies! Oh, no!" Maggie ran to the oven and flung open the door. Charlie was right behind her with two potholders. He stepped around her, pulled out the pan, and placed it on top of the stove.

They both stared in silence at the very brown brownies. Then Charlie turned to Maggie and said, "Perfect! Just the way I like 'em." He slipped his arm around her and gave her a squeeze. Maggie put her head on his shoulder and leaned into him.

"Yoo-hoo! We're all here. Ready or not."

The host and hostess disentangled themselves and greeted their four grinning guests.

"Here's your iced tea, Bob. Do you want me to get you anything else before I sit down?"

"Thank you, honey. You spoil me."

"It's the best job I've ever had, and the only one I want." Ellen bent down and kissed the top of his head before slipping into the lawn chair next to his. She eyed his khakis and sport shirt and smiled at her husband. *I'm glad I was able to convince him to change out of his sweatshirt and jeans. Maybe I can get them washed this evening.*

Wanda walked up and handed Bob a bowl of pretzels. "Did Ellen tell you about our soothing swim yesterday?"

"I don't think so. It sure is a beautiful day."

Charlie called from his post at the grill. "Ellen, when you get a chance, come on over. I want to introduce you to a native Wisconsinite."

As Ellen stood up, Wanda took her chair. "Oh, good. I can sit next to your hubby and tell him my version of the swim story."

Ellen walked over to the grill. "I don't see anyone I haven't met. Who's the mystery guest?"

Charlie pointed to a sizzling row of sausages lined up on the grill. "Meet the bratwurst—the finest, fattiest, best-tasting meat Wisconsin has to offer. If you want to get on a first-name basis with them, call them

Lydia Moen

brats. Falling in love with them is a requirement of residency."

Ellen's eyes narrowed as she leaned over the grill. Then she looked up at Charlie. "Pleasing color, satisfying aroma, enticing sizzle—I had no idea you were such a fabulous grill man."

She grinned when Maggie gave Charlie a playful nudge. "Mr. Bingham is a man of many talents. Now are the bratwursts almost ready?"

Charlie winked at Ellen. "What do you think, Wisconsinite-in-training?"

She turned to Maggie and rubbed her hands together. "How soon can we eat?"

Chapter 19

Neil Olsen sat behind the stained Formica counter in the bait shop, drinking his morning cup of coffee. He put his feet on the counter as he leaned back in his brown Naugahyde chair. He had sat in the same chair every morning for the past twenty years. It had come to fit his form perfectly, and although his wife had tried to give or throw it away numerous times, Neil refused to part with it.

Because his arm was in a sling, he crossed his left ankle over his right knee, grabbed the *Lake Breezes* off the counter, and spread the front page across his legs.

Neil's eyes widened. He dropped the paper, picked up the phone, and punched in one of his speed-dial numbers.

Joe Carnegie was heading into the big barn when his cellphone rang. He hit the talk button and put it to his ear. As he listened to his caller, he spun around and ran to his truck. He was halfway down the road when he realized he'd failed to lock up the big barn. It was too late to turn back.

Ray Hoffman parked on Lakeshore Lane. Although the trees hid his pickup, he had an excellent view of Bob's shed. *How much time can one man spend in a fifteen-by-twenty foot building? I don't have all day to wait.* He grabbed the copy of the local paper he'd taken from the truck stop. After scanning the lead article, he threw his truck into reverse and backed down the lane.

Ellen's feet crossed the finish line of her two-mile jog when she reached the end of the dock. The only thing in their mailbox was the *Lake Breezes*. She pulled it out and started reading the headline as she walked away from the lake. Her pace quickened, and she went straight to the phone when she got in the house.

Maggie dropped her Bible, startled by the ringing sound just inches from her chair. She grabbed for the phone. As the receiver fell to the floor, the voice she heard was familiar but strained.

"Ellen, is that you? Is everything okay?"

"I'll be right over."

Maggie's mind raced. *Ellen sounded so tense. Is she afraid of being caught? Why did I let her get away when she was sneaking around my shed the other morning? I should have confronted her right then. But if she is involved, why would she want to talk about it? Oh, Lord, I pray there's an explanation for her behavior that has nothing to do with the article in the paper. Please help me to keep an open mind.*

Wanda kept an eye on the mailbox while she worked in her studio. She missed seeing Charlie, but when she saw that the flag was lowered, she scurried down to the dock. She opened the mailbox and pulled out the *Lake Breezes*.

WATER'S EDGE RESIDENTS—VICTIMS OF ROBBERIES

Under the banner headline, a photo covering a quarter of the front page showed a scowling Mayor Frank Bowens and the Water's Edge director of public works, each pointing to one of two empty sign posts.

According to the article, a rash of robberies had taken place in Water's Edge over the past two weeks. A *Breezes* reporter had learned, through an interview with Mayor Bowens, that the city government was considering establishing a reward fund for the capture of the thieves and the return of the missing sign.

The article quoted Bowens as saying, "That sign has hung here since the sanitary district was established in 1947. It recognized the excellent work done by our returning veterans, who helped rebuild our fine country after the Great Depression."

Following up on the mayor's comments, the *Breezes* investigative reporter gained access to police reports detailing the thefts. The article continued:

"The *Breezes* has learned that the following items are missing from around the area:

Four-by-six-foot wooden sign, white with green lettering: 'Water's Edge Sanitary District'
- Brown twelve-foot kayak belonging to Mr. and Mrs. Lars Hansen
- Eight-foot oak bench belonging to Mrs. Margaret MacDonald
- Aluminum security light belonging to Pastor and Mrs. Alberto Santiago

- Power drill belonging to Mr. and Mrs. Robert Bailey
- Compressor, power saw, and miscellaneous tools from the storage shed behind the community center

"Only Santiago was available for comment. She told the *Breezes*, 'My neighbors and I are very concerned about the lawlessness invading Water's Edge. We can only hope the police will catch the perpetrators and bring them to justice.' Santiago did not have any photos of the security light and denied a request to photograph her with the empty light post."

Wanda walked back to the house as she finished reading. "I'm glad I decided to keep my picture out of the paper. I don't want the culprits targeting me."

She cut out the front-page story on the thefts and posted it on her refrigerator door. Before she had a chance to call Maggie, her phone rang. "Good morning," she said, pressing the phone to her ear. "This is Wanda." For the next thirty seconds, Wanda listened then said, "Okay, Maggie, I'll meet you there."

"Seriously, can you believe this? The three of us are in the middle of a crime spree and on the front page of the newspaper." Ellen sat across from Maggie in the Baileys' kitchen, the *Lake Breezes* spread out before them.

Wanda, seated at the end of the table, drummed her metallic-blue nails on the smooth surface. "I think we should call the police immediately—maybe 911 if we want a quick response."

Maggie peered over her glasses. "We are not going to call 911. That's only for emergencies, and a few thefts that took place days or weeks ago hardly fall into that category. Let's just slow down, take a deep breath, and start thinking clearly. Ellen, do you have a pencil and paper we can use?"

Ellen handed them to her, and Maggie positioned the paper where they could all see it. She made two columns and labeled them "Facts" and "Suspicions."

"Can we start with the missing tools?" Ellen curled her leg under her, sat on it, and leaned forward. "The thought of someone slinking into our shed and stealing Bob's tools makes me lonesome for the peace and safety of Washington, D.C."

"Oh, sweetie, this is the first real drama we've had in Water's Edge in forever. A month from now we'll have forgotten all about it, and the paper's lead story will be who caught the biggest trout in the annual Fisheree—our local fishing contest."

"Well, I was exaggerating a bit to make a point." Ellen pushed her glasses up on her head.

"Ellen, honey, that's so unlike you. People can take things the wrong way if you're overly dramatic. But I'm sure we're all just reacting to this frightful situation and the imminent danger we all find ourselves in."

Ellen raised an eyebrow.

Maggie tapped her pencil on the table. "Okay, ladies, let's list what we know and what we merely suspect."

"We know these burglaries started about the same time Ray Hoffman began working for Bob and Ellen. He seems like a suspicious character to me, although he does have a lovely little wife." Wanda rearranged the rainbow of beads that hung around her neck.

Ellen cringed, and she felt a hot flush spread from her throat to her face.

Maggie reached across the table and patted Ellen's hand. "We're just trying to look at all the possibilities, dear. It may not be Ray, and even if it is, you're not responsible for his actions."

"Thanks, Maggie, but I'll feel terrible if we've brought a thief into the neighborhood."

"It's not our job to determine who's guilty." Maggie pointed her pencil at her two friends. "We merely need to document what we see as the facts and what are just suspicions."

Ellen pulled her leg out from under her and sat back down on the chair. "You're absolutely right, Maggie. Let's focus on your chart."

Wanda began rifling through her tote. "When did that handyman start working for you, Ellen?"

"I'm not sure. He sets his own schedule. I remember Bob saying Ray dropped off some supplies late on a Friday night. I assumed he was on his way home from another job."

Wanda looked up. "Or from a bar." Her hands, one holding a tissue and the other a candy bar, flew to her heart. "Wait a minute! Remember the night we all woke up hearing gunshots and a truck squealing down our road?"

Maggie raised her eyebrows. "That's right! And I'll write that under 'facts.' But as I recall, Wanda, you weren't exactly sure what you heard that night. Did you even get out of bed?"

"I didn't have to get out of bed to know that someone was shooting at us."

"And that was the same night Mac's bench disappeared!" Maggie wrote as fast as the three were talking.

"And I bet that guy has access to your shed. Isn't that a fact?" Wanda began piling items from her tote on the table.

"I'm afraid that's true. Bob's been too trusting. He has a lot of expensive tools, and there's no way he can keep track of them. He's an easy target."

"Okay, I think we've covered the handyman. Who else do we need to talk about?" Maggie moved her tablet to accommodate the mounting piles from Wanda's tote.

Wanda extracted an empty soda bottle. "Ellen, do you recycle?" She handed the bottle to Ellen. "I think it's a bunch of teenagers playing pranks. Why can't they just toilet paper our trees?"

Ellen tossed the bottle in the sink. "Do kids still do that?"

Maggie laughed. "I'm pretty sure they just do it to each other. Besides, do we really think a group of teenagers could be quiet enough to pull off these heists without waking everyone within miles?"

"I didn't want to say anything before, Maggie, but the day the three of us went to the junkyard, I saw an old bench in the barn."

Maggie stopped writing. "Did you get a good look at it?"

Ellen closed her eyes and rested her head on her fingertips. "Not really. It was tucked away in a corner."

Maggie shook her head. "I've known the Carnegie family for years, dear. I don't know Joe as well—he's always been somewhat of a loner—but I'd hate to think he's involved in these robberies."

Wanda looked up from her search. "Me too."

"We'll put his name over on the suspicion side of the chart."

"What about Mr. Olsen?" Ellen hesitated a moment. "I know you don't think Joe Carnegie could be involved, but I saw his pickup pulling out of the alley next to the bait shop. Bob and I were having lunch at the marina, and we stopped by to get some bait, but the shop was closed. Mr. Olsen wasn't open for business."

"Maybe he was open for monkey business," Wanda said. "I bet he's in on it. Since his sons probably left him destitute, he's had to resort to stealing and then selling the things to Joe. Why the poor man can hardly earn enough in that bait shop to pay his monthly bills."

"I imagine he gets Social Security." Ellen watched Wanda pull yet another item from her bag, wondering if she should extend the table.

"I'd guess Neil Olsen is far from destitute, and I don't think his sons left him penniless. He merely turned the business over to them." Maggie tapped her foot. "Let's get back to the chart."

She tilted her head and looked at Ellen. "I have to admit, you've got me thinking. I went to the bait shop last week. When Joe walked in, Neil couldn't get rid of me fast enough. Before I could even get in my car, they'd closed the shop—and it was the middle of the day."

Ellen nodded as Maggie reminded them she'd seen a boat with no lights moving along the shore the night they'd heard gunshots. "I saw it too."

Wanda couldn't be quite sure, but now that they mentioned it, she felt certain she'd seen mysterious boats at one time or another.

Both Maggie's and Ellen's sightings had happened on dark nights, when it was difficult to see. Wanda was unclear on the details. Nonetheless, she voiced her opinion. "It's obvious. Neil Olsen and Joe Carnegie are partners in crime. They're stealing from the poor to make themselves rich."

Ellen laughed out loud. "I'm not sure others would think the three of us are 'the poor.' However, Neil does have ready access to pontoon boats. He captained one of them for us just the other day."

"That's right. Ladies, I think it's time to head downtown." Wanda pounded her fist on the table and eyed her two cohorts in crime-stopping. "It's our duty as Water's Edge citizens to turn our findings over to the police. Let's go!"

She held her tote up to the edge of the table and shoved everything back in it. "I give up. I can't even remember what I was looking for."

Ellen stood up and slapped her hand down in the middle of the table. "Come on, Maggie, you're next." Maggie laid her hand on top of Ellen's, and Wanda followed suit. After one more time around the table, they threw their hands in the air. "A cord of three strands is not quickly broken!"

Chapter 20

Shortly before noon, Maggie MacDonald and her crime-stopping companions walked into the Water's Edge police station and strode to the front desk. "We'd like to speak with the officer heading up the Pearl Lake robberies' investigation."

The desk sergeant told the women to take a seat and she would ask Chief Gallego to help them. A few minutes later, Alberto's cousin greeted the ladies and led them into a small room furnished with nothing but an old rectangular table and four metal chairs. He graciously pulled out Wanda's chair as he motioned for the others to take a seat.

"How is your husband doing, Mrs. Bailey?"

"He's still complaining about not being able to drive, but I know it was time for him to give it up."

The chief nodded. "I can understand how he feels."

Carlos joined the women at the table. "Now to what do I owe the pleasure of a visit from three such lovely ladies?"

"Would you mind closing the door?" Maggie whispered. After he complied, she handed him a copy of their *Facts and Suspicions* chart. "The three of us spent the morning compiling this information. We think it will be helpful in your investigation."

Lydia Moen

They all chimed in to explain the items that each had contributed to the list and how they had arrived at their lineup of suspects.

Ten minutes later, Chief Gallego held their document in front of him and peered over it at the three sleuths. "Ladies, I can see you've put a lot of effort into this. You can rest assured that we'll follow up."

"We want to be good citizens." Maggie wrinkled her brow. "Will you have to handcuff them? I'm worried about Neil. You should probably know he's suffering from bursitis, and his arm is in a sling."

Wanda tapped her fingernails on the table. "And I'm sure you'll want to keep them apart so they can't make up alibis."

Maggie noticed that Carlos kept a hand over his mouth. "Well, ladies, we need to be cautious in these cases."

"Do you think they may be dangerous?" Ellen asked, biting her lower lip.

Carlos looked down and cleared his throat. "I doubt it very much, but we need to keep the details of the investigation out of the public eye. As you know, in this country, everyone is presumed innocent until proven guilty."

They nodded in unison like three bobble-head dolls.

When they returned to the lobby, Wanda reached up and hugged the chief. "Thank you for seeing us, and do be careful, sweetie. You have such a dangerous job."

As the ladies turned to leave, the desk sergeant raised an eyebrow at Carlos and said, "You be careful out there, big guy."

The three crime stoppers returned to Ellen's house, congratulating themselves on their successful meeting at the police station. Ellen got out leftover chicken salad, while the guests put lettuce on glass plates and poured iced tea. The cord of three strands was holding fast.

Wanda offered to say a blessing, and Ellen replied, "Whatever you'd like."

All three bowed their heads as Wanda asked God to bless their food. "And," she prayed, "please be merciful to Neil and Joe."

Ellen felt her face flush at the compliments about her chicken salad. "You know, I never could have had an impromptu lunch like this when we lived in Washington. I had no idea how much fun it could be. In fact, I'm really enjoying this whole adventure. I think Chief Gallego was impressed with our presentation."

Wanda waved her fork. "Oh, I know Carlos. I could tell. He was overwhelmed."

"Well, we did our homework, and he appreciated our separating fact from suspicion. Speaking of homework..." Maggie pointed a spoon at Wanda. "How are the murals coming?"

"I've had a magnificent breakthrough." For the next five minutes, Wanda kept Ellen riveted. Eyes dancing and hands drawing in the air, the artist described each of the five murals in detail.

"That sounds awesome." Ellen clapped. "Over the years, I've bought a lot of paintings, visited dozens of galleries, and taken art appreciation classes. But I've never heard a working artist describe the process of creating a masterpiece. Using the String of Pearls to tie together the elements within each of the murals and then as a theme for the entire set of five is brilliant."

Maggie closed her eyes and brought her hand to her chest. "Wanda, I agree. It sounds wonderful. I can't wait to go over to the community center and see what you've done."

"Oh, you can just come over to the house. You too, sweetie. I've got the entire first mural laid out on an easel."

Maggie stood up and took her dishes over to the sink. Then she turned and faced Wanda. "So you really haven't started."

Ellen shifted in her chair, twisting her wedding ring.

Wanda threw her napkin down. "You obviously don't understand the artistic process, Maggie."

"You're right." Maggie crossed her arms and leaned against the counter. "However, I'm beginning to think this project is too big for one person."

Ellen stood up and cleared the rest of the table. Silence fell over the luncheon as she busied herself at the counter. When she turned back to face her friends, she held a small plate of cookies. "Dessert, anyone?"

Maggie didn't stay for dessert.

"Do you think you two will be able to patch things up?" Ellen asked Wanda.

"Oh, sweetie, we've been friends forever. This is just a snag in the pantyhose of life."

Ellen stifled a laugh and waited for Wanda to continue.

"It's not just Maggie. It's Alberto too. I was really excited when he came home from Mexico. But it hasn't been the way I pictured it would be when he was gone."

She sighed. "I know I'm a little disorganized, but he knew that when we got married. I'm an artist. My job is to be creative. I'm not a file clerk. He even had Maggie help organize my studio. I haven't been able to find a thing since."

"Wanda, you have the love of a wonderful man. Maggie lost her husband, and I'm losing mine. I hope you'll understand if I'm not completely sympathetic."

2:00 p.m.: Neil Olsen entered the Water's Edge police station.

2:30 p.m.: Neil Olsen left the Water's Edge police station.

2:45 p.m.: Joe Carnegie entered the Water's Edge police station.

3:15 p.m.: Joe Carnegie left the Water's Edge police station.

4:00 p.m.: Chief Gallego drove down Lakeshore Lane, stopped at the Bailey home, and spoke with Ray Hoffman, who was packing up his tools and loading his pickup.

4:25 p.m.: Pickup and police car departed Lakeshore Lane.

After Wanda left, Ellen walked over to the counter and packed up the remaining cookies. Ten minutes later, she arrived at the community center, checked in at the front desk, and headed down the hall to the adult daycare area.

Ellen stopped just inside the door. Bob was sitting with his back to her in the middle of a group of people. In fact, he appeared to be the center of attention. From her vantage point, she could hear snatches of the conversation:

"So how many years did he get?"

"Not as many as he deserved."

"He must have had a good attorney."

"I'd like to think so."

She couldn't see his face, but she knew he was smiling.

Ellen tiptoed over to the refreshment area, greeted the several seniors seated there, and laid the cookie tray on the counter after removing the plastic wrap.

"Help yourselves," she said in a hushed voice.

Lydia Moen

One elderly lady's eyebrows rose as she nearly shouted, "Did you make these?"

Ellen glanced at the lady's nametag then raised her finger to her lips and nodded her head, praying Betty would honor her request.

Betty's voice remained at foghorn level. "What kind are they? Oatmeal Raisin?"

Ellen leaned forward and whispered, "They're chocolate chip, Betty."

Betty turned around and shouted, "Hey, everyone! She brought cookies, and they're chocolate chip."

Ellen cringed as Bob's audience turned its attention toward the refreshments. "You don't need to get up. I'll bring them to you."

The chairs surrounding her husband were already vacated. He sat alone.

Ellen walked over to him, put a hand on his shoulder, and held a cookie out to him. Bob knocked it out of her hand. "What are you doing here? This is my office. Go home and stay there!"

Wanda looked out her studio window and saw Maggie coming through the hedge. She ran to the door and met her on the porch.

"I'm sorry."

"I'm sorry too."

Wanda loved that Maggie initiated the hug, and she held on a little longer than usual. "Do you want to go down and sit in the gazebo, my friend?"

"Before we do that, would you show me the results of your breakthrough? I've been trying to picture it, but you're right. I don't know anything about the artistic process. And I'd love to see how you're using Grandma's pearls."

Maggie had been home for less than an hour when her doorbell rang. She could tell by Sammy's barkless, wagging welcome that the visitor was a friend.

Charlie peered through the screen. "I took a chance and picked up Chinese. I hope you haven't eaten."

Maggie licked her lips. "Did you bring snow peas with water chestnuts?"

Charlie pulled a container out of the bag. "You betcha. And sizzling rice soup."

"Okay, then come on in." She laughed and opened the screen door for him.

Charlie laid out the cartons on the kitchen table and placed a fortune cookie at each of their places.

"Would you please get a couple of napkins out of that middle drawer while I take Sammy for a quick walk?"

"Sure thing."

Maggie raised an eyebrow when she came back in and saw Charlie close the drawer. "Did you have trouble finding them?"

Charlie winked. "Don't worry. I found just what I needed."

Maggie brought over plates, bowls, and glasses of iced tea. She asked Charlie if he wanted a knife and fork, but they both opted for the chopsticks that came with the meal.

He pulled out her chair, and after they were seated, she bowed her head. "Charlie, would you please say the blessing?"

He reached for her hand. "I'd be happy to."

Maggie worked her chopsticks like a stylist squeezes her scissors—

in/out, in/out, in/out. She caught Charlie smiling at her out of the corner of her eye. "What? What are you smiling at?"

"I've never seen you eat with so much gusto."

"I have to confess. I'm a Chinese-food fanatic, but I can't eat it gracefully, so you talk, and I'll chew." Maggie tipped her head up and dropped a water chestnut into her open mouth.

Charlie rubbed his chin and narrowed his eyes. "Let's see. I can tell you a funny story that came to mind the other day." When Maggie nodded, Charlie continued. "There were three of us—Jack, Mike, and me. We played on a baseball team called the Wayward Walleyes. All three of us were in the outfield, and we'd make plans for stirring up trouble during pitching changes and umpire timeouts. We weren't bad kids, but we knew how to have fun.

"One day, after a big win over the Kongsberg Killdeer, we went out on Jade Lake and caught a bunch of walleyes. There were more of them back then. We put them in my grandmother's washtub until after dark. Then we drove over to Kongsberg and dumped them in the town square fountain. Those fish were jumping around like crazy. We had to keep running after them and tossing them back in. Naturally the police showed up, but not before a photographer caught us in the act."

Charlie pulled out his wallet and handed Maggie a well-worn black-and-white photo. "I'm the one in the middle."

Maggie had stopped eating halfway through his narrative. She raised an eyebrow and peered at him over her glasses. "I had no idea I was dating a man with a criminal past."

"Dating? Is that what we're doing?"

Maggie batted her eyes. "I'd like to think so."

"So would I."

Maggie and Charlie cleared the table and took their coffee out to the porch.

"I'd like your opinion about something that happened today, Charlie."

He put his cup down and turned to Maggie. "What happened?"

"I was having lunch with Wanda and Ellen. Halfway through the meal I asked Wanda how the murals for the community center were coming."

Maggie re-created the conversation and admitted that after things got a little heated, she had left abruptly. Charlie's eyes never left Maggie's face. He didn't speak but leaned forward and nodded from time to time.

When Maggie finished relating the incident, she looked down at her hands. "Am I too critical?"

Charlie didn't respond right away. When he did speak, his words were soft, deliberate, and straightforward. "Maggie, you're the best friend anyone could wish for. You're kind, considerate, and truthful. You would never intentionally hurt someone else."

He sighed. "Having said that, you're a teacher at heart. You've spent your life helping your students grow and improve. It's natural that you'd try to help Wanda in the same way."

Maggie looked at Charlie and winced. "So I *am* too critical."

"I wouldn't use the word 'critical.' You have high expectations for yourself and others. And you want to promote excellence in anyone you care about."

"I appreciate your honesty." Maggie shook her head. "It's not my job to teach Wanda or any of my friends, but I can't seem to help myself."

Charlie reached for her hand. "Would you like to pray about it, Maggie?"

"I would. Thank you."

"Lord God, thank You for giving Maggie the skills and the opportunity to teach. Thank You for the many children who grew under her instruction. Your Son said, "I no longer call you servants.... Instead,

I have called you friends.' Guide her in her interactions with others daily and even moment by moment. Bless her with Your peace and comfort in all her relationships."

Maggie's voice joined with his. "Thy will be done. In Jesus' name. Amen."

The two chatted as they watched the horizon turn from bright pinks and oranges to softer shades of lavender and gold. When the sliver of the new moon appeared above the pine trees on the east shore, Charlie stood up. He offered his hand to Maggie. She took it and allowed herself to be pulled into his arms. "I had a wonderful time tonight, Charlie."

He placed a soft kiss on her cheek. "It was a very good date." He winked and squeezed her hand. "Let's do this more often."

A minute later she watched from the kitchen window as he drove away. Then she gathered the unused napkins and opened the drawer.

Maggie gasped. "Oh, no! I can't believe it." She closed her eyes for a moment before picking up the sheet of paper. She sank down at the table, her eyes scanning the two columns. Mac's list of assets was just as she'd written it. She giggled at Charlie's additions to his side: *Rescues beautiful stranded boaters; Provides Chinese food; Arrives bearing flowers.*

She threw her head back and laughed. "Oh, Charlie, you are so good for me."

Chapter 21

Alberto entered the Water's Edge police station and found Carlos talking with the desk sergeant. "Hi, Mary Jo. Is this guy giving you a hard time?"

She smiled at the pastor. "Nothing I can't handle, but I wouldn't mind if you kept him occupied for a few minutes."

"Consider it done." Alberto grabbed Carlos by the shoulder and led him down the hall.

When his cousin offered him a cup of coffee, Alberto smiled and waved him off. "No, thanks. You guys have the only coffee in town that's stronger than the stuff we have at the church."

They stepped into the chief's office, and he closed the door behind them.

"I understand my wife and her two cohorts paid you a visit yesterday."

Carlos nodded his head and grinned. "Your wife is an amazing woman. She has the drive and imagination to be a very good detective. And the three ladies together make quite an investigative team."

Alberto chuckled and then looked at Carlos. "Can you tell me what your department has found out about the robberies so far? Maybe there's a way I can help."

Lydia Moen

They talked for nearly half an hour. Then Alberto left the station, feeling very much like a man on a mission.

The beautiful late summer day drew Maggie to the porch. She sat down with notecards, pen, and clipboard. "Dear Ellen, Your chicken salad was delicious. I'd love to get the recipe...."

Maggie wrote for a minute or two and then looked out at the lake. After a few seconds, she nodded her head, looked down at her clipboard, and continued writing. "Wanda said the cookies were great. I'm sorry I missed them."

After a closing sentence, Maggie signed her name. Below it she wrote, "A cord of three strands is not quickly broken, Ecclesiastes 4:12b."

She addressed, stamped, and sealed the envelope. Then she picked up a second notecard and clipped it to her board. After writing the greeting, she focused her gaze on the lake for a long time. She wrote a paragraph and read it over several times. Then she put her clipboard down and walked into the house. She returned with her Bible, found the verse she wanted, and finished her writing. She took a few moments on the closing, then reread the note, addressed, stamped, and sealed the envelope.

Before going inside, Maggie took one of the envelopes down to the dock and put it in the mailbox with the flag up. She would have to mail the other one from the post office.

Ellen and Wanda sat in the gazebo sharing their morning coffee, a plate of donuts on the table between them. Wanda had picked up the treats.

Ellen set her coffee cup down and stared at the lake. "I have no idea how I'm going to fill the hours until Bob gets home. My morning jog only takes half an hour. The house is settled, and I'm sick of sewing. I've sorted through every closet and box. I'm out of projects."

"Oh, to be that organized! I'll have stuffed closets and overflowing boxes until the good Lord calls me home. Rita had to pick up a bunch of catalogs and junk mail before she could vacuum under the coffee table this morning."

Wanda reached for a second donut. "I'm going over to the community center to brainstorm with Ruth Butler about activities for Bob's office. I already have an idea for tomorrow. Why don't you ride along? Three brains spark more electricity than two."

Ellen's eyes welled up with tears. "Wanda, I can't go there anymore. You saw how upset Bob was after the boat trip."

"Oh, sweetie, I thought he'd forgotten all about that."

"He has, but I haven't. He was so jealous." Ellen threw her arms in the air. "About Mr. King? Seriously. I don't need that in my life. I was just trying to keep an old man from falling down." She shook her head. "And I haven't told you about yesterday's cookie incident. Don't even get me started!"

Wanda's pink, puce, and purple bracelets clattered as she wiped frosting from her mouth. "Those yummy chocolate chip delights you served at lunch? I knew I ate too many."

"Just the opposite. I wish you'd eaten them all. Then I wouldn't have taken them to the community center. Who knew a few cookies would set Bob off? I'm outta there from now on unless I'm picking him up." Ellen grabbed a maple frosted donut and took a big bite.

"Atta girl, a little something sweet always works for me."

The two friends sipped their coffee and finished their donuts, watching a kayaker cross the lake. Ellen sat back in her chair, her heartbeat and breathing slowed by watching the steady rhythm of the paddle.

"I need to find something else to do. My career in D.C. was being a full-time volunteer, and I loved it. I can't stay home all day. Wanda, I'm floundering. What can I do?"

"Our church has a large outreach ministry to the poor. They're always looking for donations and help."

Ellen looked up. "I have bags of clothes to give away. Maybe they'd be interested."

"They sure would. I think Maggie's going over there this afternoon. Why don't you give her a call and see if she can help you haul your things? After all, she owes you since you took all her stuff to the Treasure Chest."

"That's a good idea. I'll go call her now."

Wanda put her arm up, barring Ellen's departure. She took a donut off the plate before handing it to Ellen. "Take these home with you. If Alberto sees them, I'm in big trouble."

Wanda stretched first one arm and then the other. She rolled her head and shoulders and tried unsuccessfully to touch her toes. She'd been standing at her easel for several hours, and her neck and spine were screaming. She leaned back and squinted, first at her sketch and then at the display of pictures, postcards, and pearls on the easel several feet in front of her. "I'm liking this."

She brought her pencil up to the drawing and began shading several small trees in the foreground. She held her breath and barely touched the paper. At the sound of knocking on the door, Wanda's pencil slashed across the sketch and off the easel. She drew in a breath. "I'll be right there!"

"Carlos, what a surprise! Come on in. Do you want me to call Maggie and Ellen?"

"That won't be necessary. I'm not here to talk with you ladies about your investigation. But I would like to speak with your housekeeper, Rita Hoffman. Is she here?"

"Is she in trouble? Has her husband been arrested?" Wanda's eyes widened, and she bit her lower lip.

"I just need to speak with her, Wanda."

"Have a seat, and I'll get her."

"Thanks. I'll just wait here."

Wanda turned and ran up the stairs.

Ellen closed the back of the van and turned to Maggie. "Thanks for the help."

"I appreciate the ride. Don't let me forget to check the church bulletin board."

As Ellen started the van, Maggie fastened her seatbelt. "Do you know how to get there?"

"Actually, I've been there before, but if I start making a wrong turn, holler."

The two women chatted on the way into town, and Maggie hopped out as soon as the van came to a stop. "I'll be right back with a cart."

Ellen opened the tailgate and turned around when she heard her name. "Hi, Ellen. Looks like you could use some help."

"Alberto, it's good to see you. I've got Maggie helping me today. She's inside getting a cart."

Ellen pushed her sunglasses on top of her head. "I don't know what I'd do without all of you. Thank you so much for taking Bob to his office every day. I'm sure commuting with you has made the transition much easier for him."

"I enjoy his company. He seems to be adjusting well. How's it going for you?"

Ellen shrugged her shoulders. "Ups and downs. Adult daycare has made a huge difference. I seem to have too much time on my hands now."

"Well, my friend, it looks like you've been putting the extra time to good use." Alberto peeked into the packed van. "Are you sure I can't help you ladies unload?"

Ellen reached for a bag. "We've got it, but thanks for the offer."

The two women loaded the cart and laughed as they struggled to get it in the door and down the hall to the outreach ministry center.

"Hi. I'm Ginny Kohls, manager of My Sister's Keeper. Let me hold the door for you."

"Thanks. I'm Ellen Bailey, and you probably already know Maggie."

"Yup. She's a regular donor. Why don't you just leave the cart by the counter, and I'll show you around the shop."

"This is fabulous, and it's so well-organized." Ellen took a 360-degree visual tour of the shop. "I love the department signs. It's like Macy's."

"Well, not exactly." Ginny beamed. "But the prices aren't like Macy's either. Let's grab your cart and unload it in the back."

As they pushed through the double doors at the rear of the shop and entered the sorting area, Ellen gasped. "How do you ever turn this into that?" she asked, pointing first to the mounds of unsorted clothes in the back, then to the front of the neatly organized store.

"It takes a lot of time. As you can see, I'm way behind."

Ellen's jaw dropped. "You do this by yourself?"

"Sometimes I can get a friend to come in for a couple of hours."

Ellen looked at Maggie. "This is just what I've been looking for. Do you have to be a church member to work here?"

Ginny clapped her hands. "Just willing hands and a strong back. When can you start?"

"How about tomorrow morning?"

As Ellen and Maggie walked out the door, Ellen looked back over her shoulder and grinned. "See you at ten o'clock tomorrow, *boss*."

On their way down the hall, Maggie stopped at a large bulletin board. "I have to check the schedule for hosting the Sunday morning coffee hour. The last time I looked there were a couple of open spots." She took a pencil out of her clutch purse and wrote her name in the two remaining spaces.

Ellen scanned the board. "Amazing. You sure have a lot going on here. Do you know anything about this Alzheimer's support group? The announcement says it's open to the public."

"That must be new. Has it started yet?"

"It looks like the kick-off meeting is the first Wednesday in September." Ellen slipped one of the flyers into her purse. "I'll give them a call and check it out."

"I think you have some great ideas, Wanda. Now when would you like to have this first event?"

Lydia Moen

Wanda sat in Ruth Butler's office at the community center. "Well, my first choice would be tomorrow, since my cleaning lady was there today."

"Oh, I didn't realize you'd already sent out notices."

"Can't I do that today?"

"Oh, heavens no. We always plan at least a week ahead. But it sounds like Wednesday's a good day for you." Wanda leaned over the desk as Ruth checked her calendar. "How about next week?"

"Well, I was hoping it could be sooner, but that'll work."

Ruth wrote a note in her calendar and looked up at Wanda. "You'll need to notify the family members of your plans. Do you want to ask them to contribute anything? Food or cash?"

Wanda shook her head. "I don't think so. I can take care of all that."

"We'll send out the notice if you just type up the information and email it to me." Ruth handed Wanda her card. "My email address is on there. I'll need the details no later than Thursday. Do you need a piece of paper to make notes on, dear?"

"I always keep my lists in my head. That way I don't lose them." Wanda put her tote on Ruth's desk. "I can never find anything in here."

"Isn't it hard on your back to carry that thing?" Ruth made an unsuccessful effort to lift the bag.

Using both hands, Wanda hoisted the straps over her shoulder and winked at Ruth. "This little thing? I looked at one twice this size several weeks ago but decided I would have to put it on wheels if I got it."

Ruth chuckled. "I can believe that. This is such a nice idea. I'm sure everyone will enjoy seeing your home and being at the lake. Let me know if I can do anything to help."

"Oh, I've got it all under control. But thanks for the offer."

Wanda walked out to the lobby. "Ellen, is it time to pick up Bob already?"

"It is. I barely made it. How'd your meeting with Ruth go?"

"Great. I'm hosting another office party next week. It's going to be at our house." Wanda held up the director's card before dropping it into her tote. "You'll be hearing about it from Ruth."

"Fabulous. I'll be watching for the notice."

She smiled. "By the way, Maggie helped me take a van-load of clothes to your church this afternoon. I met Ginny Kohls, and I start working with her tomorrow. Can you believe she's been running that place all by herself?"

Wanda's hands flew to her heart. "Sounds like a match made in heaven."

"You may be right. I'm afraid I'm becoming a church lady." Ellen laughed and headed down the hall to get Bob.

Maggie handed a small cooler to Charlie. "If you can take this and the basket down to the dock, I'll get Sammy's bowl and water. The rest of the crew should be here in a few minutes."

"You betcha. Do you have the boat key?"

"It's hanging right by the door. I'll grab it." Maggie handed the key to Charlie. "Would you mind being the captain tonight?"

"Works for me."

When they reached the dock, Maggie saluted. "Permission to come aboard, Captain Bingham?"

Charlie returned the salute. "Permission granted, First Mate MacDonald and Deck Hand Sammy."

They were about to board when Sammy barked and they heard car doors closing in the driveway. "Sammy, heel." Maggie's command brought the retriever to a stop. Then he fell in step behind her and

Charlie.

Junior met them at the top step. "Hi, Mrs. MacDonald. Hi, Mr. Bingham. What's your dog's name? Can I pet him?"

"His name's Sammy, and he loves to be petted. Just let him sniff your hand first. That's how he gets to know you." Maggie turned to the other members of the Jefferson family. "Tamara, we're so glad you could come. Hello, Jessica. How are you today? And how old are you?"

"I'm good, and I'm three years old," she said as she held up three tiny fingers.

"The kids have been talking about this ever since you called. We've all been looking forward to it, Mrs. MacDonald."

"Please call me Maggie, Tamara."

"And I'm Charlie."

"You have a beautiful spot here," Tamara said as she looked from the house to the lake.

"Actually, Charlie has a lovely home on Sapphire Lake. This is where my husband and I lived before he passed away a little over a year ago. Would you like to see the house?"

"I'd love to, but would it be okay if we do that after the boat ride? The kids can't wait much longer. And neither can I." Tamara laughed.

The males led the way down to the dock. Charlie cupped his hands around his mouth. "All aboard."

"All aboard," Junior mimicked.

As soon as everyone was on the boat, Maggie put Sammy into his life vest. Then she handed one to Charlie. "If you'll help Junior get into his, I'll give Jessica a hand. Tamara, would you like to wear yours or just have it next to you?"

"I'm a pretty good swimmer. I'll just keep it near me."

While Maggie was busy casting off the lines, Junior walked over and stood between Charlie's knees. "Can I drive, Mr. Bingham?"

"Have you ever driven a boat before, Junior?"

"No, but sometimes my daddy lets me sit on his lap and steer the car."

"And how did you do? Any accidents? Any speeding tickets?"

"No, sir. My daddy wouldn't let that happen."

"Well, I won't either. When we get out a little further from shore, I think it would be okay if you sit on my lap and steer. What do you think, ladies?"

Tamara said it would be okay with her if Charlie didn't mind, and Maggie gave him a thumbs-up.

Maggie was surprised that Sammy didn't assume his usual spot, front and center. Instead he sat down right in front of Jessica. As the boat floated across the water, Sammy's new friend moved from sitting next to her mother and petting Sammy's head to snuggling up next to the golden on the deck.

Maggie set out the food and opened the cooler. "Come and get it!"

When Tamara cautioned the kids not to spill, Maggie winked. "That's why Sammy comes along. He laps up anything that falls on the deck."

"I'm just as concerned about your beautiful pale yellow slacks and sweater set." Tamara cringed. "I can just imagine little catsuppy handprints all over them."

Maggie looked down at her outfit. "These clothes have survived a slew of spills and smudges over the years. In fact, I'd actually welcome the sight of a few tiny handprints."

The two women chatted as they glided through the lakes. After they finished their hotdogs and apple slices, Junior helped Charlie steer, and Jessica took care of Sammy.

"Junior, I need some help from you and your sister. When we get to the next lake, please keep your eyes open for a bright green and gold pontoon boat. And keep your ears open for some special music." Maggie put her hand behind her ear and then lifted her nose up and sniffed. "You might even be able to smell something across the water if you raise your noses high in the air."

As if on cue, Sammy stood up and put his nose in the air.

"I think you might be right, Maggie. Sammy's already picking up the scent." Charlie laughed, and Jessica gave Sammy a hug.

"I hear the music." Junior jumped in circles and ran to the railing. "Look, Jessie. There's the green and gold boat." He pointed across the lake.

"Popcorn!" Jessica sniffed the air, stood up, and joined Junior near the front of the boat. "Mama, can you smell it?"

Tamara walked up and stooped next to her children, putting an arm around each of them. "I think we're going to have a treat," she said, smiling back at Maggie and Charlie.

"It's the Ice Cream Float," Maggie explained. "It cruises the String of Pearls all summer long. You can order anything your mother says is okay."

"I miss Daddy." Junior leaned up against his mother and scuffed his shoe along the boat deck.

"I do too." Tamara's voice cracked as she spoke.

"We'll do this again when he comes home." Charlie pulled the boat alongside the Float.

After everyone in the group had selected a treat, Maggie got out her camera. "Let's take a picture of the three of you holding up your goodies next to the Ice Cream Float. You can send it to your daddy so he knows you're thinking about him."

As the three Jeffersons enjoyed their ice cream and Sammy kept the floor clean, Maggie walked over to Charlie. She held up her camera so he could see the smiling faces she'd captured. "I wish James and Josh could be here. I wonder when they'll be home."

Later that evening, Wanda and Alberto strolled down to the gazebo arm-in-arm. The moon was already high in the sky, sprinkling diamonds on each ripple in its path from the heavens above to the shoreline at their feet.

"This is my favorite time of day." Wanda settled into the wicker loveseat next to Alberto. "I want to hear all about what you've been doing. You talk. I just want to listen.

Alberto took a breath. "Well, I—"

"But first I want to tell you about Ellen volunteering at the church. She went to My Sister's Keeper to drop off some clothes, and before she left, Ginny signed her up to work in the shop. I ran into Ellen when I was at the community center to talk with Ruth Butler about our hosting a party for the adult daycare attendees and their families."

"We're hosting a party?" Alberto frowned and ran his hands through his hair.

Wanda shook her finger. "No, no, no. Don't worry, querido. We've got plenty of time, and it's not going to be a big deal. I promise."

She grinned sheepishly. "I'm sorry. I just realized I'm doing all the talking. Tell me about your conversation with Carlos. Did he have any news about the robberies? How's the investigation going?"

Alberto opened his mouth.

Wanda threw her hands in the air. "Oh, I almost forgot the most important thing. Carlos came over here today to interrogate Rita. She left before I had a chance to talk with her. I wonder if Ray's the lead suspect now. I hope your cousin hasn't forgotten about Neil and Joe...."

Chapter 22

The door to My Sister's Keeper swung open just as Ellen approached, and she followed Ginny Kohls inside. "Good morning, boss."

"Hi, Ellen. God has blessed me not only with a volunteer but a prompt one. And please call me Ginny."

"I will, Ginny. I couldn't wait to get here." Ellen rubbed her hands together. "Where do you want me to start?"

"The first thing I do every morning is make coffee. I like to have a big pot going all day. Then if someone comes in needing conversation or prayer more than clothes or housewares, we're prepared."

Ellen twisted her wedding ring. "I'll enjoy talking with people, but I think you'll have to handle the praying."

"Perfect. We can tag team them. I'll make the coffee this morning. Why don't you walk around the shop and straighten up anything that needs it. I had to leave before I could do that yesterday. And you'll get more familiar with our merchandise as you work. Once the coffee's brewing, we'll hit the sorting room."

"Sounds like a plan." Ellen strolled up and down the aisles. She hummed as she brought order to items on the shelves and moved misplaced hanging clothes back where they belonged.

Ginny reappeared. "The coffee's on. Let's go back and do some sorting."

Ellen laughed. "I should be good at that. I've been doing it ever since we moved here. Is it okay if we're both in the back room? How will we know if someone comes in?"

"There's a buzzer back there that goes off anytime the door opens."

"Awesome. Let's do it." Ellen put a straight stack of sweatshirts back where the rumpled pile had been and made a mental note to start there when she returned.

After an hour of sorting, Ginny stopped and stretched. "I'm ready for coffee. How about you?"

"I'd love a cup."

They sat at a small round table at the front of the store. The coffee Ginny had prepared was nearby on a long counter. A plate of cookies sat next to it with a sign that read, "Please help yourself."

"I didn't see any price tags. How do you know what to charge?"

Ellen listened and nodded as Ginny explained the general operating procedures for the shop—items are free; customer confidentiality is a must; and everyone is welcome.

Ginny put her hand on Ellen's. "Working in the shop is a blessing. Every day we meet people in need, and we get to help them because of the generosity of others."

"I know what you mean. I feel lucky to be here."

Charlie couldn't remember the last time he'd gotten a letter from a girlfriend. He leaned back into the dark plaid cushions on the glider and pulled the envelope out of his shirt pocket. He could picture her standing at the blackboard as he studied her return address in classic cursive.

He reached over, took a long sip of decaf, and looked out over the lake. He smiled as he remembered the blush on Maggie's face when Neil Olsen caught them together on her boat, as well as the sight of her mouth dropping open and her head jerking back when he gunned his engine. He closed his eyes to recapture the warm look in her eyes and the satisfaction in his heart when she had handed him the keys and called him "Captain Bingham" the night before.

Charlie slid his father's silver letter opener under the flap, eased the single sheet out, and began reading. It wasn't exactly a love note, but he smiled at the way she recapped the evening—her shoveling in the Chinese food, his criminal past with the Wayward Walleyes, and their praying together about her shortcoming. Charlie gazed at the moon and its mirror image on the lake as they made their slow, steady entrance into the night before reading the letter again.

The ringing of his phone destroyed the peace of the night.

Maggie walked in the door and hung Sammy's leash on the hook. She picked up her crossword puzzle book, went into the living room, and planted herself in the recliner. Her pencil danced across the page—first horizontally, then vertically. She looked down at Sammy. "Don't you love this time of day? It's so nice just to kick your feet back and relax." Maggie laughed and clapped her hands when Sammy rolled onto his back and started kicking his feet high in the air.

The doorbell rang.

"Oh, what a surprise! Two of my favorite men. Come on in."

Charlie and Alberto followed Maggie into the living room. She spun around and faced them with a frown. "What's going on, gentlemen? Why are you here?"

Charlie took her hand and led her to the couch. "Let's sit down, Maggie."

She lowered her voice to a whisper. "You're scaring me. One of you tell me what's happening." She gripped Charlie's hand, her knuckles turning white.

Alberto spoke up then. "We don't know that anything's wrong, but we've been told that Josh is missing in action."

A long, low moan sucked the air out of Maggie's body. She doubled over and grabbed her knees, rocking back and forth and crying, "No, no, no."

Charlie put his arm around her, and she fell against his shoulder.

Alberto explained that he'd gotten a call from her son, Daniel, informing him of the situation.

"When did this happen? How long has he been missing? Is he alone?" She could feel her heart racing, nearly exploding.

"We don't have any details yet. Daniel is staying by the phone, hoping for more information. He said he'll call you as soon as he hears anything. Wanda is getting the word out to the prayer chain at church, then she'll be right over. The one thing we do know is that God is with him, and He's with you too, Maggie."

She sat up, grabbed a tissue, and wiped her eyes. "I believe that, and so does Josh. I want to pray, but I can't even think right now."

"Let's pray together." Alberto stood and reached out his hands to the couple on the couch. "Heavenly Father, You are 'the God of all comfort, Who comforts us in all our troubles.'" He prayed for Maggie, for her family, for Josh, and for those who might be with him. He thanked God for giving Maggie faith and the understanding that neither she nor Josh was alone.

Charlie added a prayer for Maggie's friends to find ways to comfort and support her.

Maggie raised her head and looked at Charlie and Alberto. "Thank you." She was quiet for a moment, but a sob escaped her throat. "I want to have faith in God's plan for Josh, but I just can't think of life without him."

Alberto nodded. "Maggie, none of us would need faith if it weren't shaken now and then, and I know you'll be strengthened by yours."

Maggie looked at Alberto through her tears and collapsed against Charlie's chest.

Wanda phoned Ellen as soon as she got the prayer chain rolling. "I'm sorry to call so late, Ellen, but I need to talk with you. Would it be all right if I came over for a few minutes?"

"Sure. Bob's already in bed, but I'll be up for another hour or so. Just come to the kitchen door, and I'll let you in."

The two sat down at the kitchen table, and Wanda told Ellen that Josh was missing in action. "Alberto and Charlie are over there with Maggie now. After Mac died, she was surrounded by her many friends—friends from church, friends from school, friends from the area. But what she really sought was time and space to be with her Best Friend."

"And that was you." Ellen smiled.

Wanda shook her head. "No, I'm not her Best Friend."

Ellen's jaw dropped. "You're not? I thought you and Maggie had been friends for years."

"We have been. But her Best Friend is Jesus. She'll need time with Him more than anything else."

"Jesus is her friend? I don't get that." Ellen pushed her glasses on top of her head and stared at Wanda.

"She just talks with Him." Wanda shrugged and flipped her hands out. "I do too. He loves that."

"What do you say?"

Wanda smiled and brought her hands to her heart. "I thank Him for things. I ask Him for help. Whatever comes to mind. I talk with Him all the time. I'll let you listen in."

With her hands still over her heart, she closed her eyes and said, "Hello, God. It's Wanda again. I'm here with my friend, Ellen. We're trying to figure out how to help Maggie. You know exactly what she needs. If You send us the ideas, we'll write them down. Thank You for being our Friend and for taking care of all of us. Talk to You later."

Ellen shook her head. "That was pretty casual."

"Oh, darlin', we've known each other for a long time."

Wanda and Ellen spent the next few minutes brainstorming ways to support their friend. Ellen served as note-taker in Maggie's absence.

"She probably won't feel much like cooking," Ellen commented.

Wanda clapped her hands. "Praise the Lord. Isn't it exciting, Ellen? He's already giving us ideas!"

The two women came up with a list of food that started with chicken soup and ended with peanut-butter treats.

"There'll be times when the poor thing just needs to do something." Wanda bounced her knee and stared at the ceiling. They developed a list of activities ranging from getting a pedicure to kayaking to lunching at the marina. Ellen volunteered to email daily "Thinking of You" cards, and Wanda said she'd keep the prayer chain updated.

Ellen wrote a quick note telling Bob where she would be. She eased the door closed behind them as the two headed over to Maggie's.

Maggie couldn't pull herself upright. She couldn't stop rocking back and forth. She gripped Charlie's hand as if she were drowning and he were her lifeline. He gave her hand gentle squeezes and rubbed her back.

Maggie didn't even lift her head when Sammy barked. Alberto answered the door and returned to the living room alone. "Wanda and Ellen are waiting in the kitchen. I'll join them there so you two can have some time by yourselves. Let me know when you're ready to leave, Charlie."

After a few minutes, Maggie sat up slowly, took a deep breath, and looked at Charlie. "Thank you. I've kept you long enough. I'll be fine with Wanda and Ellen."

"Are you sure?" Charlie reached up and tucked a strand of hair behind her ear. "I'll stay as long as you like."

"I'll be okay for now, but I'd like to feel I can call you if I need you." Her voice trembled.

"Of course." Charlie squeezed her shoulder. "Anytime. You know that." Then he smiled and patted her knee. "Let me get the girls so you three can talk."

And talk they did. Throughout much of the night, the women talked and laughed and cried.

Wanda reminisced about summer vacations when Josh spent time with his grandparents—fishing, boating, and swimming. "Remember when he and a couple of my grandchildren tried to turn our motorboat into a sailboat, Maggie? The wind caught that tarp and flipped their makeshift craft right over. None of them was hurt, praise the Lord. But the motor's still at the bottom of the lake, and they had quite a tale to tell their friends back home."

Ellen shared a few stories about the antics of her own grandchildren. Eventually Maggie, eyes brimming with tears, was able to open up. She talked about her grandson's letters and his latest phone call. She told her friends how happy she was that he'd started a Bible study group with members of his unit. But when she brought up their plans to fish together on Mac's bench after Josh's return, Maggie broke into sobs once more. "What if we never…?"

It had been four days since Maggie got the news about Josh. She forced her legs over the side of the bed and shoved her feet into her slippers. "C'mon, Sammy. I'll let you outside."

When Maggie opened the kitchen door, Sammy sat obediently beside her. "Go on, Sammy. I'll watch from here." The golden put his head down and ambled outside, looking back before stepping off the porch. Maggie leaned against the door jamb and kept an eye on him through the screen.

In moments he was back. She held the door as he padded inside. She fixed his food and set it on the floor, then wandered over to the refrigerator and opened the door. She stood staring at the pot of soup from Ellen, the casserole from the church secretary, and the salad from a teacher friend, all of them untouched. With a sigh, she closed the refrigerator door, walked into the living room, and stretched out in her recliner.

She wasn't really sleeping when the phone rang, just lying back with her eyes shut. She reached for the phone. "Hello."

"Hi, Maggie. It's Charlie. I was just going to leave for church and wondered if I could pick you up."

"Oh, Charlie. You're so thoughtful, but I just can't do it today. The truth is I don't have the energy, and I also want to stay close to the phone."

"Still no word?"

"Nothing. I can't imagine what's taking so long. Daniel calls me on his cellphone every day. I can hear the anguish in his voice." Maggie dabbed at her eyes with the already damp tissue she held in her hand. "Charlie, it seems as if all I have energy to do lately is cry."

"Even Jesus wept, Maggie."

Wanda gave Charlie a long hug after they exited their pew. "I was hoping Maggie would come today. But when I spoke with her, it didn't sound like she'd make it."

"I called her too, and I offered to pick her up." Charlie paused and rubbed a spot on his forehead. "She's struggling, Wanda. She'll be pleased to hear that Alberto asked for prayers for them in this morning's service."

As they walked out of church together, Wanda and Charlie were told over and over again, "Please tell Maggie that we're praying for her, and let us know if there's anything we can do to help."

Across town, most of the talk outside the Wesley Methodist Church was about the recent rash of robberies. Now two more items were missing from the community center's storage shed—an extension ladder and a power sander.

Unnoticed by the other parishioners, Joe Carnegie and Neil Olsen spoke privately beyond the edge of the crowd. There was nothing unusual about seeing two gentlemen talking to each other after church. If anyone had paid attention, however, they would have been surprised at the length and intensity of the conversation and the degree of animation expressed by the two normally reticent men.

Ellen spread the red-and-white-checkered tablecloth over the table in the Santiagos' gazebo. Then she arranged three matching napkins and place-settings so each of the ladies would have a clear view of the lake. She poured the iced tea and ladled *gazpacho* soup into chilled glass bowls. Finally she positioned plates of corn muffins and cheese slices in the middle of the table.

By the time Ellen had finished her task, Wanda arrived with a reluctant Maggie in tow. "I can't believe I let you drag me down here in my robe," Maggie sputtered. Then she looked at Ellen and managed a laugh. "You're wearing one too?"

"We wanted to make you feel comfortable." Wanda grabbed Alberto's robe from the bench where she'd left it before walking over to get Maggie. "Besides, if you can laze around in a robe for half the day, why can't we?"

Maggie laughed again and shook her head. "Wanda, your craziness is one of the only things that can make me feel better these days. I just can't believe you've dragged Ellen into your shenanigans!"

"I can." Ellen laughed, pulled out the middle chair for Maggie, and the three robed women took their seats. They bowed their heads for Wanda's blessing, which ended with a petition for Josh's safe return.

Maggie peered over her glasses. "This looks delicious, ladies, but I'm not very hungry."

Wanda licked off her spoon and shook it at Maggie. "You gotta try this, sweetie. It's Ellen's secret recipe. I bet she stole it from some swanky D.C. restaurant."

"Well, I don't want to encourage Ellen's criminal behavior, but it does look good enough to be illegal." Maggie dipped her spoon into the soup and raised it to her mouth. She closed her eyes and smacked her lips. "Mmm, that's delicious, Ellen. Worth whatever time it took you to prepare."

Ten minutes later, Ellen smiled and winked at Wanda as they watched Maggie lift her bowl and drain the last drops of the savory soup. "Would you like another muffin, Maggie?"

"Maybe half."

"I'll split it with you. Can you pass the cheese slices too?"

Ellen jumped up. "Oh, I almost forgot. I have a little something for you." She handed Maggie a soft package wrapped in tissue paper.

"What's this? You two are certainly full of surprises today." Maggie laughed as she opened the gift. She lifted up two pieces of light fabric, translucent except for the little kayaks on the border. "Are these curtains, Ellen?"

"They're for your shed. No one will be able to see through them, but they'll let the light in. You mentioned putting up curtains the day we took the things from the shed to Carnegie's Treasure Chest. I came over early one day and measured the window. I hope you like them."

Maggie placed her hand on Ellen's. "Thank you, dear. You have no idea how much this means to me."

Wanda leaned in and ran her fingers over the border. "Look at the tiny kayaks. They're precious."

Ellen sat back in her chair, stretched her arms over her head, and listened to her two friends. *A few months ago, I didn't even know these women. Now I can close my eyes and recognize their voices. I feel as if we've been friends for years.*

Lydia Moen

When Ellen heard her name, she sat back up and focused on Wanda. "I may not have Ellen's secret recipe for gazpacho, but I did cook up a little something for the three of us."

Ellen and Maggie looked at each other and rubbed their hands together as Wanda rummaged through her polka-dot tote. After pulling out a hairbrush, several tissues, and a couple lipstick tubes, she placed three small gift bags on the table. "I knew they were right near the top. Now we all have to open them at the same time. You two close your eyes and pull out what's in your bag." Wanda paused. "Okay. Go ahead and look."

The breeze off the lake tousled Ellen's hair as she bounced along the shoreline and up the steps. "Bob, I'm home." The words escaped her mouth before she saw him sitting in his recliner, right where she'd left him several hours earlier. She crossed over to him and kissed the top of his head.

"Ellen? I've been looking for you. I'm getting hungry. Have you fixed lunch yet?"

Ellen didn't answer but instead walked into the kitchen where the meal she'd left for Bob sat untouched. She closed her eyes, slowly shook her head, and bit her lower lip. She drew in a deep breath, and when she opened her eyes, they rested on the gift Wanda had given her. A tiny smile spread across her lips as the muscles in her face relaxed.

She turned, walked back into the living room, and put her hand on her husband's shoulder. "Your wish is my command," she said as she bowed to him. "Soup's on!"

Before she joined Bob in the kitchen, Ellen gazed slowly around the living room. When her eyes came to rest on the fireplace, she walked over and set the gift on the mantel, just below the painting of Washington, D.C. She moved away, tilted her head, and held her breath for a moment before approaching the mantel again. She inched Wanda's present forward and stepped back to view it once more. "Fabulous!"

Maggie hustled down the steps and into the kitchen. She ran her fingers through her damp hair, enlivening the curls that always showed up after a shampoo.

She sat down at the kitchen table and picked up Wanda's gift. With it still in her hands, she closed her eyes and began to pray. "Heavenly Father, thank You for the hands that made this gift and the hands that made the energizing meal. Thank You for the comfort that You continually provide through Your Word and through the friends You've sent to me. Help me to stay focused on You and rest in the assurance that You are with Josh. Keep him safe, and fill Josh and his buddies and all those who care about them with Your love and peace."

Maggie sat for a moment with her head bowed, then pushed her chair back from the table and placed Wanda's gift on the windowsill in front of her kitchen sink. As her eyes rested on it, she smiled. Then she grabbed Sammy's leash. "Come on, boy. Let's go to the dog park."

Wanda was reluctant to leave the spirit that lingered in the gazebo. She poured herself another glass of iced tea, placed it on the end table, and stretched out full-length on the chaise lounge. She closed her eyes and sang softly to herself:

What a friend we have in Jesus,

Lydia Moen

All our sins and griefs to bear!
What a privilege to carry
Everything to God in prayer!

"Father God, I can't wait to tell You about today, even though You already know every detail. Maggie didn't want to come, but You knew I'd drag her down here. Then she didn't want to eat, but Ellen's gazpacho was a stroke of genius. I hope we'll have that in heaven.

"Anyway, I see Your hand all over this. You just grab onto our hands and don't let go. And I'm amazed at what You did with my hands, Lord. Didn't You love the looks on Maggie's and Ellen's faces when they opened their gifts?

"I hope You like the spot I picked out for mine. Let's go up and see how it looks."

Wanda continued to speak with God as she walked toward the house. She held the studio door open for a moment before walking in. Then she hung the small painting on the wall where she could see it while she worked. Her eyes focused on the outline of the fish formed by three braided strands—soft rose for Maggie, pale blue for Ellen, and light yellow for herself. Bordering the fish symbol representing Christ were the words of the verse God had given them: "A cord of three strands is not quickly broken."

Chapter 23

Wanda turned the volume up when the next praise and worship CD started. She sang along with *Open the Eyes of My Heart,* as she put the finishing touches on her current sketch. "One more to go!" She danced along the line of easels, moving Grandma's string of pearls from one to the other as she went.

When the song ended, Wanda heard the answering machine kicking in on her phone. "Hi, Wanda. This is Ruth Butler."

Wanda snapped to attention, her eyes and mouth wide open. She slapped both hands on her cheeks and then ran for the phone. "Ruth, Ruth. Don't hang up. I'm here." By then *Shout to the Lord* was blaring from the CD player. "Just a minute, Ruth. I can't hear you. I'll be right back."

As she trudged back to the phone after turning the music down, Wanda grimaced, every feature on her face pulling toward her nose. *Oh, Lord, please help me!*

"Hi, Ruth. I'm so glad you called. How are you?" The artist rolled her eyes but kept a smile on her face while she did it.

Wanda listened. She tapped her pencil on the desk.

"Well, yes. You're right. I have been busy."

Wanda listened. Her eyes popped wide open, and her hand flew to her heart.

"Yes, I know that's only two days from now." Wanda held her head in her free hand. "I'm sorry about the notice. You're a doll for taking care of that."

Wanda listened and rubbed her forehead.

"Thanks for the offer, Ruth, but I have lots of help."

Wanda hardly listened.

"That won't be necessary, Ruth. I've got it under control."

Maggie put the mailbox flag up. As she turned toward her home, she saw her neighbor fishing on his dock. "Yoo-hoo, Bob! Would you mind if Sammy and I joined you?"

"That sounds good. It sure is a beautiful day."

Maggie grabbed her fishing pole and tackle box. Sammy ran ahead of her and plopped down at Bob's feet. "What are you using to attract them today, Bob?" She sat down next to him.

Bob pulled up his pole and exposed an empty hook.

Maggie raised her eyebrows. "It looks like something's biting."

Bob smiled and dropped the hook back into the water.

Maggie put a lure on her line and handed him the pole. "Is it okay if I try yours? It looks pretty fancy. I'm betting you only catch big bass with a rod like this."

Bob smiled and nodded. "Sure. Isn't it a beautiful day?"

"It is. 'He has made everything beautiful in its time.'"

Maggie did most of the talking. She asked Bob questions about his life as an attorney in Washington, and he responded with short answers and a ready smile. After a while, he looked directly at her and asked,

"How's your husband doing? I haven't seen him in a long time."

Maggie paused a beat. "He's doing just fine."

"That's good."

Maggie turned toward the approaching footsteps. "Hi, Ellen. You caught me taking a fishing break with your hubby."

Maggie put down Bob's pole. As she hugged Ellen, she whispered," I wouldn't have been able to do this before yesterday. Thank you, dear."

Ellen spoke in an equally soft voice. "It was our pleasure. Thank you for spending time with Bob."

"Ladies, freeze! It's an emergency!" They turned toward the shouts just in time to catch flashes of hot pink running toward them through the trees.

Wanda gasped for breath as she and Maggie followed Ellen up to the house. She threw herself into a kitchen chair. "Water!"

"Mercy, Wanda. What's wrong?" Maggie leaned forward and peered at her friend's bright red face.

"I'm in big trouble."

Ellen placed a tall glass of ice water in front of Wanda and sat down next to her.

Maggie raised her eyebrows. "What kind of trouble?"

"I just got off the phone with Ruth Butler. I volunteered to host a party for the adult daycare families this Wednesday."

Ellen reached back and pulled a colorful paper off the counter. "That's right. I got this notice about it. You're so sweet to entertain us."

Wanda bit her lip and tapped her fingers on the table. "Yes, yes. Well, I'm delighted to do it."

Ellen glanced at the announcement. "I'm glad you brought it up

Lydia Moen

because I didn't see a time on this. When would you like us to be there?"

"That's one of the reasons I'm in trouble with Ruth. I was supposed to send her details for the notice by Thursday, but I forgot. If she hadn't called just now, I'd still be clueless. I haven't thought about the food. I don't know what we're going to do. It's a disaster!" Wanda screamed her last statement and pounded her feet on the floor.

Maggie shook her head. "Ellen, dear, do you have a piece of paper and a pencil I can use?"

Ellen handed them to Maggie and sat down next to Wanda. "Are you all right? Can I get you anything?"

"Do you have a pound of chocolate I can have?"

Ellen started to stand up. "Just a second. Let me check."

Wanda held up her hand. "No, no. I was just kidding, and besides I'm trying to take off a few pounds."

Maggie cleared her throat and tapped her pencil on the table. "What time will the party start?"

Wanda shrugged her shoulders. "I don't know. How does three o'clock sound?"

"Three o'clock it is. How many people are coming?"

Wanda rolled her eyes. "I don't know. What do you think, Ellen?"

"Whatever. It's your party."

Wanda whined. "I know, I know. But how many people are at the center when you pick up Bob?"

Ellen narrowed her eyes and looked at the ceiling. "There are usually eight to ten seniors there, and you invited family members too. Are you including any of the staff?"

"I guess I should," Wanda groaned.

"If I were you, I'd plan for about thirty guests."

Maggie jotted the number down and looked at Wanda. "Okay, we have the time and the number of people. Now let's talk about food."

It didn't take long for the "cord of three" to string together the details of the party and divide the work. Ellen would write up information for a detailed announcement and give it to Ruth Butler when she picked up Bob. Maggie was in charge of ordering the food, and Wanda was assigned to work with Alberto and Rita to get the house ready and set up several outdoor games.

Wanda turned to Ellen. "Is Ray here today?"

"He was here earlier, but I never know how long he's staying. Why do you ask?"

"I don't have a phone number for Rita, and I'll need her to help me tomorrow and Wednesday."

"If he's here, he'll be in the shed." Ellen rubbed the back of her neck. "Do you want me to go out with you?"

"Let's all three go. We should meet the people who are working in our neighborhood." Maggie put down her pencil and paper.

Wanda pushed her chair back from the table and stood up. By the time Ellen and Maggie reached the shed, she was extending her hand to Ray. "You must be Rita's husband. I'm Wanda Santiago."

Ray pulled a rag out of his pocket and wiped off his hands. Wanda stooped down to pick up a card that had slipped out with the rag. "Here, you dropped this." She glanced at the credit card and pulled her hand back. "Oh, this is Bob's."

"Hello. You've reached Alberto Santiago."

"Hi, Alberto. This is Daniel MacDonald."

"Do you have news about Josh?" Alberto grabbed his pocket notebook.

"I do, and I haven't been able to reach my mother. Do you know where she is?"

"No, I don't, but I'm sure I can get in touch with her."

Alberto jotted down several notes while listening. He rubbed his brow and closed his eyes. "We're praying for all of you, Daniel."

As soon as Alberto hung up the phone, he picked it up again and called home. When Wanda didn't answer there or on her cell, he rushed out his office door, spoke briefly to the secretary, and headed for his car.

"It's Bob's?" Ellen stammered and glared at the workman. "What are you doing with Bob's credit card?"

"Finally. I've been looking all over for you. What's going on here?"

Ellen jumped at the sound of Alberto's voice. "I'm glad you're here. Mr. Hoffman was just going to explain why he has my husband's credit card."

Ray's face reddened. "Are you accusing me of something?"

"Let's all just settle down and figure this out." Alberto moved past the three women and into the center of the shed. "Ray, do you want to start?"

"Mr. Bailey gave me his credit card so I could buy some stuff we need for this job. I didn't steal it."

Ellen crossed her arms. "How long have you had it?"

"I don't know, a few days."

"Who has the card now?" Alberto looked from Ray to Ellen, and she held it up.

He turned his attention back to the handyman. "So Bob has receipts for your purchases?"

"He never asked me for any receipts." Ray scuffed his shoe on the floor.

Ellen held out her hand. "I'm asking for them."

"I told you, your husband didn't want 'em. I'll check in the truck and bring 'em after lunch." Ellen stepped back as Ray pushed past her.

"I'm so glad you dropped by when you did, Alberto. That was such an uncomfortable situation." Maggie sat down between Ellen and Wanda in the Santiagos' gazebo. "By the way, what brought you to our rescue?"

Maggie held her breath when Alberto leaned across the table and took her hands in his. "I have some positive news about Josh."

"Oh, thank You, Jesus! Have they found him?"

"Not yet, but they do have more information. They know he's with his friend, Chris."

"How did you find out?"

"Daniel called me a little while ago. He wasn't able to reach you at home and wanted you to know right away."

Maggie leaned forward. "How did he sound?"

"You and Mac raised a strong son, Maggie. He's trusting in the Lord."

"Did he tell you that Chris is Josh's Bible-study partner?"

"No, but isn't that just like God? He gave us example after example of sending two disciples out together. We always have Him, but when we're going through difficulties, He often sends along a brother to strengthen us."

Maggie felt Wanda's arm wrap around her shoulder. "Or two sisters."

Ellen stood up and hugged both women. "I've always wanted sisters."

Alberto sat back and sighed. "I would love to be a part of this sisterhood, but I don't think I qualify. And besides, I need to get back to the church. So if you ladies will excuse me…"

"Before you go, querido, I need to talk with you for a minute." Wanda stood up, took Alberto's hand, and walked out with him.

When she returned, she winked at her two friends. "Alberto's going to talk to Ray about having Rita call me. He'll follow up on the receipts with him too."

Maggie smiled at Wanda and Ellen and relaxed back in her chair. "Alberto, the brother who holds our hands and cleans up our messes."

Chapter 24

"Rita, you're here! Praise the Lord. How are you feeling? Any morning sickness?" Wanda hugged her helper like a mama bear hugging her cub.

"I'm fine, Mrs. Santiago. Where should I start?"

"Let's do the upstairs first. I still have to do a little picking up, but I'll try to stay ahead of you."

The women worked together for the next two hours. When the upstairs was finished, Wanda insisted they take a break. She poured them each a glass of iced tea and set a plate of peanut-butter treats on the table. "These are very good for mothers-to-be." Wanda giggled as she passed the treats to Rita and took several herself.

"These are great! You're so nice to me. I didn't know if you would want me back after last week." Rita kept her eyes on her plate.

Wanda raised her eyebrows. "You do a wonderful job. Why would you think I might not want you back?"

"The policeman—I was so embarrassed that he came here." Rita continued to stare at her plate.

"Oh, Carlos is family. He stops over all the time. He likes my peanut-butter treats too." Wanda winked at her cleaning lady and reached for another cookie. "I hope everything got straightened out."

"He was very nice, but I don't think everything's okay." Rita took a deep breath and rubbed her temple with her hand.

"What can I do to help, sweetie?" Wanda laid her hand on Rita's shoulder.

"You're helping by giving me a job. Ray's a good man, but he's had a lot of bad breaks, and his parents didn't set a very good example. His father was an alcoholic, and his mother didn't know how to deal with it. She finally left, and Ray went into foster care. He was shuffled around from one home to another until he turned eighteen. He was all alone when I met him."

She sighed and shook her head. "He doesn't want to end up like his dad, but I know he drinks too much. Ray's smart, and yet he never even finished high school. He had a good job until the company went out of business. He hasn't been able to find steady work since."

Rita's voice cracked. "We're always broke. I don't know what we'll do when the baby comes. We have no insurance, and…" Her words got lost in her sobs.

Tears brimmed in Wanda's eyes. She pulled her chair next to Rita's and drew the young woman's head against her shoulder. Stroking her new friend's long brown hair, Wanda rocked back and forth slowly, first humming and then softly singing.

Turn your eyes upon Jesus,
Look full in His wonderful face,
And the things of earth will grow strangely dim,
In the light of His glory and grace.

"I remember that song from Sunday school, but I haven't heard it for a long time," Rita whispered.

Wanda rose from her chair and looked into Rita's reddened eyes. "Wait here. I'll be right back."

When she returned, Wanda handed Rita a CD. "When you go home today, treat yourself to a nice warm bath. Put this on your CD player and turn your eyes toward Him."

Wanda could barely understand Rita's words as they tumbled out in a torrent of tears. "I don't have a home."

Ellen smiled and waved as the boat approached the Baileys' dock. "Good morning, Charlie."

"Hi, Ellen." The postman raised his nose and sniffed. "Do I detect a little mocha in your coffee this morning?"

"You do. If you like it, I'll bring a cup down to you the next time I make it." Ellen took the mail from Charlie.

"That works for me! It'll have to be in the next couple weeks, but a cup of coffee will be mighty welcome as the days get cooler."

Ellen sat down on the bench. "Having our mail delivered by boat is one of the things I love about living on a lake. We're going to miss your morning visits after Labor Day."

"I'm always a little sad to put my boat up at the end of the season. Speaking of missing people, I haven't seen Bob since he started going to the community center. How's that working out?"

Ellen's smile faded. "It's been an adjustment for both of us. I tried volunteering there, hoping it would be something we could share, but that was a mistake. Now I'm helping out at My Sister's Keeper." The sparkle returned to Ellen's eyes.

"Good for you. Is Ginny Kohls still in charge of that ministry?"

"She's my boss, the best one I've ever had."

"I'm not surprised to hear you say that. I've always liked Ginny." Charlie tugged on his University of South Carolina cap. "Is Bob still getting in some fishing?"

"He only fishes from the dock, but he's down here every chance he gets." Ellen shook her head and chuckled.

"Do you think he'd like to join a fellow angler for an outing? I'll be going after work today. I could use the company."

Ellen's gaze turned to a lone leaf on the dock. She reached down, picked it up, and twirled it by the stem before answering Charlie. "I'm sure Bob would enjoy fishing with you. I'm just not sure it's a good idea."

Wanda grabbed the table as she fell into her chair. "What do you mean you don't have a home? Where are you living?"

"In Ray's truck. We haven't had a home since we moved here." Rita cradled her head in her hands.

"Rita, why didn't you tell me this before?" Wanda covered her mouth with her hand. Then she closed her eyes and bowed her head. *Heavenly Father, guard my tongue. Let the words that come from my mouth be words of healing. Give me the thoughts You want me to think, the words You want me to say, and the wisdom to act as Your Son taught us to act.*

When Wanda looked up, Rita was staring at her. "Mrs. Santiago, were you praying?"

"Yes, I was." Wanda's eyes locked on Rita's. "Would you like to pray together?"

As tears streamed down Rita's cheeks, a tentative smile crossed her lips, and she nodded.

Wanda reached for her hand and said a short prayer. Rita whispered, "Thank you," pulled a wrinkled tissue from her pocket, and stood up. "Now I need to get back to my cleaning."

Wanda stood too and gave her homeless helper a hug. "God will provide, sweetie." She waited just long enough for Rita to go into the living room then she sped up the steps, closed the bedroom door behind her, and dialed Alberto's number.

Ellen sat down on the dock next to Charlie's boat. She pulled her knees up to her chest and wrapped her arms around them. She didn't say anything for a minute, just stared out at the lake. Then she faced Charlie. "I'm worried because I never know what Bob will say or do. It's awesome that you want to do this, but when you get out on the lake, he might forget who you are and why you're in a boat together. He might get mad, and things could get ugly in a hurry."

Charlie leaned back and switched the motor off. He threw a line over one of the dock posts and hopped up next to her. "Ellen, I only see him for a few minutes at a time. It's different for you. Do you feel safe with him?"

"I do. He gets angry but not physical, and it doesn't last long." Ellen traced her fingers along the grain of the wooden dock.

"I'm not that familiar with Alzheimer's, but I've been told some of the symptoms are similar to those suffered by stroke victims. You may not know that my wife, Fae, had a stroke several years before she died of cancer. I asked God to help me deal with her confusion and mood swings, just the way you're learning to deal with Bob's. Shortly after, I noticed how easily she could be distracted."

"And you think God gave you that idea?" Ellen tilted her head and waited for his response.

"I don't just think He did. I know He did."

"Hmm. The same thing happened with Wanda the other day. She

asked God for ideas, and all of a sudden we had a whole list of them."

Charlie nodded his head. "He just wants us to ask."

Ellen crossed her arms. "If I ask Him to cure Bob's Alzheimer's, will He do it?"

"God always answers, Ellen, but He doesn't always say yes."

"Then how do you know He answered, or that He even heard you?"

"If you believe, He will answer, and you'll have a sense of peace unlike any you've experienced before." Charlie smiled and shook his head. "I've been praying for God to show me a way to help you two, and I think taking Bob fishing is His answer to me. Can we give it a try today? I'll take good care of him."

Ellen put her hand on his arm. "I trust you, Charlie. Bob can use a good friend, and it'll be a big help to me."

They both stood up.

"How does four-thirty sound?" Charlie asked as he stepped back into his boat.

"Perfect! By the way, what time is it now?"

"It's about nine-thirty. I'd better get back to my route."

"Me too. I'm supposed to be at My Sister's Keeper by eleven today. Don't want to get in trouble with the boss." Ellen chuckled as she waved goodbye to Charlie.

Ellen reached into the large plastic bag and pulled out the last article of clothing. She held up the maternity swim suit and smiled. "I guess she had the baby. I wonder if it was a boy or a girl. Maybe twins!"

After she folded the two pieces and placed them on top of the pile for expectant mothers, Ellen leaned back and surveyed the afternoon's work. She raised her arms above her head and punched the air. "Seven bags full are now seven bags empty!"

As she bowed to a non-existent audience, she heard the buzzer indicating that someone had come in the front door. Ellen jerked herself upright and put her hand over her mouth to stifle a laugh. She glanced around with a sheepish grin then picked up the stack she had just created and walked to the front of the shop.

"Hi, I'm Ellen. Can I help you find something?"

"The lady I clean for told me I could come here for clothes," the petite young woman replied, keeping her eyes focused on the floor.

"Well, you're in the right place." Ellen set her stack on the counter. "Are you looking for anything in particular?"

"I'll just look around, if that's okay."

"Of course. I'm kind of new here too. But I'm sure that between us we can find whatever you need." She grinned at her customer, who rewarded her with a hesitant smile in return.

Ellen wandered over to the snack area and checked the coffee pot. Then she grabbed a pitcher of lemonade from the mini-refrigerator and set it on the table next to the cookies.

She turned on the CD that Ginny played earlier. Wanting to give her customer freedom to browse, Ellen busied herself restocking shelves.

"Excuse me, ma'am. I found a couple sweaters. Do you happen to have any maternity clothes? I don't need them yet, but—"

"Oh, I guess I forgot to put them out. We got a bunch in yesterday, and they're to die for. I think she was about your size."

Ellen frowned and looked around the shop before snapping her fingers. "Here they are! I'll put them on this table. Would you like coffee or lemonade and some cookies while you look through them?"

"It would be nice to sit down for a minute, and lemonade sounds good. But my husband's waiting out in the truck, so I can't stay much longer."

Her smile was wistful. "I was really nervous about coming here, but now I'm actually enjoying it."

"It's always fun to get something new. Feel free to come back whenever you need a lift. And of course, you'll want to visit us when it's time to get baby clothes." Ellen rubbed her hands together. "We'll expect you to bring the baby in to meet us."

"I'd like that." The young woman took a drink of her lemonade.

As she sorted through the maternity clothes, she stopped and looked wide-eyed at Ellen. "Oh, I can't believe you're playing *Turn Your Eyes upon Jesus.* Mrs. Santiago was singing that this morning."

Ellen pushed her glasses on top of her head. "Wanda Santiago?"

"Yes. That's the lady I clean for."

Ellen smiled. "You must be Rita."

Alberto watched as the rusty blue pickup pulled into the church parking lot. He nodded as he saw Rita climb out and go into the building by herself. He looked at his watch, rested his elbows on his knees, folded his hands together, and closed his eyes. Then he pulled a small yellow tablet out of his desk drawer and copied down an address and phone number from his computer screen. He ripped the top sheet off the tablet, folded it in half, and tucked it into his shirt pocket.

"I'll be meeting with someone and won't be able to take any calls for a few minutes, Helen." Alberto ran his hands through his hair as he walked past the secretary's desk.

He hesitated for a moment as he approached the pickup before tapping on the driver's side window. Ray Hoffman didn't move. Alberto knocked again, a little more forcefully. He saw Ray push the dirty baseball cap up just far enough to be able to see who was disturbing his nap.

Alberto responded to the sneer on Ray's face by motioning for him to roll down his window. Ray straightened up and cranked the window wide open. "What's the problem? Do you want me to move my truck?"

"It's fine where it is, Ray. I was hoping we could talk for a minute. Why don't you come on inside, and we can sit in my office. It's cooler in there."

"I'm waiting for the wife. She'll be back any minute."

"I won't keep you long. Let's go in and cool off." Alberto turned toward the building and waved his hand for Ray to follow him.

Alberto heard the squeak of the truck door as it opened and the subsequent slam. He held the church door open for Ray and then led him to his office. "Helen, this is Ray, a friend of mine. Would you please bring us a pitcher of water and a couple of glasses? Ray, this is my right arm, Helen."

"I'm pleased to meet you, Ray. And the water's already on the table, Alberto."

The pastor glanced at Ray. "See what I mean? Thank you, Helen."

He gestured toward the two easy chairs near the office window. "Take your choice, Ray. I'm glad you stopped by this afternoon."

"I'm only here because the wife had to pick something up."

"Actually, my wife called me earlier today. Rita's been such a help to her already, and I'm hoping we can help the two of you."

"Oh, yeah?"

Alberto reached in his pocket, pulled out the yellow piece of paper, and handed it to Ray. "Here's the name, address, and phone number of a place that provides temporary housing through the church. It's right here in Water's Edge. I called earlier, and they have a private room available."

"We don't have the money right now," Ray grumbled.

"There's no charge."

"What's the catch?"

"There is none. But if you feel inclined, I'm sure they'd appreciate your carpentry skills."

"Well, I don't need a handout for myself, but Rita's gonna have a baby."

Alberto glanced outside and saw Ellen helping Rita put packages in the truck. "Then this is the right thing to do. You're taking care of your family. You'll both get three good meals a day there, and they can put you in touch with other programs in the area."

Ray stood up, turned his back on Alberto, and walked toward the door. "I don't know why you're doing this." He slammed the door and was gone before Alberto had a chance to respond.

The pastor rested his elbows on his knees, folded his hands together, and bowed his head. When he looked out the window, he saw Ray climb into the rusty blue pickup next to Rita and heard the vehicle backfire as it pulled out of the lot.

Charlie anchored the boat and turned to Bob. "This is one of the finest fishing spots on the String of Pearls. It's the cleanest water of all the lakes because it has the most springs. We can hook anything from blue gills to muskie."

"Do you really think we might catch a muskie?" Bob rubbed his hands on his blue jeans and gave Charlie a thumbs-up.

Charlie returned the gesture. "Well, I have to admit I've never caught one, but they're in there. Let's see what you've got in that fancy tackle box."

When Bob opened up the metal container, Charlie whistled. "Boy, you've got a lot of stuff."

Bob nodded. "I've been collecting lures for years. I caught a five-pound walleye on that one during a trip to Canada with some college buddies." Bob beamed as he pointed to several items and told Charlie their histories before closing the lid on the tangle of lures and lines. Then he sat back and gazed out at the water.

Charlie hesitated a moment and then reached for his own box. "Why don't you try this one?" He held up a jitterbug. "I've had pretty good luck with it. Maybe you'll snare that muskie."

When Bob didn't react, Charlie picked up his friend's fishing pole and attached the lure. He handed the pole to Bob and said, "There's a drop-off on this side of the boat. Why don't you toss your line over those weeds?"

Charlie grabbed his own rod and cast the lure out in a perfect arc. It settled on the surface about twenty-five feet from the boat. When he turned back to see how Bob was doing, the smile drained from his face. Charlie wiped his eyes at the sight of Bob's vacant stare. He hadn't moved but sat holding the rod just as he had when Charlie handed it to him. The postman slowly reeled in his line and secured his rod inside the boat.

"Bob? Bob, would you mind if we took a ride up to the end of the String? I never get a chance to just enjoy the scenery. I'm always focusing on mailboxes."

"It sure is a beautiful day."

Charlie gave Bob a high-five. "Let's do it!"

As Charlie turned around to start the motor, he caught a glimpse of a woman with short silver hair kayaking along the far shore. He released the starter cord and allowed himself to enjoy the graceful movement of her paddle. When Maggie looked in his direction, Charlie gave her a crisp salute.

Lydia Moen

Bob tipped his fishing hat. "Who's that?"
Charlie smiled. "That is one very special lady."

Chapter 25

Maggie pulled the corner of the kitchen curtain back and peeked out again. She checked her watch against the wall clock—6:30. Then she inspected the picnic basket contents for the third time. She snapped her fingers, spun around to grab a pair of scissors from the sharp-things drawer, and bounced out the door.

She returned a moment later holding several asters and fern stalks. She wrapped their stems in a wet paper towel, selected a small pottery vase, and stuck them in between the cups and plates. "Perfect!"

When she heard a car pull into the driveway, Maggie stepped over to the mirror and fluffed her hair. Then she waltzed to the door and opened it.

Charlie smiled. "I'm sorry I'm a little late."

Maggie gave him a hug. "I'm glad you're here. You're good for my morale.

"I hope it's okay if we don't go to the marina, but I thought a picnic would be a fun distraction. How would you feel about going over to Brandt Park?" Maggie peered at Charlie over her glasses.

Charlie hugged her and kissed the top of her head. "That works for me. I just went by there when I was out in the boat with Bob. It didn't look very crowded."

"How'd the fishing go?"

"We ended up touring the lakes instead." Charlie rubbed a red spot on his forehead.

Maggie frowned and looked away. "I bet Bob enjoyed that, and I'm sure Ellen appreciated your reaching out to him."

"I was happy to do it, and I don't think Bob had ever been all the way up the String of Pearls before. It was beautiful out there."

Charlie inhaled a big breath. "Is that fried chicken I smell?"

"It sure is. I remembered my mom telling me about a picnic she made for Dad when they were dating. I found her menu with the recipes attached, and that's what we're having tonight." Maggie blushed. "I hope you like it as much as he did."

Wanda turned off the hose and hustled into the house. "Alberto, where are you?"

"I'm in the living room. Come on in and join me."

"Guess what I just saw." Wanda nudged Purrdita onto the floor and plopped down on the couch next to her husband.

"I hope it wasn't Peter Rabbit munching on your lettuce again."

Wanda elbowed him while fluttering her eyelashes. "Bigger news than that! Charlie and Maggie just drove by, and she wasn't clinging to the door. They were so involved with each other, they didn't even notice me."

Alberto put his hand on Wanda's knee. "I'm glad Maggie has something to take her mind off Josh."

"I am too. Poor thing."

She frowned. "Speaking of poor things, I can't seem to get my mind off Rita. Pregnant and homeless. Who knows what she's had to eat or how that husband of hers treats her?" Wanda rolled her eyes. "Were you able to get in touch with him today?"

"Yes, thanks to your heads-up about his bringing Rita to My Sister's Keeper. The church arranged for temporary food and shelter for them. I gave Ray the contact information, and he seemed receptive. Now it's in God's hands."

"Alberto, let's pray for them."

Maggie kept her eyes on Charlie as he carried the used plates, napkins, and cups over to the trash container. She smiled as she watched him stop on his way back to chat with an older gentleman who was sitting on a bench near the lake. When Charlie gestured toward Maggie, the man turned to face her and tipped his red English driving cap. He gave Charlie a thumbs-up before shaking his hand.

When he returned, Charlie winked. "You have another admirer, Maggie."

"Does that mean I already had one?" She blushed and gave him a shy grin.

Charlie took off his cap and held it in front of himself as he bowed. "I'm just one of many."

Maggie grabbed a paper plate and fanned herself. "Oh, Mr. Bingham, how you do go on! But please don't stop. I love how you reach out to people—that gentleman, Bob and Ellen... me."

"How about if I reach out to you right now?" Charlie put his arm around her waist.

Maggie leaned her head on his shoulder. "I didn't really mean that literally, but I'm glad you took it that way."

Charlie's new acquaintance cleared his throat as he walked up to them. "You two have a nice evening now."

"Al, I'm glad you walked over. I want you to meet my friend, Maggie MacDonald."

The white-haired gentleman tipped his cap to Maggie.

"Hello, Al. It's good to meet you." She shook his hand. "Do you come here often?"

"Almost every day. I'll see you two again." He pulled the white carnation out of his lapel and gave it to Maggie. "A mere reflection of your beauty, my dear."

The picnickers watched Al walk across the grass and then returned to packing up the basket. They held hands as they ambled to the car. Charlie put their things in the trunk and closed it. Then he turned to Maggie and said, "How about if we keep Al's bench warm for a while?"

"I'm sure he'd appreciate that, and I wasn't ready for the evening to end." Maggie put her arm in his.

They sat close together on the bench, watching a chipmunk watch them and laughing about what the creature must be thinking. The small lake in front of them was surrounded by a paved walking trail, although Maggie and Charlie appeared to have the park to themselves, except for the chipmunk.

A gentle breeze came across the lake, pushing tiny waves against the rocky shore. Maggie shivered and immediately felt Charlie's arm around her shoulder. "Thank you. That feels good." She nestled up against him.

"It feels good to me too. I've been concerned about you, Maggie, especially when you didn't come down to the dock for your mail. How are you doing?"

"Much better right now, although Josh is never far from my mind. Daniel's been wonderful about calling, but there's just no more news. I don't know if that's a good thing or not. The waiting is difficult."

"Is there any way I can help you?"

Maggie fluffed her hair and nudged him. "You can take me to the park for a picnic or even to the root beer stand for hot dogs."

"That works for me, but I think I'll hold out for your fried chicken from now on." Charlie patted his stomach.

She peered over her glasses at him. "My mother was no dummy."

Maggie winced when Charlie once again rubbed the red spot on his forehead. She wrapped her arms around herself as a flash of lightning sliced across the distant sky.

Charlie jumped up and grabbed Maggie's hand. The two of them ran across the grass and hopped into Charlie's car.

Raindrops bounced off the windshield as they pulled into her driveway. Charlie grabbed an umbrella from the pocket in the door and went around to the passenger side. Maggie slipped out, and together they raced for the porch.

She closed her eyes as he brushed a damp lock of hair from her face. Then she felt the gentle touch of his lips on her cheek. When she opened her eyes again, she was alone.

Wanda opened the door. "Oh, Rita, you look wonderful!"

"I feel wonderful, and I owe it all to you and your husband. We moved into the Haven last night. It was like a dream—warm food, a shower, clean sheets. We even have our own room. How can I ever thank you?"

Wanda hugged the petite mother-to-be. "Sweetie, I'm so happy for you. Now you can really take care of yourself and that precious baby. You certainly don't have to thank me. It's all in God's hands. And I appreciate your helping me give these dear people a fun time."

The two women divided up the work. Rita carried the silver from the dining room into the kitchen and began polishing. "These are beautiful," she said to Wanda as she held up the antique spoons. "Where did you get them?"

"They've been in our family forever. Grandma and I ate ice cream with them during afternoon tea parties. She'd let me wear her jewelry and one of her fancy hats. You and your sweet baby will be having tea parties before you know it." Wanda's hands flew to her heart; she closed her eyes and sighed.

She felt a gentle tap on her shoulder and opened her eyes. "Wanda, I think your husband is calling you."

Wanda slapped her hands against her cheeks. "I have to run. Alberto and I will be setting up a few games and activities outside. Call me if you need me."

Ellen covered the seven-layer dip with plastic wrap and put it in the refrigerator. She looked at her watch, grimaced, grabbed her purse, and ran out the door.

When she got back from picking up Bob, Ellen set several bags of chips on the table. "These are for the party, Bob, so don't get into them."

"No problem," he assured her. She gave the top of his head a quick kiss before heading upstairs.

She took time to light several candles and put on one of her instrumental CDs before stepping into the warm, sudsy bathtub. Ellen leaned back and let the water bathe away the cares of the day. When the water cooled and the last number on the CD came to an end, she sighed and pushed herself out of the tub.

When she glanced at the bedroom clock, she switched gears. Choosing a white shirt with navy embroidery, navy capris, and matching sandals, Ellen dressed quickly. A touch of makeup and a quick brush of her hair, and she was racing down the stairs.

She crossed the kitchen threshold and froze. Her eyes narrowed as she appraised the mess that used to be her seven-layer dip. There were no more layers. Globs of cheese, tomatoes, sour cream, bean dip, and the other ingredients littered the table. Footprints of mayo and sour cream, along with a few broken chips led to the garage door.

Ellen pulled a chair back from the table and sank down onto it. Her head sagged, her hands creating a cup for the tears streaming down her cheeks. Her shoulders began heaving as her soft sobs swelled to a crescendo. She threw her head back, closed her eyes, and wailed.

The sound of the garage door opening snapped Ellen out of her primal moment. She looked over and saw Bob entering the kitchen. He sported a broad grin and a dip-spattered shirt. "Thanks for the dip and chips, honey. It was a great surprise."

Ellen clapped her hands together and doubled over laughing.

Ten minutes later, Ellen and Maggie wedged the fruit plate between the cheese tray and the vegetable platter. They stepped back from the dining room table. Ellen turned to her coworker. "Sorry I couldn't bring the dip, but it looks like we have plenty of food."

Maggie laughed. "I don't think we could squeeze another dish on this table."

The kitchen door swung open, and Rita walked in. "Ellen, I didn't know I'd see you here today."

"Hi, Rita. I guess you've met my friend, Maggie MacDonald."

"Yes, Mrs. MacDonald and I have been working on the food together. It looks so yummy. I even sneaked a deviled egg before I brought the plate out." A flush crept from her neck to her cheeks.

"I made forty. We can certainly spare one." Maggie chuckled. "By the way, how was it?"

"I haven't had a deviled egg since I was a little girl." Rita closed her eyes. "It was scrumptious."

"I can tell you've been busy, dear." Maggie peered over her glasses. "The house looks beautiful."

"Thanks. I had a lot of fun helping Mrs. Santiago get ready. She let me polish all her gorgeous silver. It must be worth a fortune. I was a little nervous handling it, but it really shines now, doesn't it?" Rita pulled one of the spoons from the antique rack and held it to the light.

"Awesome. My mother-in-law had a collection like that." Ellen looked around the room. "By the way, where's Wanda?"

"She's upstairs getting dressed." Rita leaned in. "She's wearing something special for the party and running a little late. She wanted me to ask if you'd cover for her."

Ellen masked her giggle with a cough when she saw her friend roll her eyes.

Maggie pushed up her sleeves. "I'll keep the buffet table stocked if you'll take care of things outside."

"Sounds like a plan. I want to check on Bob anyway." Ellen stepped onto the porch and saw Bob standing next to Alberto. She walked over to them and gave her husband a hug.

A hush fell over the crowd when the hostess flung open the door and appeared on the porch. Ellen's eyes popped wide-open at the sight of Wanda in a neon multi-colored caftan. Her black ponytail draped over her right shoulder from beneath an enormous straw hat. A mélange of cornflowers, asters, dahlias, and sunflowers circled the brim, and a sparkling gold butterfly perched on the top, suspended by a wire. Her sandals glittered, a perfect reflection of the large-winged Lepidoptera fluttering just above her nose.

"'This is the day that the Lord has made. Let us rejoice and be glad in it!' Welcome to our home." Wanda's filmy, oversized sleeve floated in the breeze as she gestured toward the door. "Please come in and partake of the refreshments."

As the guests flocked into the house, Ellen edged over to Wanda's side. "Your outfit is to die for. You have an amazing sense of style." She ran her hands down her white blouse and navy capris. "Girlfriend, you are taking me shopping!"

For the next hour, Ellen supervised the beanbag throw, retrieved wayward balloons from the balloon toss, and removed prizes from the magnet at the end of a plastic fishing rod. Every so often, she caught a glimpse of Wanda snapping a picture as she floated from guest to guest.

Ellen wandered in to the dining room to get a bottle of water. "Bob, I wondered where you'd gone. Everyone else is outside. Are you feeling all right?"

He turned and stared at her. "I miss my mom. This place reminds me of home."

Ellen crossed the room and put her arms around her husband. "I can see how you'd think that. But the party isn't anything like our D.C. extravaganzas. I used to miss those, but this is more relaxing. I really like these people."

Bob squeezed her arm. "Me too. And it sure is a beautiful day."

A flash lit up the room. "Gotcha, Bobby!" Wanda's butterfly appeared to flit from flower to flower to the beat of the artist's animated chatter. "I've been looking for you two. Now I have pictures of all the office people."

When everyone had gone, Wanda put her arms around her two friends, thanked them for all their help, and gave them each a kiss on the cheek.

Lydia Moen

"It was a lovely party, Wanda." Maggie put several empty platters into the basket she'd brought the food in. "I'd like to stay and help, but Charlie and I have plans tonight."

Ellen stepped forward and gave Wanda a long hug. "Everyone had a great time. It was so generous of you to open your home to us. Now let me help you clean up."

"You've done more than enough already. Alberto, Rita, and I can take care of the rest."

Ellen frowned. "Wanda, Rita walked out a long time ago."

Chapter 26

Wanda looked up as Alberto entered her studio, briefcase in hand. "Are you heading off to the church now?"

"Not before I get my morning kiss."

Wanda set down the paintbrushes she'd just picked up and draped her arms around her husband's neck. He bent down, gave her a peck on the cheek, and started to back away.

"Not so fast, Alberto." Wanda waved a finger back and forth. "I didn't pucker up for the abridged version. I want the amplified edition."

Alberto backed up a few steps, placed his briefcase on the floor next to his feet, did three shoulder rolls, and dipped his wife into a lingering kiss.

When he released her, Wanda swooned and fanned herself with her hand. "Pastor Santiago, I can hardly wait for the sequel!"

"It'll have to be a coming attraction. I've got an early appointment today." Alberto picked up his briefcase and headed for the door.

"Have a good day, querido. You certainly got mine off to a great start." Wanda continued to fan herself while taking a dramatic swig of her soda.

Alberto turned back and cocked his head. "Oh, I almost forgot. The real reason I came in here was to ask about your grandmother's spoons. I noticed how shiny they were yesterday, but when I looked up today, the rack was half empty."

"Half empty?" Wanda steamed past Alberto and stood staring at the empty spaces where spoons used to be.

The phone rang as Alberto's car pulled out of the driveway. Wanda didn't move. But when she heard Maggie's voice on the answering machine, she reached over and picked up the receiver. "I'm here, Maggie. Can you come over?"

"I'm on my way."

A minute later, Wanda looked up to see her friend's concerned face looking down at her.

"What's wrong, Wanda? You're so pale." Maggie sat down and reached out to her. "Your hands are freezing. Are you sick?"

"I am sick but not physically. Did you see anyone taking silver spoons out of the rack at the party yesterday?"

Wanda's eyes searched Maggie's face as her neighbor first shook her head and then hesitated. "I was going to say no, but now I remember Rita took one out to show Ellen and me how beautiful it was. She was proud of how nice they looked after she polished them."

Wanda held her head in her hands. "Maggie, half the spoons are missing."

Maggie stood up and marched into the dining room. Wanda saw her eyeing the half-empty rack and heard her opening drawer after drawer in the buffet.

She came back into the kitchen and sat down across from Wanda. "Have you asked Alberto if he knows where they are?"

"He's the one who noticed they were missing."

"How about Ellen or Rita?" Maggie tapped her fingers on the table. "Didn't they help you clean up?"

"Ellen did, but…" Wanda hesitated and twisted her ponytail around her fingers. "She told me Rita left before the party was over. I never even saw her to say goodbye."

Maggie peered over her glasses at her friend. "We know the spoons aren't where they belong, but that's all we know. They may turn up before the end of the day. Or there may be a simple explanation for their disappearance. Do you want me to call the girls? I should be able to reach Rita at the Haven."

Wanda's hands flew to her heart. "Oh, sweetie, that would be a blessing. I know you'll say just the right things."

Maggie stood up, walked over, and put her arm around her friend. "I have to run a couple of errands first. Charlie and I are taking the Jefferson family fishing and on a picnic later this afternoon. That's why I was calling you. Could we borrow those plastic fishing rods you used at the party yesterday?"

"Of course. I think they're still on the porch."

"Don't get up, dear. I'll get them on my way out."

Wanda didn't get up but held out her arms. "Thanks for coming right over."

Maggie bent down to hug her. "Anytime. I'm so sorry about the spoons. Let me know if they turn up. I'll call you as soon as I've talked with Ellen and Rita."

"Oh, Neil, you're here. I'm glad to catch you in." Maggie raised an eyebrow and regarded the bait shop owner over her glasses.

Lydia Moen

"Yup, I'm here." Neil got up from his brown Naugahyde chair and walked around the counter.

"I see you've still got the sling on. How's the bursitis?"

"It's about the same. What are you looking for today, Maggie?"

"Charlie told me to get one container of earthworms and another of red worms."

"Oh, so you and Charlie are going fishing?" Neil raised an eyebrow and regarded the former teacher over his glasses.

Maggie felt her face redden. As she started to stammer out a response, she heard the back door open.

"Neil, I don't know how we're going to—"

The bait shop owner spun around and interrupted Joe Carnegie as he backed in the open door. "Just leave that outside! We'll get to it later. I have a customer."

Maggie's mouth dropped open as she watched Joe step back outside, bend over, and set something on the ground. He jerked the door closed behind him.

Wanda sat at the kitchen table for a few moments after Maggie left. Then she stood up, went into the living room, and sat down with her Bible. She closed her eyes briefly and murmured, "Worries, cares." Then she turned to the back of the book and thumbed through the concordance.

She kept one finger on the page she'd found and flipped back and forth in the Bible. As Wanda scanned the Scriptures, she sat up straighter, and the heaviness in her heart lifted as she read 1 Peter 5:7. "Give all your worries and cares to God, for He cares about what happens to you."

"Okay, God, I'm giving the lost spoons to You. Thank You for caring about me. Whether they're found or not, I trust You to do what's best."

Wanda stood up and made a beeline to her studio. She gathered the supplies for her first mural and headed for the community center.

"Oh, Ray, I didn't know you were still here." Ellen's expression morphed from surprise to anger. "What's going on in here?"

Ray backed away from the card Bob was handing him and stuffed his fists in his pockets.

"He needs to buy some stuff, so I'm giving him my credit card." Bob shrugged.

Ellen took a step forward. "Mr. Hoffman, I thought we had an understanding. If you give us a list, we'll pick up the supplies you need to finish the workshop. Bob and I are going to run errands later this evening. We'll get whatever you need while we're out."

"I don't have a list, and I'd rather pick out the stuff myself." Ray crossed his arms and set his jaw.

"I can understand that. Why don't you get what you need and bring us the receipt? I'll reimburse you right away."

"I don't work that way."

"Then I guess we have a problem." Ellen straightened her back and put her hands on her hips.

As soon as Charlie got in the car, Maggie reached out and put her hand on his arm. Then she leaned her head back, closed her eyes, and let out a big sigh.

"Tough day, Maggie?"

She nodded. "It has been. Can we just sit for a minute?"

"Of course, we have plenty of time. How can I help?"

"The way you always do, Charlie—by being with me and listening." Maggie's eyes dampened.

Charlie turned off the engine and faced her.

"It started right after you brought the mail this morning. I went over to pick up the fishing rods from Wanda, and she was almost in tears. Some of the antique silver spoons her grandmother gave them are missing. We looked everywhere we could think of, but they've just disappeared. We're afraid Rita might have taken them when she left the party early."

Charlie put his hand on Maggie's. "I can understand why that's upsetting to both of you."

"After that I went to the bait shop and had another unsettling encounter with Neil and Joe Carnegie. Charlie, they're hiding something."

"I can't imagine either of them doing anything they'd have to hide, but I wasn't there."

Maggie looked into Charlie's eyes. "I wish you had been. But you're here now, and I feel better just talking with you. Let's put all of this out of our minds for now and go have some fun."

The Jeffersons arrived at the park while Maggie and Charlie were unloading the car.

"Hi, Charlie. Hi, Mrs. MacDonald. We're here!" Junior ran up and gave Charlie a high-five.

Jessica bounced over to Maggie. "See my new dress? Mommy got it for our picnic."

"I love pink and purple too." Maggie stooped down and was rewarded with a shy hug.

Charlie handed a carton of bait to each of the children and carried the fishing poles as he led them down to the lake. Maggie and Tamara set the items for the picnic on a nearby table before moving to a bench close to the fishermen.

Junior plopped down on the sand and opened his carton. As soon as he looked inside, he jumped up and took it over to Tamara. "Look, Mommy. Worms! And they're red!"

Meanwhile Charlie crouched down on the beach next to Jessica and helped her open her carton of earthworms. She looked inside and hesitated a moment. Then she jumped up, screaming, "Snakes! Help!" and scrambled into her mother's arms.

Maggie laughed when she saw Charlie standing alone on the sand, shrugging his shoulders and shaking his head. After the initial excitement, the youngsters watched Charlie bait their hooks. He helped Junior throw his line out and threw Jessica's for her. Then he sat between them and explained how they should watch for the bobbers to sink when a fish nibbled at their worms.

Junior caught a small bluegill, and Charlie taught him the principle of catch-and-release. After his mother took a couple of pictures of Junior holding up his trophy, he let Charlie unhook the fish and send it back to its family. Jessica played in the sand with the plastic pail and shovel that Tamara had brought for her.

A short time later, Junior handed his pole to Charlie. "That was fun. Can we eat now?"

They gathered around the table and held hands while Charlie said the blessing. When he paused at the end, Junior piped up, "And help Daddy find his friends."

Maggie wrinkled her brow and looked first at Charlie and then Tamara. "Is James in the Marine reserves?"

"Yes, he is," Tamara answered. "And two young men from his unit got separated in the field. We've been praying for them ever since."

Maggie grabbed the edge of the table. "Do you know if their names are Josh and Chris?"

Tamara's eyes widened as she nodded her head.

"Josh is my grandson."

"You two need time to talk, but Junior and I are hungry." Charlie smiled at Maggie and Tamara before passing the food around. "Let's eat now, and the kids and I will clean up afterwards so you gals can visit."

Maggie reached for Charlie's hand and mouthed a quick "thank you."

The fried chicken was just as big a hit with their guests as it had been with Charlie. His fruit sticks and chocolate chip cookies topped off a great picnic.

As soon as Maggie put down her napkin, Tamara stood up, took Maggie's hand, and led her down to the bench they'd been sitting on earlier. Maggie's heart sank when Tamara told her she didn't have any new information to share. The lieutenant's wife put her arm around Maggie's shoulder. "Would you like to pray together?"

The two women spent the next several minutes with bowed heads. Tamara prayed that Josh and Chris would be quickly and safely reunited with the unit. She prayed for peace for the two young men and their families. Maggie thanked God for His amazing plan, which had placed Josh and Chris under James Jefferson's command and brought his family into her life.

When Maggie looked up, she saw tears in Tamara's eyes through the tears in her own. The two women stood and gave each other a long hug before walking back to the table hand in hand.

Junior frowned as his mother approached. "What's wrong, Mommy? Have you been crying?"

"People cry for all kinds of reasons, Junior. This isn't a bad kind of crying."

Jessica tugged on her mother's arm. "Can I kiss it and make it better?"

"I always feel better when you give me a kiss." Tamara bent down and picked up her daughter.

Junior stood on the bench next to Charlie and pulled off the postman's cap. "Look at Charlie's 'owie.' Do you want me to kiss it for you?"

Maggie drew in a breath. The spot at Charlie's hairline had turned into an angry red blotch.

He glanced up at her and then down at the ground. A flush crept up his neck to his cheeks. "Thank you, Junior. I know that'll make me feel better."

Chapter 27

The van headlights silhouetted the giant, jagged shadow of the blue pickup on the shed. Ellen stomped on the brake. "Bob, why is Ray here at this time of night?"

"Who?"

Ellen closed her eyes and gritted her teeth. "Bob, get Alberto."

"I can carry everything in myself."

Ellen slammed her hands against the steering wheel. "Please, just get Alberto."

"If that'll make you feel better." Bob scratched his head and reached for the door handle.

"Hurry!"

Bob got out of the van and sauntered down the road. Ellen groaned when she saw him stop, bend over, and pick up a dirty paper cup.

She switched the headlights off and inched the van over to the side of the road, careful to stay clear of the street light's reach. She sat stone-still, holding her breath. Her eyes darted between the windshield and the rearview mirror. Her clammy hand reached for the door handle then pulled back as if burned.

With her eyes focused on Ray's truck, she pushed the door lock. Its electronic beep shattered the silence. Ellen gasped and threw a hand over her mouth, stifling a scream as a flurry of flying feathers crashed into the windshield.

Wanda, hair dripping and tying her robe, answered the door. "Hi, Bobby, come on in."

"Hi, Wanda."

"What's up? Is Ellen right behind you?" Wanda looked around Bob as he entered the kitchen.

"I don't think so. She told me to come over here." Bob scratched his head and stood smiling at Wanda.

She put her arm around him and led him to a chair at the kitchen table. "Well, I'm glad you did. Have one of these." Wanda placed a jar of peanut-butter treats in front of him. "I'll tell Alberto you're here."

As Wanda turned toward the stairs, she clenched her jaw and quickened her pace.

As the screeching crows flew off, Ellen crouched down, expecting Ray to pull on the van door any second. She held her breath and didn't move. She couldn't hear any noise above the pounding of her own heart.

Ellen finally raised her head, looked around for Ray, then glanced over at the shed. The truck was still there, and she didn't see any movement. She groaned when she checked her rearview mirror and saw no sign of Bob or Alberto.

Ellen unlocked the van and slipped into the darkness, easing the door closed just enough to turn off the overhead light. She crept around the back of her vehicle and along the side. Then she stopped and took a deep breath before peeking around the bumper.

From that vantage point, Ellen could see light flickering out the shed window. After scanning the area, she scrambled across the lane and hid behind Ray's pickup. Using the back wheel for cover, she crouched down and wiped her forehead with her sleeve.

Ellen craned her neck to get a better view of the lane. *Where are they?* She squeezed her eyes closed for just a moment. When she opened them, she scooted over to the side of the shed, inched herself up the wall, and peeked over the windowsill.

Wanda hurried into the bedroom and found Alberto reading. "Bob's here, and I think something's wrong."

"Isn't Ellen with him?" Alberto frowned and set down his book.

"No, and that's what worries me. Ellen told him to come over here, but he doesn't seem to know why. I think you better get over there, Alberto."

Bob was sitting at the table, snacking on a peanut-butter treat when Alberto and Wanda entered the kitchen.

"Hello, neighbor. Good to see you. What's going on at the Bailey house tonight?" Alberto put his hand on Bob's shoulder, but remained standing.

"Oh, the usual."

Wanda sat down across from Bob. "Bobby, didn't you say something about Ellen wanting Alberto to come over. What does she need?"

"I'm not exactly sure." Bob reached for another peanut-butter treat.

"I'll see what's up with that lovely bride of yours." Alberto grabbed his cellphone and headed out the door.

Ellen couldn't move, couldn't think, couldn't breathe.

She was face to face with Ray Hoffman. Only the tool shed window separated the two. The man inside the shed glared at her, his dark eyes stabbing into hers like porcupine quills.

Then the pause button that had kept the two immobilized released, and Ray turned off his flashlight. Ellen spun around and darted toward the road. She tripped and staggered forward, arms flailing and hands clawing at the air. Tears broke through her bravado and spilled over onto her cheeks as she landed in a clump of ferns.

The door slammed behind Alberto as he jumped off the porch and hurried down Lakeshore Lane. His adrenaline spiked at the sight of the old pickup next to the Baileys' shed. He almost stumbled on Ellen's body sprawled next to the driveway.

Ellen moaned and pointed toward the shed. "He's in there."

"Are you hurt?" Alberto knelt beside her.

"Just scared. I don't know what he's doing here."

He helped Ellen to her feet. "Can you walk?" She nodded her head.

He raised a finger to his lips when Wanda and Bob arrived, surprised they had followed him. "You two take Ellen into the house. Stay in the shadows, and lock the door when you get inside. I'll take care of our visitor."

Alberto pulled out his cell phone and called 911. When he completed the call, he prayed, *Lord, we are in Your hands. Please keep all of us safe. Go before me so that I perform this mission according to Your will. Give me the words to speak, and control my actions and those of this intruder. Thank You for the gift of Your presence.*

Alberto lifted his head, threw his shoulders back, and strode to the shed.

"Bailey residence. This is Wanda Santiago."

"Why are you answering Ellen's phone? Is everything okay?"

"Oh, Maggie. Ellen's had a bad scare, but she's resting on the couch."

"I'll be right over."

"That's good, but sneak over on the lake path. Alberto's got Ray Hoffman cornered in the shed."

"Oh, mercy!"

"You'll be okay, sweetie. Just keep your head down and don't use a flashlight. I'll unlock the porch door and let you in."

Alberto's eyes took a moment to adjust to the shed's darkness. Before his vision sharpened, he heard someone breathing behind him.

"Hello, Ray. It's Alberto from next door. How's the work coming along?"

"What's it to you?"

Alberto flipped on the light. The handyman glared at him from just a few feet away.

"What's going on, Ray? Working in the dark?"

The handyman crossed his arms. "I'm just leaving."

Alberto leaned against the doorjamb and looked at his watch. "What are you doing here so late?"

"I, uh, forgot something and came back to check on it." Ray tapped the blunt end of a screwdriver against the palm of his hand.

"You're certainly conscientious. Maybe you'd like to help out with a couple of jobs we've got down at the church."

Ray grasped the handle of the screwdriver in his right hand and took a step forward. "I'll be moving on soon."

"Let me know if you're interested." Alberto continued to chat with Ray, asking him questions about his work, his background, his family—anything to keep him there.

When police sirens screamed in the distance, Ray pushed past Alberto, flew out the door, and ran to his truck. He was still fumbling with his keys when Chief Gallego pulled up to his rear bumper. Ray Hoffman dropped the screwdriver and threw his hands in the air before Carlos drew his pistol.

Alberto stood off to the side, while Chief Gallego handcuffed the suspect's arms behind his back. The chief patted the handyman's pockets and pant legs and then sat him down in the backseat of the patrol car. While Carlos searched the pickup truck, the garage, and the surrounding area, Alberto sat in the front seat of the squad car facing the back, talking to the now-subdued suspect.

When Maggie reached for the door, Wanda opened it, grabbed her arm, and pulled her into the house.

"I heard the sirens and saw police lights in your driveway. What in the world is going on?" Maggie sat down and put her hand on Ellen's. "How are you doing, dear?"

"I'm still shaking. I don't think I've ever been that frightened before."

Wanda's hands flew to her chest. "I would hope not!"

Maggie patted Ellen's hand, as she listened to Wanda's retelling of

Ellen's encounter with the handyman. "What a scare! I'm so sorry, dear. What can I do to help? Would you like a cup of tea?"

"That would be awesome. It might calm me down."

All three women jumped at the loud knocking at the backdoor. Maggie stood up first. "Wanda, turn off the light. I'll peek out and see who's there."

Spotting Alberto when she peered through the nearby window, Maggie opened the door.

"I'm glad you're here, Maggie," Alberto said, stepping inside the kitchen. "This has been a pretty stressful evening for Ellen."

He walked over to the table and put his hand on Bob's shoulder. "I hate to interrupt you, but Carlos would like you to come out and identify the tools he found under a tarp in the back of Ray's truck."

Bob looked up from his dish of ice cream. "Carlos?"

"He's my cousin. You'll recognize him." Alberto grinned.

"Tell him I'll be out as soon as I finish my dessert."

"I'll put it in the freezer for you, Bob." Maggie reached for the bowl.

A few minutes later, Maggie joined her friends at the table for tea. "I saw Alberto talking with your handyman, Ellen. I think he might be praying with Ray."

Ellen paused a moment, pressing her lips between her teeth. "I think it's a little late for prayer."

Maggie looked at Ellen and smiled. "I've found it's never too late for prayer."

Later that evening, Maggie sat in one of the twin chairs in the corner of her bedroom. She picked up her nighttime devotional from the table at her side and opened it to the day's date. When she finished reading,

Lydia Moen

Maggie nodded and closed her eyes.

She always pictured her Lord sitting in the opposite chair, smiling lovingly at her. She knew He listened attentively to her prayers, because He often responded through her readings and the thoughts they brought to her mind.

She thanked God for keeping Ellen and Alberto safe during the confrontation with Ray Hoffman. She asked Him to reveal Himself to the thief through caring Christians who would come alongside Ray and show him the love and peace available through Christ. After praying for the safe return of Josh and Chris, she praised God for His amazing plan to place them in James Jefferson's unit.

Maggie paused for a minute, her eyes filling with tears. "I'm concerned about that red spot on Charlie's head, Lord. Let him feel Your presence as You lead him into a physician's care. Fill him with Your love and peace. I pray the prayer that never fails: *Thy will be done.* In Jesus' name. Amen."

Charlie knelt beside his bed for several minutes, giving the day's concerns to God before tucking in. It was a habit he'd developed as a child, and the only change he'd made over the years was to use the kneeling pad his late wife had made for him. His prayer time ended with "Forgive me for not heeding Your nudges to see a doctor, for letting my fear of cancer keep me in denial. Give me the strength to protect Maggie from reliving painful memories. Thank You for little Junior's willingness to point out what I was running from. Now, Father, I run to You. Show me clearly the path You want me to take."

Chapter 28

Early the next morning, Alberto took a seat across from the chief in the Water's Edge police station. "How's your newest inmate doing?"

Carlos frowned and shook his head. "Unfortunately, if you're talking about Ray Hoffman, he's not our newest. We had a busy night."

"Sorry to hear that. It seems as if law enforcement is one of the few growth areas in the economy."

Alberto took a swig of his coffee before setting it back on the desk. "I'm glad to see you guys aren't wasting our taxpayer money on gourmet java."

"It's pretty bad, isn't it?"

"The police station is *still* the only place in town where you can get a worse cup of coffee than the church!" The chief and the pastor raised their cups to each other and chuckled.

"Well, I didn't come here to critique the coffee." Alberto sat up straighter and leaned forward. "I'd like to talk with you about what's going to happen with Ray."

Carlos rocked back in his desk chair. "His hearing is scheduled for later this morning. Based on what he said last night, I assume he'll plead guilty, and then the judge will set a date for sentencing."

Alberto hesitated. "I'd like to see Ray while I'm here today. If he agrees, I'd like to speak up for him at the appropriate time."

Carlos raised his eyebrows. "You're kind of sticking your neck out here, cousin. What do you really know about this guy?"

"We got to know each other pretty well in the shed last night." Alberto chuckled.

"And you *still* want to speak up for him?" Carlos shook his head.

"I do. His wife has become a friend since she started working for us. Rita told Wanda that Ray lost his job over a year ago, and until they moved into the Haven on Tuesday, they'd been living in his truck. I'd like to do some counseling with him…if he's receptive."

He took a deep breath before continuing. "You know, Carlos, the church has used people in the work-release program before. Do you think there's a possibility we could get Ray into it? We need a general handyman, and I'd take responsibility for supervising him."

The chief pulled his glasses down and looked over the rims. "Alberto, you and I are kind of an odd pair. I put them in cuffs, and you try to get the cuffs off. But in this situation, maybe the guy needs a break. I'll do what I can."

Alberto stood and shook his cousin's hand. "Thank you, Carlos. I hope we can change this man's life."

Carlos escorted Alberto to Ray's cell. "Mr. Hoffman, you have a visitor." He unlocked the door and the pastor walked in.

The police chief locked the door behind Alberto, started down the hall, and then called back over his shoulder, "Just holler when you're finished, Pastor Santiago. The guard will let you out."

"What do you want?" Ray frowned at Alberto from his seat on one of the two cots at the sides of the cell. The glare of the single light bulb in the ceiling lit up his forehead and nose, casting dark shadows over his eyes, mouth, and cheeks.

Alberto sat down on the cot across from Ray. He leaned forward, elbows on his knees and hands folded. "I'm concerned about you. I wanted to see how you're doing."

Ray stood up and grabbed hold of the iron bars that Alberto had just walked through. "How do you think I'm doing?" He wheeled around, a vein in his neck pulsing. "Thanks to you and your friends, I moved out of my truck and into the shelter for two whole nights before ending up in these fancy digs." Ray stretched out his arms and looked from one side of the cell to the other.

Alberto slowly got to his feet, surveyed the cement block wall, and nodded his head. "I agree, this is not a very nice place to be, and I know you've had some tough breaks. But this is where you are, Ray. And if you'd like my help, I'm here to do what I can."

Wanda dropped down onto the chair the community center maintenance man had left for her and pulled in a deep breath. When she heard the click-click-click of heels coming nearer, she jumped up and started going through her folder of transparencies.

"Hi, Wanda. I'm glad to see Ralph got the table and overhead projector set up for you."

Wanda looked up at the approaching director. "You folks are really well organized here."

"Your mural is going to brighten up this wall, and some of the people who pass by can use a little brightness in their days. It'll be fun to watch the reaction of the adult daycare attendees and their caregivers. I'm glad to see you're getting started, Wanda. Let me know if there's anything we can do to help you."

Wanda gave a dismissive wave. "It's really nothing. Coming up with the idea is the hardest part of creating any work of art. I'd like to keep it a surprise. Is there any way we can cover it up until I finish?"

Ruth raised an eyebrow. "How long do you think it'll take?"

"Just a few days. I've already drawn the sketches and had them copied onto transparencies. And I've prepared the wall, so I'm ready to go." Wanda flashed Ruth a broad grin and a thumbs-up.

"I'll talk with Ralph. He'll come up with something. Now I don't want to hold you up. Thanks again for doing this, Wanda."

After Ruth's heels click-click-clicked their way out of earshot, Wanda sank into the chair again and gazed at the empty wall before her. She sat and stared for several minutes until she heard someone else approaching from down the hall. She popped up again and started thumbing through her transparency folder.

"Hi, Wanda. It looks like you're busy, but would you have time to join us for today's snack?"

Wanda turned around and saw Mr. King's daughter carrying a box. "I really should keep working, but thank you anyway, sweetie."

"They're homemade brownies, Wanda. I just took them out of the oven."

Wanda put her folder on the chair, grabbed her magenta and teal blue tote, and gestured toward the adult daycare center: "You said the magic words. After you."

A few minutes later, Wanda was sitting at a table chatting with Bob between bites of brownie. She felt a tap on her shoulder and turned around.

Ruth Butler smiled down at Wanda and touched her own front teeth. She whispered, "You have a little brownie there."

Wanda nodded and took care of the brownie spot.

"I'm glad I found you," Ruth said with a smile. "I was afraid you'd already left."

Wanda's face burned at the realization that taking a snack break might look as if she were shirking her responsibilities. "Oh, no. I'm still here. I just came in to help Mr. King's daughter pass out the brownies. Would you like one?"

Wanda searched the room for the serving tray. Before she was able to locate it, Ruth held up her hand. "No, thank you. I don't want to spoil my lunch. I came back to tell you that Ralph will take care of covering your mural."

Wanda followed Ruth out the door. She went straight to her table and turned on the overhead projector then picked up the transparency folder one more time. Hearing the now familiar click-click-click of Ruth's heels retreating down the hall, Wanda let out a deep breath. When she looked up, Ruth was peeking at her from around the corner. The director smiled and waved before her head disappeared and the clicking continued.

Maggie hurried down the steps to the dock. "You're a little early today, Charlie. I almost missed you. Would you like to come up and try my lemon-poppy-seed muffins? They're still warm."

When Charlie hesitated, Maggie peered at him over her glasses. "Just for a few minutes? You're ahead of schedule."

"Okay...but just for a few minutes." Charlie turned off his engine, tied up his boat, and followed Maggie to the house.

Maggie gave Charlie a summary of Ellen's encounter with Ray Hoffman and his subsequent arrest. When she finished, Charlie looked down at his plate. "I'm glad they caught him and everyone's safe."

Maggie tapped her foot. "How's your day going?"

"Not bad. How about you?"

"It's better now that you're here." She fluffed her hair and winked.

Lydia Moen

Charlie stared at the lake and took a swig of coffee.

Maggie's foot kept tapping. She picked up the novel she'd been reading and thumbed through the pages. "What's on your schedule this weekend, Charlie?"

"I have a lot to do around the house." He rubbed the angry red spot on his forehead. "I better get going now. Thanks for the muffin."

Maggie reached over and put her hand on his arm. "Charlie, I'm concerned about your health. I hope you'll see a doctor soon."

Charlie stood up. "You're a good friend, Maggie, but I don't want you worrying about me."

Maggie remained seated and watched Charlie trudge back down to his boat. She waited for his customary salute, but it never came.

Ellen slammed the last drawer of her dresser and strode across the room to her nightstand. She yanked on the top drawer so hard it fell out, spewing reading glasses, hand cream, and various other items across the floor. She waved her hand, dismissing the mess at her feet, and moved on to the second drawer, shoving it shut after rummaging through its contents. She snatched up the hand cream and threw it across the room, plunked herself down on the bed, and stomped her feet on the floor.

"Ellen? Are you all right, dear?" Maggie called. Ellen glanced at the open window, picked up her pillow, and bit it.

"As promised, Wanda and I are here with lunch. Can we come in?"

"The kitchen door's open." Ellen put her head in her hands and rocked back and forth.

"Do you need any help up there, Ellen?"

"No, no." Ellen covered her eyes and shook her head. "Don't come up. I'll be right down."

"Don't rush. We'll get lunch on the table."

"Fabulous." Ellen held onto the handle and inched the bedroom door closed. Then she plodded into the bathroom, peeked in the mirror, and took a deep breath. She splashed cold water on her face, ran a brush through her hair, and looked in the mirror again. "That'll have to do." She straightened her shoulders and headed downstairs, but when she passed the D.C. painting, tears filled her eyes.

When she entered the kitchen, Maggie embraced her, and then Wanda handed her a cup and saucer. "Here, sweetie. This always helps me relax."

Ellen took the tea, but her shaking hand spilled the hot liquid on the floor. She dropped into a chair and buried her face in her hands. Wanda rushed to Ellen's side and put an arm around their sobbing friend.

"I'm sorry, ladies. I'm just a mess." Ellen could barely get the words out. Her shoulders heaved, and her breath came in gasps.

"I was so scared…that miserable thief…all Bob's tools…now my jewelry box."

"Your jewelry box?" Wanda's eyes widened, and she sat down in a chair next to Ellen.

Ellen raised her head, looked up at Wanda, and spat out the words: "Those horrible Hoffmans stole it, just like they stole Bob's tools and your spoons."

"Oh, mercy! No wonder you're upset. Have you looked everywhere for it?" Maggie narrowed her eyes.

"That's what you heard me doing when you got here."

Maggie put her hand on Ellen's. "Let's have our lunch, and after we eat, we'll go up and help you look."

Wanda put her hand on top of theirs. "Three is better than one, or even two, and we're a cord of three strands."

Wanda kept the conversation going as they ate lunch, telling her two friends about starting on her mural at the community center and getting caught eating brownies when she was supposed to be sketching.

"Brownies sound good," Maggie said. "Did you bring dessert?"

"I guess I forgot. I should have swiped a couple of brownies from adult daycare." Wanda laughed.

"There's been too much swiping going on lately." Ellen tapped her fork on the table.

Maggie and Wanda exchanged frowns, and Wanda spoke up: "You're right, Ellen. I shouldn't joke about that."

"Don't even get me started. First Rita takes your spoons, and then her husband gets caught with a load of Bob's tools in his pickup. Seriously, who are these people? It's not enough that we give them jobs—they take our stuff! Rita's over there at your party acting so nice, and she's robbing you behind your back. Are you kidding me? They've probably already fenced my jewelry."

"Mercy. I can certainly understand why you'd be upset. After all, Ray did steal your tools." Maggie tapped her fingers on the table. "But we don't really know what happened to Wanda's spoons or your jewelry box. If we're all finished eating, let's run upstairs and make sure your jewelry isn't here."

Ellen was chagrinned when she opened the door to the master suite and surveyed the mess she'd left behind. She brought her hand up to her forehead. "Oh, no! I'm so embarrassed."

Wanda stepped around her. "Embarrassed? This is the way our room looks after I've picked it up. Where do you want me to start?"

Maggie stepped in to give directions. "Wanda, why don't you take the bedroom, and Ellen, you check the bath. I'll just pick up this drawer and then start on the closet."

As Ellen rifled through her bathroom drawers, she could hear Maggie sliding hangers and moving boxes in the closet. She could see Wanda looking under the cushions of the matching easy chairs and then sitting down in the middle of the floor.

When Ellen came out of the bathroom, Wanda was peeking underneath the bed. Her friend looked up at her. "Do you have a flashlight?"

Ellen handed her one from the bedside table, and Wanda shone it under the bed. "Praise the Lord, and thank You, Jesus!" She reached under the bed and pulled out the jewelry box.

Ellen took the box from Wanda's outstretched hand and collapsed on the bed. Maggie came running from the closet and sat down next to her.

"You'd better make sure nothing's missing." Wanda watched from her position on the floor.

Ellen opened the box and looked inside. "This is so strange. All my jewelry is here." She hesitated and then raised the lid all the way. "Where did these old business cards come from? And these shoelaces? And this is Bob's favorite jitterbug lure."

While Ellen and Maggie continued to study the contents, Wanda pulled a shoebox out from under the bed and held it up. "Did you want this under here?"

Chapter 29

Later that afternoon, Wanda leaned back, her eyes focused on the community center wall in front of her. Golden rays from the skylight danced across the pines she'd drawn that morning. Her face broke into a satisfied smile as she studied the eagle she'd sketched in, soaring over the rippling waters of the lake below.

The artist whispered to herself. "Now the backdrop is ready for the stars of the show—the pearls." She turned on the projector, placed the transparency on the glass, and then eased the projector forward and back, enlarging and shrinking the size of the pearls until they fit her design perfectly.

Fifteen minutes later, the pearls were strung gracefully across the mural like the lakes across the countryside. Wanda went back to the table, selected another transparency, and positioned the image on the pearl in the center of the picture.

After transferring the drawing to the wall, she stepped back, tilted her head, and frowned. She tapped a pencil against her lips then raised it in the air. She returned to the wall and sketched quickly until a fishing hat rested jauntily on her subject's head.

Wanda set her chalk down on the table and checked her watch.

Lydia Moen

"Whew! I made it." She turned the projector off and placed her transparencies back in the folder. She took another long look at the wall, gave herself a thumbs-up, and headed for the lobby.

She picked up speed when she saw Alberto holding the door for her two friends. "Oh, my three best friends are here to see my work in progress! Come right in. I can't wait to find out what you think."

Without waiting for a response, she began giving orders. "Okay. Maggie, you stand here. Alberto, here. And Ellen, here. Now Maggie, you grab my hand and Alberto's, and Alberto, you grab Ellen's. Close your eyes and follow me." They shuffled down the hall like a group of preschoolers on a field trip. Wanda put a finger to her lips as Ruth Butler walked by shaking her head.

The artist came to a halt in front of the mural. Those in the train behind her bumped into each other but recovered without further incident. At last Wanda announced, "You may drop your hands, but keep your eyes closed until I say it's okay."

She moved down the line, positioning each of the three. She stepped to the right and ahead of the panel and clasped her hands under her chin. "Okay. You can open your eyes."

Silence fell over the hallway for a moment before the reviews came in.

Maggie walked over and gave Wanda a hug. "It's going to be beautiful, dear. You are a gifted artist."

Alberto was right behind Maggie. As he picked his wife up off her feet and whirled her around, he whispered, "It's just as you described it. So meaningful, Wanda."

The three stood together and looked over at Ellen. Her face was red and her fists clenched as she glared at Wanda. "That's Bob!" She spit the words out as she pointed a shaking index finger at the man in the fishing hat. "Who gave you permission to plaster his face on a wall outside the adult daycare center?" She spun around then ran down the hall and out the door.

Ellen dragged herself into the house and up the stairs. She plopped down on the bed and reached for the jewelry box Bob had given her at his retirement party. *How typical it was of him to honor me on a night that was meant to be all about him.* She lifted the lid and stared at the contents—a bizarre combination of beautiful gifts from her husband and items Bob's now-diseased brain commanded him to hide from everyone, even his wife.

She set the jewelry box on her nightstand before pulling the shoebox onto her lap. She closed her eyes, took a deep breath, and removed the top. One of the handkerchiefs she bought for Bob on a trip to Ireland was crumpled inside. When she pulled back the monogrammed corner, a single tear fell from her eye onto the objects hidden beneath it.

She rose and walked to the bathroom sink then returned moments later and sat down on the bed. Her hands shook as she opened the half-full bottle of pain pills. She swallowed the contents with a glass of water and lay down on her side, her knees drawn up to her chest. The last thing she remembered was the vision of what lay beneath the fine linen bearing the initials RPB.

Wanda recoiled from the pressure of Alberto's hand on her shoulder. "Don't touch me. I don't want to feel better. I'm upset, and I have a right to be upset."

Wanda stomped over to the table, snatched up her eraser, and started rubbing Bob's face off the pearl. "If she doesn't want it on here, it won't be. There are plenty of other people who'd love to have their image on my mural."

Alberto grabbed his wife and spun her around to face him. "Stop, Wanda. This is not the time for action. This is a time for prayer. This is a time for seeking God's wisdom."

Maggie put her hand on Wanda's arm. "Would you like to go sit in the courtyard for a few minutes?"

"No! I want to get out of here." The artist threw the eraser down on the table, picked up her transparencies, and headed for the exit.

Maggie had caught up with Wanda in the parking lot and now sat opposite her in a back booth of the Java Joint. "I'm going to have the special. What about you?"

"I seem to remember they make wonderful cupcakes here, so I'll just get a small salad and a cup of soup. Gotta save room for dessert." Wanda winked a puffy red eye at Maggie.

As soon as they ordered, Wanda started talking. "I don't know whether I'm mad or sad—maybe a little of both."

Maggie sat back and listened.

"I've been working so hard on these murals. I couldn't wait for you three to see the first one. Boy, was that a mistake! I feel like painting the wall purple and forgetting it. Am I being unreasonable?"

"You've put a lot of time and effort into this project, Wanda, and you have a right to be proud of it. Your work is inspired. I love the theme. I'm looking forward to seeing all of the murals when they're finished."

"I took pictures of the adults who go to the daycare center when we had the party so I could sketch them later. It never occurred to me that people might object to having their image on the mural. I love those folks, and I wanted to pay tribute to them."

"And it's a wonderful, thoughtful thing you're doing."

"That's why I'm so upset. Ellen's one of my best friends, and she couldn't even stand to look at it." Wanda's swollen eyes filled with tears again.

Maggie reached across the table and put her hand on Wanda's. "Ellen was upset before she ever saw your mural. I don't think we can imagine what her life is like now. Bob's disease is progressing much faster than I would have expected. And the incidents with Ray Hoffman last night and the jewelry box today must have been crushing."

Wanda nodded.

"It's not about your mural, Wanda. It's about her life. I'm really worried about her."

"I am too. Let's stop at her house on our way home, and then maybe the three of us can go kayaking."

The server delivered their food. "Anything else, ladies?"

"Just our check." Wanda looked at Maggie and grinned. "And three cupcakes with chocolate frosting and sprinkles to go, please."

Maggie rang the doorbell. When there was no response, she opened the door a crack. "Yoo-hoo!"

She turned to Wanda after waiting for an answer that never came. "Look in the garage window and see if her van is there."

Wanda hopped off the porch and peeked in the garage. She nodded her head. "It's here."

Maggie opened the door wider and called more loudly. "Ellen, it's Maggie and Wanda."

Wanda edged her head around Maggie's. "We've got cupcakes."

Lydia Moen

When the phone rang, the two women stepped inside the house. Maggie turned to Wanda. "Good, Ellen will get it."

After several rings, Alberto's voice came on the answering machine. "Hi, Ellen. Just wanted to let you know I picked up Bob and convinced him to stop in and watch the Brewers game with me. We'll grab a bite to eat here."

When Wanda started to pick up the receiver, Maggie shook her head. "Let's check on her first."

They turned toward the stairway. "Ellen, we've come bearing gifts," Maggie called from the bottom of the steps.

Wanda held up the pink bag. "It's chocolate!"

When there was still no answer, the two friends glanced at each other and started up the stairs. Maggie knocked on the bedroom door. "Ellen, please answer. We're concerned."

"I'm sorry about the mural, sweetie. Please talk to us."

Maggie knocked again and shrugged her shoulders. "We're coming in, dear."

Shocked at seeing Ellen lying on the bed so still, Wanda shadowed Maggie over to their friend's limp body. "Is she breathing?"

Maggie bent down and put her ear next to Ellen's face. "Yes, but just barely. I think we should call 911."

Wanda picked up the phone next to the bed, dialed the number, and asked them to send an ambulance immediately.

Maggie brushed Ellen's hair off her face. "Tell them her skin is cold and sweaty."

Wanda relayed the message. "Yes, we'll stay on the line, but I'm going to put you on speaker."

Maggie grabbed a corner of the blanket. "And could you take that box off the bed so we can cover her up?"

Wanda moved around to the other side of the bed. When she grabbed the shoebox, the lid came off. "Oh, Maggie. Poor Ellen! Look at this." Tears streamed down Wanda's face as she held up her grandmother's silver spoons.

Wanda and Purrdita looked up from the couch at the sound of Alberto coming down the stairs. "Did you get Bob settled in for the night?"

"Yes, ma'am. He never even asked why he wasn't going home. Thanks again for calling from the hospital. I can't believe Bob and I never heard the siren. We must have had the game on louder than I thought."

Alberto sat down in his recliner and looked over at his wife. "You've had quite a day. How are you holding up?"

"I'm doing better now that I know Ellen's going to be okay. I almost had a heart attack when we went into her room and found her lying unconscious on the bed." Wanda squeezed her eyes closed and shivered.

"Oh, I can't believe I forgot." Wanda ran out of the room, came back, and handed Alberto a shoebox.

"What's this?" Alberto lifted the lid. "Your grandmother's spoons! Where did you find them?"

Wanda's eyes filled with tears. "I found the package under Ellen's bed when we were helping her look for her jewelry box, but I had no idea what was inside. The spoons were wrapped in Bob's handkerchief. He must have taken them. I'm sure Ellen was horrified, especially because she was so convinced Rita had stolen them." She shook her head. "First Bob's face on the mural and then the spoons. It was too much for her. This is all my fault. We found the empty prescription bottle next to the bed. I might as well have forced those pills down her throat myself." Wanda flung herself full-length onto the couch and buried her head in a pillow.

Lydia Moen

She didn't move when Alberto knelt beside her, nor did she respond when he put his hand on her shoulder and told her it wasn't her fault. "Don't shut me out, querida. We need to talk about this."

Wanda raised her head, then her shoulders, and finally, clutching the pillow in front of her, she curled up in the corner of the couch.

"Thank you, mi esposa. This isn't easy for either of us. But it needs to be said. This is exactly the kind of thing that keeps tripping you up. I love your enthusiasm and your creativity. You have a caring heart and good intentions. But…"

Wanda sat up straighter and stared at her husband. "But what?"

Alberto cringed and ran his fingers through his hair. After waiting several moments, he took a deep breath and said, "But you should have gotten permission before you put anyone's picture in the mural."

Chapter 30

Ellen sat in the recliner and finished her hospital breakfast. She pushed the tray aside and leaned her head back. She had started to doze off when she heard a knock at the door. "Come in," she called.

She smiled when Alberto peeked in. "Is the patient in Room 113 available for visitors?"

"I'm available for you, Alberto. Come over here and sit by the window with me."

"Before you ask, let me tell you that when I left the house, Bob was sound asleep in our guest room. Did you know he snores?"

Ellen chuckled. "Yes, I'm aware of that."

"Anyway, I heard Wanda stirring, and I'm sure she'll make him a hearty breakfast." Alberto patted his stomach and raised his eyebrows. "He'll be fine staying with us for the time being."

"Thank you, Alberto. You and Wanda have been so kind to us." Ellen reached for a tissue and dabbed her eyes. "Would you close the door, please?"

Alberto did as she asked and returned to the chair opposite hers. He sat back and gazed out the window for a moment, and Ellen appreciated his sensitivity in giving her a little time to gather her thoughts

Lydia Moen

At last she spoke. "As you can imagine, I'm totally embarrassed about everything that's happened with Bob and me the last few days. My behavior at the community center yesterday was deplorable. And I guess ending up here is the last scene in a poorly-written melodrama."

"You didn't write this melodrama, Ellen. Yes, you and Bob are the main characters, but the last scene hasn't been written yet. Every good drama has plot twists. We might be at one of those points in your story."

Ellen rocked back and forth, holding herself. "I don't know how much more drama I can take, Alberto."

"I understand. But you're a strong woman, and you have strong friends who are eager to help you."

"I can't watch him every minute of every day, and neither can our friends. You've done way too much already."

"Ellen, we're happy to help. But it may be time for all of us to realize that Bob needs more help than we can give. We're responsible for his safety now because he can't be responsible for himself. Adult daycare has been a good transitional step." Alberto put his hand on hers. "But when you're back on your feet, let's talk about that next scene."

"Lakeshore Lane must be pretty quiet this morning. Alberto was here earlier, and now you two." Ellen held out her arms to embrace her friends.

"Alberto was here?" Wanda frowned. "When was that?"

Maggie gave Wanda a playful nudge. "Aren't you two talking to each other?"

Wanda snapped her head around. "Why would you ask that?"

"I was just kidding."

"Well, I don't think it's very funny."

Ellen looked from Wanda to Maggie. "He wasn't here very long. I'm sure he visits people in the hospital all the time."

"Oh, it doesn't matter. What's important is how you're feeling today." Wanda patted Ellen's hand.

"I'm feeling a lot better, thanks to you two. And, Wanda, thank you so much for taking care of Bob."

"I thought I'd bring him for a visit this afternoon." Wanda sat down on the chair her husband had vacated earlier.

"That's a nice offer, but I think it's better if he doesn't see me here." Ellen twisted her wedding ring. "I've been doing a lot of thinking this morning, Wanda."

Maggie moved toward the door. "I'm going to head down to the cafeteria for a few minutes. Can I bring you two anything?" She snapped her fingers. "Oh, the cupcakes. We should have brought them. Where did they end up, Wanda?"

The chocoholic tilted her head down while looking up at the two of them. She rubbed her tummy and grinned. "I don't think I need anything else."

"I'd love a lemonade." Ellen placed her hand on her heart and looked straight into Maggie's eyes. "And thank you."

As soon as the door closed, Ellen reached for her friend's hand. "I can't believe you came to see me after the way I acted yesterday. I'm so sorry."

"Apology accepted. And I'm sorry I didn't get your permission before I put Bob in the mural."

Ellen graciously accepted her friend's apology and then said, "But there's more." Ellen looked down and fiddled with the tie on her bathrobe. "I found your silver spoons...."

Wanda reached over and gently raised Ellen's chin. "I know. They were lying out on your bed last night. I understand, sweetie. It's the disease."

Before leaving the building, Alberto called on a member of the congregation who was hospitalized. Then he drove to the police station. Although Ray agreed to see him, Alberto did most of the talking. When their time was up, Alberto extended his hand. Ray shook it and scowled. "Thanks, Pastor. You're the only person who visits me."

Alberto heard the phone beep as soon as he came in the door. He hit the play button and heard Wanda's voice. "This is Wanda. I'm going to lunch with Maggie. Bye."

Alberto's jaw dropped. He whacked the receiver against his leg. "What is she thinking?"

He called her right back, jiggling his car keys while he waited for her to pick up. He didn't give her time to finish answering. "I'm assuming you took Bob with you."

"Why would I do that?"

Alberto closed his eyes and shook his head. "We're supposed to be taking care of him. Did you actually leave him here alone?"

"I gave him breakfast, and he was watching a fishing show when Maggie picked me up."

"You don't have your car?" Alberto ran his hand through his hair.

"No, Maggie drove."

"Wanda, your car's not here. I have to find Bob."

Alberto raced out the door and jumped in his car. When he got to the end of the driveway, he looked toward the Baileys' house and saw Wanda's car passenger-side down in the ditch. He turned off the ignition, hopped out, and sprinted toward his wife's vehicle.

His heart pounded as he opened the door. The station wagon was empty.

He scanned the area as he ran to Bob and Ellen's house. As he drew near, he heard the sound of the TV and saw a fisherman reeling in a trout before he found Bob in his gray sweatshirt and blue jeans snoring in his recliner.

"Maggie, pull over." Wanda waved her cellphone at the side of the street.

Maggie glanced in her rearview mirror, then steered the car into a parking lot they were about to pass. Wanda bolted out the door and started pacing, first muttering, then talking, then shouting to herself.

When Maggie reached her, she grabbed Wanda's shoulders. "Tell me what's wrong!"

Wanda's lips and chin began to tremble. "Bob's gone, and he has my car."

Maggie put her arm around her friend. Wanda's whole body shook uncontrollably as she allowed herself to be helped back into the car.

Wanda leaned her head back and closed her eyes. She heard her phone ring just as her friend settled into the driver's seat. "Will you get that?"

"Hello, this is Maggie MacDonald." A moment later, Wanda felt a tap on her shoulder. "It's your husband."

Wanda kept her eyes closed and shook her head.

"Thanks for calling, Alberto. I'll tell Wanda."

Wanda opened her eyes as Maggie turned toward her. "Bob's fine. Alberto found him asleep in front of the TV in the Baileys' living room." Maggie pulled the car back onto the street. "Now let's have a quiet lunch at my house."

Wanda sniffled and looked over at her. "Thanks, sweetie. That sounds perfect."

Lydia Moen

When Alberto flicked off the TV, Bob stopped snoring. Alberto turned and saw Bob leap out of his chair. He had just enough time to duck and avoid the punch headed for his face.

"Bob, it's Alberto. What's the matter?"

"Get out of here before I call the police. And leave my TV where it is!"

"Bob, I was just turning it off so you could rest. I'm your neighbor, Alberto."

"I don't care who you are! Get out of my house!" Bob picked up the fireplace poker, raised it in the air, and swung it at Alberto. When Alberto dodged the cast-iron weapon, it hit one of Ellen's Waterford vases and sent it flying across the room. Before Bob could do any further damage, Alberto grabbed his arm and pried the poker out of his hand.

"You're right, Bob. Let's get out of here. You promised to show me your dock. Are the fishing poles down there?"

"I think so."

As quickly as he had set Bob off, Alberto distracted him and steered him toward the door. They walked down to the lake, picked up two poles, and sat on the dock.

Bob smiled. "This is a great idea. I've wanted to get some fishing in ever since we got here."

Alberto closed his eyes and thanked God for calming the storm.

"Blest be the tie that binds
our hearts in Christian love;
the fellowship of kindred minds
is like to that above."

Wanda sang the words in time with the rocking of the chair she nestled into on Maggie's porch. Images of Alberto, Maggie, Charlie, Ellen, and Bob wrapped up in pastel ribbons binding them to each other, to her, and to Christ floated through her mind.

When she opened her eyes, she saw Alberto sitting on the Baileys' dock with Bob, and she realized she was weeping—tears for the frayed ribbons of relationships that were dear to her. *Have I lost my Christian love?*

The door creaked, and she felt Maggie's hand on her shoulder before she saw her furrowed brow. "Wanda, dear, how can I help?" Maggie set the lunch tray on the table.

"Just make sure I don't let 'the tie that binds' us in Christian love fray, Maggie. If I keep messing up like I have been, I won't have any fellowship that's 'like to that above.'"

Wanda leaned forward and listened when Maggie sat down and started talking. "I love how the words of that hymn take us to the Bible and Hosea's message to the Israelites to stay close to God. Isn't it amazing how the answers to all our problems can be found in the Bible?"

Maggie paused and smiled. "When my life is unraveling, spending time in God's Word mends my spirit. The fabric of my life starts to fray when I'm at my busiest, but God always gives us time for the things that are most important to Him."

"Thank you, Maggie. I needed to hear that. And thank You, heavenly Father, for my sweet friend's 'kindred mind.'" Wanda grabbed a tissue, wiped her tears, and blew her nose.

"Would it help to talk?" Maggie handed Wanda her lunch.

"Yes, if you don't mind my talking between bites. This salad looks scrumptious." Wanda's fork slid into her mouth before Maggie had a chance to answer.

Maggie smiled. "I'll be listening between bites."

Wanda glanced over at the Baileys' dock and confirmed that Alberto was still fishing with Bob. Then she leaned forward and in hushed tones revealed the conflicts that had sprung up between Alberto and her since his return.

"When he was gone, I couldn't wait for him to come back. But now that he's home, I miss being able to set my own schedule."

"I can understand that." Maggie nodded. "I miss Mac terribly, but I do like having the freedom to come and go as I please."

They talked and listened between bites. After a few minutes, Wanda put her plate down and grabbed another tissue. "I know I drive Alberto crazy sometimes." She sniffled and cleared her throat. "But lately he doesn't seem to think I do anything right. First it was not getting started on the mural. Next it was not preparing for the adult daycare party. Then it was not getting permission for the faces on the mural. Now it's not staying home with Bob."

Wanda put her head in her hands. "Sometimes I wonder if we'd both be happier if he went back to Mexico."

Wanda closed the door with her hip and carried the tray of fresh peanut-butter treats and iced tea down to Alberto and Bob. "How are two of my favorite men doing?" She set the tray down between them.

"Better now." Alberto popped one of the treats into his mouth.

"These look good." Bob scratched his head. "I don't think I've ever had them before."

Wanda paused and looked at Alberto. Then she smiled at Bob. "Well, it's about time you tried one. They're my specialty."

Wanda took the scrunchy off her ponytail, redid it, and then fanned her face. "Aren't you fellows hot down here? Let's go over and sit in the gazebo where we have some shade and a fan."

Alberto stood up. "That's a good idea. Come on, Bob. Let's get out of the sun for a while."

"I think I'll stay here, buddy, but you go ahead. It sure is a beautiful day."

Wanda put a couple of peanut-butter treats on a napkin and handed them to Bob along with a glass of iced tea. "Come and join us whenever you're ready."

She picked up the tray and smiled at Alberto. She grabbed his hand as they walked along the path between their homes.

When they sat down in the gazebo, Wanda looked over at Bob staring at the water from the end of his dock. "I'm so relieved Bob's okay. I'm sorry I left him alone. I had no idea he'd wander off."

"He didn't just wander off, Wanda. He took your car, and it's sitting in a ditch down the road. Thankfully, he wasn't hurt. I found him asleep in front of his TV. When I turned it off, he woke up and thought I was trying to steal it. He started swinging an iron poker at me. To tell you the truth, I'm not sure what made him calm down. It must have been divine intervention."

Wanda stared at Alberto, shaking her head in disbelief. "Querido, you could have been killed. Do you think it's safe to have him staying in our house?"

"I'm sure I really startled him. I think as long as we're careful, we'll all be okay. Ellen has never mentioned his being violent in the past. But she may have to come to terms with the fact that she can't keep him at home anymore."

Chapter 31

Alberto turned off the ignition and sat staring at the red brick hospital wall in front of him. He rubbed his face then kneaded his neck. He closed his eyes and leaned back against the headrest.

"Father God, I need You. Tell me what I'm doing wrong. You know how much I love my wife, but my words keep hurting her."

Alberto paused and lowered his head. He recalled Wanda's angry reaction to his offer to stay with Bob so she could go to the community center and work on the mural. He winced at the image of her crossed arms and red face.

"The book of Proverbs says, 'Reckless words pierce like a sword, but the tongue of the wise brings healing.' Give me words of healing, Lord, and help me understand why Wanda and I are having so much trouble. We trust Your plan for our lives. Did I come home too soon? Have I left work undone in the mission field that You want me to complete?"

Alberto raised his head. "Thank You, Father, for hearing my prayer and for the peace that comes from knowing You will answer it. Now help me to focus on ministering to Ellen and Bob. Let my tongue bring healing and comfort."

Alberto got out of the car and strode through the hospital doors, greeting staff members and visitors on his way to Ellen's room.

Ellen was standing at the nurses' station when she felt a hand on her shoulder. She turned around and was greeted by Alberto's warm smile.

"You're up and about. What a nice surprise."

"For me too." Ellen gave the pastor a gentle hug.

Alberto motioned to the bud vase in her hand. "Did you get flowers?"

"Yes. In fact, you're the second Al I've seen today. I'll tell you about it when we get to my room." Ellen grasped the arm that Alberto held out to her. "Thanks. I'm still a little unsteady."

When the pastor opened the door, Ellen went right to the sink and filled the little glass vase with water. She placed a single white carnation in it and breathed in the sweet fragrance. "This is from the other Al I saw today."

The two of them sat down. "Tell me about this other Al."

"There's not much to tell except that he appeared at exactly the right moment. The meeting with the drug counselor was a nightmare. I know he was just doing his job, but it was humiliating. I'm not a drug addict." Ellen looked at the floor and shook her head.

"I was a wreck when I got back to my room, and then Al showed up." She looked at Alberto and smiled. "He only stayed for a moment, but by the time he tipped his red cap and walked out the door, I felt totally different. I can't even tell you what he said, but he did leave a card next to the flower. I haven't looked at it yet." Ellen picked up the white embossed card and read the message aloud. "'Come to Me, all you who are weary and burdened, and I will give you rest' (Matthew 11:28)."

She turned the card over and read the inscription. 'To my friend Ellen. From Al.'

Her jaw dropped, and she stared wide-eyed at Alberto. "How…?"

"God works in mysterious ways." He reached for her hand. "You know, Ellen, before I came in here, I had some heavy burdens of my own. I sat in the parking lot and shared them with God. I asked Him to help me, and He did. He lifted those burdens right off my shoulders and onto His. He'll do the same for you. He's just waiting for you to ask."

"Charlie told me the same thing." Ellen raised an eyebrow and smiled at the pastor. "Have you two been talking about me behind my back?"

Alberto chuckled. "No, but we both talk with the same God."

Ellen winced. "I haven't talked to God in a long time." She looked down at her hands and began twisting her wedding ring. "I'm glad you stopped by to visit before I have to go home."

Alberto sat back in his chair. "When do you think that'll be?"

"At least a couple more days. I called Lizzy, and she's coming tomorrow to stay with her dad."

"And how are you doing, Ellen?"

Ellen smiled and raised her eyebrows. "Well, better than yesterday." She looked straight into Alberto's eyes and frowned. "To tell you the truth, I'm really afraid of what lies ahead for us."

"That's only natural. You've been thrust into the role of caregiver, and it's become a round-the-clock job. Because Alzheimer's attacks the brain, it's especially tough to deal with."

Ellen nodded. "I had no idea how hard this was going to be." She grimaced and gave her head a slight shake. "Alberto, I don't know who I'm dealing with from one minute to the next. He can be resting in his recliner when I walk out of the room. If I come back thirty seconds later, he might be out of his chair, throwing books at the TV."

Alberto's brow furrowed, and he reached over and put his hand on Ellen's. "Are you afraid of him, Ellen? Has he ever been violent with you?"

Ellen stared out the window. When she turned back to Alberto, she spoke in a hushed voice. "He's never hit me or hurt me physically. But..."

Alberto nodded. "Ellen, Wanda and I spent the last twenty-four hours with Bob. We had no idea what you've been dealing with. He needs constant supervision. As you suggested, his reality can change in a matter of seconds. Physically he's a strong and healthy man. You'd be no match for him if he suddenly perceived you as a threat."

Ellen's voice shook. "He's my husband. I promised to have and to hold him in sickness and in health. I didn't say, 'unless he has Alzheimer's.'" Her chin dropped to her chest as her arms squeezed her body.

"Ellen, I'm not suggesting you stop loving Bob or abandon him. When the situation becomes unsafe, your responsibility as his wife is to make the decisions he can no longer make."

"Evening walks feel good, don't they, Sammy?" Maggie's companion gave her a quick smile before lapping up every drop of water in his bowl. "You're thirsty, aren't you? I'll check the answering machine and then get you a refill."

She walked over to the counter, looked at the phone, and sighed. "No messages."

Sammy bumped her leg with his nose. "Okay. I'm thirsty too."

After getting water for both of them, Maggie sat down at the kitchen table and picked up the day's issue of *Lake Breezes*. She scanned the front page and then glanced up at the clock—7:30. She flipped pages until she came to the crossword puzzle. Grabbing a pencil from the catch-all drawer, she began filling in the squares. With half the spaces still empty, she glanced up at the clock again, put down her pencil, and picked up the portable phone. "Come on, Sammy. Let's go down to the dock."

The golden retriever grabbed a tennis ball from his toy basket and raced to the door. After fifteen minutes of toss, swim, and fetch, both participants were played out.

When they got back to the house, Maggie placed the phone in its base; just as quickly she picked it up again, pushed the "talk" button, and put it to her ear. When the dial tone sounded, she closed her eyes and dropped her head.

After brewing herself a cup of tea, Maggie sauntered into the living room, settled herself in a chair, and picked up her current mystery. She opened it to the final chapter and pulled out the bookmark. After reading page 292 four times, she gave up and tossed the book on the end table, knocking the phone onto the floor. As she bent over and picked it up, the dial tone taunted her.

"Okay, I give up." She dialed the number she'd committed to memory just a few months before. After several rings, she heard, "Hello. You've reached Charlie Bingham. I'm not available… "

Charlie leaned forward with one hand on his lower back and the other on the railing, inching his way down the stairs. By the time he got to the kitchen, his stomach was rumbling. "Eight o'clock and I'm just getting around to dinner. No wonder I'm so hungry." He put a frozen pizza in the oven and eased himself into his chair.

He groaned as he reached across the table and picked up the list he'd written that morning. He checked off each item:
- Vacuum and wash out boats
- Trim bushes

- Clean out gutters
- Blow pine needles off driveway
- Wash car

At the bottom of the page he wrote:
- Mow lawn
- Weed front flower bed

With a crisp nod, he checked both of them off. "Alrighty then." He wadded up the list and did a nothing-but-net shot into the waste basket.

At the sound of the timer, Charlie pushed himself up and hobbled to the stove. He slid the pizza onto the cardboard disk, sliced it, and set it on the table. He grabbed a soda from the refrigerator and sat back down.

As Charlie ate, he skimmed the day's issue of *Lake Breezes* and stopped to read the article about Ray Hoffman's arrest. Finishing the story, he put his hand up to the spot on his forehead, closed his eyes, and shook his head from side to side.

The ringing phone interrupted his thoughts. He flinched, raised his head, and looked over to see who was calling. When he saw the name, his heart raced. He reached out but quickly pulled his hand back.

"Hello. You've reached Charlie Bingham. I'm not available...."

The next morning, Maggie hopped into Wanda's station wagon. "Thanks for picking me up." She looked in the backseat and then at Wanda. "I thought Bob was coming with us."

"I was planning to bring him, but Lizzy arrived this morning, so he's back at home with her. She'll be staying for a few days to help her parents out."

Wanda fingered the large stained-glass cross that hung from a cord around her neck. "I love having your company on the way to church, but where's your regular Sunday chauffeur? Did Charlie go out of town? I haven't seen him all weekend."

Maggie frowned. "I'm not sure where he is. In fact, I called him last night just to say hello, but his answering machine picked up."

Wanda shrugged her shoulders and glanced over at Maggie. "We'll probably see him at church."

She parked the car in the nearly empty lot. Maggie tagged along behind her as they entered the church. Her friend stopped to talk with each of the early arrivals, gradually weaving her way to the second row from the front. As usual, they slid toward the center of the pew, leaving room next to Maggie for Charlie.

The organ came to life with the morning's prelude, and the growing crowd of worshipers quieted down. Maggie leafed through the bulletin, occasionally glancing over her shoulder and frowning. She picked up a hymnal and located the first hymn, slipping her bulletin in to mark the page. Then she turned around and craned her neck to see over and around the stragglers still in the central aisle.

Maggie felt a tap on her shoulder, turned around, and scowled at Wanda. "What?" Maggie asked a little louder than she intended.

Wanda leaned over, waved her palm up and down, and whispered, "Stand up!"

Maggie peeked around and popped up. She snapped her hymnal open and started singing.

Throughout the rest of the service, Maggie fidgeted beside the empty seat. In fact, the only times she sat still were when she felt Wanda's hand clamping down on her knee.

She didn't wait for Wanda when the service ended. She spied the back of Charlie's head nearing the door as she slipped into the aisle. By the time she reached the parking lot, neither Charlie nor his car was anywhere to be seen.

Maggie knocked on Ellen's door. As soon as they heard her say "Come in," Wanda nudged it ajar and jiggled a pink bakery bag through the gap.

Ellen swung the door open. "Friends bearing gifts! The long-awaited cupcakes have finally arrived." The cord of three strands tangled itself in a big hug.

Maggie stepped back. "I bet you'd love to get outside for a while. Let's pick up soft drinks in the cafeteria and sit out in the atrium."

Five minutes later, the three settled around an umbrella table. Maggie smiled to herself at the picture they made—Ellen dressed in her robe, Wanda garbed in gold, scarlet, and orange, and herself in mint green and white. Their purses were equally distinct—Ellen with none, Wanda's huge striped tote, and Maggie's white clutch purse.

Wanda opened the pink bag and handed out the cupcakes with chocolate frosting and sprinkles. "Have you seen Lizzy yet? She looked so pretty when she stopped by this morning."

Ellen shook her head. "I can't wait to see her, but I don't want Bob to visit me here. She'll come tomorrow when her dad's at daycare."

Maggie peered over her glasses. "Why don't I spend some time fishing with him so she can get here today? I don't have anything going on this afternoon." She frowned and shrugged her shoulders. "Or this evening, for that matter."

"That would be perfect, Maggie. He loves to fish, and it'll give Lizzy and me a chance to talk."

Ellen tilted her head and narrowed her eyes. "Is everything all right, Maggie? Any more news on Josh?"

"No, nothing new from overseas."

Ellen hesitated. "We haven't known each other as long as you and Wanda have, but I can tell something's bothering you. Maybe we can help."

Maggie lowered her eyes and tapped her fingers on the table. "The cord has more important things to deal with right now. I'll be fine."

Ellen reached for Maggie's hand. "I think the cord is strong enough to weave through more than one person's snag at a time."

Wanda plunked her hand on top of the other two and gave them a squeeze. "Absolutely!"

"It's Charlie." Maggie frowned and shook her head. "I can't figure him out. I don't know if he's mad at me or tired of me, but all of a sudden, he's ignoring me."

Wanda snorted and a drip of soda escaped the hand she threw over her mouth. "Maggie, for heaven's sake. The man can't keep his eyes off you."

"Are you kidding me? He's crazy about you." Ellen paused. "Something else must be bothering him."

Maggie sat back in her chair and hesitated before answering. "I don't know if it's bothering him, but he's developed a red blotch near his hairline. We've talked about it, and he said it's nothing to worry about."

Wanda leaned forward and frowned at Maggie. "When exactly did you talk about it?"

"Let me think. I told him he needed to see a doctor and get it checked out. I guess it was Thursday morning. Yes, because both Friday and Saturday, my mail was already in the box when I went down to meet him."

Ellen drew her eyebrows together. "You haven't talked to him since Thursday?"

Maggie shook her head. "He didn't even sit with us in church this morning."

"That's true, sweetie," Wanda said, "but he probably just came in late."

"Maybe, but I could swear he ran out so he wouldn't have to talk to me."

Ellen put her hand on Maggie's. "Does he always talk with you after church?"

"We sit together, and for the last few weeks, we've gone to the marina for brunch afterwards."

Wanda broke the awkward silence that followed. "It's a proven fact that chocolate is good for the mind. Let's eat."

The three friends picked up their cupcakes and pulled the paper off. The corners of Maggie's mouth crept up as she watched Wanda lick the frosting from the paper and toss it on her plate. At the same time, Ellen folded hers in half and then in half again before putting it in a napkin and doubling the napkin over several times.

Partway through her cupcake, Wanda leaned over. "Maggie, you have an abundance of patience. If you didn't, I guess we couldn't be friends."

Maggie took a sip of her soda. "What are you saying, Wanda?"

"I think you just need to be patient with Charlie. He'll come around and talk when he's ready."

Chapter 32

Charlie sat on his porch and waited for Alberto's car to pull into the driveway. Every few minutes, he lowered his copy of *Lake Breezes* and looked down the street before checking his watch. His ride arrived promptly at 9:00 a.m.

The postman hustled down the stairs but stopped short of the car. He breathed in the pleasing perfume of Fae's roses as his eyes embraced the vibrant colors of the bushes that hugged the driveway.

His hand trembled a bit when he reached for the door handle. "Thanks for the lift, Alberto. I thought I could drive myself, but I'm glad you talked me out of it."

"I am too. How are you feeling about all this?"

Charlie stared out the window. "I'm not sure how I feel. I guess I'll know better when we get the results."

Half an hour later, Charlie was wheeled into an operating room. The pungent odor of disinfectant and the glare of surgical lights against white walls and stainless steel surfaces assaulted his senses. He winced at the sting of the numbing agent invading his forehead. Even after a nurse covered him with a heated blanket, he continued to shiver.

The procedure went quickly, and Charlie smiled as he approached

Lydia Moen

Alberto in the waiting room. His friend stood up and put his hand on Charlie's shoulder. "That was fast. How did it go?"

Charlie clutched his hat in his hand and took a deep breath. "Easier than I expected. How about you? Did you get bored waiting?"

"Not at all. I sneaked down to see a couple of patients while you were gone."

Charlie frowned. "And how are they doing?"

"They're fine. Both of them should be out of the hospital in the next couple of days." He glanced down at Charlie's hands. "I see your cap is in your hand and not on your head. Does that mean you won't be wearing one for a few days because of that bandage?"

The tightness in Charlie's shoulders eased, and he rubbed the back of his neck. "Nope. I told the doctor straight out that I can't do my job without my cap. It's part of the uniform. I'll just have to loosen the back for a few days." He turned toward the elevators.

Alberto held up his hand. "You probably haven't had anything to eat since last night. How about if I treat you to breakfast in the cafeteria? Shirley whips up a mean omelet."

"That works for me!" Charlie did an about-face.

While they waited for their omelets, the men talked about plans for the fall Bible study. "It'll be great to have you leading the discussions again. You're not heading back to Mexico, are you?"

Alberto reached for his coffee and took a long sip. Then he raised his eyes. "I hope not, but we haven't made a final decision yet."

The waitress walked up to their table. "Here you go, gentlemen. Two omelets. Who has the bacon?" Alberto raised his hand, and she turned her attention to Charlie. "Then you must be the sausage. Can I get you anything else?"

Alberto lifted his cup. "Just refills on the coffee, please."

When she left, Alberto leaned forward. "Charlie, this has to be difficult for you after losing Fae and then Mac to cancer."

Charlie lowered his head and sat in silence for a moment. Then he looked Alberto in the eye. "My only concern is for Maggie. She just fought a long battle against cancer with Mac. I don't want her to go through that again." He shook his head. "I've been trying to put a little distance between us. The more time we spend together, the harder it'll be to walk away if I get bad news from the biopsy. But I have to admit, I missed her this weekend."

Alberto nodded his head. "I understand your wanting to spare her from losing someone she's close to again. You and Maggie had strong marriages that ended much sooner than you expected. But I think you can feel comfortable that she'll seek God's wisdom in this relationship. You don't have to make the decision for her."

Charlie put his elbow on the table and rubbed his chin. "I know you're right, but…"

Maggie sat on the dock, bouncing her knee and staring at the print in front of her. She let out a heavy sigh and flipped the page back over. "Let's try it one more time, Sammy. 'Madelaine spied the first northern oriole of the season that morning.'" Looking up, Maggie peeked over at the point for Charlie's boat, grimaced, and returned to her novel.

The golden retriever had been dozing in the warm sunshine but stood up when Maggie said his name. When her knee started bouncing up and down again, Sammy gently placed his soft but heavy head on her thigh. Maggie stilled her knee and bent over to ruffle her companion's ears. "Am I driving you crazy, big boy?"

Sammy circled several times then sank down on the dock, resting his chin on his owner's feet. Maggie glanced at the point again before going back to her book. "'Madelaine spied the first northern oriole of the season that morning.'" She sighed, set the book down on the dock, and closed her eyes.

Maggie didn't stir until she sensed Sammy rising to his paws. "Is he finally coming?" She bolted out of her chair and fluffed her hair, surprised at Sammy's low growl. She blinked and shielded her eyes from the sun. "Sammy, why are you growling at Charlie?"

Sammy walked to the end of the dock. When his growling turned to barking, Maggie focused on the approaching mail boat.

"Sammy, sit." She frowned and tilted her head. "Good morning, John. Where's Charlie?"

John shrugged his shoulders. "I don't know. I just got called in to take over his route today."

Wanda marched straight to the director's office when she arrived at the community center. She peeked around the doorjamb. "Hi, Ruth. I'm back to work on the mural."

Ruth stood up. "Good to see you, Wanda. Let me help you carry some of your things." She reached for the large portfolio that balanced precariously under Wanda's arm.

The director led Wanda down the hall. "You're the second Santiago I've seen this morning. I just ran into Alberto at the hospital."

"He's there all the time visiting with the patients and their families. My husband has a heart of gold." Wanda sighed. "I'm truly blessed."

Ruth nodded. "It's refreshing to see a woman who appreciates her spouse. That seems uncommon these days."

"Oh, I don't know what I'd do without Alberto. He's an absolute angel." The two women reached the table across from the mural and set down Wanda's equipment.

"When I saw him, he was in the cafeteria having breakfast with Charlie Bingham. I think Charlie must have had some kind of procedure on his forehead." Ruth smiled at Wanda. "But I suppose you know all about that."

Wanda kept her own smile frozen on her face until she heard the click-click-click of Ruth's heels going back down the hall. As she disappeared around the corner, Ruth called out, "Let me know if there's anything else I can do for you."

Wanda turned her back to Ruth and muttered under her breath, "You can call my husband and ask him what's going on with the man my best friend is dating—and why he didn't tell me." She grabbed the edge of the table with both hands, clenched her jaw, and snatched a stick of chalk from the box. She paused a moment, narrowing her eyes, then snapped the chalk in half and threw it down. Seizing a darker alternative, she whirled around and attacked the wall.

Twenty minutes later, sweat beading on her brow, she stepped back from the mural and crossed her arms.

Click-click-click.

Wanda froze, her eyes as wide as the lump in her throat. Her head swiveled toward the approaching footsteps. She lurched forward and planted herself in front of her recent artwork.

"Just checking to see if you need the overhead today." Ruth picked up the broken chalk and set it on the table.

Wanda captured a bead of sweat from the end of her nose just before it dropped to the floor. "Thanks for asking, Ruth, but that won't be necessary. I believe I'm finished for today."

"Your face is flushed. Are you feeling all right?"

Wanda fanned herself with her hand. "It's kind of warm in here. Maybe I'll come back later."

Lydia Moen

Ruth clasped her hands under her chin and grinned at Wanda. "Can I see what you've done this morning? I've never watched an artist work before."

Wanda felt the color drain from her face, and she was sure Ruth could hear her heart pounding. "Oh, I'm really not very happy with what I did this morning. In fact, I was just about to erase it." Wanda began rubbing her back against the wall.

Ruth put her arm between Wanda and the mural. "Don't do that. You'll ruin your shirt. And I'm really fascinated by how your mind works."

Wanda let out a low moan, her arms hanging at her sides. "I'm afraid my mind blew a fuse today." As she stepped away, she heard Ruth gasp. The director was standing two feet in front of Wanda's depiction of Alberto's face, sneering from behind a black handlebar mustache.

Wanda breezed by the church secretary with a wave and a quick "Hi, Helen" and then blew into her husband's office.

At the bang of the closing door, Alberto took his feet off the windowsill and spun his chair around. When he held up his index finger to silence her, Wanda stepped up to his desk, crossed her arms, and began tapping her foot.

"Let me get back to you on that, Harold. I've got someone in my office." Alberto hung up the phone, stood, and walked around the desk. "What a nice surprise. Are you here to steal me away for an intimate lunch at the Water's Edge Inn?"

Before she could answer, he put his arm around her and whisked her toward the door. Almost as quickly, he pulled his arm back, frowned, and rubbed his sleeve. "Querida, you have black chalk all over your back. What did you lean up against?"

Wanda jammed her hands onto her hips. "I'm not here to get your critique of my appearance. I'm here to find out about Charlie."

Alberto took a step back and put a finger to his lips. "Let's sit over here and try to keep our voices down."

Wanda flounced over to the chair Alberto had pulled out for her, turned her back on it, and plopped herself down in the opposite seat.

Alberto sat down and leaned back. "Wanda, what's upsetting you?"

She threw her arms in the air. "How would you feel if you found out from a mere acquaintance that your spouse was hiding things from you?"

"Wanda, what are—"

"Don't pretend you don't know what I'm talking about. Ruth Butler saw you and Charlie at the hospital this morning. She said his head was wrapped in bandages and you were comforting him. I want to know what's going on and why you kept it from me!"

She frowned. "Did you ever think about how Maggie might feel? Do you have any idea how frantic she's been? How brokenhearted she is? You should have told me what was going on, so I could have eased her mind."

"That's exactly why I didn't tell you. If Charlie wanted Maggie to know, he would have told her himself." Alberto leaned forward, his gaze penetrating hers.

"Did you suggest that to him?" Wanda fired back.

Alberto's voice rose. "Did you suggest to Maggie that she call Charlie?"

Wanda sat back and smirked. "Let's try to keep our voices down. The reason she's upset is that she hasn't seen him for days and he isn't answering her calls."

Alberto ran his fingers through his hair. "This is a matter between

Charlie and Maggie. We have enough issues of our own without taking on theirs."

"You're right. We do have issues." Wanda stood up, turned her back on Alberto, and stormed through the door, closing it firmly behind her.

As soon as Maggie's car pulled into the driveway from the hospital, Ellen heard the yelling.

"Who do you think you are?"

"I'm your daughter, and I'm telling you that you need to take a shower."

At the sound of a crash, Ellen glanced up at their bedroom window. "Maggie, will you come in with me?" They both raced to the door and ran upstairs.

Bob stepped over the broken lamp. "Ellen, where have you been? This woman is trying to make me take my clothes off."

"Mom, thank goodness you're home! I just wanted Dad to get cleaned up before you got here," Lizzy stammered through her tears. "I'm sorry you had to come back to this. I wanted everything to be perfect."

Ellen brought a shaky hand to her forehead as she looked over at Maggie and mouthed the words, "I don't know what to do."

Maggie walked over and put her hand on Bob's arm. "It's lunchtime. Let's go down to the kitchen, and I'll get us something to eat."

Bob grinned at Maggie. "That sounds good."

Ellen closed the door when she heard Bob and Maggie chattering downstairs. She opened her arms to Lizzy, and the two of them sank down on the edge of the bed. She held her daughter and stroked her hair as the younger woman's sobs turned to soft tears and, finally, to silence.

"It's okay, Lizzy. I'm sorry you had such a hard time. It's not your dad. It's the Alzheimer's."

Ellen reached for the phone as soon as the ring invaded their closeness. "Hello."

"Oh good, you're home. It's Wanda."

"Are you okay? You sound like you've been running."

"Is Maggie there?"

Ellen sat up and frowned. "She's downstairs with Bob. Do you want me to get her?"

"No, just tell her to call her son, Daniel, right away. He's trying to reach her and left a message on our phone."

Ellen stood up. "Is there news about Josh?"

"I don't know, but it sounded urgent."

Chapter 33

Charlie noticed the blinking red light on his phone as soon as he got home from the hospital. He leaned back against the kitchen counter, crossed one ankle over the other, and then did the same with his arms. He stared at the light, bringing one hand up to his chin and rubbing it. He sat down at the table and then jumped up and pressed the play button.

"Hi, Charlie. This is Maggie. I'm calling to make sure you're okay. Sammy and I missed you when John delivered the mail this morning. You don't have to return my call. I don't want to be a nuisance. I just want you to know that I'm thinking about you."

Charlie rubbed his neck and patted the bandage on his forehead. Then he hit the play button a second time and sat down. He leaned back and closed his eyes as he listened to Maggie's voice. At the end of the message, he rested his elbows on the table, clasped his hands, and bowed his head.

A few minutes later, Charlie stood, picked up his cap and keys, and headed for the car. He pulled into Brandt Park, turned off the engine, and rolled down his windows. Then he let his gaze drift over to the picnic table Maggie and he had shared. He smiled at the memory of her reaching across the table with a napkin and dabbing an errant bit of fried chicken from his chin. Then the image of her face when Junior pointed out the spot on his forehead flashed into his mind.

Charlie stepped out of the car and leaned against the door to close it. He put his hands in his pockets and, with head bent down, meandered in the direction of the lake.

"Is that you, Charlie?"

The postman turned his head. "Al. Twice in one week! How are you doing?"

Al tapped a spot next to him on the bench. "I'm fine, but you look like you've been in a fight."

Charlie sat down. "Just trying to get a little attention."

"Speaking of attention, where's your friend Maggie?" Al turned and looked toward the car.

"I'm not sure where she is."

"I wouldn't let that one get too far away. You looked a lot happier when you were with her."

Charlie tilted his head and raised an eyebrow. "So you don't think I'm looking very happy today?"

Al shook his head. "You look like a man who's wrestling with a dilemma."

"I didn't know it showed."

"The bandage was a dead giveaway." Al leaned over and gave Charlie a light poke in the arm.

Charlie winced and rubbed his arm. "Hey, man, take it easy. I've had a rough day."

They both chuckled, and Charlie noticed Al's smile fade. The older gentleman leaned forward. "Do you want to tell me about it? I'm a pretty good listener."

Charlie told Al about his biopsy and his decision to pull away from Maggie. "My pastor, who's also a friend, has me questioning that decision."

"So you're concerned about cancer, and you think Maggie can't handle it." Al furrowed his brow.

Charlie waved off Al's comment. "Oh, no, Maggie's a very strong woman. But her husband died of cancer, and I don't want her to go through that again."

"So you don't want her to suffer. Very commendable. How does she feel about that?"

Charlie paused. "I guess I don't know."

"Maybe that would be a good thing to find out." Al reached in his shirt pocket and pulled out a small white card. Embossed on one side were the words, "Love is patient and kind…. Love never gives up, never loses faith, is always hopeful, and endures through every circumstance. Love will last forever… (1 Corinthians 13:4a, 7-8a)."

Maggie looked up from her lunch with Bob when she heard Ellen hurrying down the steps. "Do you need something, Ellen?"

"Maggie, that was Wanda on the phone. Daniel called her and wants you to call him."

Maggie gasped. A shiver ran through her as she pulled out her cellphone and hit Daniel's number on speed dial.

Ellen tapped her on the shoulder. "Why don't you go out on the porch? The reception's better, and you'll have some privacy."

Maggie hustled outside. She paced back and forth, waiting for her son to answer and forcing her shaking hand to hold on to the phone. When the ringing finally stopped, she heard Daniel's voice on the line.

"Mom, they found Josh." Maggie could barely hear her son's next words through her shouts of joy. She fell to her knees, tears flooding her cheeks. She released her grip on the phone and clasped her hands together. She could hear Daniel's voice calling to her but couldn't rip one hand from the other to answer him.

Maggie looked up. "Merciful Father!" Seconds later she collapsed into Ellen's arms as her friend knelt down beside her. She watched Ellen pick up the phone and press the speaker button.

"Mom! Are you there?"

Maggie looked at Ellen and shook her head.

"Daniel, this is Ellen Bailey. I live down the road from your mother. I have you on speaker so Maggie can hear you."

"Is she okay?"

Maggie nodded her head. "She is. Just overwhelmed."

Maggie reached for the phone and spoke, her voice trembling. "I'm here, Daniel. Tell me everything."

Ellen started to stand, but Maggie put a hand on her shoulder and mouthed, "Please stay."

"Their buddies found Josh and Chris hiding in enemy territory and called for a helicopter to rescue them. They're on their way to a military base in Germany, and we've been told they're both going to make full recoveries."

By the time the conversation ended, Maggie and Ellen were sitting next to each other on the glider. Maggie leaned into the arm that Ellen wrapped around her shoulders. "Thank You, God."

"Yes, thank God they're safe." Ellen gave Maggie's shoulder a gentle squeeze.

The door swung open, and Wanda appeared. "They're safe?"

Maggie jumped up to hug Wanda. "Yes. They've been rescued, and they're on their way to Germany."

"Praise the Lord! Thank You, Jesus. Your mercies are new every day." Wanda's hands flew to her heart as she sat down across from her friends.

Maggie looked at Ellen. "Would you fill Wanda in while I call Tamara Jefferson? Josh and Chris are in her husband's unit, and she's been praying for them."

While Maggie spoke with Tamara, call-waiting beeped in. "Could you hold on a minute, Tamara? I'm getting another call. It might be about Josh." Maggie checked the number, cocked her head, and then shook it. "I don't need to take it," she said when she resumed the conversation.

When Maggie hung up the phone, she turned to Wanda. "Would you call Charlie and tell him the news about Josh? He beeped in when I was on with Tamara."

Wanda frowned and shrugged her shoulders. "Why don't you call him? I would imagine he'd rather hear it from you."

"I'm not so sure about that."

Tears welled up in Ellen's eyes as she watched her husband and daughter walk past the porch, fishing poles in hand. "Lizzy's going home tonight. I know she can't stay forever, but I don't know how I'll manage on my own. To be honest, I couldn't have gotten this far without your help, but you can't be here twenty-four hours a day." Ellen paused and looked down toward the dock. "Bob is becoming a handful. His symptoms are getting more threatening every day."

Wanda's quiet words pulled Ellen's attention back to their conversation. "We saw some of that while you were in the hospital."

Ellen put her hands up to her face and looked over at Wanda. "I was afraid something might happen. What did he do?"

"Everything turned out fine, but we had some scary moments. While Maggie and I were visiting you in the hospital and before Alberto got home from seeing you, Bob took my car."

Ellen gasped. "Are you kidding me? Did he get arrested?"

"Thankfully he didn't get that far. The car went into the ditch at the end of the road, and Bob just got out and walked home. But when Alberto found him in your living room, he startled him out of a nap." Wanda paused.

"What happened?" Ellen felt every muscle in her body tightening.

Wanda put her hand on Ellen's. "Sweetie, Bob thought Alberto was stealing his TV. He went after him with a fireplace poker."

Ellen let out an anguished moan as her chin dropped to her chest.

"Mercy." Maggie clasped her hands. "Thankfully Alberto is strong enough to take care of himself. But Bob certainly could have hurt Lizzy today, and he could hurt you, himself, or somebody else tomorrow."

Ellen raised her head and threw up her arms. "What should I do?"

With Bob settled in his recliner watching a baseball game, Ellen and Lizzy took their iced tea out to the porch and sat down on the glider.

Ellen let out a long sigh and rested her head on her daughter's shoulder. "It's been wonderful having you here, Lizzy. Thanks so much for coming. I hate to see you go."

"I'll be back, soon and often." Lizzy took a sip of tea and put her glass down on the table. "I had no idea how hard things are for you, Mom. Dad really scared me today. It was like he was a totally different person. Is he ever like that with you?"

Ellen watched a lone mallard glide past the dock and settle down on their shore. "He's never hurt me, and I don't want to believe he ever would. But I do believe your father's world is spinning out of control."

"Tell me what's going on, Mom."

"At first the problems were more annoying than frightening. I couldn't count on him. Did I ever tell you he gave Ray Hoffman his credit card? The same man who's now in jail for stealing his tools."

She shook her head. "Then things got more serious. Remember when he set the plastic soup container on the stove and started a fire? Right after that, he got picked up by the police for driving without a license. And in a single afternoon, he started fights at both the DMV and the police station."

Lizzy squeezed her hand as Wanda continued. "Last week I found Wanda's silver spoons hidden under our bed, along with the jewelry box I'd been scouring the house for."

"And you think Dad stole the spoons and hid them with your jewelry box? Why would he do that?" Lizzy stared at her mother and shook her head.

"His mother had a collection of spoons like that. I suppose he thought they were hers. He seems to be afraid that people are trying to steal things from him. I've learned that's not uncommon for people with Alzheimer's."

Ellen took a deep breath. "As hard as all that's been, it's the threat of violence I can't deal with. I had a long talk with Maggie and Wanda this afternoon. I've decided it's best for everyone, especially your dad, to move him to an Alzheimer's facility."

The sound of glass shattering on the other side of the screen door brought both women to their feet.

Chapter 34

Wanda worked in her studio all evening. Then she went straight to bed without giving her husband their nightly kiss.

The next morning, Wanda waited to peek her head out from under the pillow until she heard the bedroom door close. "Is he gone, Purrdita?" she whispered. "I don't know how much longer I can stay in bed pretending to be asleep." When she heard Alberto down in the kitchen, both she and her cat sat up and stretched.

A few minutes later, she heard the kitchen door close. Wanda hopped out of bed, threw off her pajamas, and slipped into a sweat suit. Just as she reached for the CD player's on/off switch for a dose of praise and worship music, she heard footsteps on the stairs.

Wanda snatched her PJs from the floor, dove into bed, and pulled the covers up to her chin. *What is he doing back in the house? I don't want to talk with him. Why can't he just leave me alone?*

She yawned a "Come in" to the tap on the door then held her breath, maintaining her firm grip on the covers as her husband approached the bed. "Am I waking you up?"

"It's okay. Did you want something?" Wanda yawned and blinked her eyes.

Lydia Moen

Alberto leaned over to hand her a tray of coffee, donuts, and a just-picked rose from the garden.

Wanda grasped the covers more tightly. "Just put it on the nightstand."

Wanda moved her legs over, and Alberto sat down next to her. She bit her lower lip and waited for him to speak.

"Querida, I want to talk with you before I leave for work. I know I've been making your life more stressful, and I'm sorry. I love you, and I don't want you to be miserable." Alberto hesitated. "Would you be happier if I went back to Mexico for a while?"

"Go back to Mexico? You just got home!" She blinked as unexpected tears bit her eyes.

"That's not what I want to do. I want to be here with you. I need you, Wanda. I need your spontaneity, your creativity, your passion...."

When Alberto reached for Wanda's hand, she gripped the covers even tighter. "But those are the very things you've been trying to fix!"

Alberto ran his hand through his hair. "Fix? Is that what you think I'm trying to do? You don't need fixing, querida. I just hate to see you so stressed. I want to make your life easier. How can I do that?"

"Just love me, Alberto. And pray for me."

"I've been doing that since the day I met you, and I'll continue to do that forever. Now what are you hiding under that sheet you won't let go of?" Alberto's eyebrows shot up when he pulled back the corner of the covers. "Oh, ho! So I didn't wake you up after all!"

Wanda let go of the covers and opened her sweatshirted arms to her husband. "Come here and give me a hug, querido. That donut looks delicious, but I'm hungry for a little Santiago sugar this morning."

Maggie would have known Labor Day was approaching without

looking at the calendar. The maple tree outside her living room window was beginning to reveal hints of yellows, oranges, and reds. And the zesty aroma of cinnamon, the sweet, fresh smell of apples, and the rich, earthy scent of walnuts wafted from her kitchen in a blend of autumn fragrances that had become irresistible.

Maggie put down her devotional book, stood up, and turned to Sammy. "Those muffins have to be cool by now. Let's have one with a cup of tea."

She wanted to savor the first bite but had to swallow it to answer the phone. "Daniel, I was so excited I could hardly sleep. Have you heard anything else?"

"We just got off the phone with Josh. He sounded weak and tired, but he said they're getting first-class medical care at the base in Germany. I'm running late to the office. I'll call you again when I have time. And Mom, he sends you his love."

Maggie closed her eyes, bowed her head, and sent up yet another prayer of thanks and praise. When she opened her eyes, Sammy was standing in front of her, wagging his tail and panting.

The motion of Charlie's boat pulling up to her dock caught her eye, and she knew what Sammy was excited about. "Go lie down, Sammy. We'll get the mail later." The golden obeyed but kept his ears cocked and his eyes on his mistress.

Maggie turned off the light on the table next to her. She watched Charlie take frequent peeks up at the house while he sorted and re-sorted his mail. Finally he beeped his horn and called out her name.

At the sound of the mail-boat horn, Sammy barked and ran to the door. Maggie didn't move.

She watched with tear-filled eyes as the postman pulled his boat away from her dock. "Come and lie down, Sammy. We're not going to see Charlie today."

Lydia Moen

Ellen wasn't sure if the bird calls had awakened her. She kept her eyes closed, listening to the cheerful songs of the robins, chickadees, and nuthatches. The warm lake breeze caressed her face, carrying with it the smell of pine wrapped in the fragrance of the clematis that climbed the trellis outside her window. She yawned and stretched under her blanket.

Her senses aroused, she opened her eyes, frowned, and then turned her face up a bit. She listened for the familiar snore from the other side of the bed but didn't hear it. Anticipating the musky scent of Bob's aftershave, she breathed in deeply but didn't smell it.

Ellen turned over and propped herself on her elbow. She flopped back down on the bed with a groan. "Oh, no. He's already up."

She dragged herself out of bed, threw on her robe, and clattered down the stairs. When Ellen spotted the open kitchen door, she ran outside. She circled the house, glancing down at the lake, checking the workshop, and looking up and down the lane.

Ellen stood at the end of the driveway, crossing her arms and rubbing the sleeves of her robe as images flashed through her mind—Bob wandering in the woods, lying at the side of a road, at the bottom of…

She ran to the garage and punched in the code. Both cars were inside. She tugged on the handle of his sedan, then cupped her hands to her eyes and looked inside. She ran to her van, swung open the driver's door, and spied a rumpled form in the dimly lit backseat.

"Bob! Is that you?"

Alberto pulled into the parking spot reserved for clergy and approached the stately main building of The Harbor at Water's Edge. As he crossed the spacious porch, its roof supported by solid round pillars, he spoke to several residents.

"Good morning, Mrs. Johnson. Has your grandson gone back to the university yet?"

"He goes down to Madison next week to start football practice."

"Go, Badgers!" Alberto held up his hand and received a spirited high-five from the elderly woman.

He exchanged a personal greeting with each senior he met before heading inside to the director's office. Don Carey was standing at the receptionist's desk with two cups of black coffee when Alberto walked in.

The pastor reached out one hand to grab a mug and the other to shake the director's hand. "Best free coffee in town. Thanks for seeing me on such short notice."

When they were seated in Don's office, Alberto handed the director a piece of paper. "I think you'll find most of the important details here."

Alberto watched his friend's eyes scan down the page. "Robert Bailey, fifty-three. Lakeshore Lane." He peered up at Alberto. "That's right. You said he's your neighbor. And this would be an emergency admission?"

Alberto nodded. "As of today, if at all possible. Ellen Bailey left a message on my answering machine last night, asking me to help find a place for Bob right away."

"We do have a room available. We'll just require basic insurance information to get him in here. Mrs. Bailey can complete the rest of the paperwork in the next day or two."

Alberto stood up, looked the director in the eye, and reached across the desk to shake his hand. "I really appreciate your making this possible, Don. They need your help."

Don stood up. "That's what we're here for. Let's go downstairs, and

I'll show you the available room."

Alberto followed him out of the office and down to the Alzheimer's unit. As the two men entered Bob's room, Alberto went straight to the window. "What a view!"

When he turned around to Don, the director had a gleam in his eye and a satisfied smile on his face. "It took a lot of planning, but we found a way to give every resident a window facing the lake."

When Alberto turned to leave, he recognized the large painting on the wall across from the bed. It depicted an elderly gentleman wearing a fishing hat, standing on a dock, and reeling in a big bass. "Perfect. Bob will begin and end each day seeing a reflection of himself. He'll catch that whopper a thousand times."

Ellen shoved the door open and jumped into the van. "Bob, wake up! What are you...?" When her hand grasped the limp blanket, she sank onto the backseat among the clothes she'd intended to drop off at the cleaners. "Oh, Bob, where are you?"

Ellen backed out of the van, slid the door shut, and stumbled into the house. She grabbed the phone and collapsed into a kitchen chair.

When Wanda answered, Ellen cried out, "Is Bob with you?"

"No, he isn't. Have you checked with Maggie?" The anxiety she heard in Wanda's voice heightened her own fear.

Ellen's words spilled out through her tears. "I was going to, but could you?"

"Yes, and we'll be right over."

At the sound of steps entering her kitchen several minutes later, Ellen looked up and raised her eyebrows. When only Maggie appeared behind Wanda, she bent over and cradled her head in her hand.

After they joined her at the table, Ellen lifted her head. "He's gone."

Wanda leaned forward. "We're here to help, sweetie. Can you tell us what happened?"

Ellen nodded her head and cleared her throat. "Bob overheard Lizzy and me talking about a care facility for him. He was furious.

"Lizzy wanted to stay, but I made her leave. Bob and I argued for a long time before he finally got tired and went to bed. I went up half an hour later, and he was sound asleep." She sighed. "But I couldn't sleep. I tossed and turned for hours. I remember checking the clock. It was two-thirty, and Bob was snoring."

Ellen shook her head. "The last time we had an argument like this, Bob had forgotten all about it by morning. I thought he'd forget about this one too, but evidently he didn't. I think he ran away. He's terrified, and I don't blame him."

Maggie grabbed a notepad and pencil from the counter. "Do the police know he's missing?"

Ellen wrinkled her brow and looked at Maggie. "Are you kidding? They won't do anything about a missing person for forty-eight hours."

Wanda stood up and pulled the cellphone from her pocket. "The authorities are a little more flexible here. Besides, I happen to know the police chief has a soft spot for your hubby."

Ellen closed her eyes. "Thank you."

Once Wanda was connected with Carlos, she put the phone on speaker and described the situation.

"Is Mrs. Bailey with you now?" Carlos asked.

Ellen's voice trembled. "Yes, Chief Gallego, I'm here. We're at our house. Maggie MacDonald is here too."

"I'm sorry to hear your husband is missing, but I'm glad you called us."

Carlos asked if Ellen knew when Bob had disappeared, what he was wearing, and whether he was on foot, in a car, or in a boat.

"Our cars and boats are all here." Ellen shrugged her shoulders. "But I don't know exactly when he left or what he was wearing. He was sound asleep at two-thirty. He probably just pulled on jeans and a gray sweatshirt. I can check to see if those things are missing and get back to you."

"We'll get patrol cars and boats out looking for him right away. It's a small town, and the guys all know him. If you have different information about what he's wearing, we can radio that to them. The best thing you can do is stay right where you are. What phone number should we use to contact you?"

Ellen gave him her home and cell numbers, thanked him, and hung up.

Maggie's eyes widened. "Have you tried Bob's cellphone?"

"No!" Ellen grabbed the phone from the table and punched in his number. She glanced from Maggie to Wanda. "It's ringing."

The electronic melody of *Anchors Aweigh* drifted down the staircase. Ellen dropped the phone and started sobbing.

As soon as Maggie picked it up and ended the call, the music from Bob's phone stopped.

When Ellen came downstairs after a quick shower, she heard her friends' voices out on the porch and joined them. "That felt good." She looked at the muffins on the table and asked where they came from.

Ellen smiled when Wanda waved her thumb in Maggie's direction. "Thanks, Maggie. I didn't realize I was hungry, but I am."

Maggie passed her the muffins. "Did you find Bob's sweatshirt and jeans up there?"

Ellen shook her head. "No, and they were lying on the chair when I went to bed. He must be wearing them. They've become his uniform." Her lip trembled, and Maggie handed her a tissue.

Maggie turned to Wanda. "Were you able to reach Alberto?"

"Yes. He's out looking for Bob now. When I spoke with him, he was just leaving The Harbor."

Ellen tilted her head and furrowed her brow. "He must have gotten my message. Do you know anything about the place?"

Maggie set her teacup on the saucer and leaned toward Ellen. "It's a beautiful care facility on Jade Lake. I have several friends living there, and they love it."

Wanda nodded. "Alberto's over there all the time. It's one of his favorite stops. He met with the director, Don Carey, this morning."

Ellen stood up and walked over to the railing, closed her eyes, and took a deep breath. "What did he find out?"

"They have a room for Bob…if you want it."

Ellen turned toward Wanda but kept her eyes on the floor. "How soon could he move in?" She wiped a tear from her cheek and looked up.

Wanda returned Ellen's gaze. "Today."

"I don't think I can do this," Ellen sobbed.

She felt Maggie's arm around her, guiding her back to the table. "This is a heavy burden for you, Ellen. We want to help you carry it. But this is a burden the three of us can't carry on our own. Could we pray together?"

"I haven't prayed for a long time. I don't know what I'd say."

Ellen felt Wanda's hand gently grasping her own. "You don't have to say anything, sweetie. God knows what's in your heart."

Ellen looked over at Maggie and extended her hand. Maggie enfolded it in hers, and the three women bowed their heads and closed their eyes. In the silence that preceded the prayer, Ellen felt an unfamiliar stirring. She squeezed her friends' hands and smiled when they returned the gesture. Then she heard Maggie speak.

"Heavenly Father, we thank You for joining us together as a cord of three strands. Ellen is carrying a heavy burden. Bob is lost, Lord, but You know where he is. Please bring him home safely."

When Maggie paused, Ellen heard Wanda's voice. "We know You have a plan for Ellen and Bob. Please show her Your plan and help her to follow it. Give her the strength that comes only from You and the peace that comes from walking side by side with You."

Maggie joined Wanda in saying, "Thy will be done. In Jesus' name. Amen."

Ellen felt the burden lifting from her shoulders. "Amen."

When Maggie stood up and started clearing the dishes, Ellen put her hand over the muffin plate. "We can get these later, Maggie. Let's move to more comfortable seats. We don't know how long we'll have to wait."

Ellen watched Maggie and Wanda rock back and forth on the glider. Just as she closed her eyes and tipped her head back, the front doorbell rang. Ellen flew out of her chair and raced inside, her heart pounding. Then she spied a policeman's hat through the glass at the top of the door. She grabbed the knob, bowed her head, and took a deep breath before turning it.

Chief Gallego touched the brim of his hat. "Mrs. Bailey, we found your husband."

Ellen leaned over to peek around the officer. "Where is he? Is he okay?" She held her breath.

The chief removed his hat and spoke quietly. "He's fine. He's in the cruiser, Mrs. Bailey. I wanted to talk with you for a minute before he comes in."

As she opened the screen door and stepped back to let Carlos in, she saw her two friends standing behind her. "They found him. He'll be in shortly."

Wanda raised her arms above her head. "Praise the Lord!"

"Amen," Maggie added.

When Ellen nodded her head and smiled at the women, Maggie said, "We'll head home now, dear. If you need us for anything, just call."

Ellen stepped forward and gave each of them a warm hug. "I'll see you later."

Then she turned back to Carlos. "Would you like to sit down?"

"Thanks, but this will just take a minute. We found your husband walking along the highway north of town. He was very confused but didn't resist getting in the car with us. If he was willing to come with us, he might get in the car with anyone."

He paused a moment before continuing. "I'm concerned about his safety. Have you considered putting keyed locks at the top of your doors or installing other devices that would ensure he couldn't leave without your knowledge?"

Ellen nodded her head as she listened to the chief. "I realize now that he needs supervision twenty-four hours a day. Your cousin, Alberto has made arrangements for Bob to move into The Harbor today." She couldn't hold back her tears any longer.

Carlos put his hand on her shoulder. "You've made a wise but difficult decision. You must love your husband very much. Now if you'll excuse me, I'll get him."

Ellen followed Carlos out the door and stood on the stoop. She clasped her hands to her chest, looked up at the sky, and whispered, "Thank You."

When she looked down, Bob was approaching her. "Hi, Ellen. I'm home."

Ellen wrapped her arms around Bob's neck and buried her face in his sweatshirt. When he took a step toward the house, she kept an arm around his waist. "You must be starving."

Bob stopped mid-stride and looked down at his wife. "Now that you mention it, I am."

Ellen smiled, stroked the side of his face, took his fishing hat off, and placed it on the kitchen counter. "Why don't you go put your feet up? I'll fix you something and bring it to you."

Five minutes later, Ellen walked into the living room with a sandwich, fruit salad, and a glass of iced tea. Bob was asleep. She decided not to wake him but set the tray down on the end table next to his recliner and kissed the top of his head.

She pulled up a hassock and perched on the edge, elbows on her knees and chin resting in her hands. She studied the rhythm of his chest rising and falling and the vein in his neck pulsing slowly but steadily. She noticed his cheek bore a smudge of dirt, and his chin was covered with the morning stubble that had been spared the razor's edge today. He looked older, more fragile, more vulnerable.

Ellen didn't realize she was crying until the tears dripped onto her hands. "God, Maggie and Wanda say You have a plan for us, but I can't see it. An hour ago, I felt Your presence. It was amazing. Now I just feel sad. Help me to believe that You're here and that You care."

Bob stirred in his sleep as Ellen continued to pray. "Did You keep him safe? Did You bring him home?" Ellen paused and looked out at the lake. "Was it Your plan that brought us to Lakeshore Lane? Did You know Maggie and Wanda would become my friends?"

Ellen rose without making a sound and walked to the window. "You knew there would be a place for Bob at The Harbor, and I must believe that You love us and You'll take care of us."

Chapter 35

Ellen's eyes panned the white expanse of Bob's new home. The green shutters that framed the large windows gave the impression of a southern estate. And the window boxes overflowing with red geraniums, blue lobelia, and trailing vinca reminded her of pictures she'd seen in landscaping magazines.

She hung back a bit as Alberto introduced Bob to residents enjoying the afternoon warmth on the spacious porch. She moved up the steps when Bob turned to her. "Ellen, have you met Mrs. Nichols?" He bent down a bit and put his hand on the elderly woman's shoulder. "Mrs. Nichols, this beautiful woman is my wife, Ellen."

"Looks like you hit the jackpot, Bob. Nice to meet you, Ellen."

Ellen extended a hand to Mrs. Nichols and then felt Bob's gentle nudge guiding her to the entrance.

Bob saluted the porch crowd. "We'll see you later, everybody."

An attractive man in a business suit met the trio as soon as they entered. "Hi, Alberto. And you must be Bob and Ellen Bailey. I'm Don Carey. Welcome to The Harbor."

After they exchanged handshakes, Ellen turned and took in the surroundings. "This is beautiful."

Don beamed. "One of my favorite spots on the String. May I give you the tour?"

Ellen glanced at Alberto and nodded. "We'd like that."

Don showed them to the elevator, and they went down to the restricted lower level.

Alberto drew Bob's attention to a picture of Pearl Lake. "You know, Wanda did this painting."

Bob smiled and touched the kayaks in the foreground. "Ellen and I like to kayak."

Meanwhile Ellen used the card Don gave her to unlock the door to the Alzheimer's unit. "What are the visiting hours?"

"You're welcome here anytime, as often and for as long as you wish. Lots of family members join our residents for snack time or a meal. There's always plenty."

Ellen turned at the touch of Bob's hand on her shoulder. "Honey, did you see the picture of us kayaking?"

Ellen cocked her head and looked at Alberto. He smiled and winked. "Wanda's donated several paintings to The Harbor. The one in the hall is a Pearl Lake scene."

When they stepped into the large common room, Ellen let out a breath and tilted her head back. "Bob, look at that gorgeous lake."

Ellen smiled at the young man who came over and held out his hand to Bob. "Hi, I'm Jack. Would you like something to eat or drink, Mr. Bailey? We've got snacks over at the counter."

When the two walked off, Ellen turned to Don. "I love the pastels. It's bright and airy in here. Not at all what I expected."

Don smiled. "I'm glad you like it."

Alberto put his hand on her shoulder. "Are you ready to see Bob's room?"

She lowered her head. "Bob's room. That sounds so strange. For the first time in thirty years, it's not Bob and Ellen's room."

Alberto gave her shoulder a squeeze. "This is a big sacrifice you're making, Ellen, but Bob will be safe here. I sense a real strength in you, something I haven't recognized before."

After Don lured Bob away from the snacks, the four of them started down the hallway.

Ellen grinned at the elderly gentleman walking toward them. She did a double take when he said, "Hi, Bob. I'm so glad you're here."

Ellen raised an eyebrow. "Al, how do you know Bob?"

He walked over to Bob and put an arm over his shoulder. "Your husband and I met this morning. Just did a little walking and talking together." He pulled the white carnation out of his lapel and gave it to Ellen. Then he tipped his red English driving cap. "I'll see you folks again. Have a good day, my dear."

Ellen watched their new friend until he turned a corner and disappeared.

She caught up with the others as they entered Bob's room. The director's cellphone beeped. After looking at the text message, he excused himself to go back to his office. Before leaving, he extended his hand to Bob and then Ellen. "It was so nice to meet you folks."

Bob put his hand on Don's shoulder. "Thanks, buddy. Stop by anytime."

When the director left, Bob looked at the chair in the corner. "Ah, my recliner. I'm bushed."

Ellen smiled and whispered to Alberto, "I guess he feels at home."

Bob picked up a small white card off the seat before sitting down.

Ellen held out her hand. "What's that, honey?"

Bob handed it to her, and she sat down in a side chair next to Alberto. She looked at the card. Embossed on one side were the words, "The boundary lines have fallen for me in pleasant places… (Psalm 16:6a)."

Lydia Moen

When she turned it over, she read, "To my friend, Bob. From, Al."

After Ellen got out of the Santiagos' car, she leaned in through the open window. "Today never would have happened without you, Alberto. Thank you."

Alberto stared into Ellen's eyes and pointed a finger at her. "You are a strong woman, Ellen Bailey. Try to relax tonight."

Ellen shrugged her shoulders. "A relaxing evening for me is going to be a salad and sleep. And I may skip the salad."

As she approached the stoop, she heard voices in the kitchen.

"She's going to love this."

"I hope so. I'm sure she could use some cheering up tonight."

Ellen rested her forehead against the door, closed her eyes, and wished she could disappear. Then she took a deep breath, pasted a smile on her face, and went inside.

Her two friends stood in the middle of a spotless kitchen. Wanda's broad grin made Ellen think of a smiley face. Maggie's tight-lipped smile reminded her of Mrs. Jones, her fifth-grade teacher. The dishwasher hummed, and she could hear the steady whine of the dryer from the laundry room.

Ellen walked over and flung her arms around her friends' necks. "You two must have worked all afternoon. I'm grateful and tired."

"Of course, you're tired." Wanda's hand stroked Ellen's hair. "You just rest, sweetie. But if you'd like to join us later, we're serving a five-star meal—chicken wings, chips and salsa, strawberries topped with whipped cream, and chocolate frosted cupcakes with sprinkles for dessert."

Ellen leaned her head against Wanda's shoulder and reached out a hand to Maggie. "I'm definitely the weak strand in our cord right now. Thank you for being the strong ones."

When Ellen grabbed the bannister to head upstairs, Maggie's voice stopped her. "If the phone rings, do you want us to answer?"

"That would be great. Just call me if it's The Harbor."

Ellen smiled and shook her head when she walked into her room. She had left it a rumpled mess but came home to an immaculate and inviting refuge. A vase of fall flowers stood on her dresser.

She tossed her purse on a chair and kicked off her sandals on her way to falling into the bed, now newly made with the covers turned back. She reached over for Bob's pillow and let the muted scent of his aftershave lull her to sleep.

Wanda turned to Maggie. "She's in the shower."

"Why are you talking so softly?" Maggie asked.

Wanda giggled and whispered, "I don't know."

They both laughed.

Wanda nodded when Maggie asked, "Why don't you put the other food on the coffee table? I'll stick the chicken wings in the oven."

Ten minutes later, Wanda came sneaking into the kitchen with a finger on her lips. "She's coming!"

The two women hustled to their spots at the kitchen table. Wanda leaned forward and smiled at Maggie. "So tell me, how are your tulips doing?" Wanda winced when Maggie rolled her eyes.

Maggie said, "I trust the spring tulips are sound asleep, and my fall flowers are doing fine, thank you."

Wanda looked up at the sound of Ellen's footsteps entering the room. "Oh, you're awake. Were you able to sleep?"

"I was, and after my shower, I couldn't resist putting on my PJs."

"It's a slumber party!" Wanda and Maggie popped up and strutted across the kitchen—Maggie in her flowered nightie and Wanda sporting

Lydia Moen

NYPD pajamas.

Maggie pulled the chicken wings from the oven. "Are you hungry yet?"

"I'm starving. I haven't had anything since your muffins this morning, and the wings smell delicious."

Wanda put her arm around Ellen and guided her out of the kitchen. "We set up the rest of this gourmet meal in here."

She felt a subtle resistance from Ellen as they entered the living room. After several seconds, Ellen pulled her shoulders back then walked over and sat down in Bob's recliner.

Wanda winked and nodded toward Ellen when she caught Maggie's attention ten minutes later. Wanda swallowed the lump in her throat as Ellen refilled her plate for the second time.

"I almost forgot something," Wanda said, jumping up and hurrying out to the porch. She came back in waving a copy of *Lake Breezes*. "They've solved the case of the midnight robberies!" Wanda stood in front of the fireplace and began reading.

"Water's Edge Police Solve Mystery

Chief Carlos Gallego, of the Water's Edge Police Department, brought two guests to a special press conference Monday afternoon. Neil Olsen, former owner of Olsen's Marina & Grill, and Joseph Carnegie IV, owner of Carnegie's Treasure Chest, had been questioned in the town's recent rash of midnight robberies.

According to Gallego, Olsen has been the 'midnight robber' ever since he turned over the operation of the marina to his sons, Neil, Jr. and Eddie. Olsen found himself with spare time on his hands and wanted to give back something to his community. For several months, he has taken it upon himself to restore worn or broken items removed by boat from the homes of his Pearl Lake neighbors. He usually returned the items before the owners realized they were missing.

Gallego went on to say that Olsen learned his nighttime escapades had been discovered when they were documented on the front page of *Lake Breezes*. When Olsen developed bursitis, he brought Carnegie into his confidence, and Carnegie offered to help him complete his anonymous philanthropic work. (See photo lower right.)"

Wanda folded the paper and held it up to Ellen and Maggie so they could see the picture of Neil and Joe surrounded by several restored items. She pointed to a white blur in the background. "If you look closely, you can see our yard light. And there's your bench, Maggie." Then Wanda continued reading.

"The good-works partners assured *Lake Breezes* that all missing items would be returned in working order sometime this week.

Gallego credited several women from the community with assisting police in the case."

Wanda looked around the paper and squealed, "That's us!"

Maggie raised her arms. "Praise the Lord! I'm not surprised. They're such nice men."

Wanda nodded. "I knew they were innocent all along."

Ellen had just taken a large gulp of iced tea. When she choked and sputtered, Maggie reached over. "Are you all right, dear?"

Ellen cleared her throat. "I'm just remembering our chart of facts and suspicions. I sure thought they were guilty. When we went to the junkyard that day, I was really afraid of Joe."

"They acted like conspirators the couple of times I stopped in at the bait shop," Maggie said.

Wanda furrowed her brow and then blurted out, "And we saw those suspicious boats at night."

The three women sat in silence. Then Maggie started chuckling. "I bet Carlos had a good laugh after we left the police station that day."

Ellen began giggling. "I remember saying how impressed Chief Gallego was with our presentation."

"And, Wanda, you said, 'I know Carlos. He's overwhelmed.' Yeah, he was certainly overwhelmed." Maggie bent over, holding her stomach as she laughed.

Wanda mimicked Maggie's voice. "Will you have to handcuff them? Neil's suffering from bursitis, and his arm is in a sling."

The three women laughed until they cried. Eventually Maggie stood up, grabbed a box of tissues, and passed them around.

Wanda dabbed her eyes and blew her nose. She took a couple of deep breaths. "Whew. I haven't laughed that hard in ages." She followed Maggie's gaze over to the recliner, where Ellen lay curled up in a ball, her shoulders rising and falling. It seemed her laughter had turned to tears.

Wanda followed Maggie's lead, picking up their dishes and taking them into the kitchen. The two women worked silently side-by-side, putting the food away and filling the dishwasher. When they finished, they returned to the living room.

Wanda cleared her throat, and Ellen looked up. "Thank you for giving me a little time. I've been sitting here trying to figure out this new feeling I have inside. It started when we were praying this morning."

"Can you describe it to us?" Wanda pulled a hassock closer to Ellen, and Maggie sat down in a chair facing her.

"I'm not sure I can, but I'd like to try. It was almost like when someone helps you carry something that you can't carry by yourself. It's such a relief." Her voice quavered but she continued. "I've been so worried about Bob, but when we were out on the porch this morning, I felt a sense of complete peace. I felt it later too, when I was sitting right where you're sitting now, Wanda. I don't know where it came from, but I felt sure someone would watch over Bob." She smiled. "I remembered what you said about God's plan, and I suddenly knew it was true."

Chapter 36

The ringing of the phone jolted Ellen out of her sleep. Her head snapped up, and the room spun as she pushed the speaker button. "Hello?" Her heart pounding, she threw her legs over the side of the bed and held onto the headboard to steady herself.

"Good morning, Ellen. It's Alberto. Did you get any sleep last night, or did those two wild friends of yours keep you up all night?"

She glanced at the clock and winced. "They kept me up late enough that I slept in until nine—something I never do."

"I just got back from The Harbor. Bob and I sat on the patio having coffee, and he's doing great. His assigned caregiver said he had a good night's sleep. You made the right decision, Ellen."

As Alberto gave his report, Ellen closed her eyes and rubbed the back of her neck. "Thank you for checking on him. I've been so anxious to hear how he's doing. If Wanda and Maggie hadn't been here last night, I wouldn't have gotten any sleep at all."

She chuckled. "We even had a good laugh at ourselves after Wanda read the article about Neil and Joe. I guess we're not the super-sleuths we thought we were."

She could almost see Alberto smiling as he said, "Wanda has just enough knowledge of police investigations to drag you and Maggie into her drama."

Ellen rubbed her eyes and stretched. "Are you kidding me? She didn't have to drag us. And our facts and suspicions weren't entirely wrong. Wanda read us the article about Ray Hoffman. I imagine you had a hand in getting him into the work-release program."

"You know, Ellen, Ray's had a hard life, but I believe he wants to change. Sitting in prison probably isn't the most effective way to make that happen."

Ellen nodded. "I agree, and I hope it makes things easier for Rita. She seems like a sweet girl, and I think she has potential." Ellen looked at the clock. "Thanks for all you do, Alberto. Now I think I'll head over to The Harbor as soon as I can get ready."

Alberto didn't respond right away. "You know, I don't think you have to go today. In fact, giving new residents a few days before family visits generally makes their adjustment easier. I can stop over a couple times a day and keep you posted."

Ellen gasped. "A few days? I don't know if I can do that. I have to go over to fill out paperwork today, and I was planning on spending the rest of the day with Bob." She waited for Alberto's response.

"Why don't you talk to Don Carey about it while you're there? He knows much more about working with the new residents than I do."

As soon as she hung up the phone, Ellen fell back on the bed, hugged Bob's pillow, and wept.

Wanda's nose began to twitch. She lifted her head and walked trancelike toward the combined smells of salsa, queso, and refried beans. "Alberto?"

"*Sí, señora. Tu esposo estás aquí.*"

Wanda smiled at his response then peeked around the corner and fluttered her eyelashes. "Oh, Pastor Santiago, are you making a house call?"

"I am. And I come bearing gifts."

Wanda squealed and raced to his side. "I know what's in the to-go bag. But what's in the other one?" She tried to snatch the pink bag out of his hand, but Alberto held it over his head.

He waggled a finger back and forth in front of her face. "Not until after lunch, querida. How would you like to eat in the gazebo?"

"I'd love it!" Wanda grabbed a couple of sodas out of the refrigerator and placed them in a basket, along with paper plates, napkins, and silverware. She smiled and held out her hand. "Let's go!"

Alberto transferred the bags to his left hand and squeezed hers in his right as they headed to the shore.

The two didn't talk much over lunch. They didn't need to. Near the end of the meal, Wanda turned and gazed into her husband's eyes. "We're back, aren't we?"

She leaned forward as his arms drew her nearer to him. He lifted her chin and whispered, "We never really left. I love you, Mrs. Santiago." He pulled a cupcake with chocolate frosting and sprinkles out of the pink bag.

Wanda gasped and reached for the treat, but Alberto took her hand in his. Then he extended the cupcake to her lips. She took a generous bite before plucking the cupcake from her husband's hand and holding it up to his lips. "I love you too, Alberto."

Ellen scooped up the pile of papers, straightened them, and tucked them in the folder Don Carey had given her the day before. She stood up, raised her hands over her head, and stretched. After checking the clock, she ran upstairs and put on her jogging shoes. "I'll just do a couple miles, get a quick shower, and I can still make it to The Harbor by three."

She pulled into the parking lot five minutes before her appointment with the director. When she stepped into the main lobby, she smiled at Don. "How's my husband doing? Have you heard anything?"

Don pointed to a vase in the middle of his office table. "Do you like flowers? I would guess you make beautiful arrangements. Bob is that last beautiful rose you put in the center of a bouquet. We just weren't quite complete until he joined us."

Ellen tilted her head and wrinkled her brow. "The center of a bouquet. That sounds good, but what exactly do you mean?"

They sat at the table. "Let me give you a couple of examples. We have one gentleman who always sits alone at the dinner table long after the meal is over. Last night Bob sat down across from him, and before long they were chatting like old friends. When I went down this morning, your husband was helping set the tables for breakfast. The bouquet is more beautiful because Bob's in it."

Ellen sat up a little straighter. "Bob genuinely likes other people and makes them feel good about themselves. And I'm not surprised he helped this morning. He's a hard worker."

After Don approved the paperwork, Ellen cleared her throat. "Would it be okay for me to see him now?"

She searched Don's face as he began. "I can certainly understand how eager you are to see him. And I'm sure he'd love to see you too. But he's making an amazingly smooth adjustment. Sometimes seeing a spouse or other loved one can actually throw that progress off track. It won't be long before it won't be an issue, but for now, I have to tell you it would probably be better for Bob if you don't visit for a few days."

Ellen pulled a tissue out of her purse and dabbed her eyes.

Don reached over and placed his hand on hers. "That being said, there is a way you can see him without his seeing you."

Ellen's face brightened, and five minutes later she and Don were in the darkened office of the Alzheimer's unit coordinator. They stood side by side in front of a large window. "He can't see us. He just sees his reflection."

She stared at her husband as he moved around the room, dressed in a handsome sport shirt and khaki slacks. Then she glanced at Don. "Bob looks happier than I've seen him in months."

Maggie scooped the last piece of chicken out of the frying pan and turned toward Sammy as he sidled up next to her. "I thought you were sleeping. So you smelled chicken, did you? Yes, I know it's your favorite."

When the golden whined, she looked down at him and winced. "You're right, Sammy. It is a lot of chicken, especially since it's just the two of us."

Sammy turned and scampered to the door, wagging his tail. When the bell rang, Maggie followed. Her hand flew to her chest, and her eyes filled with tears.

When she opened the screen door, Charlie stepped inside and wrapped his arms around her. "I've missed you, Maggie."

She laid her head on his shoulder. "I've missed you too."

Maggie grabbed his hand and led him into the kitchen. "I can't believe you could smell the chicken all the way over at your house."

He chuckled. "Actually, I came to invite you on a boat ride over to the marina for the Wednesday-night buffet."

Maggie pointed to the platter on the counter. "How about a dinner cruise on my boat instead? But I'd like a rain check on the marina."

"That works for me. But before we leave, I have to tell you how grateful I was to hear that Josh and Chris were found."

"It was an answer to lots of prayers." She reached for his hand and gave it a squeeze. "I suspect many of them were yours."

Half an hour later, Maggie had her feet up on one of the benches and her head resting against the seat back. Her hand relaxed on Sammy's soft head, her eyes closed, lulled by the gentle rocking of the pontoon boat. Then she felt the boat lurch and heard the motor sputter. Her eyes popped open, and she sat up straight. "Charlie, what's wrong?"

She felt her wrinkled brow relax when she saw his grin. She looked at the shoreline and then back at the captain. She moved toward him and planted her hands on his shoulders. "You planned this, didn't you?"

Maggie drew in her breath when Charlie winked and pulled her onto his lap. "This is where I got my first hug. I thought it was worth trying again."

She fluffed her hair and threw her arms around his neck. "Anytime, Captain Bingham."

Charlie dropped the anchor, and Maggie set out fried chicken, fruit, and potato salad. They had just finished eating when they heard music. Charlie waved, and the Ice Cream Float drew up beside them. "I didn't get to buy you dinner. What would you like for dessert?"

Maggie stood up and looked at the menu painted on the side of the boat. "I'd love a chocolate cone."

"Make that two."

When they finished the ice cream, Charlie raised the anchor and started the engine.

Lights were beginning to blink on around the lake as they pulled up to her dock. Maggie jumped up and ran to the rail. "Charlie, the bench is back! At least, I think it's the same bench. It looks brand new."

Once the boat was secured, Maggie walked over to the bench. She held out her hand, and Charlie joined her at the end of the dock.

"Look at this." She reached out and touched the new brass plate on the back of Mac's bench.

> In loving memory of Mac MacDonald
> Present on Earth: June 29, 1947—August 30, 2013
> Present with the Lord: August 30, 2013—Eternity
> *See you when we get there, Mac!*

Charlie put his arm around Maggie's waist. "It looks like Neil and Joe added a touch of their own. Mac would like that."

The moon was rising above the trees across the lake, its reflection shimmering on the water. Maggie looked into Charlie's eyes. "Could we sit here for a minute?"

"I was hoping you'd ask. I have something to show you."

Charlie reached into his shirt pocket, pulled out a small white card, and handed it to Maggie. In the fading light, she was just able to make out the words embossed on the front. "Love is patient and kind.... Love never gives up, never loses faith, is always hopeful, and endures through every circumstance. Love will last forever... (1 Corinthians 13:4a, 7-8a)."

"Charlie, where did you get this?" Maggie tilted her head and looked up at him.

"First I should tell you that I had a biopsy on Monday. I was going to wait to tell you about it after I got the results. I had made up my mind that I wouldn't put you through another ordeal with cancer. But I missed you."

Maggie, unable to speak, clasped his hand in hers and nodded her head.

"I went to our park. It seemed like the right place to think about you and me. As I walked toward the lake, I looked up and saw..."

Lydia Moen

Her voice whispered, "Al."

She turned the card over and read it out loud. "Charlie, 'Be not afraid.' Your friend, Al."

He smiled. "I'm not afraid, Maggie."

"I'm not either." Maggie leaned into Charlie's arms, felt the warmth of his hand lifting her chin, and closed her eyes as his lips met hers.

Although Ellen appreciated the beauty of the moon's reflection on the water, she found little joy in it tonight. She looked at the empty spot next to her on the glider and grabbed another tissue to dab her swollen eyes.

She sat up straighter and took a deep breath. "Okay, a lot of other people go through this. Count your blessings." Ellen held up her fingers and tallied as she spoke.

"Bob is doing well. He's in a wonderful place. I can see him anytime I want to.

"I live in a beautiful home. It's near family. The lake view is spectacular.

"I have plenty to live on. The house is paid for. We can afford good care for Bob.

"I'm in good health. My mind is clear. I can get plenty of exercise here.

"I've made good friends. They support me when I'm down. We've become…"

Ellen shuddered, fighting the tears that would not be denied. As she groped for the tissue box, her hand fell on the present her two friends had given her the night before, and she felt the now-familiar stirring in her heart. She sank back in the cushions, pulling the Bible onto her lap.

It fell open to Jeremiah 29:11, the verse her friends had bookmarked. She smiled as she read it aloud. "'For I know the plans I have for you,' declares the Lord, 'plans to prosper you and not to harm you, plans to give you hope and a future.'"

Lydia Moen

Chapter 37

Ellen closed her eyes and raised her head toward the vaulted ceiling of Water's Edge Bible Church. Two weeks had passed since she'd made the tough decision to move Bob to his new home. She squeezed his hand. "Did you enjoy the service?"

"I sure did. That last song was beautiful." Bob turned to greet those around them as the crowd started filing out.

As he did so, Ellen felt a tap on her shoulder. Ginny Kohls gave her a hug. "It's good to see you here again. I couldn't believe all the work you got done on Thursday. My Sister's Keeper has never been so well-organized, and I really enjoyed the day off."

Ellen squeezed Bob's arm. "Ginny, I'd like you to meet my husband. Bob, this is my friend Ginny Kohls."

Bob extended his hand. "Hello. It sure is a beautiful day."

When Ellen heard someone call her name, she turned around to see Wanda waving her bulletin and pointing to Charlie and Maggie from across the room. "Ellen, wait for us outside!"

Ellen watched Bob's face brighten and break into a broad grin as Alberto joined the group gathered on the lawn outside the church. Her husband stepped forward and shook the pastor's hand. "Hey, buddy.

What are you doing here?"

Alberto smiled and shook his head. "Same thing you are, Bob. Enjoying the service and the company of friends."

Ellen noticed Bob rubbing his forehead. "Are you feeling okay, Bob?"

"I need to get back home. I have a lot of work to do."

Ellen reached for his hand and faced him, her smile quivering. "Of course, you do."

As they walked across the lawn toward the parking lot, Bob turned and saluted the group. "We'll see you later, everybody."

Wanda sat down at the large, round table on the marina deck. "I almost didn't make it past the buffet without filling a plate. Did you see the croissants?"

Charlie rubbed his hands together. "I saw you do that double-take when you walked by them, but did you smell the Belgian waffles?"

Wanda laughed and spread her arms out toward the lake. "We hardly need to eat when we can devour God's feast for our eyes. I'm glad we had to wait for Ellen to join us."

Alberto leaned over and straightened her necklaces. "I see Grandma's pearls are no longer hanging from an easel but from a much more beautiful backdrop."

Wanda caressed a string of tiny ceramic dolls that hung just below the pearls. "Querido, do you remember these?" Wanda looked at Maggie and Charlie. "My precious Alberto brought them to me from his first mission trip. Aren't they just scrumptious with this Mexican skirt?"

Charlie put an arm around Maggie and patted the shoulder of her soft pink sweater. He touched her delicate silver cross necklace. "Wanda, your outfit expresses your personality as clearly as Maggie's matches hers."

Wanda elbowed Alberto. "There's Ellen. And her navy blue ensemble could have been made just for her. We are a cord of unique strands."

Wanda's eyes softened at the smile that brightened Ellen's face when Alberto approached her. Charlie stood up and pulled out the chair between Wanda and himself. "It was great to see Bob at church today. He showed us around when Maggie and I stopped by the other day. Nice group of people, and not surprisingly, they all seem to be Bob's friends."

Wanda put her hand on Ellen's arm. "Every time I've been over to see that sweet hubby of yours, he's been hanging out with a bunch of his buddies. I've never even seen his room."

Ellen's eyes lit up. "Oh, Wanda, you'd love the painting on his wall. It's of a man catching a big fish off his dock. The guy is wearing a fishing hat, and Bob is sure the painting is of him. He points it out to everyone who comes to his room. That fish gets bigger every time he tells the story."

Wanda's jaw dropped, and she looked up at her husband. Alberto nodded his head and put his arm around her shoulder.

"What's wrong?" Ellen pushed her glasses on top of her head.

Wanda nudged Alberto's shoulder as she wiped her eyes with his handkerchief.

She leaned into his hug and smiled when he told Ellen, "You're sitting next to the artist."

Wanda stood in front of the paint-spattered tarp, looking at her four-person fan club. "I don't really have any prepared remarks, but I do want to thank you for your support. As you all know, this has been one of my most challenging projects. I'm so glad you could be here for the unveiling. Alberto, would you please turn on the CD player?"

Wanda smiled and remembered to make eye contact with each person in the audience while waiting for the music to begin. When the rather scratchy rendition of Glenn Miller's "String of Pearls" blasted out of the speakers, Wanda scowled at Alberto.

After he turned the volume down, she heard a familiar click-click-click and turned to see Ruth Butler coming down the hall.

"I hope you don't mind my joining in the festivities, Wanda."

Wanda's face flushed as she assured Ruth she was thrilled she could be there. Then she nodded to Ralph, who was clad in full custodial garb and holding a rope tied to the top of the tarp. At Wanda's direction, he pulled the rope and the tarp fell to the floor, barely missing the artist on its way down.

Wanda backed out of the spectators' field of view and held her arm out toward the mural. As Ralph scrambled to remove the tarp, the audience drew in a collective breath and then burst into applause.

The mural was just as Wanda had envisioned it, a medley of scenes: pines on the big island… boats crowding the marina… an eagle against a blue sky… kayaks stacked against a stone wall…. No people. Just scenes from around the lakes. Weaving through the depictions of natural beauty was a stunning string of pearls, each precious gem bearing a sketch of an unidentifiable senior's face.

Alberto lifted Wanda off her feet and spun her around. "*Exquisito*, querida. I'm so proud of you."

When Charlie held out his hand to shake hers, Wanda grabbed it and insisted on a hug. "Charlie, you don't have to be so formal with me. I'm still just the same woman who comes down to the dock in her husband's robe to get the mail."

She felt a hand on her shoulder and knew it was Maggie's when she heard, "Okay, Wanda, I think that's enough hugging with Mr. Bingham. It's my turn now."

When Charlie moved toward Maggie with his arms wide open, Wanda laughed out loud. "I think she meant me, sir."

Maggie threw her arms around Wanda and looked over her shoulder. "Later, Charlie."

Wanda pulled Ellen into the circle, and the three strands wove themselves into the cord they'd become.

The artist heard the click-click-click of the director's shoes before she felt Ruth's hand on her shoulder. "It's stunning, Wanda. Thank you so much." She started to leave but turned back and winked. "And I like the changes you've made."

Maggie breathed in the clean scents of the lake and the pine trees that surrounded it. She smiled at Charlie. "I've always loved Sunday evenings, especially when the rush of summer has passed." She snuggled closer to him when he put his arm around her shoulders.

Charlie whispered in her ear, "As I recall, promises were made."

"Promises were made? What? And by whom?"

She felt his arms tighten around her as he drew her to him. "Yes. You promised me a hug."

Maggie giggled and jumped to her feet. She stood in front of Charlie and pulled him from the bench. "Yes, I did. And I always keep my promises." She wrapped her arms around his shoulders and made good on her word.

"Thank you. We have reason to celebrate tonight. I have good news. I got the results of the biopsy yesterday, and it's benign."

"Oh, Charlie! Our prayers have been answered. Praise the Lord!" She put her hands on the sides of his face and held it as she gazed into his eyes. Then she pulled herself up as he leaned down. The kiss, long and tender, was a promise of hope fulfilled.

Ellen and Wanda heard the golden's bark before he and Maggie appeared out of the trees along the shoreline. "I'm glad Sammy accepted my invitation." Ellen ruffled the dog's ears and led him to a bowl of water she'd placed near the edge of the porch. "Do you think he'll be okay here alone if we go kayaking later?"

"Oh, he'll just wait for us on the dock." Maggie hugged her two friends and sat down on the glider next to Ellen. "We just got back from visiting Bob. Naturally Sammy adores all the attention, but he makes it evident to everyone that he's there to see Bob. He parks himself at Bob's side and follows him wherever he goes."

Ellen twisted her wedding ring. "How's he doing this morning?"

Maggie put her hand on Ellen's. "He seems content. We had a lovely visit."

After a brief pause, she continued. "Before I forget, Wanda, I noticed your shore light is back. In fact, it was turned on. You might want to get one of those timers like I have on mine. It saves a lot of electricity."

Wanda looked at Ellen, grinned, and rolled her eyes. "Thank you, Maggie. I'll have to look into that."

Ellen turned to Maggie. "Does that mean your bench is back?"

"I can answer that." Wanda brought her hands to her heart and closed her eyes, pretending to swoon. "It's back, and I can assure you it's been fully tested."

Maggie peered over her glasses. "Wanda Dobinski Santiago! Have you been spying on me?"

Wanda shrugged her shoulders and crossed her arms. "I was just checking our shore light."

Ellen poked Maggie's arm. "What have I been missing? I need details!"

"There will be no details." Maggie's face reddened. "Charlie and I were just celebrating good news. He got the results of the biopsy, and it's benign."

Ellen's eyes teared up as she stood and opened her arms to her two friends. "That's hug-worthy news!"

As they sat back down, Ellen clapped her hands together. "I have good news too. Lizzy and her family are coming next weekend. We're going to celebrate Bob's birthday."

While Ellen and Maggie chatted about Lizzy's upcoming visit, Wanda stood up and walked in the house. When she returned, Wanda handed Ellen a large rectangular object wrapped in brown paper.

Ellen's eyes widened. "What's this?"

"Just a little something for your bedroom wall. I didn't think Bob should be the only Bailey with a Santiago original."

Tears formed in her eyes as Ellen hugged the package to her chest. She rested her chin on top and closed her eyes. The tears escaped, dampening her cheeks. Her hands trembled as she slid a finger under the tape. When the wrapping fell away, she gasped. "This is not going in my bedroom!"

She got up and walked toward the house, cradling the painting as if it were a newborn. Maggie held the door open, and Ellen's two friends followed her into the living room. She stood in front of the fireplace for a moment. Then she turned and handed her gift to Maggie.

"Wanda, will you help me slide this behind the couch?" Ellen reached for one end of the painting of Washington, D.C., the painting she had hung when they moved to Water's Edge. Wanda took the other end.

Ellen stood back as her two friends hung the image she'd come to love over the mantel. She reached for their hands and bowed her head. "Thank You, God, for bringing Maggie and Wanda into my life. They've taught me the true meaning of the words 'love thy neighbor,' and they brought me back to You. Thank You for weaving us into a cord of three strands."

She squeezed their hands before releasing them. Then she stepped up and nudged the right side of Wanda's Pearl Lake landscape just a touch higher.

Discussion Questions

1. Which character in *String of Pearls* did you like or relate to the most and why?

2. If you visited Waters Edge, where would you want to spend time and why?

    a. On the String of Pearls

    b. In the Java Joint

    c. At Brandt Park

    d. Other

3. Have you ever had to relocate to a dramatically different environment? What did you find to be the most challenging adjustments?

4. Have you ever felt the need to escape as Ellen did when she returned to D.C.? What did you do?

5. How do you feel about Maggie's relationship with Charlie?

6. Have you had a friend like Wanda? What did you like best about her? What did you find frustrating?

7. What are your thoughts about Al?

Lydia Moen

8. Having read the book, what changes would you like to make in your relationships?

9. If you were writing this story, what would you change?

Digging Deeper

10. S*tring of Pearls* tells about relationships with Jesus and people we encounter in our daily lives. How are you exhibiting friendship to others and how could you strengthen your contributions to being a Christian friend?

11. Who helped you develop a closer relationship with Jesus? Have you thanked them?

12. Can you relate to Ellen's return to Washington, D.C.? Has God ever allowed something to be taken away from you or denied you something you wanted desperately? Did He have something as good or better planned for you?

13. Have you ever drifted away from your relationship with Jesus? What happened to bring you back to Him?

14. Maggie sits in her bedroom easy chair and imagines Jesus sitting in the chair facing her. Do you have a special place for doing devotions or reading the Bible? How does that help you feel closer to God?

Preview of Book 2 in the "A Cord of Three Strands" series

Coming in Fall 2015

As autumn arrives in Waters Edge, delight in the String of Pearls through Maggie's eyes. When her grandson moves in with her, the two generations struggle to find common ground. Meanwhile, Maggie's relationship with Charlie faces new challenges; Ellen strives to find a new purpose for her life; and Wanda continues to offer her unique kind of support to her friends.

Get reacquainted with Bob, Alberto, Ray and Rita Hoffman, and the Jefferson family. Get to know Josh, Maggie's grandson; Katie, his email pal; Hank, his Marine buddy; and Lieutenant Jefferson. Laugh through the meetings of the Cord of Three Strands. Share a tear as each of the neighbors faces a new ordeal. Continue to embrace God's peace and comfort on the String of Pearls.

Lydia Moen

About the Authors and an Invitation

Nancy Willich, **Ann Guyer**, and **Peggy Byers** began writing books as their second career in 2004. After retiring from diverse professions in various locations around the country, they now write at one table, overlooking the very lakes that provide the backdrop for their books.

How do three sisters who fought as kids become one author? God is good. After creating the outline together, Nancy paints the setting, Ann constructs the plot, and Peggy articulates the voice.

Overcoming such adversities as cancer, divorce, the death of a spouse, and their mother's Alzheimer's disease has brought the three sisters closer to each other and to God. Their goal is to help others find similar love, peace, and joy as they experience the relevance of Scripture, the power of prayer, the strength of faith-based relationships, and the therapy of laughter through the sisters' books.

The three sisters write under the pen name **Lydia Moen**, a tribute to their two grandmothers, Lydia Genrich and Ada Moen, and their great aunt, Ellida Moen. They would love to have you drop by their website: www.lydiamoen.com and get acquainted.

The authors' nonfiction book and audiobook, *"Your Mother Has Alzheimer's" Three daughters answer their father's call*, are available through Amazon.